Echoes of the

S. M. Porter

- Archaeological Adventures -
- Book 2 -

Echoes of the Eternal City

S. M. Porter

-Archaeological Adventures Book 2-

First published as a Kindle eBook 2018
Print version published via Amazon KDP 2018

ISBN: 9781731127167

Praise for Archaeological Adventures

THE MYSTERY OF ST. ARONDIGHT'S

"So good I missed my stop!"
Calum Maynard

"Fantastic read! Loved the mix of archaeology and adventure."
Hannah C

"An intelligent book full of high adventure and intrigue."
Julia P

"Perfect archaeology read. Wanting book 2 now, I'm hooked"
Angel

"Great blend of historical and archaeological facts, myths and fiction, with the author's own unique spin."
James

"Will leave you thrilled and exhausted by the end."
S. T. Rider

"Brilliant book, I thoroughly enjoyed it and couldn't put it down."
Vidcol

"Certainly a page turner. I stayed up late engrossed in reading it."
Prof. David Breeze

Acknowledgements

My thanks must again first go to my wonderful husband Dan, who does all the formatting and the cover design, and more importantly, puts up with me and my writing brain, providing encouragement, ideas and cups of tea.

Thanks, is also due to my Beta Readers: Lucy Porter, Kim-Marie Coon, and Joanne Wallwork, and especially to my Mum. Who made the mistake of saying she had nothing to read and ended up proofreading the whole lot, along with my Dad, who said he would edit it, but just enjoyed reading it instead.

Echoes is dedicated to the memory of the late Derek Pierce of South Trafford Archaeology Group, (S.T.A.G) who let me loose on my first archaeological site in 2001. It was the site of a moated medieval manor, and the people I met there provided the inspiration for my teenaged characters.

A brief note on the text:

There are three languages (four if English is counted) that appear in this book. These are Spanish, Italian and Latin. All can be recognised by the use of *Italic* text. Unless the speech is of direct importance to the story I have not provided an English translation. Where entire conversations take place in Italian I have written the speech in *English Italics* and indicated that the characters are speaking Italian.

Prologue

The slave staggered through the dark and rain swept alleys, a storm raged overhead. Jupiter's lightning bolts tearing holes in the darkness as the great god roared in his anger. The slave had no time for the wrath of a distant god thundering away on his mountain, rage was something the god had time to indulge in, but Tiberius, his hands slippery with rain water, his head pounding with terror, was almost out of time.

Another flash strobed the sky and for a moment the new settlement; Rome, stood illuminated in the light. Several mud huts clustered on the Palatine Hill, not much now, but one day. One day, Tiberius knew, this cluster of hills would rule the known world, but only if he succeeded tonight.

Once he had been a slave of Remus, brother of Romulus, but Remus had been defeated and executed. Now Tiberius was an acolyte of the Etruscan priestess who had promised Remus the world. But that was not his only task. For the last ten years he had been a spy for Romulus, working to bring down the scheming priestess. Following the death of Rome's founder, everything was to play for. His feet splashed through muddy puddles as he hurried on his way. They would have noticed it missing by now, but he had a good head start.

'Tiberius!' a voice called from the darkness. Castor, one of his fellow conspirators beckoned to him from a darkened door way. A carpenter's shop. Neither of them knew the owner, but he would have the tools they needed.

Sighing in relief, Tiberius ducked inside the building and dragged his heavy burden from below his tunic. The silver glowed in the dull light as he practically threw the thing away from him. It was dangerous to have, she would come for it. They had to work quickly.

Rummaging through the tools, wondering where the third member of their conspiracy was, Tiberius grabbed a chisel and hammer. Stealing it wasn't enough. It had to be destroyed. 'Castor, the door,' he hissed, anxious that they were not disturbed. The three slaves had to be ready to run at a moment's notice, although Meredius was not yet here. Could they have been discovered already? The sweat of sheer terror dripped from Tiberius's face. He could die for this. He was afraid to die, afraid of pain.

Not concentrating on his task, he miss-hit the chisel, driving the blade into his palm. Suppressing a squeak of pain and fright, he dropped the hammer and had to scrabble after it below the table. A noise outside brought him to his feet.

'Castor?' he whispered, 'Meredius?'

There was no answer, just another odd, wet sounding thump from outside. Quickly, Tiberius finished his task, breaking the silver object into three pieces. He stuffed one back under his tunic and crept towards the door. 'Castor?' he hissed, leaning out into the rain.

A flash of lightning lit up the street and Tiberius caught sight of his friend, and realised instantly what the noise outside had been. A spreading red pool was soaking into the mud of the rain slicked alley. Deep, water filled footprints led away towards the Aventine Hill.

Their conspiracy was uncovered. Meredius must be dead too. Tiberius was alone. He ducked back inside, one hand at his throat, terrified of the pain that his fellow slave must have died in, and haunted by the knowledge that he was next. 'Dearest Feronia, a slave presumes much to speak with the gods, but you at least may listen to us. I have nothing to offer but grant this slave safe passage through the foul night, and let me not rest until the shades of evil are destroyed,' he intoned, offering a prayer to the goddess most likely to listen.

Trembling with fear, Tiberius collected the other two pieces of silver and snuck out of a rear window. Slithering in the mud he picked his way quickly towards the Tiber, and hurled one of the fragments into its murky waters. The river should carry it to the sea, and the sea would carry it beyond the world. A sound behind him startled him, and in a rush, he hurled the second piece into the Tiber too. Then cursed as he saw a feral dog pawing through the mud. He had panicked and now the two pieces would remain close. He had intended burying the larger one outside Rome as Meredius would have done.

It couldn't be helped. Now he was down to the final piece, his piece, and his plan for that was simple. He just needed to reach the tomb of his true master, before it was sealed at the eighth hour of night. It was not far. Jupiter's lightning flashed again, and he saw a man ahead of him. A second flash and the street was empty.

Afraid and alone, Tiberius half-ran to the Aventine, to the tomb. Creeping around the knot of close friends and soldiers keeping watch, he inched his way inside. No one noticed slaves, particularly not slaves with no master. It was why the three of them had been chosen for the mission. But, Tiberius thought, someone had noticed them, noticed Castor and Meredius at least.

Pushing the thoughts aside, he tip-toed through the tomb, wary of the devices and curses he had been warned would be in place to trap and kill intruders. All around was death, and death was what Tiberius feared above all else.

Eventually he reached the chamber, too exhausted, tired and relieved to notice the wet footprints that indicated the presence of another in the tomb.

'Dominus,' he whispered, bowing his head before the huge stone coffin in which Romulus lay. 'It is done.'

Something hit him in the back, and with a grunt he fell to his knees. A burning pain spreading through him as he fell. Then a second blow slammed into his throat, and he stared, wide-eyed, up into a familiar face.

Meredius. The third in the conspiracy and, in his hands, the golden symbol of Rome.

Tiberius tried to speak, to gasp out a word, but all he managed was a gurgle, which drenched his chest in blood as Meredius laughed. 'You thought you could betray Remus? Simple fool, Romulus was right to trust you. But me, never me.'

Tiberius gurgled again, and clawed at his throat, he could barely hear what Meredius was saying, he could barely see. He was cold, wet and more afraid than he had ever been in his life. Meredius had betrayed him. He'd sided with the priestess, remaining loyal to Remus.

'She will find the pieces,' Meredius continued. 'I saw you throw them in the Tiber. Remus will rise again.' With a final laugh, he jammed his dagger into Tiberius's chest and hurried away, clutching his prize. The symbol of Romulus.

Summoning every last bit of strength he had, Tiberius gained his feet, staggered to the coffin and slipped the fragment of the silver eagle from beneath his tunic. His fingers fumbled as he tried to affix the catches on the armour Romulus wore, but the silver piece was in place.

'Remus can never rise Dominus,' Tiberius hissed, finally sinking into the oblivion of darkness. 'He took your eagle, but he cannot rise. She may learn that the piece is here, but she cannot enter this chamber. Rome is safe.'

When he awoke some hours later, the sound of thunder now distant, dreamlike, he was alone. The darkness was complete, the tomb of Romulus was sealed. He pushed himself up, a feeling of weightlessness settling over his cold flesh, and drifted to his master's coffin. The stone casket was sealed. Tiberius sank to his knees, resting his head against the stone. Then jumped back in fright.

His head had sunk through the stone. He'd gazed upon his master, Romulus, his silver pectoral still in place. The last fragment of Remus's soul. The priestess had lost. Once sealed, the tomb of Romulus would never be found, the city would envelop it, hide it, protect it.

Curious and frightened, Tiberius touched the stone again. His hand melted through the rock to the cold body beneath. He recoiled and drifted back towards the spot where he had woken. There was a bloodstain on the floor, a big bloodstain. He let out a moan and fell to his knees. The act dropping him partially through the floor of the cave. The Goddess Feronia had heard his words, his careless frightened words, and he would be denied rest until the shades of evil were destroyed.

I

One vice-like hand gripping her shoulder, the other holding her bags, the uniformed Royal Marine Commando frogmarched Suze across the crowded entrance of the airport terminal, his polished black boots thumping the floor with every regimented step. Unintimidated, she scanned the crowds as they scattered before the marine's authoritative stride, searching for the now familiar faces of her new friends.

'Flight number?' her imposing guardian requested, pausing in front of the departures board, his fingers keeping a tight grip on her shoulder.

'ROM246,' she replied as they both scanned the board. She sighed heavily and slumped against the marine's grip as she spotted "Delayed", in dull orange lettering, beside her flight. 'Well that sucks.'

The marine muttered a response that Suze didn't catch as she began surveying the ever-changing crowd again. A flash of red caught her eye, but immediately vanished. Suze stretched up on her toes and just about caught sight of Jerry, his lanky six foot- seven inch frame, topped with a plastic centurion's helmet, his long corkscrew curls obscured by the plastic cheek guards.

'Over there,' she said tugging at the Marine's camouflaged sleeve, 'tall guy in the Roman helmet, that's Jerry.' The crowds surged again and she lost sight of him, luckily, the commando didn't and the enforced marching resumed, the crowds parting for them like the Red Sea for Moses.

As they drew closer to Jerry's towering figure, the red-headed girl by his side broke into a broad grin and waved, jabbing the slightly shorter brunette beside her and pointing at the marine. Excited to see her friends again, Suze pushed forward, almost escaping her guardian's impressive grip, which tightened again keeping her close. Resigned, she waved back at the girls, happy to see Mell looking so bright and bubbly. She had been so despondent, reclusive almost, in the weeks following their summer adventure. Understandable of course, after what happened to her, but Suze hoped that she was starting to feel more like her old self again.

'Hey Suze, been arrested already?' Jerry asked, with a bemused expression as her military escort dumped her bag on the floor.

'Me? Arrested? As if!' Suze retorted indignantly, finally shrugging free of her big brother's grip. 'Did you really have to frogmarch me across the airport?' she hissed, turning to face him and giving her most vicious scowl.

'My orders were clear,' he replied, totally deadpan. 'Mum said, "make sure she meets her friends okay", mission accomplished.' He bent to look Suze in the eye and gave a mock salute. 'Now I'm going home, throwing on civvies, popping a beer and watching the football. Which, Nerdicus,' the marine ruffled her hair affectionately, 'I could already be doing if you'd not gotten in the way.'

'Get over it,' Suze retorted, squirming away. 'Now gimme my passport, and vanish off home like a good little soldier.'

Grinning, her brother pulled the little red book out of his pocket and slowly raised it above her head out of reach. 'If you can get it it's yours,' he said swinging it lazily back and forth. A fit of giggles erupted from behind Suze, as Sarah whispered something to Mell.

'Something funny?' Suze demanded, rounding on them.

'No, Sarah just thinks your brother's cute,' Mell giggled, twisting her long red hair between her fingers, as Sarah's face flushed a vivid shade of scarlet.

'Mell!' she exclaimed sharply, covering her face with her palm. 'That was meant to be a secret.'

With one of his legendary disarming smiles, Suze's big brother transferred her passport to his left hand, offering Sarah his right. 'Royal Marines Commando Drew Jones, at your service ma'am.'

'Sarah,' she replied, looking down at the floor before tentatively slipping her hand into his.

'Ignore him Sarah, his name's not Drew, it's Andy!' Suze hissed, swiping ineffectually at his arm, still holding the passport well out of reach. 'He's an idiot. Now gimme my passport cannon fodder!'

'Nope,' he replied ruffling her hair in response, whilst giving Sarah an apologetic look. 'Kid sisters huh?' Sarah giggled, and her cheeks bloomed with colour again.

With a heavy sigh, Suze turned pleading eyes to the only person in the group taller than her brother. 'Jerry, would you ...'

'You kidding?' Jerry recoiled in mock horror, 'he's a marine, he'll kick my ass all the way to Rome!'

'Could you do that?' Sarah asked the marine, tentatively laying a hand on his arm.

'Well,' Andy responded, casually flexing his bicep below her fingers and leaning close to whisper to her. 'I have the best stamina in my squad.'

'Alllllright!' Suze said, pushing the two apart and diffusing Andy's charm offensive. 'Duty's done soldier boy, you are discharged.'

'So's your face,' he grinned, tossing the passport over her head to Jerry. 'Have fun Nerdicus, and don't do anything or anyone that I wouldn't.' Suze stuck her tongue out in response as he walked away.

'Hey guys,' a bright voice broke in, 'who's the military hunk?' Claire was almost unrecognisable as she stepped up beside Mell, a takeaway coffee cup in one hand and an elegant wheeled suitcase in the other. Her hair, normally shoulder length and natural dark blonde, was cropped short and bleached almost white. With heavy, dark make up and sparkling nails to match, she looked like she'd walked out of a Gatsby party.

'Something's different,' said Jerry, cocking his head to one side and frowning as he inspected her face. 'Did you see a ghost? Stick your fingers in a plug socket or something?'

'What?' Claire shrugged, 'I fancied a change, get over it.' She ran her fingers through her new hair, enjoying the interest from the others. 'Although Jerry's right the colour sucks, makes my eyebrows look dark. I'll be able to get dye in Rome, right?'

The last part of whatever she said was lost under a particularly loud and incessant amount of high pitched girlish shrieking, and everyone turned to discover the source of the disturbance. A large group of glossy, giggling girls, all sporting skis and matching pastel shaded designer suitcase sets, were strolling into the airport as if they owned the place. They looked like models, almost generic in a way, each one tall and slender, with legs up to their armpits, sleek shiny hair and sheathed in designer clothes.

Suze used the diversion to snitch her passport back from Jerry. Recalling how Simon had retrieved something from the taller boy over the summer, she jammed a knee hard into the back of his, forcing him to sink to a lower height. Although, she still had to stand up on tiptoe, leaning heavily on his shoulder, to finally pluck it free.

'Ouch.' Jerry deadpanned in response, massaging his knee and straightening his centurion's helmet, before flashing Suze a cheeky grin as he rose to his full height.

Claire glanced back at the glamourous girls wistfully. 'I would love to afford just one of those bags,' she sighed, staring at the designer suitcases. 'But they run to nearly two thousand pounds and that's just for the small ones. Those girls have a whole set each.'

'Two grand! For that!' Suze exclaimed in disbelief, bordering on horror. 'My rucksack holds more … cost a fiver.'

Claire stared at her then shrieked with laughter. 'Oh Suze you really don't get it. It's not about what it holds, it's the statement it makes.'

'Can we blow off Rome and go skiing instead?' Jerry asked, staring at the ski girls. 'They look like fun.'

'You don't know how to ski,' replied Sarah, fixing him with an angry glare.

He shrugged. 'Who needs to ski? I'm all about the wooden panelled chalets and hot tubs. Dark log panelled bar, snow outside, roaring fire inside, cheap fizz, job done.'

'You're a pig,' Sarah retorted looking away and shaking her head.

'Sticks and stones may break my bones,' he sang softly, jabbing her with his elbow. 'But you still fancy me,' he snapped his fingers in a gun shape, pointing at her.

'In your dreams Jerry,' she shot back. Folding her arms defensively across her chest.

'Frequently,' he retorted, grinning inanely as she flushed bright red, and he had the last word.

The others watched their exchange curiously. Jerry and Sarah had gotten close over the summer and it was unclear if something had been going on. Only Suze knew that Jerry had kissed Sarah, but only to snap her out of paralysis and save her life. At least according to her. Although, given Suze's own experience with Simon over the summer, which was the source of the fluttering butterflies in her stomach right now, she wasn't convinced by Sarah's declaration that Jerry was just an idiot boy. Jerry himself was harder to read, by his own account a serial womaniser and king of the one night stand. A statement which everyone else, obviously, took as false bravado.

Sarah was saved from the increasingly tense situation as Claire's attention was caught by something much more interesting than designer suitcases. 'Hey guys look at the car that just arrived, super swanky!' her voice was loud, sending a ripple through the airport as everyone craned their necks to catch a glimpse of the potential celebrity. 'It must be someone important, or famous, they don't roll those things out for just anyone.' She stretched up on her toes, impatiently trying to see through the thronged airport, whilst simultaneously hunting through her bag for a mirror.

Just outside the glass fronted doors of the airport a very large, dark green vintage Bentley, with tinted windows in the rear and the personalised plate "JDM 1", pulled to a stop. As they watched, a liveried driver in an equally dark green suit and cap with white piped detailing got out. He walked slowly around the car and, opening the nearside rear passenger door, offered his white leather gloved hand to the occupant inside.

From the dark recesses of the vehicle, an elegant female hand with vividly pink painted nails appeared. She rested her fingers lightly on the chauffeur's glove before displaying first one, then another impossibly long leg, clad in tight cream jeans, accessorised with strappy, silver skyscraper heels.

'Whoa, she's hot!' Jerry's mouth hung open, and he stared unblinking, as the luxuriant blonde Venus finally emerged, to be greeted by a crescendo of screeching from the ski girls.

With practised disdain, the girl flicked her long hair and fiddled with a bracelet fitting as the driver began to unload her copious amounts of baggage; yet another set of the pastel coloured cases. Suze stared at her, trying to quell the niggling feeling that she had seen the girl somewhere before.

'I don't envy that guy,' said Mell, looking back at the car. She indicated a tall dark-haired man with a perfect olive tan, wearing an expensive looking navy-blue sports jacket, who had emerged from the other side of the car.

'Long suffering boyfriend?' guessed Claire, watching as he exchanged words with the uniformed driver. 'Wish we could see his face. Although, with arm candy like that, he must be a millionaire. A really ancient millionaire, they always have beautiful girlfriends.'

Mr. Millionaire took a moment to ensure that all of the violet-shaded cases and skis were loaded on to the driver's trolley, together with his own simple black holdall, before offering his arm to the blonde goddess and escorting her into the airport. The screeching of the ski girls became unbearable as the glamorous pair drew closer, and Suze realised with a groan who the man in the expensive jacket and wraparound sunglasses was, and, by extension who the blonde girl was.

'Is it a celebrity?' said Sarah peering at them curiously, along with half the people in the airport.

'It's just Simon and his girlfriend.' Suze replied, watching the glittering couple parade over to the elegant girls. 'Surprising to see him use one of his father's fleet cars though.'

'So it is,' said Mell, looking closer. 'Perhaps we should go and check in, looks like he might be a while. Jerry!' she snapped, realizing he was still staring hard at the girl who they now knew to be Simon's girlfriend. 'For God's sake, close your mouth and put your eyes back in your head, you look like a goldfish.'

'Say what?' he mumbled. Sarah elbowed him hard in the ribs. 'Ouch!' he rubbed his chest and glared at her. 'What was that one for?'

'You're eyeballing Simon's girlfriend,' she hissed.

Jerry's eyes widened slightly and he swung back to look at the group of girls again. 'No way,' he breathed, 'lucky bastard.'

Although in theory, the group trip to Rome was intended to be a cheap holiday, with five of them pooling their hard-earned wages from weekend work to book a relatively cheap hotel; Simon, reluctant heir to his father's commercial empire, had insisted on booking the flights and upgrading their hotel from a two to three star. Which is how the teenagers found themselves ushered into the J.D.M first class lounge, surrounded by the brand's distinctive British racing green and white colour scheme. Their flight further delayed, the five found a secluded spot by the window and settled into the huge squashy sofas to wait for Simon to escape his girlfriend and join them.

Only moments later the tranquillity of the lounge was broken as the large group of elegant ski girls arrived, laughing and giggling at their own private jokes. A dark-haired girl in a fashionable blue pant suit and blazer detached herself from the group, glancing around as if searching for someone, and then fixed her gaze on the door.

'Lady Hayworth,' she called outside softly, although loud enough for the whole room to hear. 'As your delectable *Señor* Matherson's father owns this establishment, would it be within his power to procure us some light refreshment?'

'They make a gorgeous couple,' Sarah sighed, watching as Lisa and Simon strolled arm-in-arm into the room in deep animated conversation. The five watched almost mesmerised as Lisa touched Simon's shoulder lightly and said something. He responded with a subtle bow, striding confidently to the bar.

'Oh my god, did he just bow to her?' Claire's eyes were wide in disbelief. 'That is so…'

'Poncy,' finished Jerry, flopping back into a chair and dangling his legs over the arm rest.

'The word is chivalrous Jerry,' said Sarah, fixing the tall boy with a pointed glare, 'you could learn a thing or two from Simon about being a gentleman.' Jerry snorted and began to play chords on an imaginary guitar.

'He really does behave differently, doesn't he?' Mell spoke quietly, as she watched Simon return to his girlfriend with two sparkling glasses of champagne, whilst the bar staff scurried to serve the other girls of the group.

'Different social circle,' Claire retorted looking at her phone. 'His girlfriend is an Earl's daughter...'

'He's being a proper snob, just like we always thought he was. He was nothing like that over the summer,' Jerry complained loudly.

'Keep your voice down,' Mell hissed. 'If he hears you going on like that he may well be embarrassed. And Claire stop cyberstalking him.'

'Posh nob,' Jerry muttered, pulling down his centurion's helmet and scowling into his long, dirty blond curls as Claire reluctantly put her phone away.

Several of the girls had glanced at them as Jerry's outburst reached a crescendo, and Suze felt herself shrink slightly under their looks of haughty distain. She had seen Simon this way once before, over the summer when forced to meet him at a polo match. He'd said that he hated the masked indifference of the upper echelons, but he slipped into the role so effortlessly. Unwilling to see more she dragged her guidebook to the Colosseum out of her bag and busied herself reading.

Half an hour later, the call came for a flight to Switzerland and the giggling girls began to leave. Lisa, of course, was one of the last, seemingly unwilling to leave Simon. The five travellers couldn't hear but he seemed to be reassuring her of something, before taking her hand and saying goodbye with a formal, but obviously lingering kiss to her right hand, as an older lady, that they had not previously noticed, loitered close by.

'Oh, how sad,' Claire intoned softly, turning back to the others, 'they've not once kissed each other.'

Moments later a shadow fell over the table, as Simon finally graced the group with his presence. '*Buenos días,*' he said softly in his native Spanish, before, somewhat formally, offering his hand to Jerry.

Jerry ignored it and waved at a chair. 'Dude, there's no need to stand on ceremony, just say hi and park your ass in a chair, you're with the common folk now, no more flowery hand kissing and junk.'

With evident relief Simon sank into the free chair, raking a hand through his dark hair. 'Thank God. It is good to see you all again, and thank you so much for getting me out of that ski trip. I hate skiing.'

'Really?' said Claire, 'that's not what your bio says.' She brandished her phone at him.

Simon slipped her phone from her hand and scrolled down the page shaking his head. 'You should really stop reading this junk. It is deliberately inaccurate, I value my privacy.' He handed Claire's phone back to her and turned his attention to Mell. 'Melody, how are you? I believe I have not had the pleasure of your company since early September.'

'I'm surviving,' Mell replied. She would have said more but she was rudely interrupted by a female voice calling Simon's name, the sound unexpectedly loud in the now quiet lounge.

'Lisa!' he scrambled back to his feet. 'Honey, what are you doing here,' he glanced back at the door. 'Where is Nina?'

Lisa bit her bottom lip. 'Nina is indisposed, and I forgot to give you this.' She handed him a small black box. 'Because I will not see you tomorrow.' Lisa stood on tiptoe, and wrapping her arms around his neck, kissed him passionately, pressing her body up against his. 'Happy Birthday, *mi amor*,' she whispered, and giving his hand a final squeeze, ran lightly back towards the door.

'So, I guess now you know my birthday is tomorrow.' Simon said, flopping back into the chair and closing his eyes. 'When the hell does our flight leave?'

II

Reclining on the leather sofa, clad only in her newly bought black lace and satin lingerie, Messalina Della Fontinanii topped up her wine glass and lit a cigarette. She was finally alone, and although still waiting for a late group of tourists, she was determined to make the most of it. Her husband, a weedy fellow with stringy hair and a face like an emaciated rat, was, thankfully, away for the first time in a month. But without his assistance, running the hotel, moulding the building into her vision of luxury, was a time-consuming task and she was exhausted. Well, not too exhausted, with Stefano safely out of the way she was planning on spending a few hours with Luigi. He was inexperienced and clumsy, but young and energetic and the idiot was utterly in love with her, so what did it matter?

She supposed it didn't, though she dreaded being found out simply because having an affair with the pool boy was such a cliché. Unfortunately, divorcing the useless Stefano would lose her the business that she had worked so hard to build. Mentally she cursed the events that had forced her into marriage with the ugly little businessman. The seventh ugly little businessman she'd been forcibly involved with at the behest of others. Her dalliances never usually lasted long and ended messily, not her fault, but she seemed to have been trapped with Stefano for years. She took a deep drag from the cigarette, if this week went well it was almost certain that she'd be able to get rid of him without losing the new empire she was working on.

Exhaling a bored smoke ring she reached lazily for her laptop, enjoying the sight of her scantily clad reflection in the polished table top. She still looked good, she didn't need Luigi to know that, Messalina could turn heads anywhere.

She clicked her laptop on and brought up the last page that she'd been looking at. The news from the past week. An archaeological excavation near the Colosseum a few months ago had discovered a partial silver legionary standard, the bird was missing its wings. The Capitoline Museum would be unveiling it in a display on the twins, Romulus and Remus, tomorrow. She tapped black polished fingernails against the keyboard and smiled. It was perfect, the world knew Rome was founded in April but few outside of the *Lupa Cultum* knew that the twins had been discovered by the she-wolf in October. Messalina blew

13

another smoke ring and reached for her wine glass, carefully considering her next move.

As if scripted, the brassy ding of the reception bell penetrated her thoughts, followed by the low murmur of people. Rising, Messalina pulled on a thin wrap dress and crossed the room. With a hand on the doorknob she paused to check her reflection in the mirror as she eased her tired feet into elegant high heeled shoes. She fluffed her long black hair, ensuring that it fell just right and, with the hand still holding the cigarette, slicked on an extra layer of red lipstick. Before rubbing a smudge of mascara from her cheek and opening the door to the reception.

'*Si, Si, Si, appena un momento.*' She made a show of hurrying out with her cigarette still elegantly poised in her hand and pausing behind the desk, took a deep drag, collecting herself before surveying her new customers. As the booking had specified there were six of them, all teenagers; four girls, two brunettes, a blonde with a god-awful dye job, and a red-head, all dully English, and none particularly striking. Although the shorter of the two brunettes had a strange intensity to her, perhaps trying to act more mature than she really was. Unimpressed, Messalina turned her attention to the boys. One, freakishly tall, blond and English, although oddly accented and wearing a Roman soldier's helmet, was stood by the door, staring out towards the Pantheon, or maybe the karaoke bar across the street. The dark handsome one at the desk though, he was different. Continental European, with a strong face, imperious almost. In fact, there was something unsettlingly familiar about him. The way he stood, carried himself, his dark eyes as he caught sight of her, he reminded her of someone. It was such a shame she had a rule about sleeping with the guests.

'*Signora di buona sera.*' To her surprise he spoke Italian, and not the broken guide book type, he was fluent and without trace of an accent as he apologised for the lateness of their arrival. Feeling excited butterflies in her stomach at the prospect of flirting with the handsome young man, Messalina elegantly stubbed out her cigarette and blowing out a final smoke ring, leaned forwards on the counter. Allowing the neckline of her dress to shift slightly, revealing a flash of black lace. Rules were, after all, made to be broken.

To her dismay, he kept his eyes firmly on her face as they spoke. Over his shoulder the other five were idly checking out the décor in the reception. Trying a different track, she gave him a soft smile and dropped her eyes to check the pile of passports under her hand. All were red, and in varying states of use. One looked very new, unused, another was battered almost to the point of falling apart. She slipped that one to the bottom of the pile and quickly checked through the rest, glancing down at photos and up at the group. The new one belonged to the tall boy. She liked his photo, he had an open and friendly face. She could tell he was the funny one just by the picture, mischief sparkled in his eyes. The bleached blonde had been pretty before she'd had the terrible dye job, very pretty. One of the other girls had a visa for the USA stamped in the back. Messalina picked up the old tatty one carefully, almost afraid of breaking it, noting the crest of Spain rather than Britain on the cover.

'*C'è un problema?*' the Spaniard asked her, glancing away from his friends and noticing that she had lingered over his passport. In truth, his name had given her pause, like the boy himself something seemed familiar about it, but she couldn't place it.

Embarrassed at having been caught, she spotted a get out clause and turned his passport to show him. Placing her finger delicately on the page, she indicated that the document was due to expire in the next few weeks. As he smiled and thanked her for pointing it out, she handed the pile of documents back, taking great care to accidentally brush her fingers against his. '*Nome della prenotazione?*' she asked, flicking her hair back suggestively and running her finger down the log book.

'Matherson,' he replied absently. Fingers tracing the line of his nose, which, she noticed, slanted slightly to the left.

Messalina gave the Spaniard her best flirtatious smile and, still trying to work out why his name was familiar, she checked through Stefano's terrible, scrawled handwriting for the booking. Then selected three room keys for the top floor, below the roof bar, and sashayed around the reception desk, ensuring that the short skirt of her dress revealed as much thigh as possible, accentuated by her stiletto heels. Stalking across the marble foyer, it came to her. Matherson was the name of the hotel and transport tycoon who owned the JDM brand. The revelation took her completely by surprise. The young man in her reception looked nothing like the arrogant business man, and she tripped, slamming a hand into the wall to keep her balance. '*Scusami, è stato un giorno lungo,*' she covered herself with the excuse of a long day. '*Seguimi prego.*' Playing her cards right with the young man could be well worth it, if indeed he was who she suspected he was, it was surprising enough that he had booked into her hotel when there was a JDM in town. Her mind working furiously over how to use this opportunity, alongside her other plans for the week, Messalina indicated that her guests should follow her.

She walked slowly, gesturing around the reception, showing the group the location of the on-site spa and the small subterranean pool. The Pantheon was right outside the door and from there it was an easy walk to anywhere, or there were metro stations between attractions. The blonde girl with the terrible dye job seemed more interested by the spa than the fact that ancient Rome lay right on the doorstep, although the rest of the group were chatting quite knowledgably about the Romans. Messalina wondered briefly whether to warn them about the soldiers by the Colosseum. They were harmless, but photographs with them were expensive.

A plan beginning to formulate in her mind, Messalina positioned herself close to the group and started to lead them up her newly installed white marble staircase towards the rooms on the upper floors. The marble only went as far as the first floor, sweeping up out of a corridor to the left of her reception desk, to a balcony that ran in a square around the open entrance and foyer below. On the regular stairs to the second floor, she made her carefully planned stumble, landing her hand with exact precision on the young Spaniard's arm.

His response was to catch her elbow, and ask her, in Italian, if everything was all right, before insisting that they could probably find their rooms alone. She waved his concern away, whilst taking the moment to study his face. He definitely did not look like his father, if of course, she was correct about who he was. Taking the opportunity, she slipped her arm easily through his and began talking to him about the Renaissance façade of the building and her plans for it, in animated Italian, before casually mentioning John Matherson.

Instantly the Spaniard's body tensed up. His whole demeanour changed and Messalina got the feeling she had just made a terrible mistake. He swiftly reclaimed his arm from hers, fixing her with an icy, piercing gaze. His jaw worked momentarily as if he wanted to say something, but instead he bowed his head to her, turned curtly on his heel and strode quickly away up the stairs towards the roof bar. Messalina froze, conscious of her other guests and that she must have made a huge error, but uncertain what she could have done that would result in such a terrible reaction. The other five were a little way back down the stairway, perhaps she'd been lucky and they had not noticed her faux-pas. She glanced towards them as a loud bubble of laughter reached her, and saw that they were busy giggling about something, then she caught the tall boy's words.

'Betcha anything, she asked him for a quick one.'

Messalina rolled her eyes as the red-head elbowed him in the ribs and told him to be quiet. She didn't mind too much if her guests thought she'd been flirting with the handsome Spaniard, she had been, at least before everything went wrong. She would simply have to apologise the next time she saw him. Shaking her head, Messalina smoothed down her dress and picked an invisible speck of dust from her waistline. She ran her fingers through her hair as the five approached, suddenly feeling very conscious of her heavily accented English.

'These are you. Twenty-two,' she gestured towards the first door and handed the key to the girl with the red hair, 'next door, twenty-four,' she passed a key to one of the dark-haired girls, 'and here, twenty-six.' She gave the final key to the tall boy hoping that she'd worked things out right and that there were no romantic pairings within the six. The sun had gone down about an hour ago but Rome was still impressive in the darkness, and as the teens unlocked their doors, Messalina gave them her final parting spiel. 'The rooms at the front of the hotel have a shared balcony, and there is a rooftop bar up the stairs that way. I think your friend headed up there already. If you need anything, zero on *telefono* anytime, if no answer, please come to reception. Enjoy your stay. *Buona sera.*' With a final smile, she stalked away down the corridor, one stilettoed foot after the other, hips swaying in an exaggerated fashion, courting the admiration of the tall boy.

Exhausted, the five weary travellers piled into their rooms, barely noticing the lights that marked the centre of Rome. They stumbled through the entrances and across the rooms barely aware of the opulence of their surroundings as waves of tiredness swept over them.

'Anyone want a coffee or something?' Sarah asked, wandering out onto their adjoining balcony, and staring in wonder at the *piazza* below and the majestic Pantheon.

'I'm sure Simon will want one,' Suze called back.

'I'll have one,' Claire said, sweeping an approving gaze over the view as she joined Sarah on the balcony. 'This place is nice, I was a little gutted when Simon refused to stay at the JDM. I've always wanted to stay in one of those.'

'It's just a hotel,' Suze replied, 'albeit a posh, fancy hotel where you feel like you're permanently on display and being judged.'

'I forget that you stayed in one with him,' said Mell, dropping into a spacious chair.

'Spent every moment thinking they were gonna throw me out,' Suze admitted. 'Can I still drink tea in Italy or is there just coffee?'

'I could have coffee,' Simon groaned from the doorway to the room he was sharing with Jerry, and there was an audible crack as he stretched his shoulders out and massaged his forehead. 'My head is pounding.'

'Your hangover is your own fault,' Mell scolded. 'Don't blame the plane because you tanked too much champagne in Manchester.'

'I did not drink so much,' he replied defensively. 'Besides champagne gives me less of a headache than the sedative.'

'A sedative?' Claire said with amusement. 'What on earth do you need a sedative for? You scared of flying or something?'

Simon's phone chirruped into life, saving him from having to answer Claire, and he shook his head. Although his tired smile, and the way his body snapped to rigid attention; standing straight, his left hand moving to rest automatically behind his back, betrayed the fact that the caller was Lisa. Everyone else flopped down into the comfortable looking sofas on the wide balcony, looking towards the lights of Rome. After a few moments Jerry gave a loud yawn, followed almost immediately by Mell, who glanced longingly towards the bedrooms.

'Do you think the Eternal City will forgive us if we sleep first?' she asked no one in particular.

III

Lisa Hayworth-Mills stood at the top of the slope in the early morning sunshine, staring down at the crisp snow below. Her ski poles were jammed in the snow beside her and she leaned on one whilst staring into space, lost in her own thoughts. She'd been so excited about this holiday with her friends, a gossipy, girly week full of fun, frolics and harmless flirting with her ski instructor. And now she was here, all she could think of was her boyfriend, in Rome, with four other women.

She'd known he was going, he'd told her three weeks ago. She'd just naively assumed it was a rugby lads' week of fun and hi-jinks, then Louisa had told her that Tobey knew nothing about it, so it couldn't be a rugby club thing. Simon had just said that he was going with friends, she'd never considered that his friends would be female. She desperately hoped that he wasn't cheating on her. Her mind kept playing over their final goodbye, before she'd had to run for her flight. She'd gone back to give him his birthday present and they'd all been there, relaxed, joking. Simon had seemed so tense when he stood up to meet her.

At the time, she'd told herself it was nothing. For someone who shuttled often between England and Spain, Simon had a severe phobia of flying, of course he was tense. But he must have known that she felt threatened, she'd never kissed him in public like that before. His response had been chaste, not unresponsive but she would have appreciated a little more passion. Although that was just him, how he'd always been when people were watching. Lisa only ever got true passion out of him when he was certain that they were alone. She closed her eyes remembering how it felt when Simon held her close and tried not to cry imagining that he could hold someone else like that.

'Lisa?' A voice interrupted her thoughts and someone lightly touched her arm. 'Lisa, is everything all right? You've been broody since we arrived.'

'Come on Lisa,' said another voice, 'we've been over this, your prince charming is not off hooking up with those other girls in Italy. The man barely even acknowledges that other women exist. He is not his father, you can trust him.'

'Louisa, he never even mentioned that his friends were girls,' Lisa's voice was pained.

'In his defence, I doubt he noticed that they were girls, I certainly didn't,' Sofia sniffed. 'None of them looked half as attractive as you honey. Your man is sound.'

Lisa shook her head, trying desperately not to cry and mist up her ski goggles. 'I do not trust these new friends of his. Simon never mentioned them prior to the summer and I have no idea what they did last time they were together but he returned with strange bruises and a broken nose.'

'Lisa your boyfriend is always covered in bruises, he plays rugby for goodness sake,' Louisa folded her arms with a smile. 'Tobey probably elbowed him in the face in a scrunch, or whatever they call it.'

'That is what father said,' Lisa replied, although the expression on her face suggested that she did not believe it. Unwilling to discuss it further she reached for her poles and pushed off down the slope, letting the wind blow their words away.

She was an accomplished skier and the run was easy, and all too soon she found her mind wandering again as she slalomed down on auto-pilot. It was all too overwhelming by the time she reached the bottom and with a sob, she tore her goggles off and threw them into the packed snow and tugged at her gloves, desperate to unclip her skis and get off the slope, back to her room to be alone.

'Lisa are you all right you look like you're about to cry!' exclaimed Miranda, stepping out of the café and folding her in a perfumed embrace. 'What is it honey?'

'She thinks *Señor* perfect is off to Rome for a promiscuous affair with four other women,' Louisa said harshly, sliding to a graceful halt having followed Lisa down the run. 'Tell her she's crazy, the younger Matherson barely even acknowledges the existence of other ladies.'

'Sweetie, Simon would never do that to you,' Katrina gasped in horror. 'When was the last time you two were alone together?'

Lisa baulked slightly. 'It has been a few weeks, Nina is always there, and I am certain father knows and has asked her to keep a closer watch on me. I am surprised that she did not insist on coming on the slopes with us.'

'You know what you could do,' Miranda whispered conspiratorially. 'If we kept Nina busy, you may be able to sneak off, go surprise him in Rome.'

'That would be perfect,' squealed Sofia, 'You said it was his birthday today. You should go and surprise him.'

'Ohmigod do it,' Louisa said excitedly, clapping her hands. 'We can go shopping, the village is nearby, we can find you a really sexy dress, or two.'

'And new underwear, you have to have new underwear,' Miranda insisted, 'something uncomfortable and very sexy.'

Lisa gave a wobbly smile. 'It would never work; besides I cannot use daddy's credit card to buy underwear, he'd notice.'

'He may notice the store name, but I hardly think Earl Hayworth is going to question his darling daughter purchasing satin panties in Switzerland,' Katrina snorted.

'You do not know father, it would be terrible,' Lisa insisted.

'Oh Lisa, use my credit card, we have to do this,' said Sofia insistently as they began pulling their ski boots off. 'Between us all we can fix you a flight, a dress and some sexy satins, and your father will never know.'

'And when you get to Rome, wear the outfit we pick, it has to be the first thing Simon sees you in. Save the sexy dress for dinner and a hotel room floor,' said Miranda with a wink.

'Oh, and when Simon asks why you are there, be all mysterious and tell him that you have another gift for him to unwrap,' Louisa prompted.

A nervous smile crossed Lisa's face. 'Do you really think I can do it alone?' she bit her lip as Nina, her ever-present chaperone, gestured for her to come indoors.

Louisa beamed back and squeezed her hands. 'You can do anything babe,' she said. 'Now, go tell Nina that Sofia and I want to go shopping and we'll be back in three hours.'

Lisa ducked into the café, sharing a few brief words with Nina and then re-joined her friends in the snow outside. Their plan could work, she had never been totally alone before, but it would just be for the duration of the plane to Rome and getting from the airport to Simon's hotel. She knew a little Italian, not as much as he did, but surely enough to procure a taxi. She just had to find out where her boyfriend was staying, it certainly wouldn't be his father's hotel, Simon actively avoided all contact with his father, the fact that he had flown to Rome with JDM had been unusual. The hotel was a problem easily solved though, she could innocently call him to wish him Happy Birthday and ask about his holiday accommodation. True, she'd called him last night to ask about his flight, but a call on his birthday wouldn't raise suspicion. Lisa smiled secretively to herself, if she had the time she would buy new makeup, and curl her hair before she saw him. She just had to be confident in her own abilities. She pulled out her phone and called him, her whole body relaxing as she heard his accented voice at the other end. Simon would never expect her in Rome; the plan was perfect.

*

The morning sun was golden, the sky empty, the air still and silent. Suze stood on the wide shared balcony breathing in the crisp morning air and relishing the near silence. Focussing on the view of the Pantheon, she wandered around the balcony, pausing before the statue of two-faced Roman God Janus that adorned the small area. Actually, looking closer it was possibly the twins, Castor and Pollux, rendered as Gemini. Or something else, one of the figures held an eagle on an outstretched arm, the other cradled a small bird in cupped hands and they both stood on the back of a wolf.

Her scrutiny was interrupted as Mell and Claire emerged bickering from their shared room. 'Claire, this is Rome not Milan …'

'There are still boutique shops, fashion exists, I don't see why we have to spend all our time looking at ancient Roman crap. All I want is an afternoon in Prada,' Claire was practically screaming.

'All you think about recently is shopping,' Mell retaliated, spiky hand gestures mimicking her words as she spoke. 'This is the Eternal City. Rome. As in Romans. As in Empire. Or Borgias, the Vatican, da Vinci, Michelangelo, half the world's history in one city!'

'As in yawn,' Claire replied over her shoulder as she drifted towards the room the two girls shared. Those outside could still hear her muttering before she slammed the bathroom door. 'Look at the state of my hair! I need a deep condition, and this blonde is disgusting.'

'Suze, Sarah,' Mell groaned, slumping into one of the chairs on the balcony. 'Could one of you swap rooms with me, if I have to hear Claire complain about her hair one more time, I'm gonna kill her,' she took a deep breath. 'Oh god like I …'

'We know what you meant,' Suze said quickly, interrupting the dark direction of her thoughts. 'One of us can swap, it's not a problem.'

'I don't know what's going on with her right now, the haircut, the crazy dye. She talked nearly all night about nothing but fashion, eligible millionaires and how cute your brother was,' Mell confessed. 'She's driving me nuts. I swear, her obsession with millionaires, if Simon was single she'd be all over him.'

Sarah giggled. 'I'll swap. Wanna do it now whilst she's in the shower or later?' she paused listening. 'Can you two hear that? Jerry's singing.' She was right, a soft melody was issuing from the direction of the boys' room, obscured by the sound of the water pump. 'He's actually really good,' Sarah elaborated, a slow smile brightening her face. 'You guys should have seen him in Dover, he had the entire pub on their feet, he's awesome.'

'I knew it,' Mell grinned slyly, 'you quite fancy him, don't you?'

'Urgh, no,' Sarah protested, scowling and dropping into a chair. 'Definitely not, the man is a complete ass basket, he has no respect for women.'

'Or for people trying to sleep,' Suze agreed with a grin, recalling from the summer how much Simon hated being woken early. 'I bet Simon's not happy, although he was pretty chilled out yesterday. I think he's enjoying being away from England.'

'Well he is continental, I guess Italy must feel more like home than Britain does,' Sarah replied as the balcony door to the boys' room opened disgorging clouds of steam, from which Jerry emerged like the rock star he was pretending to be. A fluffy white bath towel hung low around his hips, his long dirty blond hair scraggled in tendrils around his angular face and the glistening red dragon of Wales stalked proudly across his skinny, naked chest. Oblivious to the world he strode across the balcony, still belting out an old rock song, his fingers playing imaginary chords on a guitar as he bounced his soaked curls to the rhythm in his head.

Suze grinned as she watched his performance. Sarah was right, Jerry was good, not just karaoke good, he could really hit and hold a decent note. He suddenly caught the girls watching and flashed them a huge cheeky grin and a wink.

'*Buongiorno* ladies,' he grinned widely. 'Jukebox Jerry is open for requests.'

Suze laughed, at least someone was enjoying the morning.

'Put some clothes on,' Sarah demanded, with a lot more venom than the others were expecting. Rising from the sofa and heading into the room she shared with Suze to turn the kettle on. 'No one wants to see your gangly twig body this early in the morning.'

'I'm not a twig, I'm a sapling,' he replied, striking a pose that threatened to dislodge the already precarious towel. 'Towering like a mighty oak.'

Mell started giggling. 'I'd forgotten what a wonderful idiot you are,' she smiled.

Jerry made an obscenely flamboyant bow. 'I aim to please ...' he was interrupted by a gentle knock at the door to his room. 'Don't everyone move at once,' he chided half-heartedly, checking his towel was secure before leaning back into the room and hollering that whoever it was could come in. A second or two later their polished Italian hostess stepped gingerly out onto the balcony.

She ran an appreciative eye over Jerry's chest before raising a shapely eyebrow in approval and brandishing an envelope. '*C'è una lettera per Signore Matherson*,' she held it out and peered curiously around Jerry, presumably hoping to catch a glimpse of Simon.

'Not here,' Jerry replied, 'I'll take it.' He plucked the cream envelope delicately from her hand, letting his damp fingers linger against hers and, fixing her with his most charming grin, allowed his towel to slide just a little lower. His flirtatious efforts were rewarded with a slow smile and low throaty chuckle. She left the letter with him and sashayed gracefully away, very aware that he was watching.

'What do you mean Simon's not here?' Suze demanded as soon as she vanished. 'Where is he?

'How the hell do I know?' Jerry replied, tossing the crisp envelope onto the coffee table, almost losing his grip on the towel that was beginning to reveal a little too much. 'He wasn't here when I got up, and I didn't hear him leave.' Jerry dropped into the nearest chair and put his feet up on the coffee table.

'Jerry,' Mell hissed, 'take your feet off the table.'

'Fine,' he dropped his feet to the floor shifting his legs as he did so and both girls immediately giggled and looked away.

'Is that a new tattoo?' said Suze, suddenly catching sight of something on Jerry's right calf.

'Uh, yeah,' he moved his right foot back onto the coffee table to show off his double headed battle axe, entwined with a green ribbon upon which the word *Honour* was emblazoned. 'Reminds me of Gawain, and it covers the scar,' he grinned cheerfully, inadvertently exposing more of what lay below the towel.

'Jerry, I really think it's time to go put some clothes on,' said Mell. 'And where do you think Simon is?'

Jerry shrugged, 'Your guess is as good as mine.' He relaxed back into the sofa, resting his hands behind his head and closed his eyes. 'So … why is Rome called Rome? Cos its inhabitants are always romin' around,' he laughed.

'You dingbat,' Suze laughed, 'you know it's named for Romulus.' Rolling her eyes, she got up to make a cup of tea.

'Ahh yes, King of the Romulans,' Jerry deadpanned, eyes still closed. 'Roman Mowgli. Didn't he have a brother? Rebus?'

'Remus.' A soft accented voice corrected him. Simon had returned as quietly as he had left.

'Well don't you look gorgeous this morning!' Mell exclaimed, taking in his tailored black suit and white shirt. 'Where've you been? A James Bond convention?'

'Today happens to be Sunday,' Simon replied, removing his collar studs and cufflinks, loosening his tie. 'His Holiness was giving morning Mass at the Vatican. I took the liberty of assuming that none of you would be interested.'

'Didn't know you were Catholic Si?' Jerry offered sleepily, forgetting his less than casual attire and shifting his position slightly.

'Jerry! For god's sake get dressed,' Sarah shrieked, as she returned to the balcony and caught an eyeful of what lay under the towel.

'Make me,' he replied, finally getting up. 'Besides that's blasphemy ain't it Si? Sarah watch your language you might offend him.'

Simon laughed. 'I am hardly devout, I only ever attend Mass if I happen to be on the continent and only on Sunday. Unless I happen to be at home where the local Padre is a close family friend. In England, I rarely bother.'

Inside her shared room Suze glanced back towards the balcony, Mell was right, Simon did look dashing, suited and booted as he was. As she waited for the water to filter through the coffee strainer she watched him remove a simple gold crucifix from under his shirt and sighed. There was still so much about the elegant Spaniard that they didn't know, but she did know that he liked real coffee and it was his birthday. Collecting the full cups, she wandered back outside. 'Happy Birthday Simon,' she said softly, handing him a large mug of black coffee.

'*Gracias*,' he replied, wrapping his fingers around the steaming mug and inhaling deeply as he leaned back against the stone rail of the balcony.

'How come you didn't tell us?' Sarah asked accusingly. 'Your eighteenth is a big deal.'

Simon glanced up blankly, taking a sip of his coffee. 'The matter seemed irrelevant. Anyway, you were talking about Romulus when I came in. The *Museo Capitolino* has a new temporary exhibition about the twins and the foundation of Rome. They are also exhibiting, what is believed to be, a silver legionary eagle found about a month ago in the Ludus. We could go and have a look, I have some tickets held on reserve.'

'So, no massacring Christians at the Colosseum then?' Jerry yelled from their bedroom.

'Maybe later,' Simon called back with a smile.

IV

The afternoon sun was warm as Mell, Simon and Sarah sat on the edge of the fountain in front of the *Palazzo Senatorio*, in the *Piazza del Campidoglio*. At Sarah's request to see something less Roman in Rome, Simon had taken both of them via the Borgia palace to the Spanish steps and the house of the Romantic poet Keats. Before ushering them onto the metro, down to the other end of the city, and into a graveyard, where he'd quickly hunted out the graves of both Shelley and Keats. Then they'd grabbed *gelato* on the way back, ducking into various basilicas on the way up to the Capitoline Museum.

Waiting for the others, they watched the crowds milling around the *piazza,* they needed the rest. Rome was breath-taking, in more ways than one. She was an exhausting riot of history and modernity. A simple walk to the museum had left them almost dizzy. The Eternal City certainly lived up to her name; it was almost as if time had stood still, as if the Roman Empire were still there, simply veiled by a gauzy curtain that could be pushed aside. The same for the Renaissance period, if one turned the right corner perhaps Raphael or Michelangelo would be sat before an easel or working a block of stone into sculpture, or Lucretia Borgia would be holding one of her famed parties, perhaps by the Spanish steps writers would be dramatically declaiming poetry. Rome scooped up tourists, whizzed them in a blender of history and left them dizzyingly exhausted. Her magnificence was almost a physical assault on the eyes and mind, there was no direction to look in and not see her glory. Even the museum buildings had been designed by Michelangelo. In the centre of the space a bronze rendered statue of the emperor Marcus Aurelius sat astride a horse, his benevolent gaze watching the thronging tourists.

Sounds of a disturbance came from the *via di San Pietro in Carcere* to their right and seconds later Jerry and Suze hurtled into the crowded *piazza* as if an army were chasing them. 'You are such a dork!' Suze yelled, just about managing to keep up with Jerry's long-legged stride.

Jerry, still wearing his plastic centurion's helmet, twisted to look back over his shoulder. 'We are in Rome! The term is Dorkus!'

'The term is I'm gonna kill you!' she screamed back, launching a half reasonable rugby tackle towards Jerry's legs that brought them both to a tangled heap on the ground beside the trio sat on the edge of the fountain.

'Ungh, Suze gerroff,' Jerry hissed as she sat on him, pinning him to the floor.

Mell shook her head and took a sip of her cold lemonade. 'You two are a pair of Dorkusus.'

'Dorkii, perhaps?' Simon said absently, then shook his head realising that either way made no sense. 'Suze, that was, without doubt, one of the worst flying tackles I have ever seen. Promise me that you will never play rugby, at least not against my team.'

'What did Jerry do this time?' sighed Sarah, leaning back and trailing her hand in the cool water of the fountain, tilting her face back to the sun.

'Because of course it has to be my fault,' said Jerry, rolling Suze off his back and standing up. 'Something happened, it must be Jerry's fault, couldn't possibly be anyone else.'

'But it was your fault, Jez,' Suze said, oblivious to the tension between Sarah and Jerry. 'You were pretending to be a Roman soldier down by the Colosseum, and the real ones chased us cos you were stealing their revenue. So, we didn't get into the Colosseum and we sprinted past the forum,' she slumped down on the floor, leaning against the fountain between Simon and Sarah, her Colosseum guidebook clutched in her hands. 'There is so much stuff here, I love it! But I have no idea where to start, I want to see everything!' she leaned back and closed her eyes losing herself in a daydream.

'What is she doing?' said Sarah quietly, as Suze moved her hands. Her left, holding the book, came up as if holding a shield, her right making deft parrying movements.

Simon shushed her, recognising Suze's actions from Caerleon. 'Playing gladiator,' he said in a half whisper, answering Sarah's question. The group watched her for a few moments longer, then with a smile Simon leaned down beside her clenching his left hand into a fist before her face and whispered softly in Suze's ear. 'His imperial majesty is still not impressed.' As Suze's eyes flew open, Simon twisted his wrist to give the thumbs down indication from the emperor to finish a downed gladiator. The same as he had done when he caught her daydreaming at Caerleon over the summer. The other three laughed, Suze flushed scarlet, annoyed at having drifted off in their company, and opened her book trying to escape.

'What's so funny?' Claire asked finally joining them. She had still been in the shower when the other five left the hotel, and despite numerous entreaties to go sightseeing with them she'd wanted to go shopping and try the spa.

'Just Suze, falling asleep,' Mell replied. 'How was shopping?'

'Fantastic,' Claire's eyes sparkled. 'I wish I was a millionaire, I could have spent thousands, there were these really cute shoes in Prada, but they were like four hundred euros. Which was a little out of my price range. Although I did buy something.' She flashed a huge smile in Simon's direction, 'I found the most beautiful dress for dinner tonight, it's gorgeous.'

'And a huge hat,' said Jerry, looking curiously at the enormous floppy brimmed sun hat that Claire was wearing. 'Wanna swap?' He offered her his centurion's helmet.

'Are you seriously going to wear that all week?' said Mell, pushing her sunglasses down her nose and looking at him over the rims like a stern school teacher.

'Yup,' he replied. 'Although I could switch with Claire.' He stretched across and swiped playfully at the brim of her hat, knocking it sideways and eliciting a scream of rage.

'Jerry! You moron!' Claire grabbed at her hat, missed, and knocked it off completely, revealing her now bright green hair. She'd clearly been hiding it. Jerry burst out laughing.

'It's awful,' Claire groaned. 'I was trying to go back to a more natural blonde, but the dye reacted with the bleach.' She reached for her hat again.

'It's kinda funky,' said Mell. 'Like a computer game character.'

Claire looked at her blankly. It's hideous. Okay, I look a mess. And I have no idea how to fix it. It's green for god's sake.'

'I like it,' Simon said. He sat on the edge of the fountain, elbow resting on his knee, chin on his knuckles. 'It is bold, daring. Although the orange shirt may have been a mistake.'

'You like it?' Claire removed her hat again and shook her hair out, running her fingers through it, straightening it after having kept it stuffed under the hat for most of the morning. 'Really? It doesn't make me look stupid?'

Simon's response was a clearly well-honed routine of agreement. Perfected by hours of inane questions about appearance from his demanding girlfriend. '*Sì, sì, no.* You look fine.'

'Ohmigod thank you!' Claire threw her arms around him in a hug that he clearly wasn't expecting and with a splash that showered the entire group with water, they both ended up in the fountain.

Roaring with laughter the other four could only watch as Claire apologised and tried to help Simon out of the fountain. He was soaked, but seemed to take the incident in good humour as he hauled himself, dripping, over the lip of the pool and back onto solid ground. The day was warm, it wouldn't take long for either of them to dry off.

A barrage of unintelligible, screamed and frenzied Italian, broke through the group's laughter and they turned to watch as two museum security guards awkwardly man-handled a squirming figure out of the *Palazzo dei Conservatori*. The third figure was an old man, ragged and bony with a long, matted beard and wizened features, likely one of Rome's many professional beggars, or one of the genuine destitute. Either way he was spritely, the guards were having trouble holding him as he shrieked, squirmed and wriggled like a fish.

'What's going on?' Mell asked, discretely gripping Simon's wrist as she felt a hollow fear begin to rise in her stomach. 'Is he likely to be dangerous?'

Simon shook his head, scattering water droplets onto the paving. 'I doubt very much that he is dangerous, perhaps he has a less than tenuous hold on his sanity.' He listened for a moment to the jabbered Italian. 'Apparently he believes that something in the exhibition is evil.'

'Well I suppose the enemies of Rome may have seen their eagles as a symbol of evil,' Suze said with a shrug, before relaxing back against the fountain again.

'Vikings are so much cooler than Romans,' replied Jerry. He ruffled the red crest on his helmet and changed the subject as the old man sat on the floor and continued to yell obscenities at the museum doors. 'Si, did you get that letter the hot Italian lady brought up this morning?' he grinned, 'Illicit love letter, was it? She definitely wanted a piece of you last night.'

Simon stared at him for a second dumbfounded, and then burst out laughing. 'Nothing so sordid, it was a birthday letter and small gift from *mi abuelo*.' He held up his left hand, indicating the signet ring on his little finger. 'Symbol of the Spanish house of de Valentia.'

'Abuelo?' Sarah asked.

'My grandfather. Sometimes I forget that you do not understand Castilian,' he took in his friends' uncomprehending faces and rolled his eyes. 'Oh, come on, that was an easy one. It is what you would know as Spanish,' he clarified, glancing towards the museum entrance. 'I no longer seem to be dripping, shall we go in?'

They rose, heading for the *Palazzo Nuovo,* which housed the Roman artefacts and statues, thinking to avoid the old man by visiting the temporary exhibition later, but unfortunately, he had watched them move. Staring with wild unfocussed eyes he pointed at each of them in turn and in lilting Italian projected his ire. *'La falso aquila è stata rivelata, la profezia della Sacerdotessa si avvicina al completamento e non ho altro che sciocchi con cui affrontare il malvagio.'*

'Simon what's he saying?' Claire asked, slipping her hand into his as he stood up.

'Same as before, something about a priestess and some gibberish about the evil one. We should just ignore him and go inside,' he replied, deftly disentangling his fingers from hers.

The old man hissed at them as they moved by. Then stepped back, thumped his chest, and threw himself prostrate at Simon's feet. *'L'erede di Cesare ritorna a Roma, non tutto è perduto. Deve essere distrutto. Distrutto!'* Without warning he snatched at Simon's trouser leg and wrapped a bony hand around the eighteen-year-old's ankle.

'Did he just call you Caesar?' Suze asked, glancing at Simon.

'No,' he replied, his native Spanish accenting the familiar word as the colour drained slightly from his face. He stood perfectly still, the old man still wrapped around his leg, muttering in Italian. 'Can one of you find a security guard,' Simon hissed keeping his voice low. He seemed in control, although Suze noticed the nervous twitch in his left hand.

Most of the *piazza* had now stopped what they were doing and had drawn back to watch the spectacle. The old man continued to holler as he clung to Simon's leg. *'Ave l'erde di Cesare! Ave! Ave!'* Mell had run off to find the museum security, but the rest of the group could do nothing as the old man snatched at Simon's left hand and dragged it down, apparently to inspect Simon's new signet ring.

'What the hell is going on?' said Claire, as across the *piazza* the security guards began to push their way through the crowd.

Sensing that his time was limited, the old man finally relinquished his hold on Simon's leg, kissed his signet ring and threw himself prostrate on the ground again. *'Perdonami Cesare,'* he muttered, before scrambling to his feet and fleeing before the guards could catch him.

V

Dressed in a long, black hooded robe Messalina moved silently as a shadow through her annex, she knew where all her staff should be and the hotel was not busy. Most of her guests would be in Rome, but still she moved stealthily through the rooms until she reached the large private dining room, behind the hotel reception. It was her favourite room in her private space, adorned with its racy frescoes, copied from the brothel at Pompeii and several nude marble statues. She had designed it herself, in fact she had designed most of the annex in which she and her detestable husband now lived, but this room was her sanctuary. She took perverse pleasure in the obvious discomfort that the explicit frescoes inflicted on many visitors, and an even greater pleasure from entertaining her many lovers in the charged atmosphere generated by the images.

She crossed the room quickly, heading for the darkest corner, in which lurked a naked and rather well-endowed satyr, almost hidden by the trailing leaves of a pot plant. Brushing the plant aside Messalina's fingers tenderly caressed the image, her fingers landing delicately on the satyr's groin, which formed a hidden lever jutting out of the wall. With a soft click, one of the marbled paving stones slid down and sideways revealing a wooden trap door below. She paused again listening, but the house remained silent. With practiced movements, she reached for the iron ring, lifted the panel and descended into the darkness below, making certain that the stone slab slid back into place behind her.

Wrapped in the darkness of the secret basement Messalina stood still, breathing quietly, feeling her heart beat quicker in a mixture of anticipation and revulsion. Reaching for an alcove she knew to be on her left, she grasped a candle and moments later it flared into life, wreathing her face in quivering shadows. Slowly, almost reverently she descended the short flight of steps into the basement proper, before removing her shoes and slowly walking the perimeter of the room, lighting several large wax candles and two incense sticks placed strategically around the small space. The only sound was a soft swish as the hem of her long black robe brushed against the cold stone floor. The candles lit, Messalina paused in the centre of the room, her large dark eyes surveying her equally dark domain.

On the back wall, in the centre of her black draped altar was a female skull, crumbling with age and painted with black charcoal swirls and symbols. She had been the Etruscan priestess of Remus, founder of the *Lupa Cultum*. Legend had it that she had been killed inciting the rabble of Rome, forever known as Remus's rabble, to overthrow the kings of Rome. The Etruscan priestess had succeeded, the seventh king had perished, but the republic which followed him had not set right the grievous mistake of the past. Nor had anything since. Either side of the skull stood a bronze statuette, one; Janus, God of Time and Doorways. The other, a fairly nondescript man in Roman dress with a small bird on his shoulder. He bore no name.

Composing herself before the intimidating presence of her deities, Messalina raised the cowl on her robe, ensuring that her head was reverently covered, and knelt, bowing her head and splaying her arms out towards the altar.

For a long time, she knelt in silence; waiting, listening, her knees feeling the chill of the stone floor, breathing the incense, absorbing the silence, feeling the chill of the basement seep into her skin. When she spoke, it was as if in a trance. Her natural Italian, slightly slurred, mixing effortlessly with its more ancient Latin roots as she raised her head to see the glowing deities before her. On her knees, she called them forth from the mists of the netherworld.

The candles guttered in a draft that arose, and the air in the tiny windowless cell grew colder, but still Messalina knelt on the stone, head bowed in supplication, listening for instructions from the realm beyond. A woman's voice, thin and papery, barely there, whispering in her ear. Invisible cold hands touched her body, assessing, appraising, with teasing caresses, like when she was introduced to the cult. They who had inducted her had never truly believed that their aims could be achieved, they had simply been going through the motions, as they had for hundreds of years. Messalina though, heard the words of the long dead Etruscan priestess. Since her first ritual she had been favoured by the ancient priestess. A feeling of ecstasy washed over her and she threw herself back succumbing to the disembodied voice in her head.

Eyes half-open, anxious to please her gods, Messalina reached gently into the folds of her diaphanous robe and withdrew the small, barely breathing body of a brown bird. A wren. Dropped in her doorway by a passing cat just an hour ago. The small bundle of feathers seemed fortuitous, a symbol of her nameless god. She moved, still kneeling, towards the altar and laid the tiny body down on the black cloth, levering the bird onto its back. Removing two of her hair pins, she splayed the wings out and fixed them firmly in place, nailing the wretched creature to the dark altar. There was a flash of light on metal as she retrieved a sharp scalpel from her robe. Slowly, reverently, Messalina examined her blurred reflection in the blade, she looked like a keeper of mystery, like the *Lupa Priestess* herself. Filled with a sense of greater purpose she plunged the sharp scalpel into the barely quivering breast of the bird, feeling the spurt of hot blood on her fingers.

With the practiced movements of a haruspex she teased the warm entrails from the feathered body. Her fingers, slippery with blood and mucus, danced quickly along intestines, feeling the bumps of the poor creature's last meal. She sought out the lungs and heart checking for defects, interpreting each shadow and lump of muscle with a skill divined from the gods of old.

She could see something strange in the shadows of the creature's heart. A dark-haired man, mature beyond his years, red and gold in his background. Uncertain of what she saw she checked the slithery intestines again, each bump confirmed her reading. Only when she was truly certain of what she had read did she sit back, dropping the remains of the bird onto the soaked and bloodstained black cloth. As she had suspected the time was right for her to begin. Problematically though the new exhibition at the Capitoline only had part of what she needed, the other part lay buried, hidden from the world, under guard, inaccessible to her but attainable through the man with the penetrating eyes, shrouded in red and gold. Her Spanish guest. The reason was unclear but with the right leverage, her readings indicated that he could be persuaded to do her work, to enter the place where she could not go herself.

From somewhere far away she heard a door open, followed by the clack of heeled shoes across marble paving. Messalina raised a hand to her head, as if to ward off a headache and forced her eyes open. The voice of the priestess resisted, she was not done yet. Messalina felt her hand move, gripping the scalpel once more, plunging the blade down into one of the clay tablets she kept on her altar for this purpose. Her actions were automatic, uncontrolled, as another hand possessed hers and etched the jagged words into the clay. From above, the ding of the reception desk bell echoed through the hotel. Messalina's eyes flickered, she had to regain control. She pushed back against the control of the priestess's voice and blinked herself awake.

'I have guests to see to,' she said forcefully to the silent, yet presence filled basement. The familiar, repeated brassy ding of the reception desk bell supported her words and with a reluctance the priestess relinquished her hold. For the moment anyway. With each basement visit the long dead spirit grew stronger.

Messalina, rose quickly and raced up the steps, blowing out candles and casting her long robe and the clay tablet aside, as she entered her erotically decorated dining room. As the bell rang again, she plunged her blood-soaked hands into a basin of water below the mirror beside the partition door, rinsing the remains of the bird entrails from her fingers and doing a final make-up and hair check before stepping out into the reception. But not before she noticed an unfamiliar, dark glittering menace in her eyes, the priestess had not completely left her this time.

The sight of her latest guest brought an inadvertent, tight-lipped smile to her face. The girl was beautiful. Tall, thin, with a dramatic cascade of blonde hair, sparkling blue eye shadow emphasised the blue of her eyes and a soft peach tinted her full lips. Her white dress was scandalously short and held what little curves she had in all the right places. An expensive looking necklace; a golden rose, with a sparkling diamond dewdrop, completed her elegant appearance. She was a girl well used to her looks and even more aware of how to use them. Messalina disliked her instantly, it was like looking at a younger, blonder version of herself. The radiant girl made her feel old.

The girl stood with her hands on her narrow hips, an expression of clear irritation on her face at having been kept waiting. '*Buongiorno,*' she said icily, glaring down her nose at Messalina.

'Good afternoon,' Messalina replied in accented English, the single uttered word of Italian greeting had been enough to convince her that Italian conversation was out of the question. 'You are looking for a room?'

A flicker of relief crossed the girl's face. 'You speak English. Excellent.' Then remembering her own importance and annoyance at having been kept waiting she continued. 'I am Lady Lisa Hayworth-Mills, I would like to enquire as to one of your guests.'

'You have a meeting? Messalina looked down at her diary, she had nothing scheduled, and given that she knew one of her guests to be important, she was wary of the pretty, but stuck-up English girl.

'Actually, I am looking for a person who happens to be staying here. He is not expecting me, I was hoping to surprise him,' the blonde replied twisting her fingers in her hair.

Messalina raised her eyebrows. 'I do not rent rooms by the hour, take your business elsewhere.'

The girl looked scandalised. 'No,' she shrieked, 'I am not,' she dropped her voice to a low whisper, although there was no one else around to hear them. 'I am not a … a prostitute.'

Messalina folded her arms. 'My guests are not to be harassed.'

'Look,' Lisa stood up straight. 'My boyfriend is a very important man with a big name, and I know he is staying here. Quite why, I cannot imagine when there is a perfectly good JDM in the centre.' She drummed her fingers impatiently on the counter.

Messalina frowned, she'd rather hoped her important guest was single. She had been hoping to make amends for whatever she'd done that had caused so much offence the previous evening. 'Ahh, *lui è Spagnolo*? Staying with the four ladies?' she waited for Lisa to nod, noting the hurt look that flittered across her face. 'Top floor, adjoining rooms twenty-two, twenty-four and twenty-six.' The blonde reached for her wheeled suitcase and turned towards the stairs.

'But you will not find him there *Cherie*. He left with two of the ladies this morning. I believe he was meeting the others at *il museo di Capitoline*, this afternoon.' Messalina glanced up at the clock. 'They will likely be there all afternoon, you could catch them.' As the girl turned away again a sudden dart of pain flashed through Messalina's head, like the start of a bad headache, but instead of a throbbing pain all that was left was an idea, clear and fully formed. A product of the priestess and her recent session, the girl was the key to getting what she wanted. '*Un momento, Cherie*. You can leave your case behind the desk, I can show you the way to the museum.'

Ducking quickly back into her private quarters to collect her bag, Messalina began to work through her plan. Hopefully the blonde girl's jealousy would be enough, but she had other means of getting what she needed.

VI

'Wow!' gasped Mell, as the teenagers entered the first exhibition room through a blast of icy air conditioning, and came face-to-face with Roman frescoes and other such decor extending as far as the eye could see. A sheen of bronze gleamed in the filtered sunlight cascading into the next exhibition room, barely visible through an open archway. 'This could take us a long time.'

'Well, it's Simon's birthday,' said Claire, twisting a strand of green hair around her fingers and glancing up at Simon. 'What do you want to do first?'

'Hmm?' he replied, as his phone blared into life and, squinting at the screen, he debated whether to answer or hang up, before swiping left and shoving the offending item back into the pocket of his jeans.

'I want to see the legionary eagle,' Suze said, although if she was honest she wanted to see everything that the museum had to offer, to leave no display case unseen.

'The eagle is in the other building,' Simon replied, groping back into his pocket for his phone, as a distinctly Spanish sounding tune filled the air. He silenced it without looking and went to slip it back in his pocket when it rang again.

'Dude, who the hell is calling you?' asked Jerry, dragging his attention away from the goggle-eyed expression of the emperor Constantine that he'd been trying to mimic, to see what the noise was about.

'Earl Hayworth,' Simon replied with a tight-lipped grimace. 'I should really take this, go on inside, I can catch up with you.' He stood up straighter taking a deep breath before answering the call and moving away from the others. '*Buenos días Señor* ...'

'Who is Earl Hayworth?' Claire asked, as the group moved on into the museum.

'Lisa's father,' Suze replied with a sigh. 'Simon plays polo with him.'

'Interesting,' Claire replied, pulling a compact mirror out of her bag and checking her make-up, whilst shoving her hat into the bag, letting her green hair flow loose around her face. 'Wonder why he's calling Simon?' Suze just pulled a face and shrugged.

Agreeing to meet in the Hall of the Emperors in an hour, the group split and drifted through the museum, each taking it at their own pace. Mell and Sarah headed straight to the third floor to find the sculpture of the Dying Gaul, which Simon had told them was the focus of a verse in Byron's poem *'Childe Harold's Pilgrimage'*, and so would fit nicely with what they had seen earlier in their non-Roman tour of the city. Jerry, having packed excessively lightly and being in possession only of the clothes he stood in, headed straight for the gift shop in the hope of finding a new T-shirt. Claire and Suze remained close to the entrance way poking about, looking at some of the smaller display cases. Suze because she wanted to see everything, Claire for reasons of her own.

'Hey look at this,' Suze said, spotting something. It was a small silver bird, a robin perhaps, or maybe a sparrow, fashioned like a legionary eagle, wings back, feet forward. 'Claire?' Suze glanced up, she'd vanished. Then she spotted her green hair through a doorway to another room. Claire was talking to Simon, her head tilted sympathetically to one side, her hand stroking his arm. Suze looked away immediately, what on earth was Claire playing at? The man had a girlfriend. A spoiled, vain and beautiful one, but a girlfriend all the same.

Suze focussed her attention back on the display case. Irritated that Claire's flirtations, along with whatever argument Sarah and Jerry, were or weren't having, were probably going to break up the little group. Or would at least cause some sort of fight in the next day or so. The artefact's label was in Italian. She didn't know Italian but her rudimentary Latin allowed her to at least work out that the little bird was silver and came from Nero's palace. 'Neronian table ware huh?' she guessed.

'Dovrebbe essere distrutto!' The creaking voice at Suze's shoulder startled her, she'd not noticed the old man's reflection in the glass.

Apprehensive, she turned and came face to face with the derelict old man, who had grabbed Simon's legs outside. Evidently the wily old fox had found his way inside this wing of the museum. His Mediterranean featured face was well worn, creased with deep roads of wrinkles. A matted white beard hung, almost touching the floor, clinging to his chin as a stalactite to the roof of a cave. His patched and ragged clothes hung shapeless on his gnarled and bony, yet somehow proud body.

'Distruggilo!' he hissed at Suze, the fingers of both hands curled into devil horns.

She had no idea what he was saying and stepped back away from him, watching warily, as his eyes took on their crazed glaze again. He began to chant softly under his breath, wafting one hand as if holding a sistrum. An ancient soothsayer trapped in the modern world. Perhaps he wasn't crazy, just out of time.

'Hey babe, there you are,' Mell's voice cut through the building tension and a moment later her arm landed across Suze's shoulders. 'Been looking everywhere for you sweetie,' she said, doing her very best girlfriend impression, leaning her nose against Suze's hair. 'Is this man bothering you?'

Shaken from his trance the old man lunged suddenly forwards, grabbing Mell's shirt. '*Lo scricciolo è la chiave. Ricorda.*'

Taken unawares Mell let out a gasp and lunged backwards, her bravado gone as memories of Richards and her vulnerability flooded her mind. Her knees buckled, and her sudden weight forced the old man to drop her. Suze dropped instantly to the floor beside her and gently reminded the red-haired girl to breathe, as she started to tremble.

'Come on Mell, you're okay, you're okay. He's not going to hurt you,' Suze murmured, encouraging her friend to stand. Mell's shirt was damp and beads of sweat stood out on her face as she gasped her way out of a panic attack. There was a noise across the gallery as two security guards appeared. Like before, the old man wriggled and hollered unwilling to be taken away. Eventually the guards gave up trying to silence him and simply dragged him, still screaming and cursing, down the corridor.

'Mell, are you still with me?' said Suze giving her a squeeze, 'we should probably think about meeting up with the others.' She pointed out a doorway where the colossal head of Constantine loomed, staring goggle-eyed at everyone who passed through into the imperial domain. 'Unless you want to step outside?'

Mell shook her head and grabbed a bottle of water from her bag. 'I'll be alright,' she insisted. 'Just a crazy guy in a museum, no different to Manchester streets on a Saturday, right?'

'Right,' Suze punched her shoulder lightly and the two of them followed the others into the Hall of the Emperors, where they were staring at the portrait bust of an intense looking young man.

'Handsome, isn't he?' Sarah mused, gazing up at the sightless eyes of the marble face.

'Who, Jerry?' asked Mell, then with a wicked grin desperate to take her mind off Richards. 'Or Suze's brother?'

'Neither! Julius Caesar,' Sarah replied, indicating the statue, although her cheeks flushed with colour.

'Actually Sarah, that is Caesar's nephew,' Simon said, appearing at her shoulder. 'Named Gaius Octavius, following Caesar's assassination and in conjunction with the Roman laws of adoption, he took the name Gaius Julius Caesar Octavianus. When *the* Julius Caesar was deified in 42BC he dropped Octavianus and added *Divi Filius*; Son of the Divine. Thus, becoming *Gaius Julius Caesar Divi Filius*. In 38BC he dropped his *Praenomen* and *nomen* in favour of the title Imperator, as hailed by the army, and so became *Imperator Caesar Divi Filius*. Finally, after Actium and the defeat of Marcus Antonius in 31BC the Senate voted a final adjustment to his name in 27BC; *Imperator Caesar Divi Filius Augustus, Princeps of Rome*. Or Augustus as most know him.'

'Did you eat encyclopaedias as a kid or does the internet just download straight to your brain?' said Jerry, pretending to stagger under the weight of Simon's imparted knowledge.

Claire giggled. 'I love that he knows so much,' she gently touched Simon's hand to catch his attention. 'It means we never need a guide book, makes the museum much more interesting.'

'Hey I know stuff,' Jerry feigned hurt. 'Good stuff, way more interesting than Simon's tedious academic babble.'

'Oh yeah?' Sarah challenged, folding her arms. 'Prove it.'

Jerry took a deep breath. 'Caligula was a cross-dressing transvestite, who made his horse a senator and had the army fight the sea. Among a whole heap of other weird insanities.' He adopted a crazed expression, rolling his eyes, his tongue hanging out the left side of his contorted mouth and twirled his index finger towards his right temple. 'Fruit bat. But I bet his/ her/ their parties were fun.'

'His name was Gaius and he probably had a stroke or something, plus those tales are probably all later propaganda designed to disgrace him …' Simon tried to argue.

'Aww Si, spare us the intellectual un-biased viewpoint. I happen to like 'em barmy. There is no fun in neutrality,' Jerry groaned in response. 'Besides bad PR or forward thinking, I love that Caligula ran around in a dress, Hadrian was gay, Elagabalus had a sex change and Nero thought he could play guitar.'

'Lyre,' Simon corrected.

'Nah-ah, I read it somewhere,' Jerry protested.

'A lyre's an instrument Jerry,' Mell said giggling. 'But I do love the idea of Nero playing bass, whilst Rome burned.

'Before building his big palace, his gold statue and graciously bestowing his name on a chain of coffee shops,' Jerry finished, grinning triumphantly at Simon, who shook his head, although an amused smile did creep across his face.

'Simon, ignore Jerry, I was interested,' said Claire, slipping her arm easily through his, and leaning close, quietly asking him to repeat what he had said about Caligula. He looked a little surprised but dutifully responded to her request.

'Is she flirting with him?' said Sarah, watching closely, a look of disapproval on her face.

'Think the more important question is; how long until Suze beats her up?' said Jerry. Suze moved to punch him and he caught her wrist with a laugh. 'Can't believe you rise to my insinuation every time. You clearly fancy him.'

Suze wrenched her wrist free and shoved him aside, folding her arms defensively across her chest. 'I do not. But Claire should watch what she's doing. He has a girlfriend.'

They moved on, heading for the other wing and the temporary exhibition. It was less crowded over there and they headed straight in, past the rooms of Papal statues and Renaissance paintings to a large open area enclosed in glass, towards the rear of the museum.

'It's cold in here!' said Claire rubbing her arms and shivering in an exaggerated manner. 'I guess they have temperature control on for conservation.'

Wordlessly Simon passed her his sports jacket. It had been draped over his arm since coming into the museum. Claire smiled gratefully, instantly wrapping herself in the expensive material. It was obviously too big for her, but she looked delighted. 'Simon you're so sweet,' she breathed in deeply. 'I like your aftershave.'

'That, would be Lisa's perfume,' he replied, turning his attention to the nearest display cabinet.

'Hey look over here,' called Sarah, 'I've never seen this before.' She pointed out a huge mosaic covering almost the entire rear wall of the temporary display room. 'It's the story of Romulus and Remus in mosaic story board form.'

'So, these guys are the story behind the Gemini constellation, right?' Jerry asked.

'That's Castor and Pollux,' Claire replied, rolling her eyes as Jerry sniggered.

'Pollux,' he grinned and laughed again.

'You are so immature,' she hissed at him. Jerry shrugged and stuck his tongue out.

'Simon can you translate this please?' said Suze indicating the placard beside the mosaic.

He skimmed over the wording. 'Paraphrasing: "Romulus and Remus are born to the Albion King, it is prophesized that they will grow up to overthrow him, so he orders them killed. The twins are left in a basket by the Tiber, where they are found by a she-wolf, who raises them, until they are found by a shepherd, who takes them as his own. Unaware of who they are, the twins go to Albion, learn their true identity, kill their father, re-instate their uncle as king and wander off to find their own land to rule. Reaching the seven hills, Romulus choses the Palatine, Remus the Aventine. They fight, Romulus kills Remus, takes both fledgling hill tribes and founds the city of Rome".'

'Well then this is wrong.' Jerry was scrutinising the mosaic. 'Remus is killing Romulus here. So, it's an alternate universe where Remus's settlement on the Aventine, supersedes that of Romulus on the Palatine. And Europe is conquered by the Remans. Who apparently bring death.' He pointed at a character on the mosaic who was dressed like the grim reaper.

'That's nonsense,' said Sarah looking at the mosaic. 'You must have the twins the wrong way around, and that's a priestess.'

'Hey Claire, you should come and look at this,' Mell called from a display case. 'There is a whole case of Etruscan jewellery over here.'

'In a minute,' Claire called back softly. 'Simon,' she threaded her arm through his again, 'did you have plans for dinner tonight, only I spotted this really chic looking restaurant with outdoor tables in front of the Pantheon, they were advertising dinner and dancing, it looked like a great atmosphere. It would be a fantastic way to celebrate your birthday.'

'Actually, I already had a place in mind,' Simon replied when she paused for breath. 'A fairly small, intimate place on the other side of the Colosseum. They do an exquisite swordfish and have an excellent stock of vintage Champagne.'

'Sounds perfect!' Claire breathed flirtatiously, earning herself a funny look from Mell and Sarah.

Simon's left hand pinched the bridge of his nose. 'Listen, Claire …'

'SIMON JAMES MATHERSON!'

Whatever he was about to say was spectacularly cut off as a clearly horrified female voice screeched his full name across the crowded gallery. With a muttered Spanish curse, Simon dropped Claire's arm. He counted to ten under his breath before straightening up, turning toward the voice and executing a perfectly timed bow as his elegant girlfriend, Lisa Hayworth-Mills, materialised in front of him. '*Mi Señora*,' his voice was even as he took her hand to bestow his customary kiss to her fingers.

'How the hell does he do that?' Mell hissed to Suze, marvelling at how calm Simon's reaction had been. 'I'd jump out of my skin if someone screamed my name across a museum with no prior warning.'

Lisa, snatched her fingers back away from him, eyes blazing. 'Oh no, do not think your Spanish charm gets you out of this one.' She planted her hands on her hips and glared at him, before flashing a look that could kill Medusa in Claire's direction. 'Who is she?'

Simon straightened up, his left arm automatically curving to rest his left hand against his back, and met her fiery gaze with his own calm intensity. 'Do you really want to make a scene here Lisa?' he murmured in response. 'You just screamed my name, my full name, across a museum. People noticed.' He offered her his right hand. 'Claire is just a friend.'

'A friend,' Lisa didn't look convinced. She folded her arms, as her lip trembled and her eyes began to glitter on the verge of angry tears. 'She is far too pretty to just be a friend and she's wearing your jacket.' She turned her full attention to Claire, stalking around her like a cat toying with a mouse.

'Lisa,' Simon said softly, trying to deflect her attention from Claire. 'It is me that you are angry with. Leave her alone.'

Standing behind Claire, Lisa glared at her boyfriend and jabbed a finger at Claire as she spoke. 'Explain then Simon, how exactly did *she* come to be wearing *my* boyfriend's jacket?' Shaking her head, she continued with her circle around the interloper and finally halted in front of Claire, lowering her voice and addressing the girl directly. 'If you're trying to steal him you may as well give up. You recall, he dropped you, forgot you, as soon as he saw me.'

'Leave her alone,' said Mell, stepping in and giving Claire's shoulders a squeeze. 'The gallery is cold and Simon is a nice guy. He'd have loaned any of us his jacket. You have nothing to worry about, except for how much of a spoilt, petty brat you are.'

The ice blue eyes flickered once, awarding Mell the briefest of assessments, and with a barely concealed laugh of indifference, Lisa turned back to Claire. 'Simon would never look at you twice anyway. I mean look at you, distinctly average, and the green hair? It's like someone sneezed on you,' she sneered.

'Lisa! That really is enough. What has gotten into you?' Simon said, embarrassed by his girlfriend's behaviour.

An indignant look of fury crossed her face and she pushed her pouting lips out further in a scowl that transformed her features into a picture of pure displeasure. 'Sure, defend your harem. I should have known that you were exactly like your father.'

She'd hit a nerve. Simon tensed up, hands curling into fists at his side. He stood taller, jaw squared, his normally soft brown eyes hardened to an imperious flinty stare. 'I am nothing like my father!' he practically spat the words out.

'Claire, Mell, come on,' Suze's voice was a lot calmer than she felt, cutting quietly through the tense silence as Lisa recoiled from Simon's intense anger at being compared to his estranged father. 'We should go and look at the eagle in the next room.'

'Good idea,' Sarah whispered, giving Jerry a jab in the ribs to make sure he followed as the four girls quickly moved away from the developing disagreement.

'Did you see how many people reacted to his name?' Jerry said with a low whistle. 'Is Si famous or something?'

Claire stared at him. 'Jerry, his father owns like, a third of the world's hotel and transport industry. His name is famous.'

'I think people just reacted to someone screaming in a quiet museum.' Sarah said, before letting out her own shriek of surprise as she clapped eyes on the gory spectacle of the eagle display.

In place of the legionary standard, surrounded by shards of glass, was a large bird of prey, wings spread, thrown back, talons forward. Its head was missing, the dripping blood spray on the side of the case indicating that it had been killed, in the room, very recently.

VII

Lisa stared at her boyfriend. She'd pushed too far comparing him to his father, she should have known what his reaction would be. Simon and John Matherson had a strained relationship at the best of times, John's repeated philandering was one of many issues of contention between father and son. Lisa almost couldn't believe that she had said it but she was hurt, feeling betrayed, the other girl had been wearing his jacket for christsake. Unwanted tears sprang to her eyes as Simon's friends hurriedly made their exit. 'Simon, I … I did not mean …' she trailed off, lowering her face a little so that when she looked up at him, it was through the veil of her eyelashes.

Simon raked a hand through his hair. 'We can discuss your perceptions on my fidelity later,' his tone was hard, and he met Lisa's eyes easily. She looked down and away, her shoulders giving a small shrug as a sob escaped her lips. Simon exhaled deeply and bit his tongue, before realising something. 'Lisa, where is Nina?'

She turned her huge, glittering eyes up towards him again as a huge smile crept across her face. 'Switzerland!'

'You came here alone?' his question was rhetorical, Simon already knew Nina was in Switzerland, Earl Hayworth's call earlier had been one of panicked concern as to his daughter's whereabouts. 'Darling, why on earth would you do that?' Simon paced back and forth in front of her. 'Anything could have happened to you, your father has been frantic. I really should call him and let him know that you are here and safe.'

As Simon reached for his phone, anxious to do the right thing and put his girlfriend's father's mind at ease and stay on the Earl's good side, Lisa laid a restraining hand on his arm. 'Or,' she said softly, 'you could understand how truly alone we are right now.' She bit her tongue waiting for it to register with him, she'd ditched her chaperone, her father had no idea where she was, and even once they located her it would be hours before anyone official arrived to act as guardian and chaperone. They could finally be alone as a couple and not just snatched half hours in the stable block or the folly on Earl Hayworth's property, always alert to the prospect of discovery.

'Ah *mi amor,* you are incredible!' Unable to believe that she had managed to both surprise him and get rid of her chaperone, Simon took her hands and with a wide smile spreading across his face, he glanced towards the eagle room. They so rarely had time unaccompanied, he was not going to waste it being annoyed with her, hopefully his friends would understand. 'Five minutes Lisa, five minutes and I am all yours, I promise.' He raised her hands to his lips and kissed her fingers, before moving quickly towards the eagle room and his friends, intending to make his excuses and spend some time alone with Lisa.

Alarms blared out across the museum as he reached the others on the threshold of the eagle room. At a glance, he could see that the silver eagle was gone. Over the sound of the alarm people began to scream as a loud bang crashed through the room. As the group made their way quickly back towards where Lisa waited by the wolf and twins mosaic, a flaming projectile sailed across the gallery. From off to the left came another crash and suddenly the room was flooded with thick blueish-green smoke. The museum was under attack.

*

Shrouded in the blue-green smoke Messalina knew she had precisely two minutes until the smoke began to dissipate. She'd experimented with the home-made smoke bombs before, although never in a room this big. Considering this, she amended her time to a minute and a half. What she needed to do shouldn't take long, the pretty blonde had provided enough of a distraction for the first phase of her plan, which meant that she had one extra smoke bomb if things got difficult.

Placing the stolen eagle in her bag and lodging it beside a display case, she pulled her black robes around her, using the hood to hide her face and walked purposefully through the smoke towards her target. Keeping her eyes on the six figures moving towards her she made a calculated lunge for the isolated seventh. No one saw her until it was too late. Lurching out of the smoke Messalina threw a black clad arm around the elegant blonde girl's shoulders, bringing the blade of her dagger up to rest against the girl's slender throat.

'Lisa!' Messalina watched as the Spanish boy lunged towards her as if to play hero and take on his girlfriend's assailant. But two of his friends, the tall boy and the red-headed girl grabbed him and held him back. The Spaniard seemed stronger though. Messalina had the distinct feeling that he may dislocate his shoulder to escape them, given half a chance. His passion would certainly work in her favour, but right now she needed to keep him and his five friends at bay.

'Any closer and I kill her. Understand?' Messalina spoke through a voice changer, her careful words sounding hollow and metallic. To emphasise her point, she pressed the blade harder against the girl's throat, feeling her terrified fluttering pulse in the vibration of the blade. The Spaniard stopped struggling and Messalina mentally praised the blonde, she had her man well trained.

Her time running short, Messalina kept her eyes on the six teenagers and tightened her grip on the girl with her dagger wielding arm, she needed her other hand to retrieve the inscribed clay tablet from her robes. This was the dangerous part. She wished that she'd been able to catch the couple alone, six teens could more than likely overpower her and the shorter of the two brunettes appeared to be eyeing up the situation. She may turn dangerous or simply cause a distraction enough to ruin Messalina's plans.

She fumbled quickly through her robes and felt the rough edge of the clay tablet, warmed slightly by her body heat. Gripping it between her fingers she spoke again, keeping the teens' attention on her, and the blade. Through the distorter her voice seemed detached, otherworldly and loaded with menace, she almost scared herself.

'The time draws near for the rightful twin to take his place, for the silver eagle to fly.' She threw the tablet at the girl with green hair, an improvement on the bleached blonde but still terrible. Not expecting it, green-hair fumbled the catch and almost dropped the piece, which would have been a disaster as it was the only copy of the priestess's words and the only clue to what Messalina needed. If they broke it or couldn't work out the riddle, no one would get what they wanted and the blonde girl would die.

The attention of all but the Spaniard on the clay tablet, Messalina wrapped her free arm around the blonde's shoulders again. Her final words she spoke directly to the Spanish boy. 'Retrieve the silver wings, or in six hours, she dies.'

With a speed she hardly knew she possessed, Messalina brought her stiletto dagger around, inflicted two small punctures on the girl's lower back and shoved her towards the group of teens. As their attention was thus occupied, Messalina fled the scene, shrugging out of her robe and retrieving her bag with the eagle, before inserting herself into the exodus of people streaming out of the museum. Just another visitor caught up in what the news would later call a terror attack on the museum. She kept her head down and once free of the press of people, slipped between the arriving police cars and into the back alleys of Rome. There were now just six short hours left until the silver eagle was complete and her summoning ritual could begin. She did not dare think that the teens would fail, the Spaniard would move the heavens to save his girlfriend. Her plans would succeed.

VIII

The instant the cloaked figure vanished, Simon wrenched himself free of Mell and Jerry and sank to his knees beside Lisa. The girl had collapsed when released and was sprawled face down on the floor, twin scarlet stains dotting the back of her dress. 'Lisa?' Simon touched her face gently. 'Sweetheart, can you hear me?'

'Simon, don't move her,' Mell ordered, her eyes searching the room for the first aid box that she knew must be close by.

He stared after her, raking both hands through his hair in frustration. 'Melody!' his voice cracked, high and tight, betraying his panic. A soft groan from Lisa pulled his attention immediately back to her. 'Lisa?' he offered her his hand and, ignoring Mell's instructions, pulled her gently into his arms. 'Sweetheart, are you hurt?' She shook her head and buried her face against his chest, anxious that no one should see her cry.

Simon twisted her hair gently around his fingers, sliding his other hand down her back, feeling her sharp gasp as she pressed closer to him when his hand brushed the puncture wounds on her back. His fingers came away sticky and covered in blood, and he shot an anxious look over Lisa's head to Mell.

'Claire, what does the tablet say?' Sarah spoke so quietly it was uncertain at first that she had spoken at all. Wordlessly Claire handed the inscribed clay tablet over, her eyes fixed on Simon, narrowed in jealousy at the panicked yet affectionate attention he had for Lisa. Mell, Suze and Jerry crowded close to scan the five jagged lines of Latin.

FLAMMEUM FACES OF CHRISTIANI MARTYRIO, UBI
QUONDAM REGIA ARTIFICIS STETIT,
UBI A SALAMIS CECIDIT AD TURBAS ET MUNDI, RARA INTER
ANIMALIA, QUAE FIT PER FILIUM, QUOD MILES REGI.
IACET CONDIDIT AQUILAE GEMINORUM

'Why is it that the stuff you need to read, the really important bit, like; "don't touch that lever" and instructions for putting the genie back in the bottle, is always written in an illegible language?' groaned Jerry, leaning over Sarah's shoulder and staring blankly at the inscribed words. 'It will take all day to deal with that.'

'Or we could use Google,' Claire replied, forcing her attention away from the couple on the floor and dragging her phone from her bag.

'Simon's faster than Google,' Suze said, grabbing the tablet from Sarah and watching him reassure Lisa, speaking softly in Spanish, holding her close. His right hand rested low on his girlfriend's back keeping pressure against her weeping wounds.

Barely aware of what Suze had said, Simon glanced briefly at the tablet that she brandished at him and absently read the scrawled words, translating without thinking, his attention clearly on the traumatised girl in his arms. '*Marcas de fábrica llameantes de los cristianos martyred, adonde una vez que el palacio del artista se colocaba, donde los Salamis cayeron para las muchedumbres encante, en medio de las bestias raras, labradas por el hijo del rey. Allí águilas entombed mentira de gemelos.*' His natural Spanish was rapid, and softly spoken, the words almost running into one another. Beautiful as it was, the others, lacking his multi-lingual talent, were no closer to understanding the jagged message scrawled on the mosaic.

'Any chance of getting that in a real language Si?' Jerry quipped, but Simon's full attention was immediately diverted back to Lisa as she let out a gasp of pain that would have shamed the best theatre actors.

'We should really look at those wounds,' said Mell. She'd located the museum's first aid box and, being the only member of the group with any first aid training, was trying to assert some authority, keeping her eyes on Lisa's back, where thin rivulets of blood were starting to seep between Simon's fingers.

'You stay away from me,' Lisa spat, rising unsteadily to her feet. 'I am going back to the hotel.' She threw a look of contempt in Simon's direction. 'You can call my father now, I shall not be staying and if these are your chosen friends then you and I are through.' Tears of pain and rage pricking at her eyes she began walking away and then groaned, raising her hand to her forehead as a lightning bolt of pain flared behind her eyes, almost forcing her to her knees.

Simon was on his feet immediately. 'Lisa!' he caught her as her knees gave out and pulled her tightly against him, burying his nose against her neck. 'Lisa, *amor*, please let me take you to the hospital, we need help.'

'No!' she shrieked, twisting in his arms, fighting her way free and delivering a stinging slap to his chest. 'Stop saying that,' she clutched her head, 'every time you say hospital or doctor it hurts.' Seeing an opportunity, she slapped his chest again, 'that one is for letting another girl wear your jacket. And this,' she moved against him, a coy expression on her face, running her fingers through his hair, 'this is for your birthday.' Rising up on her toes she slipped her other arm around his neck and kissed him, pressing her lips harder against his as he responded to her.

'The interweb has a translation,' Claire proclaimed triumphantly, drawing everyone's attention away from the lovers. 'But it makes no sense, listen; "Christian fire of the artist, collapsed house in Salamis," then something about a soldier's tomb and the constellations of Aquila and Gemini.'

'It's the wrong time of year for Gemini, isn't it?' said Sarah absently, watching the door to the gallery, although she was thinking of the star sign, rather than the constellation.

'That's assuming it means the constellation Gemini and not the myth of Castor and Pollux,' Suze replied as Jerry sniggered and immaturely muttered 'Pollux' under his breath. Ignoring him she continued. 'And what was the myth behind the Aquila stars?'

'Zeus's pet eagle, killed by Prometheus, after Herakles freed him from the rock,' Simon replied, disentangling himself from Lisa's uncharacteristically amorous embrace, concerned by the amount on blood on his hands. 'Lisa, honey, you are losing a lot of blood.'

'Not a hospital!' she screamed. Then, as if her energy was spent she collapsed, trembling, into his arms again muttering something about six hours. 'Simon what did they mean?' she grabbed a handful of his shirt. 'What did they mean when they said you have six hours?'

Simon kissed her forehead, whatever panic he might be feeling was hidden behind a smooth mask of confidence. 'Just an empty threat *mi amor*, you will be perfectly safe. I promise.' He glanced over at Claire and mouthed the word, 'jacket.' With a sigh of frustration that could rival Lisa's and a scowl to match, Claire wriggled out of his sports jacket, screwed it into a ball and threw it at his face. Simon simply responded with a hard stare and draped his now crumpled jacket around Lisa, hiding her bloodstained dress beneath the expensive blue fabric.

'So, how much of this do we believe?' said Suze, as they began picking their way out of the museum, the guards mostly ignoring anyone who could walk in favour of those who had been injured. She began ticking off the facts on her fingers. 'A crazy old man outside the museum calls Simon, Caesar, a weirdo with a voice changer steals the eagle, leaves a headless real bird in its place and demands that we find some silver wings in six hours or Simon's girlfriend gets it,' she drew a line across her throat. 'And we only have a crappy translation suggesting Salamis to go off.'

'Where is Salamis?' asked Sarah, as they emerged from the museum into the late afternoon sun and crowded *piazza* full of tourists desperate to catch a glimpse of the chaos inside the building.

'Off the south coast,' Claire replied, furiously tapping at her phone, and elbowing her way through the crowd towards the narrow alley that would lead away from the *piazza* onto the *Via de San Pietro* and towards the forum. 'At least some of us are trying to solve the problem.' She broke off to send a vicious stare at Simon, as he guided Lisa through the diminishing crowds, one hand holding hers, the other around her waist, his eyes constantly on her, clearly still concerned about her wellbeing.

'Claire, have some dignity. Control yourself,' hissed Mell, unimpressed by the other girl's jealousy. 'You knew he was with her. Did you honestly think you had a chance?'

Claire fluffed her hair with one hand, and shot Mell a sceptical look. 'I have no idea what you're talking about,' she raised her voice as the crowds thinned out closer to the forum. 'I just thought that given it's his damn girlfriend who dies if we don't find these wings, that Simon may have been a little more productive in helping us!'

Lisa's screech was ear splitting, half the street stopped to stare at her, as she collapsed screaming and sobbing against the base of the statue of Julius Caesar.

The look Simon shot Claire could have melted stone, and was scarily close to the ambivalent stare of the statue above him. *'Gracias* Claire,' he hissed through clenched teeth, dropping to kneel beside Lisa.

She immediately grabbed a handful of his shirt, and choking back a sob asked 'Is she right? Am I going to die?'

'No,' Simon replied, his hand closing over hers, pressing her hand against his heart. 'I swear it, on my honour, no one will hurt you,' he brushed her hair back from her face. 'I wish that you were not caught up in this.'

'So, the battle of Salamis?' Sarah said bringing the others' attention back to the puzzle rather than Simon's distraught girlfriend.

'A collapsed house in Salamis,' Mell replied, reading the translation off Claire's phone, 'and something about a soldier's tomb. But I don't know much about Salamis.'

'A naval battle between united Greek city states and Persia in September 480BC,' Simon said, helping Lisa to her feet. 'Why are we discussing Greeks?'

'The writing on the tablet mentioned Salamis, and had something to do with Christianity and the stars,' Claire replied, passing him the tablet so that he could read the Latin text again.

'And a fire apparently,' Mell added. 'Did they burn Christians in Salamis?'

'They burnt Christians at the Colosseum,' Jerry quipped, indicating the elliptical building that dominated the view ahead.

'Jerry, can you stop being an idiot for just one minute. This is serious, we may not like her, but Lisa's life is at stake,' Mell snapped, eliciting a whimper from Lisa, who squeezed her eyes shut and clutched Simon's hand in an effort not to scream again.

'How are we supposed to get to Salamis?' said Sarah, tactfully trying to cover up Mell's accidental truth.

'We have no need to go to Salamis,' Simon interrupted, focussed on the jagged lines in the clay, either ignoring, or oblivious to, Mell's remark. 'Salamis is written in the past tense, it is being used as an example of something, not as an actual location.'

'Well if you'd have translated it into English instead of randomish we might have known that,' Jerry shot back.

'I thought I did,' Simon replied, with genuine confusion.

'*Castilian, Castellanos*,' Claire replied, trying to be clever and pronouncing it wrong.

'*Castellano*,' he corrected, 'my apologies, my mind was elsewhere.' He glanced at Lisa's tense face before looking back down at the tablet, taking longer over reading this time, considering what was at stake and who he was translating for. 'Interesting, "*Flaming brands of martyred Christians, where once the palace of the artist stood, where Salamis fell for a crowd's delight, amidst rare beasts, wrought by the son of the soldier king. There lie entombed*," he paused in his translation for a moment. "'*Aquilae Geminorum*" ... Eagles of Twins.'

'Eagles, as in birds?' said Mell confused. 'Are we looking for bird skeletons?'

'No,' Simon replied. 'Birds would be twin eagles, the possessive phrasing, "Eagles of Twins" suggests something else. Eagles owned by twins, entombed with twins,' he paused massaging his forehead. 'But that cannot be right, the eagles are not that old.'

Jerry's eyes lit up at Simon's implication. 'Legionary eagles?!'

'Introduced by Marius, during his army reforms in the later republic,' Simon said, shaking his head. 'Before that we do not know what the standards were, the first eagles are Marian, the first reference to the Legions as the Eagles is Caesarean or later.'

'So, why'd Marius pick an eagle then brainiac, why an eagle in particular?' Jerry shot back.

'Because it was the sacred creature of their founder?' Sarah theorised.

'Oh, come on,' scoffed Simon, 'the eagle is the king of the birds. It has been a power symbol throughout history, look at the American President, Romans, the eagle of Saladin, even the damn Nazis, everyone has used it. It is even here,' he said gesturing at the signet ring on his finger, where an eagle embossed in gold stretched its wings within a red stone. 'Besides which, Rome's sacred founding creature was a wolf, *Lupus*, you all saw the sculpture.'

'Silver wings, for the stolen eagle,' Jerry said. 'I thought the eagles were bronze, who had enough cash for silver ones.'

'Look dingbat,' said Sarah, reading from the slump of Simon's shoulders, that he really wasn't in the mood to deal with Jerry's relentless questions. 'We know what we are looking for. Silver wings. It doesn't matter why it's an eagle, or even whose eagle it is. What matters is where we look for it and we find it, fast. So, any bright ideas about the palace of the artist?'

Jerry's shoulders slumped. 'No!' he droned. 'But I maintain that Christians were martyred at the Colosseum.'

'And just about anywhere else it was possible to do so,' replied Simon sarcastically, massaging his forehead. 'The Christian angle will not help, you may as well search the vaults of the Vatican. The key is in the other clues, particularly Salamis…'

'Nero,' Suze said interrupting.

'The ugly one?' Claire asked, tapping into her phone again, 'looks like a frog?'

Suze nodded, 'considered himself an artist…'

'Fiddled whilst Rome burned,' Jerry added, miming a violin.

'Blamed the Christians for the fire and built himself a vast palace. The palace of the artist,' Suze continued, glancing at Simon for reassurance that she was right and encouraged by his expression as he considered the direction of her train of thought. 'A palace knocked down by Vespasian. The soldier emperor.'

'How does Salamis come into this?' Mell said, twisting her long red hair around a finger as she too worked through Suze's thought process.

'The Flavian arena, completed by Titus, son of the soldier king, could be flooded for naval battles, like Salamis,' Simon completed Suze's thought train and leaned back against Caesar's plinth, drumming his fingers against the stone. 'The bloody Colosseum. It would appear that Jeremy is smarter than all of us.'

'Boom!' Jerry grinned, 'I beat the smart kids.' He made guns out of his fingers and fired them at each of his friends before blowing off the imaginary smoke. 'Dude,' he nudged Simon's elbow and nodded in Lisa's direction. 'She okay?'

Lisa's eyes were glazed as though she were in a trance or a dream and a soft, breathy moaning escaped her parted lips. Simon shook his head, 'I should get her to a doctor.' Lisa's face contorted as he spoke and her breathy moan became a shriek of pain as he suggested medical aid.

Mell watched curiously. 'She reacts badly any time you suggest something that is not taking us in the direction of this riddle,' she paused, staring at Lisa her mind turning over the facts. 'Si, hold her, I need to see those wounds.' Her tone brooked no opposition and with Lisa in a trance and unable to object, and Mell's fierce expression suggesting that she would argue until she got her way, Simon gave in and gently lifted Lisa to her feet.

Mell peeled the blue sports jacket away from Lisa's back and prodded gently at the two bloody holes in Lisa's dress. The blood was congealing, a good sign, but within both red-brown drying stains was a streak of black. Mell dropped the jacket back into place covering the stains. Her mind was churning, first aid courses only covered so much, but it was enough that she understood the situation. The hooded person had been very specific, six hours. Lisa had been poisoned, but the stuff didn't seem to just be toxic, it apparently caused the girl pain if they deviated from their instructions. She glanced up and accidentally caught Simon's anxious gaze, he wanted to know what she thought, of course he did. His affection for his girlfriend was genuine, much more so than Mell had initially thought. But could she really tell him this. She bit her lip. 'Sarah, can you take care of Lisa for a sec?' she beckoned Simon away from the group.

'So?' he asked instantly. Mell shushed him and gently gripping his wrist pulled him a little further away from the group.

'Simon this is bad. I don't know what it is or how to fix it. There are black streaks in the bloodstains, she's been poisoned,' she paused allowing her friend to absorb what she was saying.

'The six-hour window? That is how long it will take?' Simon's voice was calm but pain flickered across his face. Mell shrugged, she couldn't be sure of the answer to that one, the hooded figure could have gotten their estimate wrong. 'The Colosseum then.'

'You can't just break into what is probably one of the most protected archaeological sites in Rome, if not the world,' Mell hissed.

Simon shifted uncomfortably mulling over his response. 'Money ... talks. With the right people.'

'What about the Ludus,' Suze offered, she'd been eavesdropping and would probably catch hell for it later but she had an idea. 'There was a passage connecting the gladiator school to the Colosseum. There are excavations on at the moment, it's where the stolen eagle was found, we should be able to get in.'

'It is true the passage once existed, but it has most likely been destroyed,' Simon argued.

Suze shrugged. 'Only one way to find out.'

IX

At four thirty in the afternoon on the last Sunday of October, the Colosseum had closed its gates. As the teenagers hurried through the *piazza* beside it, heading for the little known Ludus located on the eastern side of the massive monument the clock ticked over to five p.m. The last of the tourists were being ushered out, the Roman soldiers had left and a low drizzle was misting the air.

Simon didn't care, it was almost an hour since the incident in the museum, which meant that Lisa now only had five hours left. She had come around from whatever trance she had been in and seemed fine, a little grouchy and definitely not happy to be surrounded by girls that she did not know, but generally fine. Unaware if the others were even following him, knowing that he could never ask them to do this, Simon shouldered through the unlocked gate to the Ludus and taking the wooden steps two at a time raced into the ruins. Desperately hoping against all hope that the gladiator passage still existed, otherwise they would have to find another way into the Colosseum and as Mell had pointed out, security at the monument was beyond tight. Especially after a potential terror attack on the museum.

'Dude!' Jerry's hand landed on his shoulder, his long legs allowing him to keep up with Simon's speed easily. 'Slow down huh? We're all here, we're all in, okay?'

'The help is appreciated Jeremy; however, time is in short supply,' Simon replied, barely pausing and forcing Jerry to grab his shoulder again.

'Call me Jeremy again and I swear I'll lamp you,' Jerry grinned, enjoying the confusion on Simon's face. 'Mancunian for "punch your lights out". No one calls me Jeremy these days.'

Simon remained silent, massaging his temples as the girls arrived at the Ludus, and began making their way down the rickety wooden steps into the ruins. Lisa walking alone, ahead of the other four, too dignified to be part of the rag-tag group she considered so beneath her own standing. Simon groaned softly and met Jerry's eye. 'Best get used to it, I can hardly be so informal as to call you Jerry with Lisa here. Count yourself lucky that in the heat of the moment I neglected to refer to you as Mr Llewellen,' he held his hands up already expecting Jerry's repost. 'I know the situation is hardly ideal but what else can I do?'

'Wait, you're planning on dragging her around the Colosseum with us? You're insane! Send her back to the hotel,' Jerry darted a look in Lisa's direction. 'Look at her, she doesn't want to be here.' He grinned to himself as he thought of a solution, it wasn't every day he got the chance to make Simon feel awkward. 'Why don't you take her back to the hotel, make use of that massive double bed in our room, and me and the girls will find these wings for you? After all, not every guy gets a girl that indescribably beautiful for his birthday!'

'Do you think if that was an option I would not already be there?' Simon replied, twisting his signet ring around his finger with a sigh, almost absently noting the fact that Jerry found his girlfriend attractive. 'You saw how she reacted to the idea of getting those wounds looked at,' Jerry nodded, as Simon continued. 'We just need to find these god damn wings,' Simon gave a half laugh, 'dangerous history seems to be becoming a bit of a habit.' Jerry snorted his agreement and together they moved off through the Ludus looking for the entrance to the current excavations.

At the bottom of the stairs the girls were looking around the ruins with some interest. Only Suze had known of their existence and then only because she loved gladiators, but even she was avidly reading the tourist plaque explaining the partial building. She heaved a sigh of relief when she read that the place had been built by Domitian, the second son of the soldier emperor. They were still on the right track; her guess had been good. She didn't like Lisa, but having overheard Mell's conversation with Simon, she didn't particularly want the girl to die. Then there was the thrill of being on the trail of something again, if they could get into the arena it would be empty. They would be alone in a monument of vast international importance and steeped in so much history the walls could probably weep blood. Even so, she had never heard of anyone being interred below the massive edifice of the Colosseum.

'This is only part of it,' said Sarah, bringing Suze's thoughts back to the present with an unwelcome dose of reality. 'Look, the area is cut in half by the modern road, it's a solid concrete wall. Surely if the passage existed it would have been at the end of the Ludus closest to the Colosseum. It's gone, unless it still exists below those buildings.'

Suze looked around in dismay, Sarah was right, her great idea of getting in through the Ludus was doomed to failure. The only part of the gladiator school visible was the quadrant furthest from the arena. Balling her fists, she glanced over at Lisa, the stuck-up blonde girl was perched on a broken piece of wall staring at her boyfriend as if he'd gone mad, as Simon and Jerry frantically searched the ruins for any sign of the passage.

'Why are we even here?' said Claire, still loitering at the top of the stairs, hands on her hips. 'The Colosseum is over there, besides I thought we were going out tonight? What are we doing getting mixed up in some crazy cult thing? Don't any of you remember what happened last time? I nearly died!'

'No one is forcing you to be here Claire,' Suze replied in a low voice, slowly climbing the stairs towards the girl with the green hair. 'If you want to go back to the hotel that's fine. You're right, none of us asked to be caught up in this mess, but we're a team now. We stick together and we look out for each other.' She looked back at the Colosseum and grinned. 'Besides, who doesn't want to break into a national monument out of hours?'

Claire closed her eyes and sighed deeply. 'Okay, I get it. We're stuck. She needs help and without knowing a thing about her we are all expected to just get on board with this. It's a bit much to ask, especially as she's been so horrible.' She sighed again and looked at the Colosseum, then down at the Ludus. 'I guess I do owe Simon though, it was his knowledge that saved me.'

'That a girl,' Suze replied, clapping her friend on the back. 'Come on, the sooner we help save her and get these wings, the sooner we can ship her off back to Switzerland and get our fun version of Simon back.' She darted down the steps with Claire following reluctantly behind, and made her way through the ruins, to where Mell was pretending to read a sign but in reality, was studying Lisa.

At the opposite end of the ruins, Simon was struggling to keep his temper. Suze's idea had been good, great even. The gladiator school had been home to the fighters and there had been a passage to keep them away from the crowds and provide easy access to the arena floor. The problem was that only a quarter of the Ludus still existed and it was the part furthest away from where the tunnel would have been. Two sides of the gladiator school ended in sheer concrete walls almost three meters high, and topped with the modern road. If the passage still existed at all it was likely in someone's basement and they did not have time to knock on doors.

'Hey Si!' Jerry was yelling, waving his arms to attract attention. 'Over here, idiots just used plastic fencing and road irons to cordon off the dig, easiest thing in the world to slip through. We can even put it back up once we go in and no one will know we were here.'

'Jerry, you genius,' Simon croaked, looking at his watch before joining his friend by the orange fence. He had completely missed the doorway through the concrete, and the bright orange plastic fencing. His racing mind too frantic to focus on what he was doing. Excited, Jerry ripped one of the road pins free of the ground and opened the fence, allowing Simon access to the underground chamber beyond. He ducked inside and immediately found the next obstacle. 'So much for easy access,' he grunted. 'There is a gate here, Jerry.'

'Aww bollocks!' came Jerry's cheery response. 'Give me one sec, there is always one lazy bastard who doesn't put their tools away properly. There'll be a mattock around here somewhere, I'm sure of it.'

'Looking for this?' asked Mell, catching the end of what he said and almost tripping over someone's neatly stacked, yet not properly stored, tools. She leaned down and, moving the shovel aside, procured the mattock from beneath it. 'It's a little blunt,' she said handing it over to Jerry.

Jerry shrugged in response, offering Simon the tool, but Simon shook his head. 'We cannot go smashing padlocks. That is beyond the law.'

Jerry raised his eyebrows at Mell. 'You can tell this one ain't a real Manc, right? Get outta the way Si, I'll do it.' Jerry raised the mattock and once Simon had moved, swung the heavy iron head at the padlock. The metal sparked and left a dent but the padlock remained intact.

'Give it here,' said Mell, taking the mattock back from Jerry. 'You should hit the weak part, dumbass.' She swung the mattock and one of the links in the chain twisted and sheared. 'Let's go,' she pushed past the two speechless boys, through the gate and into the underground excavation below the road.

'Did she just …' began Simon.

'Yeah, she just,' Jerry replied. 'Mell's a badass.'

Alerted by the sound of the breaking padlock and raised voices, Suze, Sarah and Claire were drifting over to join them. Unable to resist the urge to poke fun at Simon, Jerry gave a swaggering theatrical bow to each of them as they passed him, before following them into the underground site, leaving Simon with the unenviable task of convincing Lisa to follow them underground.

Through the gate, below the road was a somewhat messy underground excavation site. Low walls ran at ankle height in all directions, ready to trip an unwary visitor, and tools lay neatly stacked or sprawled, depending on the individual excavator, by partially excavated archaeological features. Here and there a label bearing a number was visible in the light of their phone torches.

'This must be where they found the eagle,' said Suze quietly as they gazed around at the underground remains of the Ludus, her excitement growing. 'Perhaps the passage does still exist.'

'If it does, then surely it will be over there,' said Sarah, playing her phone light further into the dig site, in the vague direction of the Colosseum. A blueish light further along suggested that Mell had already had the same idea. An ominous drone suddenly echoed through the space and everyone glanced up nervously.

'Cars,' Simon's voice was low but reassuring in the enclosed space, although cut off immediately by Lisa's demanding tones.

'Don't you dare think that you are leaving me out there, Simon James Matherson.' She had a way of saying his full name that implied a level of seniority and almost scorn on her part, as if his lack of a double-barrelled surname made his name less impressive. 'I am more than capable of playing this little game your friends seem to have devised.'

'Lisa,' his voice was soft yet commanding, 'This is not a game.'

She laughed. 'I have seen you, and the rest of the rugby club do these silly little scavenger hunts so often. I know one when I see one, the girls and I do them too,' she giggled. 'Do you remember the time we had Hilary pull apart the bar in the ballroom at Lord Richmond's looking for the vouchers to the Dior launch? It was so funny.'

Mell moved behind Simon and spoke in a low voice. 'If she thinks that this is a game it may make things easier. At least she may not panic so much about the poison if it starts to take effect.'

Simon responded to Mell with a pained look then, with a resigned sigh, offered his hand to Lisa. 'As you wish, my Lady.' She took his hand and stalked past his friends, still behaving every bit as though she were at an elegant party, not about to descend into the bowels of the earth. Suze stared in amazement as the pair moved through the group, deeper into the site. Lisa still wore Simon's jacket, her tiny, tight white summer dress, so short that from the back it appeared that she was only wearing the jacket. And her heeled shoes, dainty, high and so totally inappropriate for the task in hand.

The rest of the group requisitioned tools and torches from the piles around and followed the couple through the darkened space, stepping carefully over low walls and avoiding the half-excavated postholes which hid in the shadows of the uneven ground threatening to trip the unwary. Sarah almost twisted her ankle by misplacing her foot on more than one occasion and it was a miracle that Lisa got through unscathed in her heeled shoes. Eventually they came to what looked like a random rock fall, although with closer inspection it was clear that the blockage was man-made.

'So now we dig,' said Jerry, hefting a mattock and immediately wincing as the metal head clanged against the roof of the enclosed space and thunked heavily into his shoulder. 'Well that's me out, Jones?' he offered the mattock to Suze in exchange for the shovel that she was carrying.

Suze rolled her eyes. 'Such a wimp,' she muttered, taking a swing at the blocked entrance. Dust puffed up with every swing and the air was soon full of it. The excavation team must have an air filtering device in order to work in the enclosed space.

'Suze, stop,' said Sarah coughing. 'We can't work like this.'

Suze obediently dropped the mattock and inspected the tiny hole she'd made in the blockage. 'Too right, have these guys never sharpened their tools, this is the most useless mattock ever,' she groaned.

'That's not what Sarah meant,' Mell replied, flashing her light around the space, 'There must be a generator somewhere.'

'We can't use that!' Claire immediately countered. 'Someone will hear and we'll be arrested, creeping around down here fine, it's no different to what we've done before, but actively advertising the fact?'

'She has a point,' said Jerry, pulling his T-shirt over his nose and jabbing his shovel half-heartedly at the hole Suze had made. The metal rang loudly in the enclosed space as he hit a stone and bounced off, driving the shovel deeper into the dirt pile and causing a mini avalanche.

'Jerry, you idiot,' coughed Sarah. 'You made it worse.'

'Actually,' said Simon softly shining his torch at the rubble and wafting the dust motes out of the beam. 'I think the hole may be big enough for us to squeeze through.' He put his torch between his teeth and hauled himself up the rubble, vanishing head first through the narrow gap that Jerry and Suze's combined efforts had created.

Lisa crinkled her nose in disgust. 'You are not serious? Simon?'

'It is clear on this side. Come through!' Simon's voice floated back to the assembled group. Lisa hesitated for a second, then as Claire moved forwards, she threw herself at the gap, scrambling to be first through, unwilling to leave Claire alone with her boyfriend for even a second. Claire followed her, apparently still unwilling to accept defeat. Mell gave a shrug and let Sarah go ahead of her, leaving Suze and Jerry at the back.

'Think positive Jones,' muttered Jerry, giving Suze a sly sideways look. 'Maybe both of them will fall down a shaft somewhere and leave him for you.'

She punched his arm. 'Shut up, or I'll push you down a shaft and make everyone feel better.' Jerry laughed, and let her go through ahead of him, knowing how awkward it would be to fit his tall but narrow frame through the small gap.

Once past the rubble, the passage, intended to enable the movement of armoured gladiators, was large enough for the teens to walk side by side and only a few hundred yards long. It was dark, although there was a dusky light emitting from the opening into the Colosseum, which illuminated the discarded beer cans and other detritus indicating that the tunnel had not always been closed. A warm but stale breeze wafted through the space.

At the farther end of the passageway their access was briefly barred by a simple iron door, wedged slightly. A leftover legacy from previous plans to open the passage to the public. One by one the group sucked in their stomachs and inched around it and found themselves opposite the arched gladiator's entrance to the arena floor.

X

Stepping into the Colosseum at the level of those who fought for the entertainment of the Roman public was both terrifying and exhilarating. Devoid of tourists, the walls reared to the heavens, trapping the vast expanse of sky in an unreachable oval. The enclosed sky and oppressive silence left the teens feeling small, insignificant, like fish trapped at the base of a deep well. As they moved slowly further out into the arena, onto the partial stage that now covered the eastern end, the silence deepened, falling like a heavy blanket, broken only by the unnaturally loud click of Lisa's heels as she stalked across the stage like a prima donna. Everyone else paused, awestruck, staring around at the arena from this new perspective, the perspective of the condemned.

'Qui morituri te salutant!' Suze thumped her right hand against her chest, speaking the historical salute of the gladiators as she gazed around the ancient killing ground. 'Wow, this is so much better than Old Trafford!'

'We doing this or what?' Jerry's voice cut through the silence. Unfazed by the majestic awe of the place, he was already hanging off the wrong side of the stage railings above the basement level. 'Someone is gonna see us if we hang around.'

'Jerry be careful,' Claire warned, watching him clambering along the railing searching for a suitable wall to drop down to.

'Geez, relax mam,' he groaned, and then with a grin, let go of the railing and dropped out of sight.

'JERRY!' she shrieked, racing over to the railing, followed quickly by the rest of the group, who were concerned in varying degrees about Jerry's safety. Sarah was noticeably the last to join the others looking down.

He was fine, sitting cross-legged on the paved floor of one of the hallways below, staring up at them laughing his head off. 'Your faces, priceless,' he grinned.

'Such a tool,' Sarah shook her head and turned away, unwilling to be further involved in whatever game he was playing.

'How did you get all the way down there so fast?' asked Mell, slightly concerned.

Jerry shrugged. 'I'm like a foot taller than the rest of you, less far to fall. You guys can use the wall and I'll give y'all a hand down.'

'Awesome,' Suze grinned, throwing her leg over the railing, anxious to get started looking for the wings, although even more excited at the thrill of entering an area restricted to the public. Although summer had been dangerous and they had all been scarred in one way or another, Suze often found herself missing the excitement that their accidental summer quest had brought. She dared not say anything aloud, especially not in earshot of Simon, but she was secretly delighted that they seemed to be in the middle of something again.

As the rest of the girls began climbing the railings, preparing to follow Jerry down to the lower levels, Lisa tugged lightly at Simon's sleeve catching his attention. 'Simon, will I be safe with him around, he …' she paused and examined her pink painted nails, 'he seems somewhat crass.'

Simon let out a rather loud sigh of relief, for an awful moment he had thought she may have realised that Jerry found her attractive and have been worried about it. 'Jeremy tends to mask things with humour,' he replied, 'but underneath it all he is a good friend. I trust him. Besides he is not the one you have to worry about,' he mentally cursed himself as soon as the badly phrased words were out.

'Oh,' Lisa folded her arms and stared at him, her blue eyes turning to ice. 'So, which one is she? Or are you sleeping with all four of them?'

Simon crossed to her, as she turned away from him. There was no one else around, it was just the two of them. Alone in the ancient arena, watched only by the golden, sunset tinted walls of the amphitheatre. Moving behind Lisa, wary of the hostile squaring of her shoulders, he wrapped his arms around her, nuzzling his twice broken nose against her neck, the fingers of his left hand splayed protectively across her stomach. 'Lisa darling, why are you so jealous? You know that I love you.' She froze and he felt the catch in her breath as she registered what he had said. The three little words he had never uttered in English before. One of her hands found his, the other moved to tangle in his hair as she turned her face up to his, finally allowing him to kiss her, although the moment was all too brief for both of them.

'Hey Si! You guys coming down here or what?' Jerry hollered from below. 'Don't make me come back up there!'

With no one to see them and no need to pretend that nothing had happened, the couple took a little time to break their embrace and make their way over to the railings to begin the climb down. Although, Simon felt a flutter of panic that he struggled to suppress when he caught the time on his watch. It had taken them far too long to get into the Colosseum, two hours had already passed.

On the lower level the others were growing tired of waiting. Knowing that time was of the essence they couldn't understand what was taking Simon and Lisa so long.

'We probably need to go deeper,' mused Sarah, looking around at the maze of corridors open to the sky without the arena floor. 'I saw a program once that suggested that there were lifts and other floors.'

'Where they kept the animals, and stores you mean?' Suze said, as Simon finally dropped down off the stage to join them, promising Lisa that he would catch her if she followed him down.

'There were almost forty elevators utilised in the arena, most big enough to take a lion,' Simon confirmed lifting Lisa down from the wall. 'If we search this level we should be able to find one suitable, although I doubt the capstans still work.'

'Best stay out of sight then?' Mell suggested turning away from the centre of the arena and back into the darkness of the corridors below the modern stage. No one wanted to risk being spotted and everyone followed her swiftly, turning on torches as they went.

It didn't take the group long to find a lift shaft, a yawning void of deeper darkness in the dingy half-light below the stage. A half-hearted attempt, in the form of a ramshackle, aged trellis, had been made to safely block access to the ancient lift shaft. It was so rotten that a single joint tug from Simon and Jerry brought the whole thing away from the wall, leaving only a rusty stain and a solid guard rail across the centre to imply its presence.

'How far down do you think it goes?' Suze asked, peering tentatively over the guardrail and aiming her torchlight into the gaping void.

Jerry knocked a loose stone over the edge and stood silently, waiting for the thud but heard nothing. 'Bottomless seems to be the answer,' he said nervously.

'How are we going to get down? The pulley system seems to be out of order,' Claire said, indicating a rusting metal hook and wheel embedded in the floor. The ropes for which were long gone.

'You are not seriously suggesting that I go down there, are you?' Lisa said, catching Simon's hand. 'It will be filthy and we already climbed through that dirt pile. Look, it smudged my dress.'

He ignored her, twisting his fingers free and kneeling by the lift shaft, playing his more powerful torchlight over the walls.

'Simon, I don't think we can get any lower without help,' Mell said indicating the modern lift doors behind them, which stood silent and out of place in the ancient brickwork. A security panel glowed red beside the closed doors.

'You either know very little about Roman architecture, or you give up far too easily,' said Simon, stretching flat out across the narrow corridor on his front. 'Would someone hold my torch so that I can see this wall, I require the use of both hands.'

'Simon!' Lisa was horrified. 'Your shirt will be ruined!'

Taking his torch, Suze knelt beside him, playing the light over the walls of the rectangular shaft below. Simon inched his shoulders out over the void and stared down into the darkness. Slowly he moved his hands down from the edge, searching along the wall for something.

'What on earth do you think you are doing?' Lisa screeched, 'I insist that you stop scrabbling around on the floor at once.' Everyone, including Simon, ignored her, intent on what he was looking for and how they could move further into the ancient building.

'Hey! Careful,' Mell scolded, grabbing hold of his legs as he inched further forward.

'*Gracias* Melody,' Simon replied, scrabbling further down the wall. 'Suzannah bring the light this way a little.' Scowling at the use of her full name, Suze obediently swung the light around following the direction he was indicating until he said stop. Seeing Mell struggling to hold Simon's weight, Jerry elbowed her out of the way and took over, groaning as he realised that the shorter boy was heavier than he looked.

'Simon, what are you looking for?' asked Claire squatting down next to Suze, as Lisa continued to prattle in the background.

'As with modern elevators, the Romans had a means to climb into the shaft to make repairs, a ladder of some sort. It is most likely to be a series of niches cut into the stonework. Provided I can find them, we should be able to descend to the next level relatively easily this way,' he replied, his voice echoing down into the void. Then a louder exclamation in his native Spanish indicated his discovery of the first niche.

'About time,' moaned Jerry, dragging him back up.

'How stable do you think this ladder of yours is?' asked Sarah, checking her backpack for any climbing gear she might have brought with her. She usually carried a rope or two, and a few climbing clips, but having packed light, she had nothing like crampons or picks.

'The niches are carved into the rock of the shaft, they should be fairly solid, and are at least a hand width deep, the odd one may be slightly crumbly perhaps, but if we take it slowly and carefully it should be just like climbing a ladder,' Simon replied.

'I don't like it, there's too far to fall,' said Claire, stepping back, her fear of confined spaces had already been pushed getting through the underground part of the Ludus and the covered corridors of the Colosseum itself weren't much better.

Lisa nodded, for once in agreement with her considered rival. 'I am not going down there,' she said firmly, staring wide-eyed at the yawning lift shaft, arms folded, signalling the end of any discussion.

Simon shook his head. 'Sweetheart, there is no way I am leaving you alone up here in a restricted area of the Colosseum. Any of the guards could be prowling around, and we have no idea how long we might be down there.'

'But, it will be filthy and disgusting,' she grabbed his shirt. 'There might be bugs down there. Besides I've never used a ladder in my life.'

'Lisa,' he caught her hands between his and kissed her fingers, 'a ladder and a bit of dirt will hardly kill you. Just follow the others and be careful.' He moved away from her and as she continued to protest, he carefully slid his body over the edge into the abyss, searched for the niche before settling his weight on it. He glanced up at Jerry. 'Rear-guard?' Jerry gave him a salute in response.

Sarah swung into the shaft second and Suze followed her a moment later, feeling her legs hanging in the air before finding the carved hole in the stonework. She gritted her teeth. It would be a little scary, but not too hard, just like a ladder. She kind of wished Sarah had set up a rope or something though, fearless as Suze wanted to be, even she had to admit the darkened abyss below was just a little nerve wracking.

Voices echoed up the shaft, but Suze was unable to work them out, and remained focussed on finding the next niche with her feet, until her right foot hit air. Unprepared, she flailed a little before realising that she must have reached the opening to the next floor, and lowering herself down. An arm slid around her waist, pulling her forwards into the corridor and she felt a small fission of excitement at finding herself so unexpectedly close to Simon. A shriek in the shaft forced her to squash the feeling as he leaned back into the darkness to call encouragement to Lisa.

Although it was Claire who slithered down next, with Lisa immediately following. The girl was pale and clearly glad to be back on solid ground. Watching Claire attempt the ladder had been the trigger for her to try it herself, much as she hated the green-haired girl, Lisa would not be beaten by her. Mell followed them and Jerry slithered down last. Tall enough to rest his toes on the base of the opening whilst still holding the last niche, he lazily offered a hand to Simon, who dragged him in and together the group stood silently in the dark corridor lit only by the light of Simon's torch.

'It's like the labyrinth of Crete. Where's the Minotaur?' remarked Sarah.

'Urgh, Sarah don't, it's really creepy down here. Besides, those Gladiator statues look scarier than any Minotaur,' said Claire, shivering in the damp, silent subterranean air, trying to control her breathing so that no one noticed how scared she was. Mell glanced her way and gave a small "thumbs up" sign asking if she was okay, Claire responded with a weak smile, Mell would understand, she had been at Tintagel.

'Do we have any more lights?' asked Simon hovering his light over the statues that Claire had spotted. They stood in two neat rows, flanking the corridor to the left. As his light passed over the closest one he caught the name at the statue's base, "Flamma". The most famous gladiator ever to fight in the arena. Interested he shone his torch further down the passage illuminating more figures.

'I still have dad's lighter!' Jerry proclaimed triumphantly as everyone else retrieved their torches and phones.

'What are they?' Lisa asked quietly as she moved, almost trancelike to walk between the warriors.

'Heroes of the arena, condemned to a dusty corridor, never to see the light of day. Sad really,' Simon replied reaching out, intending to catch her hand and pull her back to the group, but she evaded his grasp. 'Lisa, I think you should stay with us,' he said, watching her movements. There was something disturbingly sensual about the way she was moving, dancing her fingers over the tines of a trident, running her hand over a muscled stone bicep and moving just a little too close to another. 'Lisa?' Simon called, his concern over her strange behaviour rising as she caressed the face of another gladiator, before pressing her lips against the unfeeling stone. Conscious of his friends' enquiring glances and very confused about Lisa's uncharacteristic behaviour, Simon strode down the corridor between the gladiators and gently grabbed her shoulder, breaking her lip lock with the stone warrior. 'Lisa, what are you doing?'

Her eyes appeared glazed, then she blinked, as though rising from sleep and raised a hand to her head. 'Where am I?' she groaned quietly, allowing Simon to slip his arm around her waist and escort her back to the group.

'Where do you think we start looking for this tomb then?' said Mell playing her borrowed torch over the three passageways that they could see. 'Any idea which way?'

'What's up Simon?' asked Sarah, noticing his frown of concentration.

He motioned for silence and listened. From the left, the corridor with the gladiator statues, so quietly it could almost be nothing, came a series of soft thuds, followed by the sharper almost familiar scrape of metal on stone.

'Strange for a security guard to be all the way down here,' said Sarah, shining her light down the central passage.

A louder crunch, like breaking stone, came from the gladiator passage, followed by a thud and a metallic clang. Simon swung his torch back around illuminating the statues again and another metallic clatter rang from the depths of the corridor. More thumps came from the darkness and a long rasp of metal as one of the gladiators lowered his weapon.

'Run!' hissed Simon, grabbing Lisa's hand and roughly dragging her down the right-hand corridor, tailed closely by Claire, as Jerry shot down the central corridor, Sarah immediately behind him.

'Come on Suze,' said Mell, heading into the right corridor in the same direction as Simon, Lisa and Claire. 'Let's go.'

XI

The flame of the lighter sputtered in Jerry's hand, making deep shadows leap and dance across the narrow space. Beyond the flickering pool of light, all was darkness, deep soundless darkness. Pausing, Jerry cupped a hand around the delicate flame, throwing the way ahead deeper into shadow.

'Well, this blows,' his voice was loud in the enclosed space.

'Less than half an hour underground and we're all split up again, seems a little familiar, doesn't it?' a female voice replied.

Jerry turned, the rapid movement almost extinguishing the tiny flame in his hand. 'Oh, it's you,' he grinned, as the flickering light fell across Sarah's face, 'just my luck to get stuck with you again …'

'Well, you weren't exactly my first choice either,' Sarah interrupted with a scowl, switching on her own torch, bathing the narrow, enclosed space in artificial light.

He stared at her, a frown creasing his face before realisation slowly dawned. 'You're pissed off about what I did with your sister the other night?' he saw the look of horror creep onto her face. 'That came out wrong. But, jeez, Sarah let it go, I had a good reason,' he rolled his eyes and gestured at the space around them. 'Besides, bigger things right now, huh?'

'Yeah, cos you're one to think about the bigger picture,' she retorted, 'and no matter what you say there is no good reason for what you …'

'Shhhh!' he silenced her mid-sentence, clamping a hand over her mouth and locking his blue-grey eyes on hers. From somewhere behind came the soft scrape of metal against stone, its sound dulled by the distance and thick walls. Jerry dropped his hand from Sarah's face, 'Let's move,' he hissed softly.

Sarah said nothing, simply fixed him with an angry stare, before shouldering past him and striding quickly into the darkness ahead.

'Well-handled Jerry,' he sighed to himself, snapping off the lighter, plunging himself into darkness. Only to spark the flame immediately back into life as a muffled scream reverberated down the corridor from the direction Sarah had gone. 'Please don't let her be hurt, just be a rat, please be a rat.' he repeated as he hurried down the corridor, hand cupped protectively around the sputtering flame.

*

'Simon, I insist that we cease this physical exertion!' Lisa's voice was a high-pitched whine in the darkness. 'I think I threw a heel.' She wrenched her fingers free of his and, resting a hand on the wall for balance, stood elegantly on one leg, folding her left ankle up behind her and examining her precious shoes. Sure enough, there was a scuff along one side of the delicate white material and a large gouge in the stiletto, big enough to render the heel liable to break off. 'Ohmigod! Simon, you brute, you ruined my Jimmys!!' her shriek of anguish was like a siren in the enclosed space.

'Who or what is Jimmy?' Simon replied absently, playing his torch light across the walls of the narrow corridor, looking for anything to indicate a tomb and keeping an ear out for any further noise.

'Jimmy Choos, you moron!' Claire retorted, 'amazingly expensive, wonderful, beautiful, classy shoes.'

'Is that all? I thought it was something serious,' he replied.

'It is serious!!" Lisa's voice was shrill. 'These are my favourite, it took me an age to persuade daddy to buy them.'

'Well maybe you can ask your brute of a boyfriend if he might buy you a new pair for Christmas, right now we have other things to deal with,' Simon's tone was harder than he'd intended. Everything was taking far too long and now they were all split up. 'Claire, have you seen anything?'

Ignoring Lisa's look of distaste, Claire shone her own light around the narrow space. 'Nothing, Mell and Suze were following us but I think they ducked down a different passage back there,' she paused as a muffled scream echoed eerily through the dense air, followed by what may have been a second scream further away. The narrow twisting corridors amplified and toyed with the sounds making the origins unclear, the second scream was so indistinct that it may simply have been a reverberating echo of the first from a different direction. 'That sounded like Mell, she and Suze may be in trouble,' Claire said quietly.

'Believe me, Suze can more than take care of whatever the problem is,' Simon replied with a slow, but very genuine smile. A smile that earned him a hefty slap on the chest from his nervous and strung out girlfriend.

'She's Suze now?' Lisa screeched. 'Simon, you really are far too familiar with these girls, I do not approve.' Lisa stood back, planting her hands on her narrow hips, fixing her boyfriend with a haughty stare. She wanted to sound commanding and in control, a lady should always be in control, but her voice trembled and she stuttered over the words. 'Bad enough that you drag me into this filthy hovel, for nothing but a treasure hunt, but you bring me here with these … these …'

Simon hushed her, holding up a hand for silence as if she were a common servant, cutting her off mid flow. It was most unbecoming behaviour towards a lady of her high rank and she opened her mouth intending to indignantly remind her boyfriend that she was the daughter of an Earl and her status outranked his, when she was roughly thrown aside by the green-haired girl.

'Simon!' Claire screamed, dragging him away from Lisa, giving the blonde girl a hefty shove in the other direction. She'd seen a movement on the edge of the pool of light cast by her torch, a brief flash as light caught edged metal. She recognised it from events below Tintagel over the summer, a sword raised for attack. She'd acted without thinking, throwing the couple apart as a wicked looking, curved blade swept mercilessly through the space where they had stood.

'*Gracias!*' Simon exclaimed breathlessly. Claire's fingers remained tight on his arm, her other hand resting lightly on his chest. She could feel his heart racing through his shirt. Although, outwardly he was calm, his eyes were fixed on the vicious looking weapon embedded in the stone surface of the corridor. The rules of the hunt had changed, retrieving the standard was no longer a case of finding it in time to save Lisa. Pressed against the wall on the opposite side of the corridor Lisa stared in wide-eyed horror at the sword that could have killed them, and began to scream as she realised that this was not a game.

*

In the dim light that their torches provided, Mell and Suze raced down the narrow tunnels, twisting and turning through the cold, damp, darkness, stumbling over uneven stones until they could run no further. Flattening themselves against the wall they waited, catching their breath. Through the darkness came a soft, almost inaudible slithering sound, close by.

Wordlessly they exchanged concerned looks, both wanting, yet not wanting to know what was making the strange sound. Suze's light began to flicker, and she cursed herself for not charging her phone. Mell squeezed her arm gently, diverting her attention from the dodgy light. Something had moved in the hazy shadows. A humanoid shape, barely discernible outside the small halo of light cast by their torches.

Another move, more strange slithering, and bronze metal glinted in the stronger white light of Mell's torch, as the triple barbed tip of a trident came into view, followed by a strong and muscular body. The huge hand holding the trident protruded from a thick leather vambrace which encased the whole bulging muscular arm, up to a wide metal flange that reared upwards towards the bare head, protecting the shoulder and bull neck of the *Retarius* gladiator.

'Gladiator,' Suze said hoarsely, pointlessly, as they stood watching him curl his arm back ready to cast the weighted net that they now knew was the source of the slithering sound.

'Think we can outwit him?' said Mell sizing him up. 'Trident looks unwieldy, and he's likely more brawn than brains. If we rush him we could take him down.'

Suze glanced at her in the half light. Mell's face was set, grim and determined. She'd fought off the violent advances of the vile henchman Richards over the summer and was determined never to allow herself to be at the mercy of a man's strength again. But the *Retarius* was a formidable foe.

'We can't,' Suze replied, hating how powerless she felt, but she knew gladiators, 'The *Retarii* always win. The trident is not the problem, it's the weighted net that kills you. If he catches us with it, we're toast.'

Mell swallowed, her throat dry enough to emit a loud click. 'Okay,' she hissed, her hand landing on Suze's wrist again. 'Ready? Run!' She turned and dragged Suze along with her, fleeing through the narrow, darkened corridors of the labyrinthine bowels of the arena. Rounding a corner, they heard a scream and paused, trying to determine its whereabouts, but the reverberating echoes made detection of the source impossible.

'Best keep moving,' Suze gasped, slowing her pace unable to run any further. Slowly, cautiously, the pair continued through the maze, staying alert, looking for the others and wary of the gladiator they knew to be prowling around. From somewhere deep inside the warren of passages came a muffled yell and then the deathly silence resumed. The two girls pushed on, not daring to speak, until ahead, they made out the end of the tunnel in the gloom.

'We need to find the others,' Mell suggested, and then gasped in horror as the huge *Retarius* stepped out of the shadows, blocking the exit. For seconds, everything stopped. The opponents faced each other, then the gladiator raised his trident and began to walk slowly towards the two girls, the weighted net slithering over the stone floor of the passage, hissing death.

Knowing that fighting in the confined space was futile, the *Retarius* would never miss with the net in such a small enclosed space, Mell and Suze fled back down the corridor as fast as they could, all the time hearing his lumbering footsteps and slithering net behind. Quickly they darted down a side tunnel hoping to lose him. A glance back showed nothing, then Mell screamed and grabbed Suze's arm again.

The corridor ended abruptly in a gaping hole. Centuries of disuse and periodic earthquakes had left their mark on the unseen areas of the Colosseum. Both stared at the space where the floor should be in dismay, there was no way across. They could never jump it and there was no way around it as the void stretched from wall to wall. A stone crunched behind, and whirling round they saw the gladiator. He stood quietly, calmly knowing that he had trapped his prey.

'Shit this is bad!' said Mell, gritting her teeth, glancing from the gladiator to the hole in the floor. 'Think we can jump it?'

'Are you insane?' Suze replied, eyeing the distance, 'although it beats death by gladiator.' Slowly the pair inched as close to the fighter as they dared, trying to gain the space for a run up, as he began to swing his net around.

'Ready?' Mell asked, exchanging a final look of mutual fear with Suze, and without waiting for an answer, sprinting towards the chasm, hurling herself forward off the edge. Suze followed immediately, screwing her eyes shut as she threw herself into space.

*

Jerry paused, he could see a shadow across the wall ahead of him. A figure, too large to be Sarah, or any of the others, this person was huge in every sense of the word. Not tall, although shadows could be deceptive, but squat and muscular. Cupping the lighter to conceal the flame, Jerry tip-toed closer, pausing only once as the shadow shifted. He hoped Sarah was okay, he'd heard nothing more after her scream and had expected to find her by now. Giving himself a mental shake, he stepped forward around the corner, and clapped a hand over his mouth to stop the yell of surprise that threatened to spill out. Not a rat. Definitely not a rat.

The gladiator stood at the junction of three passages, mercifully with its back to him. From where he stood, Jerry could see the knotted, scarred muscles of a powerful back and broad, wardrobe sized, shoulders crossed by wide leather straps, below a thick neck and large domed helmet. Shifting a little, he spotted Sarah across in one of the other passages, she was pale and staring straight at him, her torch trained on the gladiator. It was her light that had thrown the shadow down his way allowing him to stay out of trouble.

It appeared that she wasn't angry enough to put his life in more danger than necessary, and for that he was thankful, but he had no idea how to help her. Slowly Jerry snapped his lighter closed, an almost silent click the only indication of his presence. With a growl of intent, the gladiator turned towards the sound, giving Jerry a brief glimpse of a shiny and distorted face before it began lumbering towards him.

'DOWN!' Sarah's shriek was ear splitting in the confined area, but it saved his life as the gladiator raised its right arm and punched a large, half-moon shaped blade into the wall just above Jerry's head. He stayed still, crouched, silent as a statue, taking in the odd weapon. The gladiator's right arm was encased in a steel tube to the elbow, from the "fist" emerged a small narrow tube ending in a flattened, razor sharp, half-moon shaped blade. Hardly daring to breathe he noticed a small dagger in the gladiator's left hand.

The beast remained still, standing over him, waiting for him to make another noise. Jerry's nose was filled with the nauseating smell of unwashed sweat and dirt, and his vision filled with the tree trunk legs which jutted out from below a dirty leather skirt. Above that was a huge chest encased in an ornate and distinctly female breastplate and above that, the strange face, which he could now see was covered by an eyeless face plate, detailed to appear as a goddess, shining metal curls surrounding an angular, blemish free face. The eyes were solidly carved so that the gladiator had to rely on senses other than sight. Squeezing his eyes shut Jerry realised why Sarah had simply been standing there, the gladiatrix, would track every sound that she heard, and so he had no way of moving.

He remained uncomfortably crouched by the wall, staring at the grotesque Amazon standing over him and regretting every time he'd fantasised an Amazonian as a kick ass, yet still significantly hot woman. Twisting, he risked a glance in Sarah's direction, silently willing her to do something, anything, crouched pressed against the wall was uncomfortable and Jerry was unsure how long he could sustain this position. The gladiatrix was too close to miss should he make a sound.

Sarah for her part was watching the scene with a degree of fascination, she'd heard of female gladiators, but had never imagined one to look like this great hulking monolith. It was only when she caught Jerry's anxious and imploring gaze that she realised it was up to her to do something. She wrapped her hands around the cheap torch, borrowed from the dig, squeezing the plastic as she thought through her options. There were two, maybe three; she could attract the gladiator's attention, although that would result in her being chased and Sarah didn't fancy her chances against the strange blade. Second; she could leave Jerry to whatever fate would befall him if he made a sound. It was tempting, although, leaving him to the mercy of a gladiator was a little extreme, even if she did like the idea of him being beaten up by a woman. No, it would have to be the third option. Giving her torch a final squeeze she stepped quietly forward and hurled the plastic light as far down an empty corridor as she could.

The move plunged them all into strobing flashes and then darkness as the light wheeled away into the corridor. Sarah could hear her heart hammering in her ears as the gladiatrix unleashed a defiant roar and, with a sound like a freight train at full speed, lumbered off in pursuit of the torch.

Just as the darkness was becoming unbearable, the tiny flame of Jerry's lighter sputtered into life and she saw him slumped against the wall. Slowly, quietly she stepped over towards him. 'Not sweet talking your way out of the gladiator's wrath then?' she asked innocently.

He sat slumped against the wall looking shell shocked, the flickering flame creating angles to his face that she'd never noticed. 'Uhhh, Jerry don't play well with lesbians,' he replied in a half-hearted attempt at a joke. 'They are immune to his charms.' He laid a hand on the wall to push himself up and let it slide again, rapping his knuckles against the floor.

'And I suppose all lesbians look like that, do they?' she shot back, her anger quick to flare up again.

'No, they're usually phenomenally hot, why? Jerry arched an eyebrow questioningly. 'Something you wanna tell me?' Sarah shrugged, and offered an enigmatic smile in response as Jerry's eyes flicked up and down giving her an appraising once over in the firelight. 'Nah,' he concluded. She just shook her head and began to walk away. Jerry awkwardly hauled himself to his feet watching her move. 'Nah,' he repeated, but less certain.

XII

'It's a gladiator,' hissed Claire.

'*Therax*,' Simon replied, his innate need to use correct terminology overriding any fear he felt as he regarded the large warrior standing in the torchlight. The deadly looking blade swept in a curve up to a right hand and arm encased in tight fish scale armour. The chest was bare, and powerfully muscular behind the small square shield held in the left hand. Ornately carved greaves covered the solid legs from ankle to knee, and a large helmet, with bulging grills for eyeholes and a mock legionary crest, protected the gladiator's head. 'Take the torch and stay behind me,' Simon ordered, passing the light to Claire, whilst behind the gladiator, Lisa continued to shriek with terror.

Glad to have something to keep her occupied, Claire kept the light trained on the muscular figure blocking the corridor as he pulled the lethal blade free from the stones. Tentatively, Simon moved further into the corridor, trying to keep in the warrior's sight line, whilst drawing him away from the girls. The gladiator however, had other ideas, and in one rapid movement swept the blade down the corridor to his right, towards the shrieking figure behind him.

'No, no, no!' Simon yelled, watching the sparks dance down the wall as the metal blade impacted with the stone. 'Lisa get down!' he commanded, sighing with relief as she actually obeyed him and the blade zinged the wall above her head. He threw himself after the gladiator, slamming his shoulder in just above the great brute's thick waist hoping to throw him off balance. It almost worked but the *Therax* was a solid mass of fighting muscle, he stumbled a step, then with a roar of rage righted himself and hurled Simon backwards with one powerful arm.

'Simon!' Lisa shrieked his name in terror as the gladiator brought the deadly curved blade around. The first swing missed, and she stared open-mouthed, unable to tear her gaze away as the large armour-clad figure jabbed the curving blade repeatedly at her boyfriend. She was terrified, more afraid than she'd ever been in her life.

'Claire, keep the light on him!' Simon yelled, stumbling over a loose stone in the darkness as the gladiator pressed him backwards. The last swing had brought the blade too close for comfort. Simon pressed his hand against the wall and righted himself, just in time to see the curved metal aimed for is head. '¡*Mierda!*' he hissed, his natural Spanish beating the English curse to his lips, as the loose cobble tripped him again and sent him sprawling to the floor. The blade clanged against the stone less than an inch from his shoulder, and the light vanished as the gladiator's bulk blocked it from his view.

Claire was frightened and confused, she knew that she could deal with the situation and was desperately trying to think, but Lisa's incessant screaming was jangling her nerves and shattering her concentration as she tried to keep the light steady for Simon. She wasn't physically strong like the guys, or stubbornly headstrong like Suze and Mell, but she could hold her own. She'd proved that to herself over the summer, both with the skeletons in the crypt and again with the mercenary Royce below Tintagel. She just had to think. She shifted quickly around behind the gladiator, doing her best to allow Simon some light, that he might avoid the sword, but as she did so something caught her eye.

Sprawled on the floor, Simon inched slowly backwards as the *Therax* raised the sword over his head, and with a growl of menace swung it downwards, the metal whistling through the still air as the faint circle of light vanished completely. Instinct rather than anything else made Simon roll to his left, the sword raising a cluster of sparks as it clanged off the stone behind him. 'Claire, I need the god damn light!' he screamed, rolling to his right. 'What the hell are you doing?' More sparks rose from the floor as the blade wedged itself into a tight crack in the cobbles.

Claire heard Simon's yell and briefly swung the light back around. 'Still alive?' she called, hoping he would reply.

'Just about!' he gasped back, staring at the blade, now embedded in the ground between his legs, the vicious point mere millimetres from his groin.

'Good,' Claire said, breathing an internal sigh of relief, and plunged him into darkness again, trying to ignore the mix of fear and anger in his voice as he called her name. She'd seen something, she just needed to get it; it was lying on the floor, rusty and forgotten. A gladius. She flashed the light up at Lisa hoping for some help, but the girl was a quivering wreck, curled up against the wall, knees pulled against her chest, twin tracks of mascara down her face. Claire tried anyway. 'Help me?' Lisa simply closed her eyes and shook her head, letting loose another scream as a dull thud came from the darkness followed by a winded grunt of agony.

Claire whirled around flashing the torch down the corridor with one hand and groping for the forgotten sword with the other. In the hazy light, she could see Simon on his knees; doubled over, choking, retching and gasping for breath. The curved sword was still stuck in the floor, the gladiator must have punched him with its armoured fist. 'Lisa, do something useful and hold the light,' Claire demanded. Forcing the torch into Lisa's cold, trembling hand, she wrapped both her own hands around the gladius and wrenched it free.

In Lisa's trembling hands, the torch light strobed crazily around the walls. Claire watched Simon drag himself upright, leaning heavily against the wall, wiping blood from his bottom lip. The gladiator waited, watching, allowing his prey to stand before unleashing a triumphant cry and hurling himself forwards again. Simon threw up an arm protecting his face and managed to dodge several of the hefty, armoured blows.

Silently, gathering her nerves for her intended action, Claire moved behind the preoccupied gladiator and taking a deep breath, thrust the sword into his back with as much strength as she could manage. It was surprisingly difficult. She had to push hard against his muscle, and her resolve was weakening. With a groan of pain the gladiator swung round, knocking Claire into the wall with a flailing fist before staggering backwards towards Simon, who dragged himself along the wall as the gladiator's solid hulk collapsed almost on top of him.

*

The jump had been foolish, both Suze and Mell knew it, but the horror of the fall was not fully realised until they were flying through the air and able to see just how far it was to the floor below. They were not going to make it. Both screamed as they hurtled towards what must surely be death, or at the very least broken limbs. In a final effort Mell stretched her arms forward, her grasping fingertips touched the edge and with a shriek that was part terror, part triumph, she managed to hold on.

Suze had been moments behind with her jump; and her searching hands missed the edge but caught Mell's outstretched arm. Mell clamped her fingers around Suze's wrist as she started to slide downwards, and dangling from the edge of the broken floor, they heard the terrified shriek of the gladiator, who had stupidly pursued them over the edge, followed by the sickening thud of his body hitting the floor below.

'We made it,' Suze gasped with relief, unable to believe it.

'I wouldn't say that just yet,' Mell answered, struggling to hold both of them with just her left hand. 'Grab my waist or something, I need both hands to hold us.'

Fully aware of the predicament, Suze wrapped her arms tightly around Mell's waist, leaving her right hand free to grab the edge. Once clamped on with both hands Mell attempted to pull them up, but she wasn't strong enough to lift them both. Defeated, the pair hung between the floors unable to move. 'Now what?' Mell hissed gritting her teeth. 'We can't hang around here all day.'

Suze grunted an agreement and twisted to look downwards, a shadow on the wall below had caught her eye. Tightening her grip on Mell's waist she leaned out a little further, it looked almost like a wing, an outstretched eagle's wing.

'Suze, what are you doing, I can't hold us if you keep squirming,' Mell gasped, almost losing her grip.

'I can see something!' Suze replied excitedly. 'An eagle. It's carved into the wall on the floor below. It must be the entrance to the tomb, or at least another clue.'

'How far down?' Mell asked, looking down through her tangle of red hair.

'Too far,' Suze answered. 'The fall killed the gladiator, but that must be the tomb, we're so close ...'

'Yet so far,' Mell agreed, clenching her jaw and letting out a moan of pain. 'We need to do something. Can you climb up?'

'No,' Suze replied instantly, knowing her own limits and feeling the dull ache in her arms that suggested she couldn't hang on for much longer. 'Sarah probably could, but I really can't.'

'Try!' Mell hissed, the words swooping out in an agonised breath.

With a sigh, Suze reached tentatively for the older girl's shoulder, wrapping her legs around Mell's. The second Suze's weight settled on her left shoulder, Mell lost her grip on the floor. Both girls screamed as they swung crazily, hoping Mell could hold on with her right hand. Eventually she clamped her left hand back down on the edge of the broken floor. 'Okay,' she said breathing heavily, 'let's not do that again. But we need to come up with something.'

They hung, swaying slightly for a short while between the two floors. The situation seemed hopeless, they were simply waiting either to fall, or for the others to stumble across them. A situation that seemed less and less likely to happen.

'What do you think of our chances if I just let go?' Suze groaned, the pain was intense and she could barely feel her fingers anymore, she didn't want to think how much Mell's arms must be aching. 'You can climb up and I'll try to land on the gladiator.'

'Shh!' Mell hissed, 'I can hear voices.'

*

'Simon!' Lisa screamed her boyfriend's name into the eerie silence of the corridor, and gave him no chance to respond before shrieking his name again. Her fingers clawed madly at her hair, at her dress, along the walls, not caring if she tore her nails, and she shrieked again. Beyond her own mad panic, she could hear nothing, she was terrified, trembling, cold, and her heart was beating so loudly she could feel it reverberating through her head. 'Siiiiimon!'

Through the thick fog clouding his head Simon was dimly aware of someone screaming, although more pressing was the issue of the immobile body of the gladiator pinning his left arm to the wall, and the pain in his stomach. He groaned and shifted his position a little, slowly dragging his arm free. The gladiator slumped sideways, away from him. 'Claire,' he groaned, spotting her slight form sprawled on the floor in the flickering light. 'Are you all right?' he gasped as he spoke, still winded from the rib shattering punch the gladiator had delivered.

'I'm okay,' she replied, pushing herself up, a bruise already purpling on her cheek. She raised a hand to her head, moving a hank of green hair out of the way and resting her palm against her forehead. 'Your girlfriend however, appears to have the lung capacity of a whale, with the pitch of a dolphin,' she moaned, gesturing into the darkness of the corridor beyond.

'Lisa,' Simon shoved himself off the wall, staggering two steps before finding his balance. Lisa continued to scream, even as he moved towards her. The shrieks no less loud, but punctuated by loud hitching sobs as she struggled to catch her breath. 'Lisa, sweetheart.' She barely registered his presence and flinched when he touched her arm, screaming even louder in the enclosed space. The walls bounced the echo back and it sounded as if every stone of the amphitheatre was screaming in torment. 'Lisa,' Simon caught her wrists in a light grip, but she struggled against him, her ragged fingers clawing at his face as she screamed, wept and struggled.

'Oh, for god's sake. Shut. Up!' Claire raised her arm, cracking Lisa sharply on the back of the head with the pommel of the rusty gladius. The shrieking ceased instantly and Lisa collapsed, like a puppet with severed strings.

There was a moment of silence as they both stared at the girl in the white dress lying crumpled on the floor. 'I ... I cannot believe you just did that!' Simon's voice was faltering, his Spanish accent grating on the words as he wrapped his arm around his bruised ribs, unable to tear his gaze away from his unconscious girlfriend.

The sword fell from Claire's hands with a clatter as her hands flew to her face, equally unable to believe her own actions. 'Simon, I'm so sorry, I don't know what came over ... I ... She just wouldn't stop screaming,' she finished lamely, there was nothing else to say.

Simon turned to look at her, the expression on his face somewhere between confused concern and an overwhelming desire to laugh. 'Claire, you just rendered the love of my life unconscious. *¡Con una espada!* He knelt by Lisa's side and gently checked her over, frowning as his fingers felt the already swelling knot on her skull, thankfully there was no blood.

'Oh gods, I'm so sorry,' Claire pressed her hands to her mouth in horror and leaned back on the wall for support, her hazel eyes wide with shock. 'Will she be okay?'

Simon did laugh then, a short sound that he instantly bit his lip to hold in. 'Well there is no blood. I expect that she will most likely have one hell of a headache when she wakes up,' he looked up at Claire, his expression unreadable. 'You know I expect that kind of behaviour from Suze, but you seemed so much more sensible.' He scooped Lisa gently into his arms, nestling her head against his chest and brushing his lips against her cool forehead. 'What the hell is going on with you Claire? You fight with Mell, snap at Jerry, flirt, badly by the way, with me. Now this.'

Claire smiled weakly in response, but her face flushed a hot scarlet in the darkness. 'Come on Si,' she said softly, 'you and I both know Suze would have hit her with the other end of the sword.'

'Then let us be grateful for small mercies. But, you need to sort your head out. Figure out what is bothering you and talk to someone.'

'I know what's bothering me! I was lying to Gary about what happened over the summer and I couldn't face him anymore, so I ended it. I was shot, I nearly died. How could I tell him that? How the hell do you do it? How do you lie to her and still have a relationship?' she gestured at Lisa's limp form. 'Mine is ruined.'

'Okaaay,' Simon drew out the sound, wishing he'd not said anything. 'Firstly, now is not the time or the place for this discussion. Secondly; I never lie to Lisa …'

Claire cut him off sharply. 'She thinks you broke your nose playing rugby!'

'Her father told her that, I simply chose not to correct him. I did not lie to her, I would never lie to her,' he caught Claire's scathing look, 'All right, I may be somewhat economical with the truth occasionally. But, rugby is far more plausible than the truth.' He frowned and closed his eyes as if to block out something unpleasant, and Claire watched as a muscle twitched repeatedly in his jaw, and realised that he was dealing with his own souvenir demons from the summer.

*

'Can you hear that?' Sarah asked, walking beside Jerry in the darkness. They'd decided against using the lighter, trying to save the limited amount of fuel it held.

'Yeah,' Jerry replied. 'Sounds like Si's girlfriend, the drama queen, screaming again. I wouldn't worry about it. Si can take care of himself.' The screaming came to an abrupt halt. 'That however, might be something worth worrying about. Keep moving; the noise will have attracted the Amazonian monstrosity.'

'Maybe we can reach them first. Come on,' hissed Sarah.

'Wait, I heard something,' Jerry caught her arm and cocked his head to one side listening. Sarah sighed in exasperation, a scowl on her face, although the sound made her pause. It was indistinct, but sounded like someone screaming Jerry's name.

Jerry grinned, and cupped his hands around his mouth. 'Oy-oy!' he hollered back unsure where the voice had come from.

'JERRY!' It was Mell, somewhere close, and clearly in pain.

'Well that sounds bad,' he said. 'Go find Simon and Claire, they can't be far away. I'll deal with this.'

'She'll be coming …' Sarah replied, 'and now that Lisa's gone quiet we can hear Mell, and if we can …' She spun and raced quickly into the darkness towards where they had last heard Lisa's screams.

Jerry ducked into the left passageway and whistled softly, clicking his lighter back into life. Close by he heard his name again. Following the tunnel, he reached a gaping hole in the floor. 'Damnit,' he swore turning away.

'Jerry! Jerry we're here,' Mell's voice came from somewhere close to his feet. Looking down he saw her white knuckled fingers, barely keeping a grip on the stone floor, and dropping to his knees he let out a low whistle. 'What on earth are you two doing down there?'

XIII

'Don't just sit there staring like an idiot, help us!' Mell demanded. Her arms were aching and the relief she'd felt at seeing Jerry had rapidly vanished as she realised he was alone.

He turned and yelled something back over his shoulder, although there was no response. Scratching his head, he looked back down at the two dangling girls, assessing the situation. 'S'okay I'm here, everything'll be fine. Mell, you good?'

'Do I look it?' she gasped through gritted teeth.

'Aww, you've looked worse,' he joked and glanced back at a sound in the corridor. Which was when Mell's grip finally failed. The united screams of his friends jolted Jerry into action and he moved without thinking, throwing himself on the floor and reaching down to grab Mell's arms. The sudden jolt as they stopped swinging, almost dislodging Suze from her precarious hold on Mell's waist.

'Not entirely sure I've helped,' Jerry groaned, feeling the weight of both girls suddenly pulling on his own arms. He'd managed to grasp Mell by both arms just above her elbows, supporting her weight as she clamped her cramping fingers back on to the stone. With a grunt of effort, he tried to drag them both to safety. But his position, prone on the ground, didn't allow him the leverage to lift their combined weight. 'New plan; Mell I keep one arm around you, and I pull Suze up with the other,' Jerry groaned.

'That's stupid,' she hissed. 'Pull Suze up first.'

'Mell,' he spoke gently staring down into her face with intent. 'The second I let go of you, you're going to let go of this edge again, we both know it.'

'I can't hold on,' she sobbed, 'it hurts too much.'

'Hey,' his voice was sharper, 'Jerry's got you okay? Jerry's got you and he's not letting go.' She turned red-rimmed eyes up to him, tears threatening to spill down her cheeks. 'I promise,' Jerry finished, shifting his weight on the ground. A noise made him glance up. 'Which ever one of you guys that is, get your ass over here now!' he called back over his shoulder.

With a muttered Spanish curse, Simon immediately offered his assistance, reaching down to grab Suze, taking her weight from Mell, allowing Jerry to haul her up. Groaning with effort, Jerry slowly pulled Mell up over the edge. She gasped and screamed with pain as he dragged her up, her shoulders and chest scraping uncomfortably against the broken stone.

Alongside Jerry, Simon's strong fingers closed like a vice around Suze's wrist, and reflexively she returned the gesture, locking them together, before he dragged her up enough to slip his other arm around her shoulders, and haul her over the edge. Before Suze could even say thanks, Simon's attention was distracted by a distinctly feminine groan behind him.

'I'll be fine,' Suze said brusquely, elbowing her way past his unasked question to collapse in a heap against the wall, whilst Jerry wrapped his arms in a tight embrace around Mell, rubbing her back and arms, muttering nonsense in her ear as she sobbed against his chest with relief.

'Simon?' Lisa's voice was groggy and confused. 'Simon, what happened?' she raised herself awkwardly up off the floor and sat leaning against the wall.

'Lisa!' he was at her side instantly, crouching beside her, cupping her face gently in his hands. 'How are you feeling?' he asked, his dark eyes studying her pale features.

'I have a headache,' she moaned, massaging a knot on the back of her head. 'And my throat hurts.'

Simon gazed down into her eyes, brushing a strand of blonde hair away from her face. 'Unsurprising sweetheart, you hit your head rather hard when you fainted.'

'Liar,' hissed Claire quietly behind her hand.

Suze shot her a questioning look, and, shielding her lips from Lisa's view, Claire mouthed the words; 'I hit her,' and gestured to the gladius leaning on the wall. Clamping a hand over her mouth, Suze stifled a giggle and swallowing hard, mouthed 'well done,' back.

'We should move,' said Sarah quietly, 'it's not safe here, there was so much noise.'

'What do you mean?' asked Mell, as her adrenaline ebbed and she began to untangle herself from Jerry.

It was Jerry who answered. 'There is a huge Amazonian thing out there that hones in on sound, what with you guys yelling for help, and Simon's pet banshee over there I'd be willing to bet that she's in the vicinity.'

A furious look crossed Lisa's face, and she took the chance to reassert her position. 'That rake just called me a banshee,' she crossed her arms and pouted as Simon stood up.

'I heard,' he replied, brushing dust off his trousers and offering her his hand.

She slipped her hand in to his and allowed him to help her up, leaning on the wall for support. 'What are you going to do about it?' she demanded drawing herself up, chin high, jaw set, blue eyes boring into her boyfriend's face.

Simon sighed. 'Nothing,' he replied planting a soft kiss on her fingers as she snatched her hand away.

'Nothing!' she shrieked, landing yet another slap to his chest. 'Simon James Matherson, you are supposed to defend my honour against all slander. I demand that you do something!' she stamped her foot to emphasise her point.

Simon dragged his hands down his face. 'Jeremy, kindly refrain from referring to Lady Hayworth-Mills as any kind of loud female creature of mythological origin.' he glanced at Lisa, 'Happy?' she gave him a look of contempt and stalked away, only to emit another skull shattering screech as soon as she was out of sight.

'Banshee point proved,' Suze grinned, hi-fiving Jerry.

'Miss Jones, you are not helping,' Simon shot her a dark look, to which she stuck her tongue out crossing her arms. But her stupid grin died as a roar of intent issued from the adjacent corridor and Lisa reappeared, throwing herself into Simon's arms, gesturing at the monstrous thing, clearly Sarah and Jerry's Amazon, behind her.

Recalling her previous encounter with a gladiator, Lisa pressed closer to Simon, and he wrapped his arms around her shoulders allowing her to bury her face in his chest, all anger between them forgotten.

'Bollocks!' hissed Jerry, as the grotesque gladiatrix thundered into the corridor, waving the deadly half-moon blade that formed the fist of her right arm.

It slammed with pinpoint accuracy into the wall, exactly where Simon and Lisa had been standing. Lisa was fortunate that her man had fast reactions. He'd turned as the gladiator swung around, moving to the left and placing Lisa between himself and the wall. They now stood motionless beside the blade, eyes pinned on the hulking monster when Jerry spoke again.

'Bigger bollocks!'

A second gladiator, the *Therax*, sword still stuck in its back, stepped into the corridor behind the Amazon, trapping the teenagers with their backs to the gaping hole in the floor. There was nowhere to hide and nowhere to run.

The sound of Jerry's voice had roused the female fighter and she whirled towards him with frightening speed, raising the strange curved blade. The teenagers scrambled to get out of the way, pressing themselves against the walls as the *Therax* raised his blade and with a roar of defiance, halted the blind Amazon in her tracks.

The atmosphere changed as the gladiatrix turned her sightless face towards the new threat. Slowly, the teens began to move, inching along the walls towards the corridor entrance, past the two silent gladiators, away from the gaping hole in the floor. The *Therax* attacked first, swinging his blade in an overhead arc, aiming to hack into the Amazon's bulging shoulder. But her short dagger and quick senses caught his blade, forcing him off balance as her deadly curved weapon shot forwards. The *Therax* jumped back, eliciting a scream from Lisa as his solid body slapped into the stone beside her, spraying her with sweat.

The scream momentarily distracted the monstrous woman, and her curved blade would have impaled Lisa, had Simon's reactions been any slower. A narrow line of blood welled up along his arm, he'd not been as fast as the gladiatrix.

'We have to get out of here!' Mell called above the noise of the gladiators crashing together again.

Remaining in the cramped space as the gladiators sought a greater victory over one another, was not an option. Moving as stealthily as possible, wary of the speed of the blind gladiatrix and the skill of the *Therax*, the teens crept past the battle.

Breathing hard, Suze ducked under the arm of the *Therax*, feeling the heat rolling off his body, trying not to breathe in the reek of man sweat. He slammed into the wall behind and she felt warm droplets, *blood or sweat?* land in her hair and trickle unpleasantly down the back of her neck. Then she was free, out of the confined space and into the next dark, narrow corridor.

Mell and Jerry were already there, huddled in the sputtering flame of Jerry's lighter as they waited for the rest. Claire was next, an expression of absolute disgust on her face, showing that she too had been caught in the *Therax's* sweat shower. Sarah slipped out on the opposite side of the corridor and waited there alone, catching her breath and watching the ongoing battle behind. Simon and the no longer immaculate Lisa were last. He seemed okay, save for the long sliver of blood along his right arm, but she looked terrible. Still wearing Simon's jacket, Lisa swayed in her pointed heels and almost turned her ankle as she staggered forwards, hands groping for the support of the wall.

'What are you guys waiting for? Go,' said Simon as they re-joined the group.

XIV

Quickly, they moved through the warren of subterranean passages, hoping that they were heading towards the outer face of the arena rather than towards the centre, but in the dark maze there was no way of knowing which direction they were going. Behind, the grunts and metal clattering of the gladiatorial battle faded as the group raced further away.

In the dim torch light, they almost missed the elevator shaft. Jerry had already walked past it, eyes intent on the path ahead, but Mell spotted it. 'Here,' she said. 'Do you think it's the same one we came down?'

'Does it matter?' Sarah replied. 'Surely they all go to the surface.'

'We can't leave,' Suze replied, glancing at her watch. 'We don't have the wings, and we're running out of time. It's almost half seven. That's four hours gone. Besides, I think I know where the tomb is!'

'Suze, there might be more gladiators, or worse in the lower levels,' said Claire. She lowered her voice. 'I'm not great at the action stuff but I can probably handle it, but she can't,' she indicated Lisa, who was still stumbling along the corridor looking miserable.

'She has to,' Jerry interrupted. 'Ain't no way we can leave her anywhere, we all saw how she reacted when Simon suggested a doctor. Besides if she's with us, no one else can get at her, so she's safe.' Unseen by the others Mell bit her lip, if Lisa was poisoned as she suspected then it really didn't matter where she was, or who she was with.

'A great reason to be in danger.' Claire huffed. 'Saving the life of some blonde brat, who couldn't care less about us, she just happens to be dating our friend.'

'Claire,' Sarah's voice carried a warning note as Simon and Lisa came within earshot.

With a scowl, Claire turned her attention back to the couple and had to stifle a laugh as the heel on one of Lisa's stilettos snapped, pitching her sideways with a shriek. Fortunately for her, Simon was right by her side, and she landed, almost as if carefully staged, in his arms.

'My shoes,' she whimpered softly, staring up at him on the verge of tears. With a sigh, he carefully lifted her back onto her feet, feeling a twinge in his stomach muscles, which had taken the full force of the *Therax's* armoured fist earlier. Luckily, he'd just been winded, nothing broken.

'Si!' said Jerry watching his friend struggle, unsure if he should help or not. 'Suze reckons she knows where the tomb is.'

Simon glared angrily at Suze as Lisa sank to the ground with a sob. 'How long have you known? Time is important here Miss Jones.'

Blood rising, Suze snapped back at him. 'Jesus, Simon, would you take the stick out of your arse for a moment, it's Suze, nothing else, just Suze. And don't treat me like an idiot. I know time is important,' she shot a disinterested look at Lisa, who was just noticing that her boyfriend had left a smear of blood across her dress. 'I saw the tomb when we were dangling between floors. When exactly did I have the chance to tell you before now?' she turned angrily away, leaving Simon speechless.

'Well I'm going down,' Jerry grinned, already wriggling his way into the shaft searching for the hand holds.

'For pity's sake Jerry! Be careful,' Mell scolded, grabbing his belt before he could plunge headfirst into the darkness.

'Just excited to be going first for a change,' he retaliated, twisting around and beginning the descent. Shaking her head Mell followed him, and as Lisa began to complain about the blood and dirt on her dress, Claire swiftly followed.

Simon sank to his knees beside Lisa, attempting to coax her into at least standing up. No one envied him the task of getting her to come down into the further depths of the Colosseum. They all wished that she wasn't mixed up in this, but there was nothing to be done about it now. Suze shook her head trying to dismiss the irritation she felt at having Lisa here, and focus on the idea of locating an undiscovered tomb in the cavernous space below. The thought suddenly gave her a visceral thrill, a feeling she had not felt since discovering the forbidden lake that summer. Smiling to herself she followed Sarah into the ancient lift shaft. The climb was easier this time, the shaft ending at the next level, requiring only a short drop from the final hand-hold to the floor.

'We waiting for Romeo and Juliet up there, or moving on?' Jerry asked glancing back up the shaft to try and spot Simon.

'Moving on gets my vote,' Suze said, trying to get her bearings and recall the route back towards where she thought the tomb might be. 'We came to the shaft from the left, so we should head that way first.'

'Suze, wait,' said Mell. 'There could be more gladiators or worse down here. We should wait for Simon and Lisa, and stick together,' she was right, of course, but it didn't stop Suze and Claire, from scowling their disapproval.

It seemed an age before they arrived. Despite his bruised ribs, Simon had carried Lisa down the shaft in a fireman's lift over his left shoulder. Her face was streaked with mascara, the heels of both her shoes were missing and there was a large tear up the side of her dress that had not been there earlier.

'Still alive?' Jerry directed the question at Simon, whose response was a tight half smile and barely perceptible nod as he lowered Lisa to her feet.

Reunited, the group moved quickly through the corridors flashing their remaining lights down each side tunnel hoping to catch a glimpse of the carved eagle, the collapsed floor or the fallen gladiator. After several false starts and feeling ready to give up, they rounded a bend and came across a broken statue lying amid piles of debris.

'Recognise this?' Jerry yelled picking his way through the rubble and triumphantly waving the gladiator's trident. 'Must be here.'

Suze gazed up at the hole in the ceiling trying to recall where she and Mell had been hanging. 'That wall,' she said pointing to her left as Mell brought her light closer, playing it over the stonework.

'I see nothing,' she said, running her hand over the ancient stone wall.

'Move the light back,' said Simon, stepping over the stone gladiator.

Obediently Mell swung it back and they watched as Simon scuffed stone dust out of a shallow groove on the wall.

'Can we widen the beam on that light?' Claire called from further back. 'I think I see what Simon's getting at.'

'We can use two lights,' Sarah replied, borrowing Simon's torch so that a larger part of the wall was covered. There was nothing obvious until she stepped to her right a little and suddenly there it was. A large eagle, wings outstretched was etched into the stone, only visible with the light on the correct side to produce a shadow. It had to be the entrance to the tomb.

'How do we get in?' asked Claire.

'That, is the million-dollar question,' replied Simon, running his hands thoughtfully over one of the eagle's wings looking for a switch or opening of some sort. On the other side Mell did the same.

'Si,' said Jerry, 'looks like a doorway has been blocked, see, around the eagle?' He drew the shape in the air.

'You may be right,' replied Simon, stepping back and sizing up the space. 'How do you propose to open it?'

'Oh, like this,' Jerry stepped back from the wall, shrugged his shoulders, and hurled himself towards the eagle. There was a dull thud as his shoulder impacted with the solid brickwork.

'Owwwww!' he hollered, staggering, clutching at his battered shoulder.

'Smooth,' said Simon, pulling a face as the rest of the group smothered laughter.

'Then how do you propose to do it smarty pants?' challenged Claire.

'Like this,' he replied, slotting his fingers into the groove of the eagle's tail feathers, and pushing the concealed handle that he had spotted. The door moved a little, then stuck. He glanced back at Jerry. 'Now we try it your way.'

'But I already broke my shoulder,' moaned Jerry in response, although his eyes shone at the prospect of entering an undiscovered tomb, one that, in his head at least, would be filled with treasure.

'Go on three?' Simon checked, Jerry nodded his agreement.

'Three!' they both yelled, slamming into the brickwork together. Nothing happened. Jerry screwed his face up in pain and Simon swore in Spanish. 'Once more.' he groaned massaging his right shoulder as they both geared up to try again. Their second attempt was more successful.

There was a dull thud followed by a yell and an earth-shaking crash as the doorway collapsed. Simon lost his balance and landed heavily on the other side among the collapsed bricks, Jerry came to an abrupt halt and sank cross-legged to the floor in the now open doorway, distorted by the billowing dust clouds. They were in.

XV

'Simon!' Lisa's scream ripped through the dusty silence, and she quickly, but gingerly, picked her way through the fallen stones and crouched awkwardly beside him, tenderly pushing his dark hair from his face. The tight little dress, although ripped, still hindering her movement as she desperately tried to keep her knees off the cold, hard floor whilst trying to ensure her boyfriend wasn't seriously injured.

'Do you think anyone heard that?' Claire whispered, coughing on the disturbed dust.

'We are three floors down,' stated Simon, painfully detaching himself from the floor, as Lisa fussed around him. 'No one heard a thing. Sweetheart, it is just a graze, leave it alone.'

'But you are bleeding,' Lisa protested reaching for his arm again.

Simon glanced down at his torn, scuffed skin. The stone had been rough, tearing open the neat slice of the gladiatrix's blade, but it was little more than a nasty graze. He'd had worse on the rugby field. He caught Lisa's hands between his and fixed her with an earnest smile. 'I promise you my lady, I will live.'

'Blegh!' Jerry mimed throwing up, 'when you're done with the icky, sicky, romance crap perhaps we can get back to the treasure? Not that I see any,' he stood up dusting down his jeans, 'for a tomb this is very empty.'

'Icky, sicky romance?' said Claire. 'Remind me never to date you.' Jerry shrugged and pulled a face, he'd never been the romantic type.

'Jerry, use your head,' said Sarah, 'if he's an emperor, or someone important they're not going to bury him behind the first wall. Think of the pyramids; full of tunnels and false doors.'

'And all robbed,' he retorted, turning his attention to Suze, who was excitedly running her hands over one of the walls, pressing every other brick hoping for a secret passage to simply appear under her searching fingers.

'There's something here,' Mell said. Unlike the others, she was looking at the floor rather than the walls. She'd nudged some debris away with her foot and noticed a bright orange patch, where the floor had been cracked by the falling masonry during the boys' aggressive entrance. Moving slowly, she crouched by the odd patch of floor and ran her hand over it. 'This is tiling, ceramic slabs plastered to look like stone!' A loud crack came from beneath her foot and she froze. 'Shit!'

Another loud crack caught everyone's attention. Mell kept perfectly still, breathing slowly, her eyes flicking across the floor, searching for the seam between the real stones and the painted tiles.

'No one move,' said Simon, still kneeling in the debris of the collapsed door. Another loud crack echoed through the space as Mell shuffled one of her feet.

'Mell, can you reach me?' Suze stood on the edge of the seam between the stone and the tile and extended her hand towards the older girl. With a relieved smile Mell reached for her and the floor cracked again. This time completely giving way under her right foot, dropping her leg into the void and sending her sprawling to the floor with a scream. Suze dropped with her and managed to grab Mell's wrist. The floor creaked ominously.

'It's going!' yelled Claire, retreating slowly backwards, as Mell tried to spread her weight over the remaining tiles.

'Come on Mell,' Suze hissed, 'commando crawl. You can do it.

Fighting the urge to laugh at, what were clearly Suze's brother's words, Mell breathed out and gently inched her way across the floor, dragging herself forwards with her elbows, imagining that every creak would see the whole floor collapse. Her left knee broke through a tile and unable to stand the tension any more, she thrust herself forwards onto the stone, hearing the crash of breaking tile on the floor below, feeling her legs dangling into the void.

'Wow!' Suze gasped, staring down into the darkened chamber below, where a sea of metal points gleamed in the torchlight. 'Those are some industrial sized caltrops down there.'

'Ouch,' Mell agreed, looking down. 'But that's not all, look.' Something was sparkling in the light thrown by her torch. 'Maybe we need to get down there.'

'I have a climbing rope,' Sarah offered. 'I can go down, I just need someone to act as my anchor, there is nothing solid enough to trust in here.' She dragged a black and white striped rope from her bag and pulled her climbing gloves on.

'You came prepared,' said Claire, staring at Sarah's backpack. 'All I have is my makeup bag, a mirror and a hairbrush.'

'I can be your anchor,' Jerry offered, holding out his hand to take the rope. Sarah gave him the briefest of glances before offering the rope to Simon. 'Simon, would you?'

He looked puzzled but nodded, taking the coil of rope and moving closer to the ragged hole in the ground. Sarah spent a few moments checking his grip, before satisfying herself that she would be safe, and slowly lowering herself down into the hole towards the sea of metal spikes below. The air in the chamber hung thick with dust and Sarah tried to keep her breathing shallow as she shinned easily down the rope and dropped between two spikes onto the floor below.

Alone, at least twelve feet below ground and surrounded by waist high metal spikes, Sarah dragged Simon's torch from her back pocket and slowly scanned the space looking for the glittering object that Mell had spotted from above. There, to her left, something glinted and she moved gingerly through the vicious points towards it, then threw her hand up to shield her eyes as the entire left wall seemed to burst with light.

'Sarah, what happened?' Suze yelled down, unable to see what was happening.

'It's nothing, there are crystals or mirrors or something embedded in the wall, the torch light just caught several of them,' Sarah called back, lowering the light and moving closer. Below the sparkling gemstones, or whatever they were, she'd spotted something else. Words. Holding the torch steady, she read the four lines of crudely scratched jagged text.

SICVT SVPERIVS, ET INFERIVS

MORTALE EST, ALTER IMMORTALEM

NON EST QVI POSSIT SINE ALIO

GEMINOS

'Superior, inferior, mortal and immortal, something possible. Gemini,' she said softly to herself, working out a few obvious words. 'Bloody Romans. The crystals are stars. I need the constellation of Gemini.' She shone the torch around counting the sparkling stones in the walls, there were twenty-two. Certain she was right Sarah looked at the text again. 'What the hell does Gemini look like?' She muttered to herself. Closing her eyes and cursing her shyness, she took a deep breath and yelled up to the others. 'Simon, I need you!' A hot flush coloured her cheeks instantly, 'could have phrased that better Sarah,' she berated herself.

Above the spike pit Lisa flashed a look of pure fury in her boyfriend's direction as he handed his rope holding duty over to Jerry. Already conscious of her simmering resentment towards his friends, Simon tried his best to diffuse it.

Inclining his head towards her and dropping his gaze to the floor. 'With your permission, my lady.' he said quietly.

'Hmph,' Lisa huffed, 'as if I have much choice.' She rubbed her arms, feeling cold. 'But, thank you.' He gave her a smile and quickly dropped out of sight, joining Sarah below ground. 'I cannot believe I bought new underwear for this,' Lisa muttered, smoothing her ruined dress over her hips, and pushing her chest out, although no one was paying her much attention, besides a still jealous Claire, who quickly turned away wishing she'd not heard it.

The rest of the group, with little to offer in terms of assistance slumped on the ground around the hole they'd created, fishing through backpacks for water and possible snacks, although none of them had been prepared for the dramatic shift that the afternoon had taken. Mell, concerned about Lisa's apparently deteriorating condition offered the girl some chocolate that she'd found lurking in her bag. Lisa was hesitant but hungry and needed little persuasion to take the offering.

'How are you really feeling?' Mell asked, desperate to help the girl. 'Look, I promise, I won't say a word to the others, or to Simon if you don't want me to. I just may be able to help you.' Lisa simply threw her a look of contempt and stalked off to sit on a piece of broken stone away from the group and the hole in the ground.

Below ground, Simon picked his way through the spikes to where Sarah stood, trying to figure out the constellation map on the wall. 'You wanted me?'

Sarah flushed scarlet again and stammered her way through a response. 'I … not like … yes but … translation,' she finished lamely, pointing at the wall and staring at the floor as Simon started laughing.

'Do I frighten you or something?' he asked, curious about her response.

'No, yes, god,' Sarah covered her face. 'You're a little intimidating,' her voice was muffled behind her hands. 'And I'm useless at banter,' she lowered her hands, but fixed her eyes on the floor. 'Can you just translate that and tell me that I'm right and we need to make the constellation of Gemini on this wall. And then what Gemini looks like?'

'*Ciertamente,*' Simon replied, turning his attention to the jaggedly etched words. 'Interesting, "As above, so below. One mortal the other immortal. One cannot exist without the other. Twins." Gemini.' he glanced over the gem inlaid wall and drummed his fingers against the inscription. 'One mortal, one immortal, one cannot live without the other. Castor and Pollux, the Gemini,' he looked up at the wall again. 'Sarah, you are half right,' he said pulling out his phone. 'Argh, no signal. Castor was mortal, Pollux was immortal, when Castor died, Pollux gave up his immortality so that his brother could live. They are not the constellation of Gemini, but the two brightest stars within it.'

'How are we going to find two stars? I don't even know what the constellation looks like,' said Sarah, playing the torchlight over the studded wall.

'Here, it looks like two stick figures,' Simon enlarged an image on his phone and showed her. 'What?' he asked, noticing the smile that crossed her face. 'I keep a star map on my phone.'

'And here was I thinking that you had resorted to an internet search,' Sarah grinned, 'that maybe you don't know everything.'

'No, I know everything,' Simon smiled back, and held his phone up against the wall. 'We are looking for the stick figure heads, Castor right, Pollux left.'

Together they scanned the wall, listening to the restless complaints of the others above ground. 'There!' said Sarah, spotting a cluster of studs that looked like the stick figures on Simon's phone screen. She brought the torchlight up and illuminated the star that Simon indicated to be Pollux.

The gem stone glittered with a blueish light, but nothing happened. With a sigh, she moved the light over to illuminate Castor, and a low rumble trembled through the room. Startled she grabbed Simon's arm as the others began to yell from above.

'The wall is opening,' Jerry shouted, 'looks like there is a passageway behind it.'

In the darkened spike-filled room below, Simon glanced over at Sarah's flushed face. 'Well worked out,' he said, staring at the wall as though working something else out.

'Couldn't have done it without your help,' she replied. 'Come on, let's get back topside.' She lowered the light and the rumbling stopped, exclamations came from above. The wall was lowering again.

'We need to leave the light,' said Simon. 'Go up, I'll fix it somewhere to keep the wall open.' Sarah nodded and yanked the rope, making sure that it was still anchored, before hauling herself back up into the room above.

'Awesome! Let's go,' cried Jerry, hauling the rope up after her and heading for the newly revealed passage.

'Uhh, guys … Are you forgetting anything?' Simon's disembodied voice floated up out of the void.

Jerry grinned and winked mischievously at the others. 'Think we need Mr Encyclopaedia anymore, or has he outlasted his usefulness?'

'We know where he is if we need him,' Suze replied playing along.

Mell shook her head. 'We don't have time for this. Get him out,' she ordered as Lisa vented her own frustrations.

'You can't leave him down there!' she squealed, unaware that Suze and Jerry were just mucking about.

Simon, although not in the room, was at least on the ball. 'Mr Llewellen and Miss Jones are just making a badly timed joke … I think,' he paused, counting seconds. 'Jeremy, come on, get me out of here,' he demanded when the rope didn't reappear.

'Aww all right,' Jerry said capitulating and unfurling the coiled rope again, bracing himself against Simon's weight as the elder boy scrambled back up.

'*Gracias*,' Simon said absently, looking at his watch, then at his girlfriend. 'Lisa *mi amor*, are you hurt?'

'Hurt?' she turned big blue angry eyes on him. 'I was assaulted in the museum. You've dragged me into a hole in the ground, it's cold, it's damp, there were men with weapons upstairs and you destroyed my Jimmy's …'

Simon held a hand up interrupting her flow. 'Physically Lisa, are you physically hurt. You are bleeding all over my jacket.'

He was right. The front of Lisa's little white dress was grubby and smudged with dirt but on her back, soaking through the dark blue material of his jacket were two spreading patches of blood.

'It's probably yours from earlier. I broke a nail,' she complained holding out her hand for inspection.

'We should move on,' said Sarah, tactfully moving towards the newly opened passage. 'The sooner we find these wings, the sooner we can all get out of here.'

'The rest of you go on ahead. I need a minute alone with Lisa, please,' Simon's face was tight, betraying his concern.

Yelling something about fortune and glory, Jerry hurled himself into the passage first. The others followed at a more sedate pace and eventually Simon stood alone with Lisa.

'Simon, I can't do this, please don't make me play this game anymore, I'm exhausted,' she said, dropping her act of bravado once everyone was out of sight. 'I don't like any of this, and I'm so cold, can we just go back to the hotel?' she sniffed, tears close to the surface.

'I am so sorry Lisa,' he groaned, raking both hands through his dark hair. 'You should not be in this mess, but I swear, I swear I will get you out of it,' he paused looking at her face. 'Are you sure that you are not in pain? You look so pale.'

Lisa shook her head. 'Simon, what's really going on?' The concern on her boyfriend's face terrified her. 'This isn't a scavenger hunt, is it?' Simon shook his head. 'Oh god,' Lisa whimpered, her eyes beginning to shine with tears. 'I … I might really, I might …' she couldn't bring herself to say the word.

'I will never let that happen,' Simon promised fiercely. He leaned his forehead against hers, slipping his arms around her back, pulling her close. 'Lisa, I would move the stars to protect you,' he kissed her, feeling her lips, soft and yielding against his own, feeling a familiar heat rise through her chilled and clammy body as she responded to his touch.

He didn't want to let her go and it was Lisa who eventually broke their kiss. 'So, what do we do?' she asked tearfully, wincing as a pain shot through her head again.

'We find the tomb,' he replied. 'We find the eagle's wings, or whatever the hell they wanted, and they lift whatever curse is on you.' He shrugged, aware of how insane it sounded.

'Curse!' Lisa hissed, her mood, her focus shifting again. 'Simon, I think one too many scrums have collapsed on your head. Things like this happen in movies, not in the real world,' she turned and walked slowly away from him, covering her face. 'Maybe I'm just imagining all this, I fell and hit my head on the ski slope. It's a dream, I'm in a coma,' she laughed, and banged a palm against her head. 'Wake up Lisa,' hysteria edged her voice as she slipped his jacket off draping it over the pile of discarded bricks.

'Dream or not, dearest love, you are bleeding,' Simon said, staring at the growing blood patches on the back of her dress. He moved behind her, gently placing his hands on her shoulders, before sliding them down to her waist, desperately wishing they were alone under better circumstances. 'Lisa,' he whispered softly in her ear, closing his eyes and reviling himself for what he needed to ask. 'I need to see your back, about here.' He pressed one hand into the small of her back, his fingers came away sticky with blood.

'Well then, I guess it's a good job we're alone,' she replied, closing her eyes and reaching behind for her zip. Her fingers closed on it and without hesitation she pulled it down and shimmied her shoulders free of her dress, allowing the material to fall only as far as her waist. 'How bad is it?' she asked, crossing her arms over her chest and hearing his sharp intake of breath, before the warmth of his fingers caressed her skin.

'Bad,' came his one word response as his splayed fingers touched two puncture wounds in her back. A black substance was spreading from them, flowing like black rivers across her back. 'Are you certain that you feel no pain at all?'

'None at all,' she replied in a dreamlike voice, moving slowly, as if in a trance towards the newly opened passage.

'Lisa, your dress,' Simon said, watching her with a growing sense of dread. She was slipping into this trancelike state more frequently and once in it always seemed to want to push forward. She glanced back, her eyes glazed and continued to walk, her dress still hanging around her waist. Simon moved, catching up with her easily and although she continued walking he was able to drag her dress straps back to her shoulders and refasten her zip, and wrap his jacket back around her shoulders

'What are you doing?' she said, suddenly herself again. 'We should follow your friends, the one with green hair will certainly be wondering what we're up to.'

Simon frowned, 'Lisa, I ...'

'I'm joking, you handsome idiot. Now come on, but first, tell me I look okay?' she held out her hand, a tense smile on her smudged lips.

Simon thought she looked beautiful, she always looked beautiful, even with her hair a mess, her lipstick smudged, covered in dirt and dust. 'Lisa, you are the most beautiful creature on God's earth,' he laced his fingers through hers. 'You look divine, as always.'

XVI

The newly opened passage descended into the earth down a long ramp eventually becoming more hewn rock than man-made, and ending abruptly in a huge pair of ancient, studded wooden doors. An eagle of monstrous proportions was carved into the ancient timber. Above it, etched into the bedrock of Rome herself, was a single word.

ROMVLVS

'Does that mean Romulus, as in the Romulus, mythological founder of Rome?' asked Mell, gazing at the intricately carved eagle, its wings thrown back, talons grasping at air. So lifelike, it could almost emerge from the wood at any second.

'I always thought he was just a story and Rome got her name some other way,' said Suze, staring up at the door. 'Can you believe it? The tomb of the founder of Rome. Under the Colosseum all this time.'

'Amazing,' Claire agreed. 'But how the hell has no one ever found this?'

'They have, they just didn't live to tell about it,' said Mell, indicating the base of the door where a broken stud lay on the floor clasped in the bony fingers of a hand.

'Eww gross!' shrieked Claire. 'Where's the rest of him?'

'As above so below,' Sarah said muttering to herself, spotting a bluish light on the door. 'Step back, there's another spike trap. That's probably where the rest of him is,' she looked up at the door. 'I need a torch, and where's Simon? I need his phone.'

'He's still with Lisa,' Suze replied offering her battered phone, but Sarah shook her head. She wanted the star map, she had to be certain before illuminating the stud and opening the door.

'Does anyone have a star map?' she asked, 'I know how to open the door, but I need to be absolutely certain of which stud is Pollux,' behind her Jerry sniggered. 'For Heaven's sake Jerry grow up it's not that funny,' she screamed, losing her temper as Simon and Lisa arrived.

Jerry held his hands up. 'Jeez, sorry I'm alive,' he muttered.

'Pollux is that one,' said Simon, spotting what Sarah had seen straight away. 'We need a light, mine is keeping the other door open.'

'I still have mine,' Mell offered passing it to Simon.

He passed it straight over to Sarah. 'Your turn.'

Tentatively she took the proffered light and moved the beam slowly up the door, careful not to touch any of the other studs with the light. 'Are you certain?' she whispered. In response Simon pulled out his phone and let her look at the image of the Gemini constellation again. Pollux was to the left. The bluish dot of Castor, already illuminated, glowed to the right. 'Okay.' Feeling more certain Sarah played the torchlight over the stud they had identified as Pollux.

A second blueish light appeared as the stud began to glow, and then along the door eighty-five smaller studs began to glow blue creating the twin stick figures of the constellation. '*Geminos*,' Sarah breathed as Simon gave her shoulder a squeeze and the doors began to creak. The giant rusted hinges groaned and squealed as the ancient wooden doors painfully inched their way open. Revealing the burial chamber of Romulus.

'Right, let's complete the challenge, grab those wings and rescue the girl,' said Mell, checking her watch and keen to get moving.

'Wait!' said Simon, throwing his uninjured arm across in front of her. 'Remember the crypt at St. Arondight's? The dead are not always welcoming.'

Warily, recalling the events of the summer, the group crept slowly through the doors into the yawning black chamber beyond. Lisa following at a distance, stumbling as though she were drunk. The fading light from Mell's torch combined with the tiny flicker of Jerry's lighter cast pale, dancing shadows deep into the gloom. The air of the chamber was laden with the heavy silence of death, even their slow footsteps made no noise.

Suddenly a light flared in the darkness ahead, followed by another and another. Tall flaming torches burst into life, moving in sequence from one in the centre of the far wall to pairs running up to the giant doors, bathing the hallowed but very small chamber in flickering light.

'Jerry?' said Claire, remembering that it had been the tall Welshman who had triggered the skeletons at St. Arondight's.

'I didn't do nothin', I swear!' he yelled as a loud creaking began. 'This is Sarah's fault, she opened the door.'

'That's a good one Jerry,' Sarah yelled back over the rising creaking, squealing sound.

'The doors!' Suze yelled, suddenly realising what was happening. The massive doors were moving as if pushed by unseen hands, gradually gaining momentum, until they slammed together, resealing the tomb.

Both Lisa and Claire let loose high-pitched screams, Claire immediately clapping a hand over her mouth and breathing heavily through her nose, trying desperately to control her claustrophobia. Mell grabbed her other hand and meeting her friend's frightened eyes, began talking her down in a soothing voice.

A second bloodcurdling scream from Lisa reverberated back off the walls, filling the cavernous tomb with wailing echoes, as, turning deathly pale she swooned elegantly into Simon's arms.

As Simon found himself with his hands full again, the rest of the group turned their attention to the tomb of Romulus. It was a small barren space, a natural cave devoid of decoration and completely empty save for the large translucent casket that Lisa had spotted, below the first torch that had flared into life. The transparent crystalline stone allowing a distorted view of its ancient occupant. The reason for her second scream.

'Is that Romulus,' asked Suze, staring at the shadow in the casket. 'Is that him, the first ruler of Rome? Creator of the Eternal City.'

Cautiously the teens approached the coffin. It was magnificent, a giant casket hewn from a single block of crystalline stone, polished to near transparency and edged with gold. The resident within the stone could be made out as a dark blurred shadow with pale limbs, flesh against dark cloth. The blurred shadow held their attention, all, with the obvious exception of Lisa, recalled the crypt below St. Arondight's with its undead skeletal guardians. Moments passed, nothing happened, the shadow within the stone lay still.

Glancing through the lid, Mell let out a gasp of horror and staggered back three paces. She clenched her fists at her sides and screwing her eyes shut took three deep breaths, before giving herself a shake and stepping back up to the coffin.

'It's not him Mell,' said Claire sensing the reason for her friend's distress and anxious to return her help.

'I know ... I just ... I saw that moment again, the look of surprise on his face.' She stared down through the blurred crystal, making herself look. 'Looks nothing like Richards,' she berated herself. Surprising everyone by saying his name.

'Simon, what is she babbling about?' Lisa slurred angrily as she regained consciousness. He looked as though he was going to respond but she held her hand up stopping him, and pushed herself away from his chest. 'I do not care. Why is there a wax effigy in a crystal box, and why are you all staring at it like it might bite you? It's an effigy, it's hardly going to get out of the box, is it?' She placed a hand against the lid and gave it a shove. It slipped soundlessly sideways a little, releasing a rich aroma of honey, flowers and an indistinctive but slightly acrid tang.

Simon caught her wrist and dragged her hand away. 'Sweetheart, I really would not do that,' he spoke to her, but his eyes remained fixed on the unmoving body of Rome's founder.

Lisa laughed, a harsh unfeeling sound in the silent tomb and freed herself from his grip. 'What are you so afraid of Simon? He's hardly going to wake up and come after me,' her voice had changed, it was light and musical, breathy and alluring, unlike her. 'Besides, darling I thought we came for the eagle's wings.'

'Lisa, *amor,* are you, all right?' Simon, searched her face, clearly concerned by the change in her demeanour. She was even walking differently, as if that last collapse had taken Lisa away and replaced her with someone else.

'Oh, I am much better than all right, my Spanish prince,' her words were breathy and she walked her fingers up his chest as she spoke, biting her lip and looking up through her long lashes to meet his eyes.

Simon snatched her hand away. 'Stop it. Now is really not the right time. Lisa, this is not you.'

'Suit yourself,' she pouted, smoothing her dress over her breasts and hips with a distinctly sexual moan of pleasure. Leaving him staring uncomfortably after her as she stalked away swinging her hips in an exaggerated manner.

'Uh Simon,' Jerry coughed trying to catch his friend's attention. 'When you two are done with your weird little foreplay, Romulus ain't mouldy.'

'You know, you are insufferable sometimes,' Simon groaned raking a hand through his hair and staring at Lisa's back, noting that the bloodstains had spread further, he'd also noticed the black webbing begin to creep across her chest and neck earlier.

'Nah-ah,' Jerry replied with a grin. 'I'm incorrigible. But Romulus is incorruptible.'

'Jerry's right, it looks like he's asleep,' said Suze, warily eyeing the healthy pink skin with suspicion.

Romulus, if it was Romulus, lay within his ornate coffin dressed for battle. His leather armour, just visible through the space that Lisa had opened, gleamed. It was well oiled and appeared freshly tanned, with the metal fittings highly polished. Romulus himself looked good, healthy, pale but pink skin, dark hair just beginning to grey at the temples.

'If this is Romulus then he is supposed to be a decedent of Aeneas, perhaps the Trojan's mummified their dead,' Simon suggested, watching Lisa move around the room. She kept touching her face and moaning.

'Simon, that's not mummification,' said Sarah. 'Even the best mummies shrivel and look like leather. He looks like he died this morning.'

'Help me!' Lisa suddenly screamed. She had gone deathly pale, a sheen of sweat across her face and visible on her arms, she closed her eyes and raised her hands to her head. 'I don't feel well …' she whispered, swaying in her broken shoes. 'There is someone else in my head!' she clawed her fingers through her hair as her breathing quickened into short panicked gasps.

'Simon, catch her she's going to faint,' said Mell, spotting a streak of blood running down the back of the girl's leg.

He only just made it. Lisa's knees crumpled and she dropped like a stone. He just caught her, cushioning her fall against his chest and lowering her softly to the floor. 'Lisa, darling come on, stay with me,' he brushed her hair back from her face.

'Aaaaand she's fainted, again. Great,' Suze groaned leaning on the coffin lid and giving it a shove. It didn't budge. 'Jerry, come give me a hand.'

He obligingly loped over and together they grasped hold of the translucent coffin lid. The stone was pleasantly warmer than either were expecting and polished smooth, they shoved it. Nothing happened. Lisa had moved it with a single handed, barely forceful, push, so neither had really gone hard at it, but it should have moved.

'Again,' said Jerry, 'and how's about putting a little effort in this time Jones, huh?' Together they threw their weight against it and were rewarded with a grating screech as the lid slid a little further.

'Come on you guys, Lisa moved it on her own,' Claire said, joining them, 'It can't be that heavy, there's nothing of her.'

'You wanna give it a go?' Jerry grunted shoving it again, the lid emitting another screech as it moved, inch by painful inch. This time revealing a glimmer of silver laying across Romulus's chest. The eagle's wings. 'Simon!' Jerry hollered, his voice booming around the chamber. 'Stop wasting time, bring your rugby muscles over here and help with the lid.'

There was no response, he was too preoccupied with Lisa. He kneeled, feeling helpless, on the floor beside her as she clawed at the front of her dress tearing the material, her breathing coming in ragged little bursts. She was unable to speak and just stared at him with wide terrified eyes. 'Mell!' Simon's voice cracked as he called her name. 'Melody, please!'

'I'm here,' she said gently, squeezing his shoulder as she slipped her jacket below Lisa's head as a pillow. 'I thought we had more time,' she said, keeping her eyes on Lisa, as the girl hovered on the edge of consciousness.

'We have an hour,' Simon replied, kneading the heel of his hands into his eyes. 'One hour left, no wings and only Romulus is here. I should never have brought her down here.' He pressed Lisa's small cold hand between his and kissed her fingers. '*Lo siento mi amor.*'

'You had no choice, whatever is inside her wouldn't let you get her somewhere safe,' Sarah said gently.

'Is that supposed to make me feel better?' he snapped, rounding on her. 'I have one hour to save her life, one hour to find the tomb of Remus, as we so spectacularly managed to find the wrong twin. And I have no idea where to look.'

'Simon, I know you're upset but that is no reason to yell at Sarah,' Mell reprimanded him angrily. 'And for god's sake, you act like you're the only one trying to solve this. We are all here, we are all trying to help. And if you knew we needed Remus why didn't you tell the rest of us? How the hell do we know what the stranger meant by rightful twin? Now move out of the way and let me see if there is anything I can do.'

He scowled at her. 'No one. Ever. Speaks to me like that.' But he shifted over all the same, never letting go of Lisa's hand.

'If you're going to insist on behaving like an ass, I'm gonna treat you like one,' replied Mell, crouching beside Lisa's sweat drenched form. 'There's nothing you can do here, go help Suze and Jerry with that coffin lid.'

'You are terrifying sometimes,' he said, placing a soft kiss on Lisa's hand before laying it gently by her side. Then scrambled quickly backwards as her eyes briefly flickered open. 'Mell, tell me you saw that?'

'Saw what?' Mell asked, examining Lisa's cold hands.

'Her eyes … Those were not Lisa's eyes,' Simon's voice sounded tight, his accent grated over the vowels.

'Probably just the light in here,' said Claire, moving closer.

'I know my girlfriend's eyes!' Simon yelled back. 'Lisa has the most beautiful sapphire blue eyes,' he stepped away staring intently at his semi-conscious girlfriend. 'Those were not even human.'

'Look dude, if you're too strung out to recognise reality, we got a problem,' Jerry said, abandoning the coffin and moving towards Lisa. Then he paused. 'You may have a point,' he said slowly. 'That is weird, slightly seductive, but very weird.'

'What on earth is going on?' Sarah was lost.

'He's right, her eyes aren't human, they look almost feral, like a wolf,' said Jerry still staring at Lisa's face, unwilling to look away now that the yellow predatory canine eyes were fixed on him.

'That can't be possible,' said Claire, shaking her head and backing away.

'No, he's right,' Mell said quietly, moving slowly away from where Lisa lay on the floor. 'It must be a side effect of the poison.'

Suze nodded a response, then froze, as the corpse of Romulus took a rattling breath. At the same time Lisa unleashed an animalistic howl and sprang to her feet, kicking the remains of her shoes away. Yellow predator's eyes swept the room and she raced immediately towards the coffin, knocking Claire and Suze viciously aside.

From the coffin came another rattling breath as the corpse of Romulus rose to face the half-wolf, half-human Lisa.

Unable to move, the others watched spellbound as Lisa bounded onto the partially open coffin lid and snatched at the silver wings of Romulus's pectoral, teeth bared in a menacing snarl, fingers curved like claws. Unable to fully exit his coffin, Romulus drew his sword.

'Si, stop you idiot,' Jerry made a grab for his shoulder and missed, as Simon threw himself at Romulus, knocking him out of the coffin and trapping the corpse's sword arm between himself and the wall of the chamber. Saving Lisa from a killing strike.

Lisa turned, and clutching the wings to her chest, raced for the vast double doors to the tomb. Her wolfish nature giving her the speed and strength of a wild beast.

'Someone stop her!' Sarah screamed. Suze and Claire moved to oblige, but Lisa was already hauling at one of the doors, dragging it slowly open.

'*Teneo!*' bellowed the Roman, throwing Simon off and stretching a hand towards the doors.

The small gap that Lisa had managed to open, slammed closed and she whirled back to face the room, a predator's grimace on her normally beautiful face. Trapped, she threw back her head and howled, an unnatural sound, guttural and loud.

'She's like an animal,' Claire exclaimed in horror.

'Lisa?' Simon ventured painfully from the floor, briefly attracting the attention of the resurrected Romulus. Lisa's wolfish eyes flicked to him, but registered nothing.

A movement caught Suze's eye and she turned to watch Romulus rising to his feet again, Lisa noticed it too, and a feral snarl escaped her barred teeth as her eyes searched for a way out. The Roman crouched, sword ready. Lisa sprang forward.

'*¡No!*' Simon pushed himself up off the floor, and towards the Roman, tackling him and hurling them both to the floor as Lisa shot past, bounded up the coffin lid and scrabbling at the wall, reached a narrow fissure near the ceiling, into which she vanished.

'What the hell just happened?' said Jerry.

'I have no idea,' Mell replied dumbfounded, staring at the space where Lisa had vanished.

Lying on the floor, his sword out of reach, Romulus overpowered Simon and pinned him to the floor, a brawny forearm pressed tightly against the Spaniard's throat as his other hand groped blindly for the sword. '*Licet tu Remus aquilam fugiat!*' he growled, an expression of fury on his face.

XVII

The Roman scrambled for the sword, keeping his arm pinned tightly against Simon's throat. Blotting out the guttural choking sound of Simon struggling to breathe, Suze dived for the sword, snatching it away from the resurrected Roman. Feeling the odd distribution of weight through the blade she adjusted her grip and slipped easily into a fighting stance, as Jerry circled quietly behind Romulus.

'What are they doing?' Claire hissed, unable to tear her eyes from the scene. 'She'll get herself killed.'

'Shh!' Mell replied sharply. The Roman had not yet noticed Jerry and the tall boy was trying to follow Suze's minute signals, to work with her in overpowering Romulus.

Crouching in the Roman's eye line Suze held the heavy but short and badly weighted blade out at arm's length, threatening. 'Let him go!' her voice was steady and, surprised by an unexpected threat, Romulus relaxed his grip on Simon and looked up. A flicker of surprise crossed his face, and then Jerry pounced, attacking from behind and catching the unaware Roman in a headlock.

'Gotcha!' he yelled triumphantly. But his euphoria was short lived as the corpse went limp in his arms. The deadweight pulled him off balance, sending him crashing to the ground on top of Simon, who let out a grunt of pain as Jerry's elbow hit him in the chest.

'Well that's a new one,' said Mell, watching the boys untangle themselves. 'The last dead guys were far more resilient.' She stared at the unmoving corpse unable to believe that it could have been so easy to defeat.

'Never mind the dead Roman, what happened to Lisa? All those black lines on her skin, and her actions. It's like she was possessed,' said Sarah concerned. 'And how she got out? She was like an animal climbing the wall over there.'

Simon crossed the room and clambered up onto the coffin lid trying to see how Lisa could have left the chamber. Busy grappling with Romulus he'd not witnessed his girlfriend's impossible escape. 'Are you sure that she got up there?' he asked in disbelief.

'We all saw her,' Claire replied. 'You took down Romulus, probably saving her life, and like some kind of animal she clawed her way up that wall. I would hate to see what her fingernails look like now. You realise that she has no shoes, right?' she pointed at Lisa's discarded, broken shoes.

'You are absolutely certain, that she left that way?' Simon knelt and retrieved Lisa's shoes, running his thumb over one of the broken heels, before discarding them. The things were so battered they were beyond saving. He was confused, having not seen her leave, and looking at the sheer walls of the chamber, what his friends were suggesting was impossible. Yet, there were marks, like claws, gouged into the rock. He shook his head, it was so far beyond the abilities of the pampered lady he knew so intimately. 'She could not have done that … Lisa is … I mean she … The only sport Lisa does is horse riding and …'

'Horizontal aerobics,' Jerry chimed in with a grin, trying to lighten the mood.

'Jerry can you stop treating everything like a joke,' Sarah screamed, finally really losing her temper with him. 'Everything is a game to you. You never shut up, you never care who you offend, hurt or insult. You are so immature.'

'Well you're the one constantly in a foul mood,' he shot back, her show of temper taking him by surprise. 'I'm just trying to lighten things up here. You're all so goddam serious. Look at us, we are in an undiscovered tomb, in the middle of Rome, we should be excited, we should be having fun.'

'Uh guys!' Suze ventured. She wasn't listening to the unfolding drama, instead her attention was fixed on the felled corpse of Romulus. She had a feeling that he wouldn't stay down, the way he had just flopped when Jerry touched him hadn't seemed right. She risked a quick glance up but the other five were ignoring her, Sarah and Jerry finally having the argument that seemed to have been brewing since before they got to the airport. With a sigh, she turned her attention back to the corpse, its hand had moved.

Sarah, usually the shy, quiet one was in full flow now, she needed this fight. 'No one appreciates your humour,' she screamed, flinging her words at Jerry. 'And no one appreciates your sleaze.'

'Sleaze!' Jerry hollered incensed. He had no idea what he'd done to deserve this tirade of anger. 'You didn't think I was so sleazy when I saved your life in Dover.'

Sarah stared back at him agog. Clearly, he remembered things in Dover very differently to her. 'Saved my life?' she screeched. 'Jerry, you just got drunk, snogged a barmaid and lolled around naked in the tent! I saved you!' her blood was pounding so hard she could feel it pulsing behind her eyes.

'Guys, seriously,' Suze tried again as an awkward silence fell across the room, but no one was listening. 'Shit,' she twirled the blade around her hand once and focussed on the undead Roman.

'Oh Sarah, sweetie,' said Claire, a look of half horror, half sympathy on her face 'You didn't sleep with Jerry, did you?'

'NO!' Sarah screeched horrified. 'Anyway, you're one to talk, until Lisa arrived you were desperately trying to find a way to get off with Simon.'

Claire flushed a furious shade of scarlet, horrified that she'd been caught out so brazenly. 'Don't turn this on me.'

'Enough!' Simon's voice was like a gunshot across the squabble, commanding attention. 'Can we at least try to focus on the problem in hand? We are stuck several floors below the Colosseum, in a sealed room. Lisa, has somehow left, and we have,' he glanced at his watch, 'twenty minutes to find her before she dies.' There was a steely, detached determination in his voice, a practiced mask of indifference on his face, hiding his true emotions.

Suze's attention was still focussed on the Roman. A bluish transparent glow had appeared briefly above the body, then vanished. She watched closely, it was almost imperceptible, but the Roman was moving, very slowly. The right hand, still splayed, was looking for the sword. Ignoring the others, Suze breathed deeply, weighing the blade in her hand, feeling the heavy pommel and grip and the unbalanced transfer of weight through the blade, she prepared.

With a defiant roar she lunged forward, catching the attention of the others as she slammed the point of the blade into the ground between the splayed first and middle fingers of the twitching undead hand. The body stilled, a shimmer of blue flickering above it and vanishing.

'God damn it Suze!' startled by her shout, Simon raked a hand through his hair. 'Quit mucking about.'

'He moved,' she replied, and poked the limp body with the blade. 'We're not done here.'

'Whatever,' Simon shook his head and turned back to the others. 'Sarah, Jerry, I neither know, nor care what is going on between you but can you deal with each other long enough to try and follow Lisa up there?'

'Sure,' Sarah replied, glancing towards Jerry. He just shrugged, scuffed his boot along the ground and moved towards the coffin ready to boost her up the wall. Without speaking Jerry made a step out of his hands and at her signal, boosted her as far up the wall as he could. Her fingers scraped against the rock, but without climbing clips and crampons there was no way that she was getting any further. She traced her hands over a fresh gouge, Lisa must have had inhuman strength to dig her fingers in and climb. 'Put me down Jerry, whatever gave her the strength to move that coffin lid must have given her the strength to climb out. We can't leave that way.'

Jerry helped her down slowly and punched her lightly in the shoulder once she was back on the ground. 'Hey, whatever I did, I'm sorry. We cool?'

'It's not what you did Jerry, it's who,' she replied, walking away from him. 'We should search for another way out, come on perhaps we can open the doors …' A scream from Claire interrupted her, and in the tense silence that followed, Mell started laughing.

'Oh god Claire, you're as bad as Lisa,' Mell giggled, then stopped as the source of Claire's scream became clear. Floating to one side of Romulus's ornate coffin was a pale fuzzy figure tinged with blue. He appeared short, but gangly with a long face and sad features, dressed in the simple belted tunic of a Roman slave.

'Is he a ghost?' Suze asked quietly, pulling the gladius free of the floor. The spectral figure let out a nervous squeak and vanished again.

'Stand down Suze,' Simon said raising a hand towards her, approaching the spot where the figure had been. With obvious reluctance she dropped the sword, but remained within arm's reach. '*Bonjourno!*' Simon spoke Italian first, then getting no response tried Latin. '*Salve?*'

'*Salve,*' a small, uncertain voice replied, although the spectral figure did not reappear. '*Licet tu Remus aquilam fugiat.*' It was the same thing that Romulus had shouted earlier, but delivered by a voice with far less power and confidence. Simon let out a half laugh, and covered his face, sinking to the floor.

'What did he say?' asked Mell, massaging her forehead and catching the time on her watch. There was now less than twenty minutes left before Lisa's time ran out.

The blue glow reappeared beside the coffin, the human form slowly becoming clearer as the ghost spoke. '*Ego Gaius Tiberius Decimus,*' he proclaimed, introducing himself, as his appearance solidified into a thin man with dark hair, wearing a short white slave's tunic edged with a darker stripe. '*Praetor de Romulus.*'

'He says his name is Tiberius,' Simon translated wearily. 'Apparently he is the guardian of Romulus and we have just let the eagle of Remus escape.'

'I thought this was the tomb of Romulus?' said Jerry, folding his arms and scuffing his shoe along the ground. 'Why is the eagle of Remus in the tomb of Romulus?'

The ghost, Tiberius, stared at the group. 'You do not know the legend?' he said slowly, disbelief on his face. 'How can you be here if you do not know the legend? How can such be possible?' He floated back and forth before the coffin muttering to himself.

'The ghost speaks English?' said Jerry wondering if he was hearing right. 'The Italian, Roman ghost speaks English with some kind of hybrid American, Australian accent.'

'I educated myself listening to *turisti*,' Tiberius paused and beamed at the teenagers, proud of his linguistic achievement. 'But this is the first chance I've ever had to practice. No one comes down here, and no one has noticed me up there for centuries.' He looked wistfully upwards and drifted out of focus again.

'Is he talking about the legend of Romulus and Remus?' said Claire, glancing at Simon, who didn't seem to be listening to anything. 'Everyone knows the legend of the twins, Romulus kills Remus, founds Rome.'

'Traitors!' The ghost suddenly materialised in front of them again, swooping into the fallen body of Romulus. 'You stole the eagle's wings. You work for her!' The body, in possession of the ghost rose from the floor again reaching for its sword, malice etched into the furious face.

Suze was faster, snatching up the sword and levelling the point at the reanimated corpse. 'You want to attack them, you come through me,' she hissed, standing her ground, but shooting an anxious glance in Simon's direction, she was worried about him. The last thing he'd said had been a translation of the spectre's Latin words, since then he'd lapsed into silence staring at the claw marks in the wall, the fingers of his left hand clenching and unclenching. Turning her attention back to the ghost, she pressed forward a step, keeping the point raised.

'An Amazon,' hissed the ghost, 'like the faceless she-devil of the arena.' Suze was unsure whether to be angry or delighted at the comparison, but a stream of Spanish halted her before she could further act.

'*Podemos por favor centrarse en las águilas? Sólo tenemos cinco minutos para el final,*' Simon's voice was strained and from the expression of fury that crossed his face the others suspected that the Spanish tirade was supposed to have been in English. In high stress Simon's native language was quicker to his tongue.

Tiberius, however, was delighted. Forgetting his anger at the infiltration of the tomb, and that Suze had a sword pointed at him, he turned to speak to Simon. '¡Español! Nunca llego a practicar mi español.'

His delight was too much for Simon, conflicted from the outset by the collision of separate parts of his life, doubtful about how Lisa would react to his friends, and how they would deal with her. Now, concerned with Lisa's whereabouts and unsure if she was even still alive, he strode over to Tiberius and standing nose to nose with the possessed corpse of the founder of Rome, spoke a single word in several languages. 'Águila, Águia, Aigle, Αετός, Aquila, Kartal, Eagle. The damned eagle of Remus?' he slammed his fist into the coffin lid with a bone crunching thud and fixed the terrified little ghost with his imperious stare.

The body of Romulus crumpled, lifeless at Simon's feet, whilst Tiberius hovered six inches above the floor, still nose to nose with Simon, too terrified to even fade out and vanish. Held in place by Simon's steely gaze. Behind them the other five exchanged nervous glances, they had never seen Simon lose his temper and it was spectacularly frightening.

'Jesus Simon, you want to burst a vein?' Mell scolded, recovering her composure and reaching for his hand. 'Let me see that, you've probably broken your fingers you idiot.'

'My hand is fine,' he replied coolly, dismissing her without a glance, his eyes still fixed on the floating body of Tiberius. 'Tell me about the eagle, who wants it and why?' The little ghost shrank back, cowering, his arms thrown up over his head as if expecting a beating. He was terrified.

'She wants it Dominus, she has always wanted it,' Tiberius's voice was barely a whisper. 'Now the wolf-girl will deliver the wings to her, and I have failed.' The small figure sank to the floor, pulling his spectral knees against his transparent chest, an expression of utter misery on his face. 'Tell me Dominus why does one of the Julii imperil his own existence to assist the forces of Remus? For if Remus rises and Romulus cannot check him, the line of the Julii will be extinguished. All of history could change. The glory of Rome lost, why Dominus?'

Still frustrated, Simon reached out as if to grab Tiberius by the scruff, and then realising it would do nothing let his hand fall again. 'What are you talking about? Deliver the wings to whom?'

'Then you truly do not know the legend,' Tiberius rose, and moved several paces away from Simon. 'She,' he pointed at Claire, 'she knows the history of the twins, but not the legend of their standards, the gold and silver eagles.'

Jerry's eyes nearly fell out of his head. 'There's a gold one? No one said anything about a gold one.'

'No,' Simon protested, massaging his left hand with a grimace of pain. 'Marius introduced the eagles.'

'Marius was trying to resurrect the legend,' Tiberius replied. 'The first eagles were the standards of the twins. A gold one for Romulus and silver for Remus, but Remus modified his. He was convinced by an Etruscan priestess that the eagle was not king of the birds but the wren was, having hitched a lift on the eagle's back and so flown higher.'

'I know this story,' said Sarah. 'I always thought it was a British folk tale. Having been on the eagle's back the wren proclaimed himself king of the birds.'

'I don't understand,' said Claire. 'How will simply putting the parts of Remus's standard back together be enough to resurrect him and shatter the past?'

'She tricked him,' Tiberius replied. 'The Etruscan priestess was skilled in the dark magic, she convinced Remus that he would be king and when he fought his brother and lost, she tricked his doomed mind into consigning his soul to the darkness. She nailed his soul to his standard. His living sprit is fractured but living within the three pieces, reassembling the standard, will allow his soul to return. As long as there is a body for it to return to. And she will use him to change the timeline.' The little ghost darted back into the body of Romulus, lifting it off the floor and moving as though to return it to the crystalline coffin. 'Romulus tried to destroy her but failed and so before his death, ordered the destruction of his brother's eagle to ensure that her plans could never be achieved.'

'So,' said Simon in a tight voice. 'By letting Lisa get out of here with the fragment of eagle that we needed to keep her alive, we just unleashed Armageddon on the history of most of Europe and the Mediterranean. Fantástico.'

'Not necessarily,' Mell replied. 'Perhaps our hooded friend from the museum is a follower of this ancient Etruscan priestess, although we can't know that for certain. We didn't see the eagle at the museum, but surely if a wren had been attached to it, we would have known about it. It would have been part of the news of its discovery as being odd. So, the wren, the final piece, if it exists, must still be out there? Perhaps we could find them before they put the eagle back together?'

'Where, in a city as big as Rome do you propose to start looking?' snorted Claire. 'We don't know who or what sent us down here, they didn't exactly give details when they demanded the wings. Where will Lisa even be taking them, assuming that she's still alive?'

'Hey, umm. Should the floor be wet?' said Jerry. He'd been uncharacteristically quiet for a while and had noticed a slow trickle of water creeping across the floor.

'Oh, that's not good,' Suze replied, staring at the growing trickle on the floor. Behind her the great wooden doors to the tomb creaked and groaned. 'That's very not good!' she hissed, spotting water breaking through the ancient wood in hissing jets.

XVIII

With a thunderous roar the doors bowed inwards and collapsed, and a torrent of icy water rushed into the room, sweeping the teenagers off their feet and flooding the burial chamber. A persistent, percussive rumbling, like a subway train could be heard from somewhere back within the Colosseum and as the group, regained their feet the water swirled around their ankles, slowly, imperceptibly rising. The flaming torches around the room fizzled in the damp atmosphere and went out, plunging them into darkness. Claire screamed.

A bright white light came on in the darkness as Mell found her phone. She turned her light towards the doors, which hung bent and buckled from their hinges. Claire and Sarah pulled out phone lights too. 'Simon,' Mell hissed. 'How the hell do we get out of here?'

He shrugged, 'The way we came in,' he said, guessing, as he began wading towards the broken doors and back into the passageway beyond. Anxious not to be left behind, the others followed, struggling against the press of water. No one saw what happened to the body of Romulus.

It was freezing and in the inky blackness the ever-present cascading sound was terrifying as they realised that the water had to be tumbling in from a great height. In the darkness, the torchlight caught the ripples of small eddies swirling around the broken brickwork where the boys had broken through the wall earlier, and reflected them onto the brick ceiling in a waving kaleidoscope. In the small chamber, Simon vanished, diving underwater going after his torch in the submerged spike room below.

'Christ, half the Tiber must be emptying down here!' Jerry exclaimed, splashing through the broken brickwork back into the lower corridor of the Colosseum, Suze right behind him.

'What are you all standing around for? Move!' Simon hissed to the rest, surprised to still see them so close as he resurfaced with his torch, he'd hoped that they would have moved on by now. The wall remained open allowing the water to continue flooding the tomb. The weight of the water had broken the mechanism.

Together they waded out into the corridors, trying to recall which way would lead them back to the elevator shafts. The subterranean corridors of the Colosseum, dark and creepy enough to begin with, were now positively terrifying as they rapidly filled with cold river water. The shifting rippling surface caught the light beams and reflected iridescent waves across the vaulted ceilings giving the group the illusionary impression of being underwater. And ever-present was the roaring white noise of the unseen torrential waterfalls that were slowly filling the ancient building.

Jerry led the way, leaning his tall body forward trying to create a bow wave big enough to ease the way for the rest. Simon was at the back, flashing his torch down every offshoot corridor, calling Lisa's name. It was obvious that he was unwilling to leave without knowing where Lisa was, or if she was safe, but the lower floor would be completely submerged in a matter of minutes, there was no way he could search for her. More than once Mell resorted to screaming at him to come back and re-join the group.

Finally, the light of Claire's phone torch fell on a churning, frothing mass of white foam. The source of the thundering that reverberated through the ancient ruin. A waterfall. With no floor to the arena above, the water was spilling down the ancient elevator shafts. The way out was inaccessible.

'We can't get out,' Claire wailed, finally losing the tenuous grip on her claustrophobia.

Mell fought her way forwards and caught her hands, 'Breathe Claire,' she had to shout over the crash of the raging water. 'It's just like Tintagel. Remember crawling through the small cave, on the wet sand?' Claire shuddered but nodded, fixing her eyes on Mell's letting the elder girl talk her through. 'It's just like that, but no one chasing us this time. Everything will be fine.'

'Drains!' Suze demanded, hissing the word out between her teeth as they stumbled forward. 'Simon how'd they drain the Colosseum after naval battles?'

'I have no idea,' he replied, pushing an unruly comma of dark, wet hair off his forehead, and twisting to cast his torchlight behind the group. 'No one is sure exactly how the Romans filled and drained the arena. It may have been a one-time occurrence before it was completed.'

'*Dominus,* if I may?' Tiberius materialised in front of him, floating just above the water, staring at Simon with large frightened eyes. His master was long dead, but as an unfreed slave in life, Tiberius seemed to cling to his status in death and had latched onto Simon as a new master.

Simon massaged his forehead, clearly uncomfortable with the situation, but with few other options as they continued to race through the rising water. 'Speak Tiberius, you need not ask permission, I am not your master.'

'*Dominus!* You are of the Julii, you are master.'

'Tiberius, if you have something useful to say please say it, or else I'm gonna find that sword again,' Suze threatened, realising with a curse that the sword was probably still on the floor of the burial chamber.

The ghost shuddered and spoke quickly. 'The Flavian arena's drains are exceptional, I watched the construction myself. The greatest of engineering. A large one circles the whole building and the intermittent well shafts plummet deep into the earth. And are still completely water tight and accessible.'

'Still accessible?' said Jerry glancing back and raising an eyebrow in Simon's direction.

'Tiberius,' Simon spoke softly, but with an urgency. 'Do you know where the nearest access point is?'

'Of course, *Dominus*. But why would you want to go down there?'

With a resigned sigh, Simon decided to just spell it out for the offbeat little ghost. 'Tiberius, whilst you may have shed the entrapping of mortality, the rest of us have not, nor are we in any hurry to do so. The water level is rising and we cannot stay here, nor can we go upwards. Show us the drains.'

'But *Dominus* I fear the water. Gaius Tiberius Decimus cannot swim, I will drown.'

The six of them stopped and stared at him in stupefied silence. There were no words to respond to his ludicrous, although somewhat charming statement. In the relative quiet, almost inaudible above the thunder of the waterfall, a howl, echoed through the corridors. The mournful howling of a wolf.

'Lisa!' a painful look darted across Simon's face and, forgetting everything else, he waded a few paces towards the sound.

'No,' said Mell forcefully, 'don't even think about it.' She reached for his shoulder, but he managed to evade her grasp, leaving her hand to splash uselessly back into the rising water. 'Simon, for god's sake, if it is her you can't get to her before this place fills completely. And what if it's not?' she managed to grab him on her second attempt and forcefully shoved him against the wall, one hand on his chest, her face grim and set, daring him to defy her. 'Simon, we are not losing you down here too,' she looked up at the ghost. 'Tiberius, drains, now!'

The terrified ghost didn't need telling twice and awkwardly half-waded, half-swam, half-floated away from cascading water as fast as he could. 'This way *Domina,* this way, not far.' From somewhere in the darkness the wolf howled again, answered this time by the angry roar of a gladiator. Simon shrugged out of Mell's grasp, the desperation clear on his face, but Jerry grabbed him, shoving him onwards. Tiberius led them quickly through the maze of corridors and halted randomly in the middle of a blocked passage. 'Here,' he declared, and ducked his head below the water.

The swirling tug of current around their legs assured the group that this was where the water was slowly draining away. 'All is not lost *amici*, it lifts, see?' Tiberius gestured to Jerry who ducked under the water and dragged the ancient manhole cover upwards a little. Water immediately pushed its way into the new void, sucking at their legs, dragging them under.

From somewhere in the darkness the wolf's howl came again, rising and falling as it echoed through the ruins. Mell slammed Simon back against the wall again fixed him with a piercing stare before gesturing for the others to leave. Suze ducked under first, followed by Claire. 'I said, we're not losing you,' she hissed.

Simon screwed his eyes shut covering them with his right hand. 'What if it is her?' his voice was a strangled whisper and he looked up, his anguished brown eyes meeting Mell's determined hazel ones. 'What if it is her, and I do nothing? What do I tell my future father-in-law when his only daughter's drowned body turns up in the Colosseum?' he banged his already injured hand against the wall in frustration. 'Let me go Mell.'

'Jerry help me,' she cried as Simon lunged forward, he was much stronger than her and although she kept hold of his arm, she was only hampering his progress more than stopping him.

'Dude, don't make me punch you,' Jerry said awkwardly, stepping in to take Simon's other arm. 'I'll knock you out and we'll drag you out of here if we have to.' Simon tensed ready to fight as the wolfish howl echoed again, this time from somewhere above, the sound grossly distorted by the heavy curtain of water pouring down the elevator shaft.

'Try it,' hissed Simon through clenched teeth, struggling against them both. Jerry glanced over his head towards Mell. She screwed her eyes shut, struggling to hold Simon, then met Jerry's enquiring stare and nodded.

'Sorry dude,' said Jerry, grabbing Simon's other arm and shoving him downwards into the drain. 'After you,' he gestured to Mell, and dived in after her.

Once in the drain there was little choice but to go with the tumultuous flow and simply try and keep their heads above the water. The six teenagers were bounced and jolted around, tumbling over and over in the ceaseless flow, down deep chasms and along ever narrowing tubes until the water level dropped and they could finally stand.

'It's grim down here,' Jerry complained, pulling his stretched and soaking hoodie up over his nose.

'What is this place?' said Claire, shaking water off her hands.

'The Cloaca Maxima would be my best guess,' Simon groaned, raking a hand through his wet hair. He'd recovered his senses whilst partially submerged in the tumble through the drain, but his head was pounding and it was just a guess.

Claire just stared at Simon. 'You know Si, sometimes you say words and they are literally just words to me. Where are we?'

Suze couldn't stifle her laughter anymore and let out a huge snort that gave way to an uncontrollable laughing fit. 'We are up shit creek without a paddle!' she giggled.

'This is a sewer!' Claire screamed finally understanding.

'Totally gross,' Mell agreed.

Jerry shoved his hands in his pockets. 'Grim, but I think someone else has been down here first,' he inclined his head towards a series of small wet footprints ahead of where we stood. 'Perhaps we should be wary.'

Simon cupped his hands around his mouth and bellowed his girlfriend's name down the tunnel. There was no reply and the action made his head swim.

'Right let's go,' said Claire suddenly taking charge. 'That way is out so everyone quick march. I want to be back at the hotel and in the shower within the next half hour, because this,' her gesture encompassed the whole space, 'is totally gross.' She pushed past Simon and took the lead, striding out following the damp footprints.

XIX

Lisa's eyes opened slowly as she regained consciousness, darkness shrouded her vision and she blinked frantically, trying to discern any difference between having her eyes open or closed. There was nothing. 'Simon?' her voice was shrill with panic, but no one answered her. She called his name again a little louder, but still all was quiet, the only breathing she could hear was her own. She was clearly alone. Perhaps it was all part of whatever game he and his friends were playing. In future, she would have to insist that Simon see less of them, whoever they were, they were clearly a bad influence.

She sat up, wincing at a pain in her lower back, feeling the solid, cold stone of a wall behind her, immediately followed by a freezing chill as her actions moved her wet clothes against her skin. She was still wearing her white dress, although it was torn, wet and ruined, and her expensive shoes were gone, leaving her barefoot. Worst of all, she could feel her normally immaculate, soft hair hanging in lank, greasy strands across her face.

Closing her eyes again, Lisa tried to think through her actions, how on earth had she gotten here? The last thing she could remember clearly, was an intense headache and an underground chamber with a coffin. Between that and waking up wet and cold in the dark, there was nothing.

Chilled, she wrapped her arms around herself and paused, feeling heavy damp material across her back and arms. Simon's jacket. It was soaked, probably ruined. But, at least it covered her dress; white had a horrible tendency to become transparent when wet, and Lisa had no intention of flashing her new undergarments at anyone but her boyfriend. Alone and seeking comfort she pulled the heavy, wet jacket tighter around herself, burying her nose in the soggy lapels. Below the damp there was still a faint trace of perfume, *hers or the other girl's?* She let out a half-choked sob, wishing that she'd not been so liberal in anointing herself earlier. The light, familiar scent of Simon's aftershave had been completely overpowered by female perfume and wet material.

Desperate to find something of comfort, Lisa blindly groped through the folds of the garment searching out the pockets. Nothing in either of the outer pockets, but she could feel something in one of the inside pockets, inside left, next to his heart. A small, hard, square box with a faux velvet base. She pulled it out, running her fingers over it in the darkness, telling her fluttering heart to be still. It felt like a ring box, but why would Simon have one of those? A part of her wanted to open it, they'd been together a long time, an engagement ring wouldn't be wholly unexpected; but, he'd not been expecting her in Rome, and, she recalled suddenly, Simon was wearing a signet ring on his left hand that had not been there yesterday. She would have to ask him about that. If his grandfather had sent him the family ring, then perhaps Simon had finally been acknowledged as heir to the Spanish de Valentia estates, he would be titled nobility one day. She would marry him anyway, of course. With or without the titles, Simon was far more impressive than any of her friends' boyfriends, but the acquisition of a title would make it so much more acceptable.

Drawing strength from her fantasy, Lisa slipped the box, unopened back into his pocket and tried to work out where she was. Her mind was still hazy, she recalled being in the lower levels of the Colosseum. It had been dark, dirty, and cold, she remembered that much. She also remembered that the dratted green-haired girl had followed her and Simon when they had split from the group. Then, with an unwelcome jolt she remembered something else; men with weapons. Gladiators. An impending sense of fear, or terror. She shook her head. Perhaps they had played a trick on her. The group had split up, there would have been opportunity for them to try and frighten her.

Something didn't seem right though. Lisa concentrated harder. A bolt of pain darted through her head, bringing with it a flash of memory and she glanced down, unable to see in the dark, whether the black lines still covered her body. Her resolve fading again she slipped her fingers back into the pocket with the ring box, although this time she came across a folded square of leather. Simon's wallet. With a sob of despair, she pressed the soft, expensive leather between her hands feeling for his monogramed initials in the corner.

Giving up trying to see with her eyes, and gripping Simon's wallet tightly in one hand, Lisa groped around on the floor. It was stone, made up of large flags. The wall behind her felt similar. Wondering how big the space was, she made to stand, thinking that she could keep one hand on the wall and wander in each direction. But as she moved her right leg she felt something cold and heavy on her ankle, heard the sharp scrape of metal on stone. She slid a hand down her leg and recoiled in horror when her fingers touched an iron manacle.

She was a prisoner. Locked up and abandoned in a darkened cell. Her stomach swirled uncomfortably and she clapped a hand over her mouth, before she was sick. 'Simon, please come and find me. Please ...' she moaned, burying her face against her knees, and, although Lisa rarely cried without an audience, she gave in to fear and wept.

*

The electric lights bathed the hotel room in a soft glow, and voices from the still populated streets of Rome floated through the open balcony door. The group was congregating in the boys' room as, being a family room, it had a sitting area and a decent kettle.

'So, what's our plan now?' said Sarah, wandering into the room from the shared balcony, cradling a steaming mug of hot chocolate. Her shower damp, long brown hair falling in long tendrils around her face.

'What can we do? We have no idea where the eagle is, or who has it,' replied Mell thoughtfully, tapping her fingers against her own warm mug as she lounged on one of the sofas.

'Si's missus had it, we just need to find her,' said Jerry, emerging from the bathroom, shirtless and clad in only a fluffy white towel. His two tattoos stood out, colourful against his pale skin as his long, wet curls dripped rivulets of water down his bare chest.

'In Rome, a city of two and a half million people. Where do you want to start?' Sarah retorted, leaning on the balcony door and staring out at the Pantheon.

'Geez sorry I said anything,' Jerry dragged his long hair back into a loose ponytail and then shook it out again showering water droplets everywhere, before flopping into a chair. 'Any hot choccy left?'

'There is if you get dressed,' Mell replied.

'No dice,' he shot back, reclining in the chair, hands behind his head and closing his eyes. 'I'm wearing pants … I think.'

'Is Claire still in the shower?' Suze groaned, wandering in from the balcony. She was the last one waiting to shower and Claire had been in the bathroom since they had arrived back at the hotel nearly forty minutes ago.

'Fraid so,' Mell sympathised, raising her mug in Suze's direction.

Suze groaned loudly. 'God, three of you have showered in the time it's taken her to …'

'Four,' Simon interrupted on his way past, 'yours is free. Thank you, for letting me go first.' He was dressed better than Jerry, in that he'd managed to at least find some jeans, but was still magnificently bare chested. Recalling his

126

chastising comment over the summer when he caught her staring at his toned abs, Suze bit her tongue and glanced away, feeling heat rise in her face as she mumbled her thanks.

'Uh … I think I'll go get dressed now,' Jerry glanced down at his own decidedly less toned chest. '*Y Ddraig Goch* can't compete with that.'

'What is it about Italy that makes the boys think they can walk around half dressed?' said Mell, shaking her head, although she caught Sarah's eye with a mischievous smile.

'I don't mind if you ladies want to join in the shirtless theme,' Jerry called back over his shoulder.

'Firstly,' said Simon, raking a hand through his jet black wet hair, 'there is a pool downstairs. Secondly, someone hid all my shirts.' He rummaged through several cupboards searching before he finally found a pale blue one, oblivious to the appreciative looks that followed him.

'Can't imagine why,' said Sarah feigning disinterest, before mouthing, 'wow' at Mell, whilst Simon wasn't looking.

His phone rang as he dragged his shirt on and with a grimace he answered it, 'Earl Hayworth … No, your Grace, I honestly have no idea where she is,' his shirt, still open, billowed as he stepped out onto the darkened balcony to speak with Lisa's father.

'That's not a call he's going to enjoy,' Suze said gazing sadly after him, 'Perhaps one of us should go talk to him. Offer moral support or something.' She loitered, glancing out onto the balcony, wanting to say something but unable to find the words.

'You should go for a shower, I can smell the Cloaca Maxima on you from here,' said Mell, uncurling herself from the sofa. 'See if you can beat Claire out, she's been in there so long I can only assume she's trying to wash the green out. I'll talk to Simon. He seems much more in control of himself now.' With a final lingering glance towards the balcony, Suze slunk off to use the vacated shower. Mell turned back to Sarah. 'Should we be worried about her?'

'Sarah shook her head. 'She's sixteen, it's probably nothing and if it is then she'll get over it. It's Claire we should keep an eye on. I don't know what she was thinking hitting on Simon so obviously. She's lucky he was such a gentleman about it, otherwise things could have gotten awkward.'

'It was awkward enough when Lisa arrived don't you think?' Mell replied, looking up and watching Simon, deep in conversation on the balcony. 'Shame her being around makes him behave so differently. I'm not sure I like her. Although, I suppose we've not met her in the best of circumstances.'

*

Simon paced the balcony, illuminated by the lights of Rome, and listened to the tense, panicky, almost accusatory voice of Lisa's father. Whilst underground he'd missed over twenty calls from the Earl and three from Lisa's friend Louisa. Needless to say, the lack of contact with either his daughter or her boyfriend had not put the Earl in the best of moods, especially since Louisa had caved in and told Nina, Lisa's chaperone, about the plan to send her to Rome.

Nina, in her usual exaggerated manner, had assumed that Simon was in on it and immediately told Earl Hayworth that she suspected an elopement was afoot. All of which led to the current ear-bashing that Simon was on the receiving end of. Unable to get a word in he held the phone at arm's length and thought his way through a believable version of events, so as not to catch himself out in an unnecessary lie, or imply that Lisa had managed to meet him. It was one thing for his future father-in-law to think that he and Lisa had been alone together, but quite another to let him know that Simon had subsequently imperilled her life and manage to lose her.

Only half listening, he almost missed the Earl's final question and his cue to respond. 'I assure you, your Grace, that in line with our conversation last month my intentions with your daughter are entirely honourable; and, had I the unexpected pleasure of encountering her company in Rome, not only would I have immediately informed your Grace of the situation, but my behaviour would have been, as always, implacably beyond question. Personal desires should never compromise a lady's honour,' he traced the leftward slant of his twice broken nose, hating himself for both lies. Lisa had of course been in Rome and her 'honour', so to speak, was long gone. Although they had not managed time alone since she had arrived so at least there was a partial truth in his words to her father. The Earl was not to be placated, and Simon found himself with no alternative but to agree to visit the Rome JDM, to check if Lisa was there.

Desperate to leave the increasingly suffocating conversation and promising to call as soon as he knew anything, Simon hung up and sank down onto the low bench around the balcony with a groan. This was too hard; the whole situation was too hard. His friends, his love, two totally separate halves of his personality that he had not realised were so different until they collided. And now Lisa was missing. He groaned again and on impulse dialled Lisa's number, it went straight to voicemail but at least he could hear her voice. He had to find her.

'*Dominus?*' Tiberius was hovering uncertainly on the balcony a little way from where Simon sat. 'The wren?'

Simon barely glanced up. 'I am not your master Tiberius.'

'But *Dominus,*' Tiberius floated beside him and landed a cold finger on Simon's left hand, touching his signet ring. 'You are Julii, of the Caesarean line. Descended from Romulus himself. How else could you have accessed his tomb? Why else would your symbol be an eagle?'

Simon shook his head. 'The Julii, are extinct, Tiberius. The Caesarean line came to a very messy end in a Senate meeting. What you suggest is impossible,' Simon covered his face as Tiberius tried to speak again. 'Leave me,' he groaned not wanting to listen and not bothering looking up to check whether the ghost had gone, his mind was playing through what had happened in those last frenzied moments that Lisa had been with them.

'Hey,' said Mell softly, startling him as she sat beside him on the bench. He'd not heard her approach. 'How you doing?'

Simon drummed his fingers against the stone seat. 'I should never have left her alone,' he shook his head.

'Don't be so hard on yourself,' Mell chided. 'We were all there when the hooded weirdo grabbed her. What could you have done by being there a moment or two earlier?'

'Something, anything,' Simon's hands curled unconsciously into fists, 'put myself in her place.'

'Simon there was nothing anyone could have done. We were all there,' Mell replied angrily.

Simon raked a hand through his hair. 'Forgive me, that is not what I … That is to say …'

'Forget it, it's not important,' Mell waved his apology away. 'Must have been a shock for you, her just appearing like that?' she paused, recalling something he'd said as they were escaping the flooding Colosseum. 'How long have you been engaged?'

'We are not. Yet. I simply have her father's permission, although not until she is eighteen,' he glanced awkwardly at Mell, 'Please say nothing to Lisa, she has no idea.'

'Not a word,' Mell replied with a smile.

He nodded a response and rose abruptly. 'We have to go back out there. There is a third piece to the standard, and Lisa could be anywhere. She could even have left Rome, we need more knowledge about this side of the foundation legend.'

'Sure,' Mell agreed. 'Simon come inside, we can all work together to figure this out, it's just going to take a little time.' She stretched a hand out towards him intending to guide him back into the rooms.

'Mell, we cannot sit around here drinking coffee, talking through what we collectively know about Roman mythology. None of us knew this story. Besides, time is something Lisa does not have. We are well past that deadline,' agitated, Simon resumed pacing.

'She left the tomb with the wings,' Mell insisted, standing. 'She must have bought herself more time …'

'It was incomplete,' Simon shot back, cutting her off. 'She may have granted herself a reprieve but we do not know that, you saw the black veins on her skin. We have no idea where she might be, or even if she left the Colosseum.'

'She didn't drown Simon,' Mell said forcefully, taking a step towards him. 'We saw footprints in the Cloaca.'

'And when was the last time you identified someone from a footprint!' Simon turned away, angry, desperate. 'Best case scenario, she is out there in a ruined wet dress, utterly alone in the middle of the night, at the mercy of anyone who happens upon her.'

Mell, sensing that she was losing this battle, reached for his arm intending to drag him inside if she needed to. 'Simon, be reasonable. You can't search the whole of Rome for her by yourself. Let us help. We can work this out and find her together.'

Simon wrenched his arm free, moving backwards, putting distance between them. 'Will you get it through that thick skull of yours. I cannot, I will not, sit here doing nothing, whilst Lisa is out there!' Tired anger raised his voice, hardened his accent, everyone in the vicinity could probably hear him, but he no longer cared. His thoughts were in turmoil, and he needed to get out. 'I am going to the museum, do whatever the hell you like,' he strode purposefully across the balcony, through the empty room that Claire and Sarah were now sharing, and slammed the door behind him as he left.

'Well screw you too Mr Millionaire!' Mell screamed at the empty balcony. It achieved nothing but she felt better.

XX

Incandescent with rage, and nursing a bad headache, Messalina paced rapidly back and forth through her erotic painted dining room, smoking a menthol cigarette from a long holder and impatiently tapping her teeth with it. She had been cheated. All that time spent with the cult, all those … sessions. Everything she'd overcome and everything and everyone she had lost. She swept up and down the room again; the spirit of the ancient priestess had favoured her above the others, she knew it. She had heard the ancient, paper thin voice on numerous occasions, but never had the whispers mentioned a third piece of the eagle.

The silver bird stood on her coffee table, majestic, proud and completely useless. Yet another statue in her already vast collection. Albeit a much more expensive one. Pausing, she stared at it, the body and wings covered with intricate feathers, the letter 'R' delicately tooled into the bird's chest. Exactly as the cult had described, exactly as the images in all their scrolls depicted. Yet there were two notches in its back. The obvious sign that she was missing an unmentioned third piece. Frustrated she resumed pacing, heels clacking out a staccato rhythm on the polished marble floor. Either the cult had somehow never known this key fact or someone had lied to prevent the goal of the priestess being achieved.

'Nothing was said about a third piece,' she muttered to herself exhaling another smoke ring and spotting her underwear dangling from the finger of one of her statues. She snagged it and continued her pacing, balling up the skimpy black lace in her free hand.

Her headache intensified, the priestess had been with her for a longer time than normal. Once out of the museum, Messalina had raced back to the hotel anxious not to be seen, although she was unable to recall much of anything between then and an hour ago, when she had found herself inexplicably down by the outlet of the ancient Roman sewer. Puzzled at finding herself there she had felt a little frightened, then suddenly the blonde girl had appeared, dragging herself, soaking wet and barely alive out of the drain, the silver wings of Remus's eagle clutched in her hands, a glazed faraway look in her eyes. Reaching out to take the eagle Messalina had realised that she herself was somewhat damp and her arms ached with unexplainable bruises. Delighted to have the eagle she had brought the girl with her back to the hotel.

Desperate to begin the ritual to raise Remus, Messalina had immediately hauled open the secret cellar and taken both the wings and the girl below. The girl had been barely breathing, as Messalina, dressed in her ceremonial robes, reattached the wings to the eagle, before realising that it was incomplete. Without the final part, she could not raise Remus. Without Remus, she could not do the priestess's work, could not change history. Howling in impotent rage she had shackled the blonde's almost lifeless body to an iron ring and hastened from the cellar, calling for Luigi. That had been half an hour ago. And she still shook with anger. The attentions of the pool boy, whilst enjoyable, had done nothing to quell the burning rage within her. The cult was gone, she'd ensured that. Now she was beginning to wish that she had not been so hasty in her revenge. There was no one left to interrogate about the missing piece, save for the priestess herself, and she would not be forced to speak.

The clacking of her heels fell silent as Messalina organised her thoughts. The girl had made it out of the drain and wherever she had been before then, perhaps the others had too. Messalina was willing to bet that she could persuade them to locate the missing piece for her; surely the handsome Spanish one would do anything to save his pretty little girlfriend. Messalina frowned, she would need to keep the girl alive. The potion she had administered should work for now, but the girl was not cured, the poison would return.

Pulling her dress a little tighter, Messalina lit another cigarette, wondering if she should check on the girl. But almost as soon as the thought crossed her mind she realised that for a while now, she'd been able to hear muffled sobbing from the secret chamber. She would have to get rid of Luigi before he noticed.

'Luigi,' she prodded the naked young man on the sofa with a stilettoed foot. 'Luigi be gone.' He let out a snort and rolled over. Messalina rolled her eyes. Men, all the same, fall asleep immediately. 'Luigi!' it was a shout this time.

The pool boy was up like a shot. '*Si, signora,*' he stood brazenly naked before her like one of her statues, and Messalina couldn't help but run an appreciative eye over his body, but she didn't have time for a second tumble. 'Get out,' she said simply, and walked away through into the hotel reception, abandoning him to dress and leave through the back door.

Sliding into the reception chair she idly flipped through a magazine, her mind turning over the problem of the eagle's missing part. To her left, the computer beeped announcing an email and she glanced up hoping for another booking, business was slowing at this time of year and she was a little low on her profit margins, but it was just an advert. She rolled her eyes and turned back to her magazine, then looked at the computer again. Perhaps the city museums had an online catalogue, she could search for her missing piece that way, assuming it would be in a museum collection.

She moved the chair closer to the computer and pulled up a search, barely noticing as a shadow passed through the lobby, but no one spoke, it was just one of the guests leaving. She turned back to her work, then jerked her head back up, it was a little late for people to be going out. Perhaps it was someone returning and she'd been right in her assumption that the teenagers had been resourceful enough to survive, the guardians *and my little trick with the Colosseum sluices.* The whisper of the ancient crone stabbed through her thoughts. Colosseum sluices, Messalina glanced down at the bruises on her arms, it was possible she could have opened flood gates during the hazy part of her day. It would also explain why the girl was wet when she came out of the drain.

Pushing an uncomfortable thought that the priestess was beginning to possess her aside, and turning her attention back to the computer, Messalina skimmed through the pages for the *Museo Capitolini*. Useless, they did not detail the collection online, only a few select pieces, and after the afternoon's "terrorist attack", banners crossed the site stating that the museum was closed until further notice. Her mind wandered towards the British teenagers again, as she checked the city news updates. Perhaps she should go and check on her young guests, after all not only had the museum been attacked in the afternoon, but there was, she'd now confirmed, an ongoing incident at the Colosseum. Surely it was her job as hostess to ensure the safety of her guests. And of course, Remus would require a host body. She had noticed one already stored in the basement, another gift from the priestess, but it was not ideal. Of course, ideal would have been Remus's own preserved body, assuming it had survived in the tomb. But, if the Colosseum had hidden the tomb of the twins, then, with floodwater still rising, any burial chamber was likely to be inaccessible. She glanced up at the stairs, perhaps she could procure a younger model for Remus's return.

She blew a smoke ring, surprising really that Remus had been buried in Rome all these years, and below the Colosseum of all places. The heart of Rome. Romulus, foolish sap, must have really loved his twin brother. She assumed they must have been buried within the same chamber. The words she had handed to the teens had been quite specific about the twins being together. At least she thought so, she personally didn't know Latin. Pushing her chair back, she ran her fingers through her hair, adjusted her dress to flash a scrap of lacy bra and, leaving her balled up underwear on the computer table, headed upstairs.

XXI

'What was all the yelling about?' asked Sarah as Mell wandered back inside, alone.

'Si's gone,' Mell replied, sinking into one of the other chairs with a heavy sigh. 'He thinks we're not interested in looking for his girlfriend, or not doing enough, fast enough to find her.'

'But we have no idea what to do,' said Sarah, her hands still wrapped around her warm mug of hot chocolate. 'And it's late.'

'We have Tiberius,' said Mell, spotting the ghost loitering nearby and obviously eavesdropping. 'Where's Jerry?'

'Getting dressed?' Sarah replied, shrugging her shoulders. 'I have no idea, he vanished when Simon was in here.'

'What did he do to annoy you so much?' You guys were pretty tight at the end of the summer, I thought there was something going on for a while,' Mell asked, absently weaving her red hair into a twisted braid.

Sarah laughed. 'Ha, me and Jerry? No way. Angry doesn't even describe how mad I am at him about the way he treated my sister.' She put her mug down and pulled her legs up onto the sofa, wrapping her arms around her knees. Mell thought she looked more upset than angry, but decided to stay quiet and let her friend talk.

'He hooked up with her, left her a note on the nightstand with his number,' Sarah shook her head. 'It was a few weeks ago, Rach was out at a club with some uni friends, it was raining, the club was playing awful music and one of her friends had to leave early, a bit rubbish really. Jerry must have been at the same club, he seems to manage to get in anywhere without ID. They clearly met, but Rach must have been really hammered. She had the worst hangover in the morning, I've never seen her so sick after a night out. And Jerry just left, sure he left his number, but he snuck out after they ...' Sarah trailed off, staring into her hot chocolate. She'd never admitted to the others that she'd actually enjoyed being the object of Jerry's affection. She loved it when he went all goofy and spoke to her in faux medieval. He had a way of making her feel special, and he'd ruined everything in a one night stand with her sister.

Mell had listened sympathetically, willing to offer advice but elements of the conversation implied something darker, and her mind, without her wanting it to, managed to play out her every encounter with the vile Richards; from the first time he grabbed her butt, to the horrific look of surprise on his face as he died. Closing her eyes, she shook her head, taking a deep breath. She was master of her own thoughts and Richards, whilst he had hurt her, had never achieved his ultimate predatory goal. Breathing out slowly, recalling how the psychiatrist had told her to cope with the memories, Mell brought herself under control before she replied.

'Everyone does stupid stuff sometimes Sarah, I'm sure plenty of people have regretted hook ups the morning after. Although it's pretty shady to sneak out like that.' Mell paused as a tall shadow caught her eye, Jerry was leaning on the door frame listening, and even in the low lighting she could see the shocked look on his face. She dropped her gaze to Sarah again. 'Are you sure that they actually hooked up?'

Sarah rubbed her nose. 'Rach said she didn't really remember but assumed that she'd slept with him, it's what made sense,' she stared at Mell through her fingers. 'What else could have happened, she doesn't really remember how she got home.'

'But she did get home,' said Mell, picking at the point in Sarah's story that she didn't think made sense. 'Look, I know people have one night stands, but if that's the idea then I don't think you leave your number,' she looked at Sarah, trying to ignore Jerry, still listening from the bedroom doorway. 'The way I see it, one of two things happened.' She counted off on her fingers. 'One; they did hook up and he liked her enough to hope for a second date, or two; your sister was drunk and Jerry took her home. That seems more likely to me.'

'Mell!' Sarah threw a cushion at her. 'I thought you of all people would understand! She's my sister!' angry, she stormed out of the room.

Mell folded her arms and stared at Jerry, one eyebrow raised, asking without asking.

He stared back at her. 'Not guilty. Never touched her. If her sister bothered to read the note and call me I would have been happy to explain what happened that night. Same as if Sarah had asked me about it I would have told her. But no, she's content for me to be the bad guy,' he flopped on the sofa beside Mell. 'Thanks for defending me.'

Mell smiled. 'She's only so angry because she likes you.'

'Yeah, I know,' Jerry leant back and put his feet up on the coffee table. 'I kinda like her too,' he closed his eyes. 'I should really just tell her what happened, but not right now, she'll just yell at me again. Besides,' he ran a hand over his head smoothing out his curls, 'we have Lisa to find and potential Armageddon to prevent.'

'Tiberius, there you are,' Suze grinned, spotting him as she wandered through the balcony door, dressed in clean jeans and a shirt with her hair wrapped up in a towel turban. The ghost looked at her curiously, and she grinned again 'Can you do me a favour? Float over to that room there, and stick your head through that door,' she directed, pointing at the bathroom in Claire and Sarah's room next door. Tiberius gave her another curious look but obliged and poked his head through the bathroom door.

'Suze that's cruel,' Mell reprimanded as Claire screamed in shock at her ghostly visitor.

The younger girl shrugged and came into the boys' room. 'She's been in there long enough; don't we have a damsel in distress to rescue? Where is Simon anyway?'

'Gone,' Mell replied, standing and looking towards the balcony as if debating whether or not to talk to Sarah, before deciding against it and sitting back on the sofa.

'What do you mean gone?' Suze demanded turning to look at her.

'He's gone to the museum, wouldn't wait,' said Mell, twisting to follow Suze's movements as she began to pace the room.

'And you let him?' Suze screeched, turning back toward her. 'You can't just let him go like that, what if he gets into some kind of trouble.' Her fingers went automatically to the scar in her left arm, a souvenir from the summer's trouble.

'Nah, she was right to let him go,' said Jerry pushing himself off the sofa. 'Poor guy is strung out, needs some headspace. He'll come back. Can't be easy for him, trying to be normal with us, and Lisa; we know him as a different person to the one she knows.' Jerry moved towards the bedroom annex and leaned on the doorframe. 'I like Si better when she's not around, but apparently he likes her, enough to wreck his life and marry her by the sounds of it.'

'They're not engaged yet, he just has her father's permission,' said Mell, ignoring her promise to keep it a secret.

'Ohmigod that is so sweet,' said Claire, finally joining everyone and conveniently forgetting her earlier attempts at flirting. Her hair was still green. 'Such a proper way of doing things, Simon is such a gentleman.'

'He's a posh git,' Jerry countered. 'What kind of idiot asks the girl's father first?'

'Definitely not the type who just leaves their number on the nightstand,' said Sarah venomously, returning to the room with her empty mug.

'Let it go Sarah, you have no idea what you're talking about,' Jerry growled in response.

'Oh, for Jupiter's sake,' Suze groaned. 'Tiberius,' she beckoned the little ghost over, hoping to change the subject and stop everyone from arguing again. 'What do the Remans plan on doing, how do they raise Remus?'

'If they have all parts of the eagle, very easily,' he replied. 'All they need is a host. His spirit can be summoned from the underworld with the completed eagle. They just need to piece it together and call him forth with the correct ritual.'

'They may not yet have all of the pieces,' Mell said. 'We know they have the eagle and it's likely they now have the wings but what about the wren that you mentioned earlier?'

'*Se,* the wren, may not have been recovered, but if they know where it is, then it can only be a matter of time,' Tiberius replied dejected.

There was a soft knock on the door and the teenagers all glanced at one another concerned. They were not expecting visitors and were on edge, after losing Lisa and now Simon.

'Think it's Simon coming back?' asked Sarah.

'He has a key. Why would he knock?' replied Mell, getting up to answer the door.

Behind Suze, Tiberius let out a cat-like hiss and vanished, although he was still in the room, there remained a cold patch in the air where he hovered, invisible.

It wasn't Simon, it was the tall Italian lady from the reception. Even from the back of the room the drama in her voice was clear to everyone as she told Mell that there had been two terrible accidents in Roma, an explosion at the Capitoline Museum and the *Colosseo* had flooded. 'Your hair is wet *Cherie*, were you caught in the rain?'

Still talking, the Italian stalked into the room, a vixen in stiletto heels, wearing a dress that showed off too much leg and stretched so tightly across her chest it looked as though her breasts were making a bid for freedom. A familiar looking golden rose necklace sparkled in the light from the lamps. 'Did your blonde friend meet you? I think she looked for *Segnore* Matherson? Are they here? Not at *le Coloseo* I hope.'

'Well she might …' Jerry began but Mell cut him off.

'They went to the Vatican together,' she lied, smiling sweetly at their hostess. 'Shouldn't be anything to worry about, we'll call you at the reception if we need anything or if they don't come back.'

Although no one could see him everyone could feel the intense dislike emanating from Tiberius towards the woman. And Suze almost screamed in shock as she felt his icy, but invisible hand pass through her shoulder. 'Reman,' he hissed sharply.

The Italian woman shivered as he spoke. 'This room is cold, no? Feels very cold for this time of year …' she narrowed her eyes slightly, scrutinising the group as if to catch them in a lie, then brightened. 'Well if all is fine, I will leave you. Although I will send Luigi up to fix your heating tomorrow, your wet clothes will never dry.' She sashayed towards the door, knowingly attracting and holding Jerry's attention with the sway of her hips. 'Ah one last thing,' she said turning in the doorway, long fingers with polished black nails, lightly gripping the doorframe, if you see *Segnore Matherson*, please tell him I have a parcel for him at reception. Ask for Messalina.'

'Nice of her to come check on us,' said Jerry, staring after her as she left.

'I don't think she knocked on any other doors though,' said Mell, leaning around the doorframe and watching Messalina retreat down the stairs.

'How did she know our clothes were wet?' said Suze, 'it doesn't look like it's rained in Rome, why would we be wet? And why assume that Simon and Lisa might be at the Colosseum? Plus, Tiberius didn't like her.'

'What are you getting at Suze?' said Sarah, 'You don't seriously think that she had anything to do with what happened this afternoon? Where is Tiberius anyway?' The little ghost was nowhere in sight.

'No, I think Suze may have a point. Why would she assume our clothes were wet, there's nothing visible in here?' said Mell, pacing the room, thinking. 'She knew that we went to the museum because we were talking about it this morning, but why assume Si and Lisa are missing at the Colosseum?'

'It's Rome!' Sarah replied 'The Colosseum is a fairly logical place to assume that people would be.'

'It was closed when it flooded,' said Claire, 'besides, did you see her necklace? A gold rose with a diamond dewdrop, Lisa was wearing it earlier.'

'She did say she had a parcel for Simon,' said Jerry scratching the blossoming stubble on his cheek. 'You think she has Lisa?'

'Could it be possible?' Suze said quietly. 'Simon went to the museum, perhaps we should find him, what if he needs help, or worse, what if he finds the missing wren and hands it over to the Remans in exchange for Lisa?'

'Then the standard would be complete,' said Tiberius, rematerialising in the centre of the room. 'They would just need a host body to receive his spirit and complete the ritual, they may already have one. I followed her.' He looked around ensuring that he held the groups' attention. 'I sensed evil in the lower rooms, but I could not follow further, it was not safe for me.'

'Doesn't mean it's her,' said Jerry, 'could be anyone who works here.'

'They need a body?' Mell's voice rose, as she finally understood what Tiberius had been trying to tell them earlier. 'A specific body or any body?'

'His own would be preferable but any shell would be sufficient,' Tiberius shrugged.

'Even the body of a small, weak blonde girl?' Mell pressed, feeling suddenly sick, wondering if the toxic looking black lines in Lisa's skin had been the start of a transformation. She massaged her forehead trying to banish her lethargy and think. If Lisa was to become the host for Remus, then it was likely that they would have to take her out in order to destroy Remus.

'Why pick a weak girl when if you play the game right and use her as bait you could have Simon?' said Jerry, who had followed another, equally unattractive thought train.

'Shit,' Mell twisted a strand of red hair around her fingers. 'Finding Simon can't be our priority, he can look after himself. If there is even a chance that our Italian hostess is really a deranged cultist, soon to become murderess and master of history; our priority has to be finding Lisa before it's too late. Tiberius, is there a way of stopping Remus once he is risen?'

Tiberius shook his head sadly. 'Only the army of Romulus can stop Remus. But they will only rise for their true leader, and he would need the standard of Romulus to control them.'

'And where is that?' Sarah asked, sensing she may know the answer.

Tiberius hung his head. 'Meredius took it from me. We were both charged with destroying the silver eagle, ensuring Remus could never return. But Meredius's loyalty was always to Remus. When I ... when I ...' he swallowed, 'when I died, Meredius took Romulus's golden eagle. It may be buried with Remus's mortal remains, but I cannot be sure.'

'Legend recounts that Remus was buried on the Aventine,' Suze said, delving deep into her memory banks for the fact.

'You will not find him there, *amici,*' Tiberius replied. 'The Aventine is now part of Rome, and Remus must be interred outside the city. He has moved many times. A whole legion was lost the last time he was moved, but where he lies now, I know not.' The little ghost drifted in a breeze from the open balcony doors.

'Where the hell would we even start?' said Claire.

'We find Lisa,' said Mell firmly. 'We find her and the silver eagle and we stop the resurrection before it starts.'

'But the raven haired Reman, she is still there, and I may not enter her space, there is some force keeps me out,' Tiberius groaned.

'You can keep watch,' Suze ordered, 'let us know the moment that she leaves, and maybe we can get some shut eye, even if it's brief,' she added, glancing at everyone's tired faces.

Understanding dawned on Tiberius's face. 'You are as smart as *Dominus!*' he said approvingly, before vanishing completely to undertake his mission.

'Simon won't like that,' Mell smiled. 'We should all stay here, that way if either Tiberius or Simon returns we can be ready for action. Suze, any other ideas on where the tomb of Remus could be? We may need to know.'

XXII

A grating sound, almost deafening in the sensory deprived darkness, startled Lisa awake. Unable to see or hear anything she'd been in a fretful doze somewhere between waking and sleeping for time unknown. A shaft of brilliant white light pierced the darkness and hurt her eyes, forcing her to screw them shut until the grating noise resumed and the red light behind her eyelids vanished.

Blinking rapidly in an attempt to reassure her brain that her eyes were open, she stared into the darkness that was no longer absolute. The soft glow of a flickering candle bobbed through the gloom and as a second flame sprang to life Lisa realised that she was no longer alone. Pressing Simon's wallet between her hands for reassurance she opened her mouth to speak, but only a tiny rasping gasp came out. Squeezing the leather harder as a third candle sputtered into life she tried again. 'Hello?' her voice cracked and her tongue felt like cotton wool in her mouth.

The bobbing candle wavered slightly and then advanced towards her. The figure carrying it remained a dark shadow until it crouched before her and the flickering light illuminated a recognisable face, the glamourous Italian lady, Messalina, who had given her a ride down to the museum earlier, or was it yesterday. A sense of relief flooded through her body, someone she recognised, everything would be alright now.

Lisa spoke falteringly, every word feeling like her mouth was full of cloth. 'Can you help me?'

The Italian smiled. 'I could,' she rose and continued her slow tour of the enclosed space, pausing now and again to light another candle.

Lisa watched her, grateful for the gradual increase in light in the room. Candle light was so soft, so comforting. But she was still cold, still shackled and hopelessly confused, yet the lady had said that she could help. Lisa reached out again. 'Please? I, I need help, there is something in my head, some kind of poison in me.

'Oh, I know,' Messalina replied in her heavily accented English. 'Your performance was *perfetto* darling. It is not your fault that the eagle had a third unknown piece.' She retrieved something from a table that Lisa couldn't quite see and stalked back towards her captive.

'Performance?' Lisa pulled Simon's jacket tighter around herself, but cold and damp it lacked the comforting reassurance of his arms. 'Pieces of eagle? I don't understand.'

'Nor do you need to,' Messalina crouched in front of her again and reached out, catching Lisa's chin, raising her face so that she could have a good look at the girl in the dim light. 'The curse worked well,' she muttered, turning Lisa's head and running a hand down her throat and along one of the black lined veins that crossed Lisa's décolletage. 'You were my *lupa terrificante*, a magnificent, snarling spitting savage. And you saved yourself by bringing me the eagle,' she let go of Lisa's face and stood up. 'And I will remove the curse on your life, at least temporarily.' She turned back to the centre of the room and walked away, her long dark robes making a soft swishing sound on the stone floor as she moved.

Weakened by the poison in her veins but unwilling to be treated in such a casual manner, Lisa clawed her way up the wall, dragging herself to a standing position. The scrape of the metal manacle on her leg against the stone attracting Messalina's attention. With one hand behind her back, leaning on the wall for support, Lisa stood straight, raising her chin and fixed the Italian woman with an indignant glare. 'You cannot keep me here. Simon will come for me.'

Astonished by her captive's apparent resolve, Messalina let out an inadvertent cackle of laughter, after all, she knew what her blonde prisoner did not. Her handsome boyfriend was not with his friends upstairs. He was missing. She moved closer again. 'You poor naïve thing,' Messalina said, gently reaching out to tuck a rogue lock of Lisa's dirty blonde hair behind the girl's ear. 'Regretfully your handsome Spaniard will not be joining us, or anyone else for that matter.'

She stepped back watching Lisa's reaction. The girl's hands went to her heart, to her throat, to her hair. Her eyes widened with the promising sparkle of tears, and her chest heaved visibly as she struggled to catch her breath. Then she changed, the tears were forcibly blinked back and her posture straightened again, the bright blue eyes raised in defiance. 'What did you do to him?' Lisa demanded.

Messalina moved back towards her, the increasing light in the room revealing a black draped altar behind her. She laid a hand on her heart affronted. 'I?' she said indignantly, meeting Lisa's accusatory glare with an assumed innocence. 'I assure you my dear I did nothing. You're the one who retrieved the eagle, left your man and his friends alone as the Colosseum flooded,' she paused, watching her words hit home as the blonde girl visibly shrank, before her knees gave out and she collapsed back to the floor with a wail of distress.

'A pity really,' Messalina continued, drawing a long ornate dagger from the folds of her diaphanous robes, and pressing the tip against her finger. 'I could certainly have enjoyed a night with that marvellous specimen,' she raised her now blooded finger to her mouth and slowly, sensuously sucked the blood off, her eyes never leaving her prey.

Lisa felt sick, her stomach roiled and her whole body felt like ice, she couldn't pick herself up, she simply lay miserably on the floor, trying to control her breathing.

Messalina watched, concern mounting, she would have to counter the curse now or the girl would die here in her basement. She would rather not have to deal with a mess like that again. Flicking her hair back over her shoulder she raised the hood on her robes and knelt before her altar, clearing her mind and allowing the priestess in. Her voice rose and fell chanting the ancient texts and the air in the cellar dropped a few degrees.

Watching through half open eyes, Lisa saw the misting of Messalina's breath on the cold air, felt the chill penetrate her body. She knew now that she would die here on the cellar floor, cold and alone with no one to protect her. The misted puffs of breath emanating from the priestess swirled in the room. She wanted to scream but her throat was closed, in her final few seconds of consciousness she noticed a body lying on the altar in front of Messalina. She couldn't see much but it was unmistakably a male body, presided over by candles and two small statues. 'Simon?' she whispered before darkness took over.

*

Her tasks completed Messalina rose, her thoughts collecting as the room refocussed around her. The blonde girl was lying in an ungainly heap on the floor, the black lines gone from her skin. The room was still cold enough that Messalina could see the little puffs of mist from her breath. She watched the girl, worried for a moment that the ritual had taken too long and she'd failed, but no, there it was, the little misting that indicated a breath. She would be fine.

Messalina had a more pressing mission now. She knew where the final piece was. The damn wren had been in the museum all along, right under her nose. If she'd have ventured into the other wing of the museum she would have seen it right away. But the ancient priestess had told her something else, she was not the only one looking for it, and the other one was already ahead of her in Rome. She didn't need the power of second sight to know that it was the Spaniard. Smarter than his friends and driven by love he was already half way there. She would have to act fast. With a final look at the crumpled girl, young enough to be her daughter, Messalina yanked the lever to open the stone, and fled the basement.

*

Simon walked quickly through the darkened, but still busy, streets of Rome. He knew the city well and enjoyed the anonymity of being alone, the freedom of not having to act one personality or another. To finally, just be himself. He'd never fully realised what an arrogant, and insufferable bore he could be until Lisa had arrived in Rome and ruined the easy rapport he had managed to establish with his new friends. He shoved his hands in his pockets and stared at the pavement as he walked, regretting his parting words to Mell, she had only been trying to help. It was just that, as an only child, Simon was unused to assistance, he managed alone, always had, until summer, when the other five had blundered into his life, or rather he blundered into theirs. Sure, he had the St. Peter's rugby team, but they were not real friends, off the pitch they barely spoke to one another and if they did it was merely to announce their boredom at some garden party, or masquerade. Things were different with the five he'd met over the summer, they were chatty. Suddenly his phone buzzed with messages that were not just reminders to do something or, quasi-romantic, badly phrased Spanish from his girlfriend.

A soft breeze chilled the October air, dragging his thoughts back to the present and made him wish he had not loaned his jacket to Lisa in the Colosseum. It was unlikely he would ever see the navy sports jacket or his wallet again. And it was not just his wallet that had been in the jacket pocket. Frowning as he remembered exactly what he'd left in his pocket he scuffed a stone down the street. The sapphire solitaire had been expensive, he really should have had it sent to England, it was another six months until he could actually pop the question. He shook his head, with luck, Lisa would still be wearing the jacket when he found her, if he found her.

He had told Mell that he was returning to the museum, but instead he walked the opposite way, towards the towering edifice of the newly refurbished JDM hotel. It stood, a towering eyesore of green tinted glass and chrome, an alien in this city of classical marble and Renaissance art. Simon stopped across the street and stared at the glass fronted entrance with its uniformed doorman, steeling himself to go inside and trying to recall Sir John's schedule. The last thing he wanted to do was run into his father. It had been almost two months since they had last spoken and over a year since the two had seen one another. Their final argument had been spectacular and with neither man willing to back down, they had both retreated into simmering resentment.

With a heavy sigh Simon dragged his hands free of his pockets, and raked his fingers through his short dark hair, using the shadowy reflection in a window to tame an unruly quiff. Taking a deep breath, he crossed the street and strode into the hotel, exhaling in relief when the doorman failed to recognise him.

The reception was paved in white marble, British racing green adorned the walls, and all furniture was of deepest mahogany, with any detailing in the room piped in white. The same as every other JDM in existence. The decor looked good in Britain, proud and classically British but here in the Mediterranean aura of Roman night, it was dull and dingy. Simon marched straight across to the Concierge and asked after Lady Hayworth-Mills. She had not checked in, nor had anyone seen her in the lobby or bar. Leaving the man with a description of her appearance, leaving his number and asking to be notified if she arrived Simon left, pretending not to notice the flurry of activity behind him as one of the staff apparently recognised who he was.

From the hotel, he walked quickly toward the Colosseum. It was not that he had lied to Mell about where he was going, his intention was still the museum, he had an idea. But first he needed to know if anyone had seen Lisa. Even at this late hour, the *piazza* outside the arena was thronged with people and a film of water leaking from the ancient building lay over everything. Simon fought his way through the crowd to the tourist entrance where a number of bored looking *Carabinieri* officers stood.

'*Mi scusi, agente?*' Simon was glad of his fluency in Italian as the officers gave him a little more attention than they did the English-speaking tourists. '*Qualcuno è stato ferito?* - was anyone hurt?'

The reply was generic, as far as they were aware no one had been injured, the water had simply cascaded in through an old chute and without the arena floor it had flooded the lower levels, there were no *turisti* down there and the monument had been closed anyway, so no casualties. Feeling a little relieved, Simon described Lisa to them, recalling her white dress and broken shoes.

Another of the officers snorted and gestured at the crowd '*Turisti!*' he had a point. The *piazza* was crowded on a normal day, now, with the Colosseum flooded and closed, and time creeping slowly past eleven p.m., everyone wanted to be here. There was nothing Simon could achieve by staying and gently he fought his way back towards the metro station and onto the *Via dei Fori Imperali,* before heading for the *Musei Capitolini* ensconced behind the Roman forum.

He wasn't entirely sure what he wanted from the museum, just had a strong feeling that what he needed was there. Tiberius had spoken of a third part to Remus's standard. A smaller bird. A wren. And whilst Simon had no recollection of seeing such a thing yesterday afternoon, something was nagging at his mind. He strode into the *Piazza del Campidoglio.* The museum was closed, one wing was decked with hazard tape and blocked to tourists, but lacking any obvious *Carabinieri* officers. When he had been here with the others that afternoon, before the smoke bomb, there had been a strange old man, raving about the end of the world and calling Simon, Caesar. It seemed so long ago. Trying to recall more precisely what the man had been raving about, Simon returned to the spot on the floor where the group had been sitting, under the gaze of Marcus Aurelius. He propped his elbows on his knees and rested his chin in his hands, staring at the old emperor. 'Help me out here Marcus, you were supposed to be one of the good ones, the philosopher, the thinker. What am I looking for?'

The emperor remained stubbornly silent.

XXIII

'Is Tiberius sure that there's no one here?' Mell asked biting her lip as their five stealthy shadows crept across the first-floor hallway and onto the marble stairway. It was two in the morning, there was still no sign of Simon returning and the hotel seemed deserted.

'He said she'd gone,' Suze replied with a shrug. Once he'd told them that Messalina had left, the nervous ghost had muttered something else and vanished on a mission of his own. Although given his strange fear of death and general nervous disposition it wouldn't have surprised anyone if it was an excuse so that he could stay safely hidden upstairs.

'She doesn't run this place by herself though,' Claire said quietly, glancing towards the hotel entrance, 'there could be someone else.'

'Anyone asks us, Simon wanted us to pick up that parcel she mentioned,' Jerry replied, from the rear of the group. 'Instant excuse for being here.'

'Okay then, let's do this,' Mell said. In Simon's absence, she had tried to assume his role and chivvy the group in the right direction, but although she was bossy, Mell lacked his natural leadership abilities and effortless confidence. Taking a deep breath, she stepped down the final marble stair, and the others followed her into the well-lit, airy reception.

Jerry strode straight over to the desk and rapped the little brass bell several times.

'You idiot!' Sarah hissed, 'what are you doing?'

'Checking that nobody's home!' he replied, ringing the bell again. There was no response, no sound of hurrying footsteps. The whole place was silent. 'I think we're safe,' he grinned.

Slowly, with a heightened sense of trepidation the five of them crept around the large reception desk, to the staff door. Through the small frosted glass window, it was clear that the lights were still on in the private annex. But there were no moving shadows visible behind the glass, and still no indication of approaching footsteps. It seemed that the place had been left completely unmanned.

It was a good thing they weren't trying to report a leaking shower or an exploding doorknob, Claire thought, and quickly stifled a giggle.

Still leading the group, Mell reached out and twisted the polished chrome doorknob, and the door swung silently open, revealing the private residence of the hotel's owner. The view was staggering. Beyond the door was a large airy space with plush, leather sofas and some seriously chic furniture, with the addition of several neo-classical statues, but it was the paintings on the walls that caught the group's attention.

'Oh my!' Sarah exclaimed shocked, taking a step backwards.

Jerry let out a long low whistle. 'That is some serious porn.'

Painted with intricate detail on every wall were graphic images of copulating Roman characters in a variety of dress and undress, in pairs or groups, human and mythical. Both Suze and Sarah stared at the floor feeling an embarrassed heat creep across their faces. Beyond the explicit paintings there were statues adorning the room, mostly male, mostly aroused. Observation of the whole vista was a truly uncomfortable experience.

'Guess there's no accounting for taste,' said Claire, her nose crinkled in disgust. 'This place looks like a brothel.'

'Maybe it is,' Jerry said. 'Perhaps she lures single guests here for sex. You know she propositioned Simon, right?'

'How do you know? Speak Italian do you?' asked Sarah scathingly, although she kept her eyes firmly on the floor, unwilling to look at either the décor or Jerry's expression.

Jerry gave her a quizzical look. 'Si told me. He and I do talk sometimes.'

'Are we going in, or just standing here?' Mell said tentatively, her attempt at leadership crumbling as she gawped at the décor.

'S'just sex,' said Jerry strolling right in. 'Racy pictures on a wall can't hurt you, unless they come to life as sex demons,' he turned back to see the girls stood in the doorway, staring at him with equal looks of disgust and horror.

'It's a joke!' he groaned, before admitting defeat and walking further into the room. The girls slowly followed him. 'Ha, weird, this dude's getting it on with a goat,' he gestured at a particularly obscene statue, chatting inanely, using bravado to suppress the inappropriate and uncontrollable flood of teenage hormones he was feeling. Striding so confidently into the charged room had been a big mistake. Making a conscious effort to keep himself twisted away from the girls, he continued to brazen it out. 'And I'm pretty sure I've never seen a nymph with boobs this big, they're like beach balls!' he exclaimed, laying his hands on the statue's ample chest. A drawer slid silently out of the pedestal on which she stood. 'Hello, what have we here?'

'Why is it always you? What have you done this time?' said Mell sharply, striding across the room after him.

'Nothing, I din't know a secret compartment was there, I was just messing about,' Jerry replied unfazed. 'This thing looks like a key by the way. Could be a secret safe around?'

'How does anyone relax in here?' Sarah wondered, finally entering the obscene room herself. She found herself too curious not to risk a quick glance at the walls, then, immediately regretting it, stared back at the floor again as a strong discomfort overwhelmed her.

Jerry opened his mouth to respond but Mell silenced him with another sharp glare. 'Like Claire said, there's no accounting for taste,' she replied. Her tone was harder than she'd intended and she clenched her right hand digging her nails into her palm.

'I'm not even sure taste comes into it,' Claire said, her face still screwed up with disgust. 'It's vulgar.'

'Simon's not here,' Suze said, still loitering in the doorway. 'You can use normal words.'

'Oh yeah,' Claire smiled. 'It's just gross really innit mate?' her terrible attempt at mimicking Suze's harsh central city Manchester accent made the younger girl giggle, breaking some of the awkward tension in the group.

'Guys come on, we've not got much time,' Mell insisted, flicking through some papers on a table. 'And all we have to go on is that Tiberius sensed something evil, and that it must be close to the main desk because he can't actually come in here. The question is where do we start looking?'

'We could grab all the statues boobs, see if there are more hidden keys and drawers,' Jerry suggested.

'Do you have to act like you're enjoying this so much?' Sarah asked rolling her eyes at him.

'They're just statues Sarah, it's not like I'd treat a real woman this way, but seeing as I can't do anything else right,' he shrugged and groped the ample chest of another statue. 'Nothing going on here.'

'You know I think Jerry may have the right idea,' said Claire with a sly smile. She'd been examining the statuary and had a theory. 'Our hostess's name is Messalina, and what if, like her namesake, she prefers a different piece of anatomy? There really aren't that many breasts in here.'

Jerry stared at her weighing the implications of her words. 'Nah-ah,' he waggled a finger in her direction. 'I ain't touching no statue's junk.'

'Little homophobic don't you think Jerry?' said Mell, enjoying the chance to goad the group's resident joker.

'Not in the slightest, wangs just don't do it for me, but Claire's right. There are hundreds of nobs in here,' Jerry paused, realising what he'd just said. 'And what better way to hide a doorknob than with a nob.'

'Do we have to check all of them?' Sarah said timidly.

'Just the big ones,' Suze replied and promptly burst out laughing.

'Guys come on,' Mell said, although she was sniggering too, 'she could be back at any moment …' she paused. 'Can you hear that?' The others fell silent, listening. There was a muffled sound, indistinct, almost drowned out by the constant buzz of traffic carried up from the city centre.

'Sounds like it's coming from over here,' said Sarah wandering towards a large potted plant in the corner beside large patio doors, leading out onto a private solarium and pool.

'Something outside?' Suze ventured, finally stepping into the room. Sarah shook her head and continued to examine the corner of the room.

'Hey is it wrong that I want to give the guys with the biggest wangs, a seedy handlebar moustache?' said Jerry, distracting everyone and hunting through his pockets for a pen.

Sarah glared at him. 'How are you so immature and Simon is so sensible, you're practically the same age,' she shook her head.

'Not even close, Si's almost a year older than me, I ain't eighteen till July. Besides Si's got some posh bastard stick up his arse that makes him act like a mature ponce. I'm just a goofball with a guitar,' Jerry strummed some imaginary chords. 'I thought I broke into a fancy mansion, but the walls, were out of fashion …' he sang softly.

'Shh,' Suze hissed, the muffled sound was louder. 'It's coming from below us.'

'Jerry, where's that key you found? There may be a cellar door around here somewhere,' Mell said, trying to move the sofa to see behind it.

He continued singing and strumming as he meandered across the room. 'I put it back in the busty statue.'

'He really is incorrigible, isn't he?' said Claire, watching Jerry cop a feel of the statue. 'I mean he's a tool,' she corrected herself catching Suze's amused glance at her choice of word.

'Tah-dah, one key,' Jerry proclaimed, one hand still on the nymph's beach ball sized breast. 'Now which hole does it go in?' he'd spoken totally deadpan but both Mell and Claire snorted with laughter and collapsed into giggles.

'Seriously?' said Sarah, ignoring the joke. 'Guys come on, I'm sure there is someone down there, it sounds like a girl.'

'Could it be Lisa?' Suze asked joining her in the corner. The room made both of them uncomfortably aware of their relative innocence compared with the others, and, having something to focus on besides the hedonistic décor, stopped their blushes from becoming overwhelming.

Sarah was right, the sound, whilst heavily muffled, was distinctly feminine and appeared to come from below the floor. 'I don't see a door anywhere,' Suze said staring at the glossy polished paving stones.

'Maybe here,' Sarah indicated a scuffed patch on the marble floor, as though someone had moved the heavy potted plant and dragged it a little, leaving lines in the polish.

Unaware of what Sarah and Suze were up to, the others were still giggling as Jerry examined one of the frescoes. 'I mean come on, that just looks uncomfortable, you'd have to be an acrobat, right?'

'Guess it's down to us to solve this then,' Suze sighed, squatting to look closer at the scuff marks on the floor. 'You could be right, there's a seam here, almost invisible.' She traced her fingers along the line and glanced up at Sarah, colour rushing to her face as she caught sight of a particularly well-endowed character painted on the wall behind the other girl. She coughed. 'That's big!'

Sarah turned, and clapped a hand to her mouth in shock. 'Oh my! Looks like the kind of thing that requires batteries.'

Suze snorted with laughter. 'It's bigger than him!'

'Well it is a Satyr,' Sarah replied, 'their appendage is what they are known for. Not surprised they hid this one behind the plant though, he's a tad excessive.'

'Ah,' Suze blinked uncertain that she was seeing things right. 'Is his …' she gestured towards the wall searching for a word. 'Thing, sticking out from the wall?'

'That is disgusting!' Sarah shrieked.

'The whole room is disgusting,' Claire called back, 'what makes that bit worse?'

'It, sticks out of the wall,' Sarah replied.

Jerry roared with laughter. 'Doorknob,' he proclaimed, 'mostly cos I'd rather not think what else it might be at that height.'

Mell punched his arm as they both moved to join Sarah and Suze in the corner. 'You have a sick and twisted mind Jeremy Llewellyn. Sick and twisted.'

He stuck his tongue out. 'Takes one to know one.'

'Well if it's a doorknob how's about we open the door?' Suze said impatiently.

'You wanna do it?' offered Sarah.

'Eww no, Jerry?' she replied.

'I ain't touching another man's junk. Statue boobs fine, blokes junk, nope,' he sliced his hand in an underlining motion to emphasise his point.

'Oh, for heaven's sake it's just a painted willy,' said Mell, although when she pressed the lever it was with a single finger and a grim look on her face. There was a low grinding sound, and the stone slab Suze and Sarah had been examining slid down and away, explaining the scratches on the surface. Below it lay a wooden trap door with an iron ring set into it. The sound of female sobbing was suddenly louder.

Impulsively Suze reached out and, grasping the ring, hauled the trap door open. A waft of cold, damp air escaped and the sobbing grew louder, followed by a sudden rasping voice. 'Hello? … is someone there?'

XXIV

'*Nero's reyezuelo!*' Simon jolted himself awake as the memory finally came to him. He stretched out, feeling a dull ache in his legs from sitting on the cold floor in the middle of the night. It had been worth it though. He finally understood the memory that had driven him to the museum. A set of silverware recovered from Nero's golden palace, including what looked like a silver table piece in the shape of a small bird. Distracted by Claire's incessant flirting, he'd missed it when the group had toured the museum, but he'd seen it before, several years ago when he was in Rome learning to drive.

The night was warm for October and he stretched, feeling a crack in his shoulders, allowing himself a small smile, it was so unlike him to do something like fall asleep in a public place. Maybe Lisa was right, his new friends were a bad influence. Lisa. A bolt of panic flared through his chest and on impulse he looked towards the museum, straight into the wizened face of the deranged old man who had accosted him yesterday. His long beard clung precariously to his chin and its long length trailed on the floor. Letting out an involuntary yell, Simon scrabbled back a few feet, the wall of the fountain impeding his progress.

The old man stayed still, crouched on his heels, rocking slightly, his eyes fixed on the teenage boy's face. '*Va tutto bene, proteggo Caesar.*'

Reflexively, Simon inched back a little more and rose slowly to his feet, raising his hands, wondering why the aged Italian insisted on calling him Caesar, although grateful that he appeared to want to protect him rather than cause harm. Speaking slowly back in Italian, unwilling to provoke a reaction, Simon thanked him for standing guard. '*Grazie, per la tua protezione.*'

'*It is the duty of Romulinus, to protect the heir of Caesar, ruler of Rome, from the evil of the Etruscan priestess,*' the old man replied in rapid Italian, throwing himself prostrate at Simon's feet.

Uncomfortable, Simon's eyes flickered around the deserted *piazza*, searching for a police officer. The whole place was deserted, the hazard tape around the damaged wing of the museum the only indication that anyone of authority may be present. He was alone with the old man. Well, if the fellow thought he was Caesar, a thought that Tiberius seemed to share, Simon guessed he could play along. Slowly he lowered his hands, offering one to the old man. '*Rise Romulinus,*' he said looking towards the wing of the museum, where he assumed the wren must be housed. Before he could say anything else the wail of an alarm pierced the night.

It took a second to register that the alarm was going off inside the museum. The sound indicating damage to a display case, rather than the building alarm. Someone was inside. Romulinus grabbed Simon's wrist in a surprisingly tight grip and dragged him from the *piazza*. '*Come Caesar, they must not see you.*'

With a speed that belied his age, the old man forcibly pulled Simon around the side of the museum and through a partially open door in the shadow of a shrub. And that was it, they were inside. A rattling chain, followed by the clumping thud of multiple pairs of heavy boots signalled the arrival of the Italian *Carabinieri,* the military police. Undeterred Romulinus forged onwards, his grip on Simon's wrist unrelenting.

'*Wait,*' Simon hissed, almost forgetting the Italian word, as the old man nearly pulled them directly into the view of an officer. Exerting a small measure of authority over Romulinus, Simon dragged them both behind a display case of Papal regalia, and pulled the old man into a crouch as they waited for two officers to cross through to the next room.

Anxious to be on their way, Romulinus tugged insistently at Simon, clawing at his clothes and gesturing wildly that they needed to move onwards. '*All right,*' Simon relented, allowing himself to be dragged forward again, '*but quietly. Understand?*' Romulinus nodded and forged onwards. Clearly, he knew exactly where he was going, but twice more Simon had to pull them both behind a wall and out of sight of the police.

After several rooms Romulinus slowed down, and with a cry of distress that threatened to bring every officer in the vicinity to arrest them, sank to his knees in front of a shattered display case.

Breathing heavily in the darkness, Simon pulled at the old man's arm. '*Come on!*' he hissed, hearing footsteps coming closer, but Romulinus would not be moved, instead he began to wail, a high keening note of distress, letting go of Simon and throwing himself forward at the broken cabinet searching among the glass fragments for something.

'Romulinus, *come on,*' Simon tried again, eyes searching the darkness for the nearest access to the room. He could hear several officers coming closer, they would be discovered at any moment. He risked a glance at the shattered display case and realised with a jolt, that it was where the Neronian silver had been kept.

First century luxury tableware was scattered on the floor amidst the shards of glass, but the wren was gone. *'Mierda,'* he muttered, realising why the old man was so distressed. They had missed their chance to grab the last piece of the silver standard first. To his left a boot crunched on glass and a bright light swept the space. Simon threw his hands up shielding his eyes and hiding his face as the officer, blocking the main exit from the room, began to call for backup.

Without pausing to think it through, Simon threw himself across the space, tackling the *Carabinieri*, both of them landing on the floor amid the broken glass and ancient silver. They rolled on the floor, glass crunching beneath them, Simon fighting a losing battle with the soldier's superior strength, until with a grimace of distaste and sympathy he drove his knee into the officer's groin. The man released Simon instantly and curled around his pain.

'My apologies,' Simon grunted, shoving himself away from the officer and scrambling back to his feet. More lights were racing through the darkness towards them, and he jumped, startled as Romulinus grabbed his shoulder.

'Come Caesar, we go this way,' pulling at him again, the old man dragged Simon through a nondescript door and into the private side of the museum. The custodians' corridors. Away from the riot of artefacts on display the space was tranquil and quiet, almost too quiet. Simon had been through the back corridors of the British Museum before, and they were always teaming with people moving things around. After hours and deserted the space was eerie, with strange shadows lurking in corners, where artefacts had been temporarily stored.

Romulinus led Simon through the maze of winding corridors and up two flights of stairs before he finally stopped for breath. A nearby sound of a door closing had them both turning towards the noise, more police officers, or the thief, they were unsure. Pressing a wizened finger to his lips, Romulinus released his grip on Simon and crept forward, catlike, through a closed fire door and into another corridor.

Light spilled around a door at the far end of the corridor, the curator's office, and they both moved quietly forward, listening to the thuds and muffled curses that came from within. Someone was searching for something. Romulinus turned to stare at Simon his eyes growing large in the low light. *'Aquilae es clavis,'* he hissed switching to Latin from Italian. Before Simon could stop him, he bounded through the door into the curator's office beyond.

Through the open door, Simon saw a woman. Shocked by the explosive entrance of Romulinus she had stopped, an office drawer still held in her hands, staring at the intruders. Romulinus took a step forward into the room, keeping himself between Simon and the black robed woman with the dangerous glint in her eye. *'Priestess Messalina,'* the old man bowed.

'You!' the woman spat, *'I thought I killed you along with the others.'* Dropping the drawer, she drew a dagger from her robes, her glazed eyes flicking towards a small silver statuette on the table. The Neronian wren. Romulinus spied it too and they both lunged for it, knocking it to the floor.

Powerless and with the odd sense that he knew the woman, Simon stood in the doorway and watched as the world seemed to slip into slow motion. The old man reached the bird first, but the priestess had lunged with her dagger, not her hand. Romulinus grunted in pain as she buried the blade to the hilt in his side, before withdrawing and slashing at his throat.

'¡No!' Simon yelled, lunging forward into the room, but he was too late. Blood sprayed like a fountain up the wall, as the robed woman slit the old man's throat. As if in a trance, lost in bloodlust, she hacked at his face as he sank to the floor, blood pouring from his wounds.

Fighting the urge to yell for the police team downstairs, Simon darted further into the room, throwing himself across the wide desk, attempting to reach the black robed priestess as she stepped back from Romulinus's body, wiping her dripping dagger on her sleeve. He had underestimated her speed though.

Transferring her blade smoothly to her other hand she turned and swiped at him, only just missing his face as he jumped back. For a heartbeat they regarded one another, the tall Spaniard and the black robed priestess. Her eyes reminded him of Lisa's, glazed, as though hypnotised. She blinked first, eyes widening slightly as though in recognition, before the vacant stare returned and with a formidable speed and strength she threw Simon aside and fled the scene.

Simon's head hit the desk, as he stumbled backwards and tripped, sprawling to the floor. By the time he'd regained his feet, raising a hand to the bruising, the woman was gone. She had seemed almost familiar, shaking his head, he dropped back to his knees beside the old man. 'Romulinus?'

There was blood everywhere, too much blood, the arcing spray up the wall now accompanied by a growing pool on the floor. More for something to do than any real expectation of life remaining in the old man, Simon pressed his fingers against the unslashed side of Romulinus's neck and was surprised to feel the faint flicker of a pulse.

'Romulinus?' he shook the man's shoulders gently, feeling a warm spurt of blood on his hands as he did so.

The Italian gave a gurgling breath, and a trickle of blood seeped between his lips. Concerned and desperate, Simon clamped one hand to the wound in Romulinus's throat and with slippery, blood slicked fingers tried to dig his phone out of his back pocket intending to call for help.

'*Too late,*' rasped Romulinus, one flailing hand knocking Simon's phone away. With an obviously Herculean effort, Romulinus rolled and dragged himself towards the mess of papers and broken drawers on the office floor. Simon retrieved his phone, almost dropped it, as blood made his hands slick, and finally punched in the international emergency number.

Romulinus ignored him until he began talking, giving his name to the operator as James de Valentia, his real identity would probably be easy enough to discover later.

Pain written in his aged features Romulinus, beckoned Simon closer. Still on the phone, but anxious to appease the old man, Simon crouched by his side and was surprised when with a final bust of life, Romulinus snatched his phone and tossed it aside.

'*They come soon enough,*' he wheezed, and held up something that looked like a silver feather, '*Aquilae es clavis.*' The Latin phrase again. '*Aquilae es clavis,*' he pressed the feather into Simon's hand. '*Es clavis!*' Romulinus slumped back down, his eyes growing dim. His breathing was shallow and Simon had to move closer to hear the next few whispered words. '*la Gemina è con Vulcan,*' the old man's eyes grew glassy and in fright he gripped Simon's left hand, '*It ... is ... honour,*' he gasped, struggling to push out the final few words, '*serve Caesar,*' his grip loosened, and he was gone.

Devastated, Simon raked both hands through his hair, leaving blood trails that would stiffen into small spikes he wouldn't notice until much later. The low squawk of his phone reminded him that he'd been calling for help, and he rose, pocketing the key and speaking several brief words into the phone before hanging up.

As if from far away he could hear footfalls, at least one officer was venturing upstairs, the old man would be found. Kneeling again he shifted the lifeless body of Romulinus to a more dignified position, lying on the floor, and gently closed the old man's eyes. '*Requiesce in pace, mi amice,*' he spoke the words in Latin, crossing himself in the presence of death.

Quickly he slipped out of the room and into another as the police officer reached the top of the stairs. There was no way he could escape through the front door. Working purely on instinct Simon pushed open the office window as far as it would go, threw his leg over the sill and climbed out onto the narrow ledge outside. He was at the back of the museum, three floors up, balanced on a ledge no wider than his foot, but fortunately invisible to anyone. There was a large tree to his left and slowly, carefully, taking great pains not to look down, he inched that way, intending to use the tree to reach ground level, not that he was any good at climbing trees.

He froze as a dark shadow moved below him, one of the police officers. Keeping still, hidden in shadows, he waited for the officer to move on, although his luck was out as the *Carabinieri* officer sparked up a cigarette. Standing on the crumbling ledge Simon was trapped, he leant back against the wall and waited, his mind wandering back to the robed woman, and why he had felt that spark of recognition. Who was she?

Eventually the officer put out his cigarette and moved on. Leaving Simon free to escape, moving as fast as he dared along the crumbling ledge and into the tree, scratching himself badly and tearing both his shirt and a trouser leg in his haste to shin down, but desperate to be on solid ground. Just before the officer left, he'd suddenly realised why he had thought the woman was familiar, and why she may have recognised him before she fled the scene. It was the hotelier. The others were in danger, he had to get back. Pulling out his phone, and cursing at the low battery, he found Claire's number. It may not be the wisest decision, but of the five of them, Claire was most likely to have her phone on her. 'Come on Claire,' he muttered, beginning to run.

XXV

Cold but surprisingly dry air wafted up from the cellar as a hoarse female voice called out again. 'Hello? Is anyone there? There was a scuffling sound followed by the scrape of metal against stone before she spoke again. 'Please, you have to help me! My father will pay you, just please help me!'

'Lisa,' Suze murmured to Mell, recognizing the girl's voice.

Mell pulled her phone from her pocket and switched on the light, thankful that she'd been able to recharge it. She didn't want to encounter Simon's girlfriend again, any more than the others did, but at least Lisa was alive. 'Come on,' she hissed, heading down the stairs into the basement, the others cautiously followed her, Jerry, loitering long enough to scribble a handlebar moustache onto the satyr whose appendage functioned as the door handle.

'You idiot,' hissed Claire, snatching his pen. 'Now she'll know we were here.'

'So will Simon,' Jerry retorted resuming his usual place as rear-guard and ushering her into the cellar behind the others.

The scrape of a chain drew their attention deeper into the subterranean room and Mell flashed her light around, illuminating Lisa's pale form, huddled against a wall. Shrouded in darkness for so long she threw her arms up, shielding her eyes from the harsh torchlight.

'Ungh, could you lower the light please? It hurts,' Lisa's voice, was barely more than a whisper, cracked by the time she must have spent weeping in the darkness. Mell obediently dropped her phone light a little and Lisa lowered her arms. Dark mascara tracks ran in lines down her red and blotchy cheeks, her once white dress was smeared with dirt, horribly torn and clung wetly to her upper thighs, leaving little to the imagination. She had wrapped Simon's sports jacket tightly around herself but, heavy with damp, it offered her no warmth and she was visibly shivering. Her feet were bare, her shoes having been left in the Colosseum and, a large iron manacle clamped her leg, tethering her to the wall. Her huge blue eyes, devoid of the glassy yellow, predatory look she'd had at the Colosseum, stared at her potential rescuers as they huddled in the cellar.

'Where is Simon?' she demanded, rising from the floor. 'What have you done with him?' she coughed harshly, her entire body wracked with the effort.

'He went looking for you in the city, we had no idea you were here,' Mell said softly, moving closer to the trembling girl.

'Ha!' she let out a hoarse bark of laughter, her voice hardened by her time in the damp cellar. 'I thought with me safely out of the way, he'd be happy with Ms Green Hair over there,' she wrapped her arms around herself as a violent bout of shivering shook her body.

'You're freezing,' Jerry said, dragging his rock band hoodie over his head, and offering it to the soaking girl. 'Here, put this on, you need to get warm.'

Lisa wrinkled her nose in distaste and shook her head. 'I could never wear another man's clothing,' she flicked her hair. 'Simon would not appreciate it.'

Jerry sighed and thrust the hoodie at her again. 'Look Lisa, your boyfriend, he's not a total spanner,' Jerry shrugged, 'well he is, but he's not. I mean,' he brandished the jumper at her again. 'Si's not a jerk, he'll understand. I'm sure he would rather you were warm and safe, than frozen. He ain't gonna be mad if you swap his wet jacket for a dry hoodie.'

Lisa half reached for it, then drew back, her eyes narrowed slightly. 'Are you hitting on me?'

Jerry swore under his breath and sighed again. When he spoke, his voice was a little harder. 'Look blondie, you ain't my type, besides you're dating my mate. I'm trying to be the good guy here, now just wear the damned jumper,' he threw it at her.

Lisa held it for a heartbeat, feeling Jerry's warmth still within the material, then quickly slipped out of Simon's ruined jacket and into the hoodie. It drowned her slender frame, longer than her dress. She dragged the hood up and snuggled deeper into the folds of material, then as an afterthought dived back down to the jacket and started pawing through the pockets.

'You should be careful of accepting gifts from Jerry,' Sarah warned her, fixing Jerry with a hard stare.

'Oh?' Lisa replied, shooting a curious look at Jerry's tall, gangly frame silhouetted by the light from the room above.

'Ignore Sarah, she thinks I slept with her sister in dubious circumstances,' Jerry retorted, scowling in Sarah's direction.

'Did you?' Lisa's question was pointed as she burrowed her hands into the pockets of Jerry's jumper, stashing whatever she had taken from Simon's jacket.

'Of course he did,' Sarah replied, before Jerry could defend himself. 'Spiked her drink, slept with her and snuck out leaving a note like a coward,' she stood, hands on her hips, daring him to deny it.

'Sarah!' Suze exclaimed in shock. 'You don't really think that, do you?' she looked over at Jerry, who had gone deathly white.

Balling his fists by his sides, Jerry tried counting to ten, gave up, and exploded with indignant anger instead. 'Fuck off Sarah,' he stepped closer, standing ominously over her, making full use of his intimidating six foot, seven-inch height. 'I did nothing wrong, some other tosser drugged her drink. I got rid of him, sorted a taxi, escorted her home, put her to bed, with a glass of water, left a note explaining what happened and my number, asking her to call me and let me know she was okay. Then. I. Left.' He turned on his heel and stomped out of the cellar into the room above. As Sarah stared after him the reception door slammed, Jerry had left the building.

A stunned silence fell over the cellar. Jerry was not normally one for storming out, he knew how to take a hit, and usually took it well with a laugh and a snarky self-deprecating comment. But Sarah had really hurt him.

'Wow,' Lisa's voice dripped sarcasm and she folded her arms, glaring at the four girls in the cellar, her sense of superiority clearly restored. 'This is some rescue. I'm still chained up and you've misplaced both the boys. Tell me, did you annoy Simon that much too? Is that why he's not here?'

'Simon is scouring the city looking for you,' Suze snapped back, taking two steps towards the cellar entrance wondering if she should go after Jerry.

'Just get Lurch back,' Lisa replied, gesturing to the cellar opening and slumping back against the wall. 'We need him to get this chain off,' she lifted her ankle, as Mell crouched beside her looking for a way to break the chain.

'Claire go get him back,' Mell ordered. 'We already lost Simon somewhere in Rome, and I'd rather we all stuck together. Besides I think he has the key for Lisa's chain. And whilst you're up there, if you have a signal call Simon. Let him know we found Lisa.' Claire nodded and scampered quickly up the stairs, relieved to be out of the darkness and away from Lisa's accusatory stare. Mell turned her attention back to Lisa. 'And you should give Simon more credit, I had to drag him out of the Colosseum or he would have drowned looking for you. Besides being wet and cold are you injured?' Mell asked, trying and failing to keep her irritation with the girl hidden, as Suze and Sarah gave up trying to help and decided to examine the rest of the basement room.

Lisa threw her a look of contempt. 'Are you blind or just mentally impaired? I am chained to a wall in a cellar, with no shoes. My dress is ruined, my boyfriend has vanished and I have a dead body for company!' she screamed this last part.

'She's right, there is a body down here,' Suze agreed, her flickering phone light falling on a male body, likely in his late forties, on a draped table. It sagged in the middle, clearly not designed to support the weight of a person. He was naked save for a modesty covering loincloth, and there was no obvious sign of injury to the body. Although it seemed unlikely he'd died naturally, given that he was laid out in a secret basement. Concentrating hard, bodies were more of Mell's thing, Suze moved her torch light carefully around the corpse looking for any indication of cause of death.

'Suze look,' Sarah stood on the opposite side of the corpse, her light trained on the wall. More specifically on an altar recessed into the stone, on which lay an ancient human skull, covered in strange dark markings. It nestled between two small statues, its sightless eyes overlooking the partially decomposed body and splayed entrails of a small bird. Sarah shuddered, the skull was creepy, menacing even.

'Gross!' Suze responded looking up. 'Messalina is a bloody weird woman.' She moved closer to the corpse's head and resumed her examination. From between swollen lips a purplish tongue protruded. 'Mell?' she called back over her shoulder. 'Purple tongue means poison, right?'

'Not always,' Mell replied, turning away from Lisa. 'Sometimes it's just natural decomposition. Although,' she joined Suze at the corpse's head, 'some poisons can leave noticeable effects on the body. Arsenic, for example can lead to mummification.'

'Excuse me!' Lisa raised her voice. 'You ladies need to reorganise your priorities, he is dead. You should be working to help me!'

'And you could make some effort to help us, help you,' Suze replied coldly, realising that she could do nothing else with the corpse and turning her attention back to the altar that Sarah was still examining.

'Simon called, he's on his way.' Claire said breathlessly, clattering down the cellar steps with Jerry right behind her. 'He said we need to leave. Messalina is on her way back and she has the wren. Everything she needs to resurrect Remus.'

'Why did he call you?' Lisa screeched, forgetting for a moment where she was, 'You were wearing his jacket in the museum, your arm in his,' a fresh bout of tears sprang to her eyes. 'Oh god, he is cheating on me. How long has this been going on?'

Claire rolled her eyes. 'I was the only one above ground and Jerry never answers his phone. Besides, where in that dress are you keeping yours?'

'Still plugged into the wall in England,' Jerry said cheerfully, fishing the ugly iron key that he'd gotten from the statue out of his pocket. 'Not sure if this is gonna work m'lady, but I'll give it a shot,' he said, kneeling beside Lisa and reaching for the manacle on her leg. Reflexively she twitched her leg away, and then reluctantly allowed him to hold her ankle whilst he looked for the lock.

Distracted, Suze and Sarah examined the altar again, looking closely at the two small statues and doing their best to ignore the rotting bird carcass. One of the statues was immediately identifiable; Janus, the two-headed God of Doorways and New Year, always looking to both past and present. The second figure, however, was an enigma. It was male and there was a small bird perched on his shoulder, like a sparrow, so not the cockerel of Mercury. His hair was clipped short and neat in an early Roman style and he was clean shaven with a youthful face, ruling out most of the main deities of Rome.

'Claire, you're good with mythology. Who do you reckon this little guy is?' Sarah called trying to put some distance between Lisa and the girl she considered her immediate rival for Simon's affections. Nothing could be further from the truth of course, Simon was utterly devoted to Lisa, barely noticing in some situations that his companions were even female, let alone whether they were attractive. His friends weren't sure what Simon saw in her, but it was something strong enough that he'd so far almost drowned himself, and was scouring every inch of Rome looking for her.

'This key ain't gonna work,' Jerry pronounced, finding the mechanism on Lisa's leg iron. 'It's far too small for this hole.'

'Well fix it!' Lisa demanded. 'You can't leave me down here, Simon said you didn't have much time, right?'

Claire glanced up from scrutinising the smaller statue in the altar niche. 'I have no idea who this is, although based on the bird remains and what we know of the owner of the room it's possibly Remus?'

'A cult statue of Remus?' Suze asked, looking towards the exit. 'I think we should leave. If she has the eagle, the wings and a cult statue of Remus, we really need to go.'

165

'Suze, we can't leave Lisa down here,' Mell scolded, backed up by a banshee like shriek from the lady in question. 'Although perhaps we don't all have to stay, we don't want to all wind up trapped down here,' she was thinking aloud.

'Jerry, your key might fit here,' Sarah exclaimed spotting something else in the altar alcove.

'Did someone say something?' he muttered, ignoring her.

'Jerry, now is not the time,' Mell's voice was firm. 'See if your key fits over there, and then see if you can find a caretaker's cupboard or something upstairs, we could get the manacle off with a bolt cutter, or a hacksaw.'

'Who died and put you in charge?' Jerry was only mock offended. He moved closer to the altar and slipped the key into the lock, that Sarah pointed out. It turned with a soft click and the whole front of the altar popped, open revealing the silver eagle, complete, save for the wren on its back. And at its feet, the larger clunky iron key for Lisa's chains. Jerry reached for it as a dark shadow blocked the light from the room above. Messalina had returned.

XXVI

The air in the cellar seemed to drop several degrees as Messalina, clad in the diaphanous black robes of a priestess, descended the narrow steps, blocking the escape route. She glanced over the small group, huddled at the bottom of the stairs, with a critical eye and frowned, there was still no sign of the handsome Spaniard. That was a pity, she would very much have liked to resurrect Remus into that body. Ensuring that no one could force their way past her to escape, Messalina looked for the blonde girl. She stood behind the others, free of her chain, an expression of despair on her pretty face. Hoping that the antidote she had administered to the girl earlier had left enough of the poison in her system, Messalina snapped her fingers.

From behind the group of teens came a feral snarl. As one, the five turned to see yellow eyes glowing in the darkness. Lisa was still possessed by the poison in her system, and it was now obvious who the black robed figure in the museum had been, and that the poison injected into Lisa, via the wounds in her back, was a form of control, giving her the speed and strength of a wolf, but tying her to Messalina.

'Fight it Lisa, you can do it,' Mell grabbed the girl's shoulders, commanding her attention. 'Come on.'

A feminine gasp indicated that she was trying, but the guttural growl came again, her cold, yellow eyes focussed on the eagle where it lay in the crook of Suze's left arm. Lisa wasn't strong enough, she couldn't fight it, and as black lines began to creep up the side of her face, her lips pulled back in a snarl exposing teeth that were perfectly straight and white.

Suze felt a bubble of laughter rising in her chest and she smothered it with a wide grin. She was actually going to enjoy this. Tossing the eagle to Mell, she centred her weight and beckoned the possessed wolf-girl forward, roaring the universal battle cry of Manchester. 'Come an 'ave a go if yer think yer 'ard enough!'

Mell rolled her eyes at Suze's fight first ask questions later attitude and melted away into the shadows, desperate to get the eagle away from Messalina, as she spotted the silver wren in the Italian's hand.

Jerry went in the opposite direction and lunged forward, towards Messalina, his intention to keep her out of the basement. She retreated a step, waiting until he was off balance and slipped easily past him into the chaos of her subterranean temple.

*

Lisa, possessed with the speed of a wolf, leapt forwards, ragged remnants of her fake nails raking four lines into Suze's arm. Beads of blood welled up almost immediately and Suze jerked her elbow forward reflexively, catching Lisa in the chest. Almost immediately she found her legs swept out from beneath her, as Lisa floored her with a speed Suze would never have believed the girl possessed.

'Holy Hell,' Suze hissed through clenched teeth, she'd not expected to be floored by Simon's weak and pathetic girlfriend. Growling to herself, she regained her feet just in time to see Claire attempt a shot at Lisa. She failed spectacularly, missing her target and screaming in pain as Lisa shoved her against the wall.

*

'*Sugo! Ego appello tu!*' Descending into the basement Messalina began her summoning spell. She'd realised that there was no way she'd be able to hold the six teenagers long enough to complete the standard and perform the ritual. Instead she was hoping that by the time she'd completed the summoning spell she would have been able to acquire the eagle and complete the standard. '*Diabolis de nox...*'

Messalina was cut off mid flow as the tall boy raced from the shadows, hurling himself at her in the half-light. There was a thud as Messalina dropped the wren and the scrape of heavy furniture on stone as she fell heavily against the black draped table, disturbing the corpse intended for the resurrection, and almost breaking the makeshift altar. Unwilling to disturb the ritual she fought to keep her concentration as the tall boy tried to restrain her. '*Frater ad Romulus,*' she gasped out, groping inside her robes searching for her dagger.

*

Mell was slowly inching her way around the edge of the room, the eagle clutched in her hands. If she could get the standard out of the basement, then the words that Messalina was saying would be rendered meaningless.

She wished she had some idea of what Messalina was saying though. Mell had never studied Latin and of the words that she'd heard, she only understood Romulus. Which in itself, was confusing as the standard had belonged to Remus and she had thought that Messalina was attempting to raise Remus. Assuming, of course, that Mell wasn't completely wrong about the whole bizarre situation.

*

Sarah watched the scene through her fingers, unable to do anything else. Backlit by the electric light eking down the cellar steps from the room above, Jerry fought to keep Messalina away from the wren and the body on the table. With a cackle that sounded like it came from beyond time itself, the Italian dragged an evil looking dagger from her robes.

'Jerry look out!' Sarah screamed, the shriek ripped from her lungs without her even having the chance to think. She threw herself towards the battling pair as Messalina repeatedly slashed and stabbed at Jerry, mostly hitting air, as she continued to chant the words of her spell.

'*Custos de malus.*' There was a wet sounding thump, like meat dropped on a butcher's slab, and a grunted exhalation of air as one of Messalina's savage blows hit home.

'Jerry!' Sarah's scream of terror filled the stone lined room as he staggered backwards away from Messalina, fingers pressed against his collarbone.

'I think I've been stabbed,' he moaned in a thick voice. Sinking to his knees as Sarah arrived by his side, draping his uninjured arm across her shoulder. His head lolled against her, and he suddenly became a deadweight pulling her to the floor with him as he lost consciousness and collapsed.

*

Suze threw herself at Lisa again, no longer caring that she was Simon's girlfriend. She would not be bested by a blonde Barbie doll. Catching the half-human, half-wolf Lisa by surprise, Suze managed to tackle her to the floor. For the briefest of seconds Suze held the wolf-girl pinned beneath her, landing a vicious punch to her shoulder, and another to her chest, before Lisa, still in thrall to whatever possessed her, overpowered Suze and their positions reversed.

*

Mell pressed herself against the wall as Messalina strode towards her. She didn't want to give up the eagle but there seemed to be no way out of the basement, in skirting the edge of the room she'd gotten herself trapped in a corner.

169

Tightening her grip on the eagle, Mell tried to pull its wings free, but the fit was too snug. The standard may as well have been solid forged. She inched along the wall as best as she could, but Suze and Lisa were blocking her escape route.

'*Surgo, et capio tuus fatum a tu palla,*' Messalina continued her chant, her voice rising and falling in a rhythm, her eyes, slightly glazed, fixed on the silver eagle.

'Shit,' Mell hissed, there was nothing she could do as Messalina raised her bloodstained dagger. In a last effort, Mell hurled the eagle towards Messalina hoping that the weight would throw the deranged would-be priestess off balance, and that she'd be able to tackle Messalina and grab the wren before escaping.

The first part of her plan worked. The heavy eagle did throw Messalina off balance, but before Mell could follow through with the second part of her plan, she was floored from behind by Lisa. Suze had been too winded to warn her and so Messalina was holding the eagle and the wren as she finished her incantation.

*

The final piece of the silver standard slid into place as Messalina spoke the final words. '*Surgo surgo ille orbis exspecto tuus praesum,*' her ritual was complete. Noticing that all the teenagers were incapacitated, or at least not in a position to pose a threat, she snapped her fingers again, returning the blonde girl to normal.

No longer possessed Lisa dropped to the floor, gasping and coughing harshly. Messalina ignored her, stepping over her to the body which lay on the black draped table. She was worried that nothing was happening, perhaps the spell had required the standard to be whole throughout. She took a breath intending to begin her incantation again, then paused. The statues on her altar had changed. The one of Remus was bigger, and stood in the pose of an emperor, Janus had been replaced entirely by a twisted demon. The spell must have worked. She dropped her eyes to the body, no sign of life.

'You won't get away with this, whatever this is,' Lisa croaked, trying to stand, but discovering that it hurt too much. 'You might have six of us down here, but you don't have Simon, and he will never abandon me,' as she spoke, the other five were slowly trying to regroup. Suze inching towards Claire, with Sarah desperately trying to catch Mell's attention, as she struggled with Jerry's still unconscious deadweight.

Messalina fluffed her dark hair with one hand, leaving herself slightly off balance, carrying the standard in her other hand. 'How quaint. You think you understand what love is. Darling any fool can see that you do not care for him, he's just an accessory, believe me I know, you and I are the same. Men are a means to an end, they bring us gifts and we reward them with sex, so easily controlled. Besides, I left your famous boyfriend covered in blood for the *Carabinieri*,' she was cut off mid flow as Remus spoke.

'*Ubi sum?*'

Summoned from beyond the veils of time and re-born into the world, Remus, the forgotten twin, had risen. The teenagers stared in horror as the corpse sat up and fixed its bright-eyed stare on Messalina. '*Panam sacerdotem.*'

Messalina bowed her head. 'Master.'

Remus stood up, even in the stringy body which he was inhabiting he was imposing. Exuding a sense of menace, he surveyed the crowd of people in the darkened basement and waved a hand at Messalina's small statues. 'Kill all but the priestess,' he intoned. Flexing his regenerated power, as the two strange statues sprang to life.

'Master!' Messalina surprised everyone in the room with her next words. Laying a hand on Remus's arm and twisting a strand of her dark hair between her fingers she too surveyed the room. 'These ... slaves, are the ones that found your standard's wings. They may be of use to you later.'

Remus huffed, but held up a hand, stopping his own order as he contemplated her words. After a pause that seemed to stretch into eternity he nodded. 'Bind the slaves,' he ordered. 'Then back to your miserable stone lives.' The living statues leapt to action, conjuring bindings from the air and deftly bound the teenagers, using iron rings set in the floor to secure their quarry.

'Wait,' Remus bellowed, as the thing that had once been a statue of Janus made to bind Lisa. 'Not that one, she has an attractiveness,' he turned to Messalina. 'Bring her, she will be of use when I acquire my own body.'

A deep frown creased Messalina's brow as she hauled Lisa to her feet. The girl was weak, barely able to stand and Messalina was forced to half drag her up the basement steps as the trio left, to unleash whatever madness Remus intended upon the world.

XXVII

Exhausted, heart pounding and barely able to stand, having sprinted across Rome, Simon darted back into the hotel, and slumped on the bottom step of the marble staircase in the deserted lobby. The lights still blazed but the wide reception desk stood empty as he caught his breath, before rising and quietly creeping around the desk towards the private quarters beyond. The door stood slightly ajar and from beyond he could hear the distant sound of a woman's voice. The words were unintelligible but the intonation was unmistakable. A triumphant summoning, the words of someone who knows they have power within their grasp. He'd heard a similar speech over the summer, given by the deranged archaeologist, Dr Lee, on the shore of the hidden lake.

Confining the disturbing memory to the recesses of his mind, Simon quietly eased the door open and stepped through into Messalina's private sanctuary. '*¡Caray!*' he breathed catching sight of the lewd décor. The whole room was decked out like a Pompeiian brothel. He stared for a moment and then with a curse, ducked back into the reception. 'Prop Loose, Hooker, Prop Tight, two Locks, two Flankers, Number Eight, Scrum Half,' he leaned against the wall and drummed his fingers on the doorframe. 'Fly Half, Left Wing, Inside Centre, Outside Centre, Right Wing, Full Back,' he glanced back at the room, swore again and repeated the rugby field positions in Greek, his least fluent language. Being a sleep deprived, hormone charged teenager was an irritation that he would be glad to grow out of.

Re-entering the room and deliberately avoiding the wall décor Simon noticed a square hole in the floor near the large patio doors, the voice came from below. He crept closer, treading carefully on the glossy paving slabs, desperate not to make a sound, and froze when a deep masculine voice sounded from below. Remus had risen, he was too late.

Instinct taking over he dived behind one of the plush sofas, wedging himself between it and the wall, praying not to sneeze, as footsteps ascended the stairs from the basement, and he finally caught some of what was being said.

'… can only apologise for the state of the body you have to inhabit, I had planned a better one, young, strong. But it has proven difficult to obtain.' That was the hotel owner, Messalina, confirming his identification of her at the museum. 'This girl is useless now, we no longer need the wolf, we should leave her with the others.'

'No,' a thick oily male voice, it could only belong to Remus. 'I like the girl, I have plans for her …'

With a high pitched shriek a third figure crashed against the sofa behind which he was hidden. Simon tensed his shoulders, trying not to make a sound as the chair shifted and the girl that had fallen against it, slumped down beside the wall. Her head lolled to the side and suddenly Simon found himself staring straight into Lisa's face, her blue eyes widening in shock as she recognised him.

Simon gestured at her to be silent, holding his left hand slightly up and pressing a finger against his lips as he gazed at her tear streaked face. Spotting him, Lisa had frozen and he wasn't sure if she would cry out, but then she steadied and giving a barely perceptible nod, the ghost of a smile graced her lips.

Messalina, still arguing with Remus, said something about her wolf, and Lisa's eyes flickered from her natural blue to the cunning yellow wolf eyes and blinked immediately back to blue again. Simon tensed and held his breath, the wolf would surely give him away. But the moment passed, it appeared that Lisa had managed to fight it this time. With a furtive glance at the arguing couple, Lisa snaked her hand behind the sofa, her fingers brushing against Simon's knee at the extent of her reach. Simon responded, stretching as far as he dared to without moving, and tangled his fingers briefly with hers. Keeping his eyes fixed on her face, he mouthed the words, 'I will find you,' and squeezed her hand gently, relishing the feel of her cool, soft skin. She dropped his hand quickly and her gaze snapped upward, as Messalina came towards her.

As Lisa struggled quickly to her feet, desperate to keep Messalina and Remus from noticing the hidden intruder, Simon wedged himself further under the sofa and waited, holding his breath, expecting to be discovered at any moment. But his luck held and the three of them left the room. Messalina still insisting that Lisa was now superfluous to requirement.

Once certain that they were gone, he exhaled loudly and awkwardly emerged, dust covered, from his hiding place. The trap door to the cellar had been closed, his friends were trapped below and Lisa was still under the control of Messalina, and now Remus, and headed for god only knew where. At least he knew where the trap door had been. It was simply a case of finding the handle.

He stepped over to the patio doors, recalling the position of the trapdoor. The floor was smooth; so there was no ring pull or handle on the door itself, there had to be another mechanism. Massaging his temples and trying not to look too closely at the details, he surveyed the room again. Graphic scenes from the brothel of Pompeii and new, nude, neoclassical statues, appeared to be the only decoration. No levered bookshelves here, the handle or switch must be well hidden. He turned to examine the wall beside him, reasoning that the lever had to be close to the mechanism, and spotted a recent addition to the room's décor.

'Jerry,' Simon actually laughed. Only Jerry could have made the location of the lever so obvious. On the face of an outrageously well-equipped satyr, he had inked in a handlebar moustache. 'Guess the lever is this fellow then,' Simon trailed off, spotting exactly how the lever worked. Jerry was apparently not the only one with a juvenile sense of humour.

XXVIII

'What do you think Remus will do?' Claire said, just seconds after the cellar door closed sealing them into the heavy darkness. It was the first any of them had spoken since Remus had risen and demanded their deaths. Strangely, they had been saved by Messalina. She'd deemed the teenagers as potentially useful in the future, either for their knowledge, or as a way of luring in the younger body she still desired for Remus to possess. However, whilst not dead, their situation was far from ideal. Secured to iron rings in the floor of the room, they were powerless to help each other. And worse, they'd managed to lose Simon's girlfriend. Again.

'Whatever he likes I suppose,' Mell replied eventually, her mind turning the situation over, looking for anything she could have done differently. Remus and Messalina had taken Lisa, and Simon was still missing. Her attempt at leadership appeared to have only made things worse.

'If he manages to somehow defeat Romulus in the past everything will change,' Suze said morosely. She wasn't sure if her eyes were open or closed, the room was so dark. 'Imagine a Reman Empire? No Caesar, no Hadrian, maybe no Romans in Britain, an extended prehistory until the Saxons turn up … if the Saxons turn up.'

'Hold on, surely if the Roman Empire changed, even just a little bit, the ensuing changes throughout history would be so catastrophic that none of us would be here. Yet here we are. So perhaps things can still be saved?' said Sarah.

'If a spell woke him up, perhaps a spell can put him down,' said Mell, thinking furiously. 'There must be something else in this room we can use to take Remus down.'

'Who cares about Remus? Is it really going to change anything? Let him do what he likes,' Jerry groaned, from the corner of the room. 'I'm far more interested in what's going on in Suze's head. The way you smiled at the chance to take out darling Lisa. Jealous much?'

'Shut up Jerry,' she replied a little defensively.

'Ooooh touchy,' Jerry laughed, then gasped in pain, and hissed through his teeth before continuing. 'How is the hideously inappropriate crush on Simon going? Must be hellish having his adored blonde princess around?'

'Just because she's a nightmare doesn't mean I fancy Simon,' Suze shot back, feeling the heat rise to her face and grateful for the pitch darkness of their prison. 'No one gets on with her.'

'Awww Suze. You got the hots for him so bad,' Jerry laughed in the darkness and hissed in pain again.

'Will you shut up,' Sarah yelled. 'Stop teasing her, she clearly doesn't like it.'

'No one asked you,' Jerry said stonewalling her. 'I've been stabbed here and I need to take my mind off how much it freaking hurts.'

'By tormenting Suze?' asked Mell, they could practically hear her eyes roll in the dark. 'I know Simon's good looking but he's our friend, no one has a crush on him.'

'Speak for yourself,' Claire replied from somewhere close by. 'I wouldn't say no if I had the chance. The man is hot.' The emphasis on the final word was enough that all of them knew that if her hands weren't bound, Claire would be fanning herself to illustrate exactly how hot she thought he was.

'Y'see?' Jerry had to be grinning in the darkness, the girls could picture his gleeful smirk as he spoke. 'Little Suze there, has a monstrous crush on our Spanish friend with the talented tongue…'

Claire snorted with laughter in the darkness.

'What d'ya know, Claire's the one with a filthy mind,' Jerry mused. 'I meant he was good at languages.'

'This isn't helping us get out of here,' Suze said trying to change the subject, glad of the lack of light so that the others couldn't see the intense shade of scarlet colouring her face. She was so glad that Simon couldn't hear Jerry's insinuations. They were totally false of course, she had no interest in Simon. She just had a horrible habit of flushing bright red when she was in the spotlight and would hate for her attractive Spanish friend to take her blushes the wrong way. She began trying to cut her bonds by rubbing the binding against the metal ring, it was going to take a long time.

'How rich do you think he is?' Jerry asked no one in particular.

'Well his father has just been knighted and is now inside the top hundred wealthiest people on the planet,' Claire said. 'Not that I've been stalking him, or anything, I just read a few things online about Sir John and …' she trailed off, realising that she'd probably already said too much. Admitting to several hours of reading up on Simon's famous father would certainly brand her a stalker.

'That's his father, not him,' Mell retorted. 'I doubt Simon has much personal wealth at all, he is stupidly proud of having bought that bloody crappy Ford Escort he drives.'

'Melody, Melody, Melody,' Jerry shook his head and Suze realised, with a jolt that she could see him. The cellar was somehow lighter. 'Pretending to be poor is what rich guys do,' Jerry continued. 'If he paraded around wearing Armani and driving a Ferrari we'd hate him.'

'He was wearing an Armani suit yesterday morning, bespoke Armani,' Sarah cut in. 'Or was it this morning? I don't even know what day it is.'

'Do you think Simon will even come back?' Suze asked quietly, realising as she did, that she could see a lot more. The others continued their debate, oblivious.

'Depends whether he knows we're here or not I guess,' Mell replied looking up at the ceiling. 'Or whether he saw Remus and Messalina leave with Lisa. He may have gone straight after her if he did. He was so desperate to find her earlier that he wouldn't wait for us.'

'He really does love the stuck-up little snob, doesn't he?' Claire interrupted, a fierce scowl on her face.

'Only because she's hot,' Jerry deadpanned. 'Frankly personality wise I think he can do better. But he needs to date someone attractive, and for that she's perfect. You need a cold shower just looking at her. But we were debating how rich he is.'

'You were debating how rich he is,' Suze shot back trying to figure out if her eyes were adjusting to the darkness, or if there was a light source somewhere. 'The rest of us were contemplating escape.' She glanced up towards the cellar entrance catching shadowy movement in the corner of her vision.

'I bet they have a massive house in Spain, something with, like, sixteen bedrooms for no real reason,' Jerry, taking his mind off the pain in his shoulder, had warmed to his theme and showed no sign of slowing down. 'There will be sports cars, Si may drive that pile of rust but he does like a fast car. Bet there is at least one out there, left hand drive, soft top speedster. Ooooh maybe a speedboat, Barcelona is on the coast, right?'

'Valencia,' Suze corrected, eyes on the floor, still desperately trying to friction fray her way out of her bonds.

'What exactly do the five of you think I do all day when I am not with you? Take baths in molten gold and dissolve pearls in Champagne?' Simon's softly accented voice came from the stairs, where he stood silhouetted in the light that spilled through the open trap door. No one had heard it open, and so had no idea how much he had heard.

'Simon!' Claire shrieked with evident relief.

'How long have you been stood there?' Mell asked warily, noting Simon's dishevelled appearance.

'Long enough,' he replied. Descending into the basement before stopping at the base of the stairs, folding his arms and sweeping a critical eye over his friends. 'Long enough to know that the five of you do not appreciate my car, cannot stand my girlfriend, Jerry still has no idea where I come from, Claire obsessively checks how well off I am, and Sir John made it into the Forbes top hundred. Which I was unaware of.' He sank down on the bottom step and raked his hands through his hair. Dried flakes of Romulinus's blood puffed into the air and he shuddered, choosing to look at the wall rather than any of his friends. Across the room, Suze breathed a quiet sigh of relief, it seemed that he'd not heard any of Jerry's implications about her feelings.

'Did you see them?' Mell asked softly.

'*Sí*,' he replied with a sigh. 'I could never have taken Remus out alone, I had to let Lisa go…' he trailed off, dropping his gaze to the floor.

'Simon I'm sorry, we tried to keep her with us,' Suze said sympathetically.

'Don't act all heroic Suze, you threw a punch at her the first chance you got,' Claire said.

Simon glanced at the floor, then rising, hands behind his back, walked with a calculated slowness over to where Suze sat, bound to one of the iron rings. Keeping his movements slow and deliberate, he crouched in front of her and fixed his dark eyes on her face. 'Is that true?'

Unwilling to let him know how much he intimidated her, Suze shrugged awkwardly. 'Yeah,' she glanced up intending to meet his eyes with her own defiant stare, but instantly pinned her viewpoint back to the floor, cowed by his steady imperious glare. Like the statue of Julius Caesar, Simon's eyes seemed to look down and through her, even though their faces were level. 'Self-defence, she was a wolf,' Suze mumbled, shifting uncomfortably.

Simon rose and shaking his head began pacing the room. 'Suze…'

'Hey, Claire hit her with a sword in the Colosseum!' she replied aggressively. Now that he was no longer in her space, those eyes were no longer daring her to defy him, she felt able to speak up.

Simon sighed in defeat and leaned on the wall, folding his arms defensively across his chest and addressing the group. 'You really do not like her, do you?'

Sarah hurried to correct him and somehow made it worse. 'It's not that we don't like her, more that we hate the way she looks at us like we're servants and that you change so much when she's around.'

'Yeah, she turns you into a real stuck-up, snobby, arrogant, money flashing, posh, foreign bastard,' Jerry added, wincing as a stab of pain flared through his shoulder when he shrugged.

'Jesus Jerry, don't hold back, say what you really think,' Mell said sarcastically. Seeing the hurt look that flitted briefly across Simon's face, replaced so quickly with a veneer of indifference, that she was left uncertain as to whether she'd really seen anything.

'This is what I was afraid of,' he admitted, his Spanish accent stronger in defence and strangely emphasised in the dark small chamber. 'I knew Lisa would be,' he paused, 'difficult, and I had hoped that she would never have cause to cross paths with you. But…' his face showed the signs of an internal struggle as he worked out what to say. 'This is me, it is who I have to be. What I must be. It's how Lisa knows me. I could never be so informal with her as I am with the five of you.'

'So, you're faking it for us? How flattering,' said Jerry, fiddling with his bonds. 'The little rich boy likes to play in the dirt with the commoners sometimes.'

'No! Nothing like that,' Simon ardently denied it.

'Faking it with her then? Simon, that's not right,' Claire scolded. 'She of all people should know the real you.'

Frustrated, Simon paced the room as he spoke. 'I do not change so much, I simply behave a little differently as the decorum of the situation and the company in question demands. Lisa is a titled heiress. I am, at best faded Spanish nobility, at worst the son of a jumped up English salesman, she should not have even looked at me. Her father allows our relationship because I at least have the manners of the imperial Spanish court and my Spanish lineage is …' he cut himself off as if he'd started something he didn't want to finish, and made a show of retrieving his wet jacket from the floor.

'Oh, the upper echelons,' groaned Jerry sarcastically. 'Pity me, my girlfriend's father is richer than mine. Boo-hoo.'

'Guys give him a break,' Suze said, trying to win herself some brownie points. 'He has two roles to play, socialite Simon and chilled out Simon.' She glanced up at him, 'what was it you said over summer? The upper-class mask of indifference? You are phenomenally, irritatingly good at acting like you belong in a regency king's court, a brainless fop with more money than sense.' She turned her attention to the others. 'Lucky for us, we get to hang out with the best version of him.'

Simon stared at her. 'Not sure if that is supposed to be a compliment or an insult Suze,' he sighed, and tossed his ruined jacket into a corner, sliding a small box that he'd retrieved from it into a trouser pocket.

'True, we may get to hang out with the more fun version,' said Mell softly. 'But Simon, sooner or later you are going to have to choose which of your two personalities is the real you. All that acting must be tiring. Anyway, can you cut me loose, Jerry was stabbed, although I suspect not as badly as he made out.' For a brief second, it looked as though Simon may refuse, then wordlessly he reached for the ceremonial dagger that Messalina had left on her altar.

'Tis a mortal wound wench,' Jerry intoned in a deep voice, slumping against the wall as Simon cut them both free.

'Shut up and take your shirt off,' Mell demanded, reaching for the first aid pack at her waist, whilst Simon moved on to cut the others free.

A dopey grin spread across Jerry's face. 'Yes ma'am,' he obligingly pulled his shirt off. Grimacing as the blood-soaked fabric pulled away from his skin, then flinched as Mell's cold fingers touched him. 'Jesus Mell! Bedside manner, warn me if you've got icicles for fingers.'

'Sorry' she muttered absently, staring intently at the small neat cut from which blood still oozed, although slowly now, it was congealing. The light in the cellar was poor, the only illumination coming from the trapdoor which Simon had left open, but from what she could see, Jerry was fine.

'What's the verdict then Doc?' asked Claire, laying a hand on Mell's shoulder, 'Is he gonna live?'

Mell gave an exaggerated sigh. 'Unfortunately yes, it's barely a scratch, not only will Jerry live to continue annoying us with his sarcasm, poor wit and silly songs, but he will be totally and utterly unscathed by the ordeal.'

'Booya!' said Jerry getting to his feet and proceeding to dance around the small chamber, singing his triumph. 'Jerry is so awesome, Jerry is so awesome, he's so indestructible, Jerry is so awesome.'

Suze glanced involuntarily at the scar in her left arm. Even after a few months it was a raised ridge of skin, red and silky to the touch. Absently she raised her fingers to it and caught Simon watching. He raised an eyebrow and gave her a knowing smile. He had a matching scar on the inside of his right thigh, courtesy of the same blade.

With nothing more to be gained from staying in the basement the six teenagers trooped up the stairs, through Messalina's pleasure room. Stumbling out of the reception, they hurried upstairs to their rooms to regroup, grab supplies and consider their next move. Where in Rome would Remus have headed, and what was Messalina planning?

Through the open balcony doors, they could hear wind screaming through the *piazza*, funnelled by the narrow streets. 'Hey guys?' yelled Jerry. 'The big domed building has gone,' he glanced across the skyline and waved an arm towards his object of interest. 'But the Colosseum still stands, at least I think it does, it's kinda hard to tell.'

'Praise Allah,' muttered Simon, looking further into the city in another direction.

Suze looked at him suspiciously. 'Thought you were Catholic.'

'Apparently not,' he replied, indicating the visible dome of St. Peter's basilica. Above which, the symbol of the crescent moon glittered in the glow of the city lights. The past was changing.

XXIX

Remus reappearance in Rome had changed things. The Pantheon, the temple to all Roman gods, was missing from the *piazza* below their balcony, and if that was missing then anything could have changed out there. Simon checked his watch, and groaned, it was almost three a.m., nearly twelve hours since Lisa had been poisoned in the museum. The *piazza* below was deserted, although the lights still illuminated the Roman skyline. Glancing down he noticed the dark blood stains on his clothes and sighed. Romulinus had left him with two strange Latin phrases, and he had nothing else to go on.

'You need to sleep,' said Mell gently taking his arm. 'The rest of us managed to get a little downtime whilst Tiberius was watching Messalina. We couldn't search her room until she left, and we thought finding Lisa was more important than tracking down the tomb of Remus.'

It took longer to sink in to his head than it should have done, and Mell had managed to walk him, trance-like, almost all the way to his bed before he shook her hand off. 'Why would we need to track down the tomb of Remus?' his tone was somewhat more aggressive than intended and Mell took a step back, hands on her hips fixing him with her own Medusa-esque stare.

'Sleep. We'll talk when your brain works. Suze is right, you're faster than Google, but you have to be functioning.'

'I am not a bloody robot Mell,' he replied. 'Sleep is important, but not as important as finding Lisa. Besides I,' he gave a half laugh and pinched the bridge of his nose. 'I crashed out in the street by the museum,' he waved away Mell's obvious question and rubbed his eyes with the thumb and middle finger of his left hand before pinching the bridge of his nose again. 'Just get me some coffee, I will be fine. And can someone please explain why we need to find the tomb of Remus?'

'Tiberius mentioned it. He said someone called Meredius, stole the standard of Romulus and may have buried it with Remus,' said Suze, appearing as if by magic with a huge mug of black coffee. Ignoring Mell's angry scowl, she passed it to Simon. 'Figured you might need some fuel,' she grinned.

'Next question,' said Simon, rewarding Suze with a tired smile. 'Where is Tiberius?' Suze shrugged, she didn't know, no one had seen the little ghost since he'd told them Messalina had left, and that he had a mission of his own to do. There was no sign of him in any of the rooms. 'Great. Well, according to Plutarch, Remus was buried on the Aventine.'

'That's what I said,' Suze replied. 'But Tiberius said he'd been moved, that he must always lie outside the city.'

'And a whole legion was lost last time they moved him,' Jerry chipped in. 'So we need to find a missing legion.'

Simon shook his head. 'The missing legion is irrelevant, legions went missing all the time. And barely any of them are missing where people think they are missing, the famous Ninth Hispana for instance, will never be found in Scotland.' With a sigh of frustration, he ventured back out onto the balcony to drink his coffee and think, alone, away from the distraction of his friends.

'Claire, you just did that online course on mythology,' Sarah said, clutching at an idea. 'Do you know anything else about the story of the twins that could help us?'

'Well, Roman mythology is boring but, according to the standard legend, the genealogy of Julius Caesar runs back to the twins, Romulus obviously; through them to Aeneas and finally to the divine ancestry of Venus. Which made Caesar essentially a demi-god, and immediate descendent of the founder of Rome. Whether you believed in the Aeneid, or the twins and the wolf as a foundation myth,' Claire said. Shooting an anxious look towards the balcony as if expecting Simon to correct her. But he remained silent, leaning on the doorframe, staring at the changing cityscape, so she continued. 'Clearly, we are dealing with the wolf version of the myth, as Lisa is possessed by something wolfish.'

'Venus is the naked chick, right?' Jerry's voice broke the sombre mood. He was lolling on one of the sofas pretending to play guitar again, and although his question was directed at Claire, he still plucked at imaginary strings as he spoke. 'Goddess of Love, sex and all that crap?'

'That's her,' Claire replied, running her fingers through her green hair and wondering at his cynicism.

'So presumably she got around a bit?' Jerry, dropped his imaginary guitar and sat up, leaning back on the sofa resting his feet on the coffee table.

'Jerry are you calling the Goddess of Love a whore?' said Mell with a slow smile. 'And get your feet off the table,' she hissed, slapping at one trainer clad foot.

'More of an exhibitionist, but yeah,' he agreed, moving to lean his elbows on his knees. 'Who's the father?'

'Father of who?' asked Claire reaching for the coffee pot, and struggling to follow Jerry's mad thought train. 'Of Romulus and Remus? Mars is their father.'

'Interesting,' Jerry stroked his chin, miming deep thought. 'The God of War got it on with the Goddess of Love? Good for him,' he grinned.

'Mars was her preferred lover, but Venus isn't the mother of the twins. She is the mother of Aeneas, who is the grandfather of the twins,' Claire replied. Trying to straighten him out, and glancing towards the balcony door, wishing that Simon would step in with his greater knowledge base.

'So, wait, who is the mother of the twins?' Suze asked, frowning as she tried to follow the thread of Jerry's questions and Claire's reasoned replies.

'A Vestal Virgin by the name of Rea Silva, daughter of Aeneas,' Claire replied. Checking her phone for confirmation, when it was clear that Simon wouldn't be helping her out. Stood out on the balcony he was either content to simply listen, or wasn't paying any attention to the conversation within the room, lost in his own thoughts staring out at the city.

'Hold on,' Sarah said, sketching lines on the back of an envelope. 'The twins relate to both Venus and Mars?' She carefully expanded her lines, trying to sketch out a family tree for the founders of Rome.

'Yes, but I can't see how it matters,' Claire cried in exasperation. 'Venus was apparently married to Vulcan, and Mars to Nerio, but there were hundreds of temples and shrines to them all.'

'Vulcan is one of the most ancient gods of Rome.' Mell said, eyes on her phone, scanning the internet. 'Apparently one of the founding kings, Titus Tatius, dedicated a temple to him at the foot of the Capitoline in the eighth century BC. At least he did according to Google.'

'*Le Gemina é con Vulca., Aquilae es clavis,*' Simon's accented voice came from the balcony, halting the conversation within the room. 'The Gemina is with Vulcan, the eagle is the key,' he strode back into the room. 'Vulcan, the blacksmith was technically more important to Rome than mighty Jupiter, because it is the geology of Rome which brought her success ...' he trailed off. 'I need a map.' He threw open the door and seconds later the others heard his footsteps pounding down the stairs.

With no more than a glance at one another, the others abandoned the room and hurtled down the stairs after Simon, unwilling to let him disappear off on his own again. Together they skidded into the lobby, but Simon was nowhere in sight.

'Where the hell did he go?' hissed Jerry heading for the door to the street.

'This way,' Sarah called, spotting him in Messalina's brothel room. Swallowing her discomfort, and determined not to look at the walls, she followed him in. The others close on her heels.

'Simon, I don't follow your thinking,' said Claire, watching him rummage through Messalina's bookshelves. 'Vulcan has nothing to do with the foundation myth.'

'Not the mythology no, but everything to do with the reality,' Simon replied, dragging a large map from the shelf and unfolding it across the polished coffee table. 'Everyone knows that Rome is seven hills and the valley,' he paused glancing at the group for confirmation that they understood. 'The seven hills of Rome are not the only ones. Here,' he jabbed at a point on the map to the south-east of the sprawling city. 'The Alban Hills, like Rome herself are...' he snapped his fingers and stepped back from the table, a frown on his handsome face.

'Are what?' Sarah asked softly, turning the map so that she could see better.

Staring down at the map, Simon snapped the fingers of his left hand repeatedly and pinched the bridge of his nose with his right. He cleared his throat and paced the room twice before coming back to look at the map again, still insistently snapping his fingers. 'Well this is embarrassing,' he groaned, covering his eyes with his right hand.

Jerry laughed. 'He's forgot the word. Oh, that's funny, that is proper funny.'

'Is that it?' Mell asked in disbelief, catching Simon's eye. 'Have you forgotten the English word you need?' she tried, and failed to keep the amusement from her voice.

'It is not a regular occurrence,' Simon replied defensively, a slow flush beginning to creep over his face. He shook his head. 'I hardly ever...'

'It doesn't matter,' Claire said smiling broadly. 'Jerry's right, it is kinda funny. We've never seen you stuck before.'

Seeing that his friends found it amusing, Simon allowed a half-hearted smile to grace his face. 'Lisa cannot stand it if I mislay an English word, she finds it mortifying to be associated with me on the odd occasion that it happens. Needless to say, Sir John also disapproves.'

'Why on earth should they be upset by it?' Suze said, incensed on his behalf. 'It's not like English is your first language. I bet Lisa doesn't even speak Spanish.'

'Lisa's Spanish is exceptional,' Simon replied, automatically leaping to his girlfriend's defence. 'Although,' he relented, 'her pronunciation can be a little off centre.'

'What were you trying to say, perhaps we can work it out,' Mell offered, trying to alleviate Simon's obvious discomfort.

'It was Claire's mention of Vulcan. Rome is built on tufa, *volcánico* rock, the mountains are *Volcanes*,' he replied, tracing the leftward slant of his nose.

'Volcanic,' Sarah said, understanding immediately. 'Rome is built on volcanic planes, and the Alban Mountains are the closest volcanic range to the city.'

'Volcanic?' Simon shook his head and raked a hand through his hair again. 'The words are practically the same, that is an unforgivable mistake.'

'You're tired Simon. Mistakes happen,' said Mell, giving his shoulder a squeeze, 'Why are volcanic mountains important?'

'Vulcan was important to the founders of Rome; the city is built on volcanic rock and it is that volcanic rock that allowed the creation of concrete. Romulus is credited with having a close relationship with Vulcan. Romulinus, the old man from the museum mentioned Vulcan too. He said "The Gemina is with Vulcan". I had no idea what he meant, but,' Simon looked up and smiled in Claire's direction. 'Claire is right, the blacksmith of the gods was married to Venus, who loved Mars, the twins are sons of Mars. Is it not possible that Vulcan should play host to the tomb of the son of his wife's lover?' Simon laid out his theory.

'That is very convoluted Simon,' Mell said, raising an eyebrow and shaking her head. 'Tenuous at best. Are you really putting your trust in the ravings of an old, possibly ill, Italian man?'

Simon dragged his hands down his face. 'A dead old man. He got me into the museum, we were both after the wren,' he dug a silver feather out of his pocket. 'We surprised Messalina in the curator's office, and she killed him. Actually, she seemed to think this was the second time she had killed him. Perhaps they were once in the same club. He gave me this, and said "the eagle is the key" and "The

Gemina is with Vulcan." Then he died.' There was a pause as Simon seemed to realise he was still covered in the old man's blood. He shook his head. 'I should change my shirt.

'Question,' said Jerry raising his hand like a child in class and waiting until he had everyone's attention. 'Are we serious that the idea of the one sensible genius among us is to drive out to the middle of nowhere and hope for the best?' He shrugged, 'I'm in.'

Simon elaborated. 'It is not completely the middle of nowhere. The dominant peak, Monte Cavo, was home to a sanctuary of Jupiter and was where the consuls came during the republican period, when awarded a triumph. As far as I know the temple is gone but the roads, the *Via Appia* and *Via Triumphalis* still exist,' he traced a finger down one of the roads marked on the map. 'Perhaps the tomb of Remus is out there too and we can destroy what remains of him, or find the other eagle,' he left the room, throwing his last words back over his shoulder. 'We need transport.'

XXX

Whilst Simon vanished off upstairs, strangely followed by Claire, who insisted that she also wanted to change, Suze shoved open the patio doors at the back of Messalina's erotica room and stepped out into the private land behind the hotel. She moved forward slowly, heading for a gate that would let her out into the alley behind the building and its private yard. As she reached for the gate latch she paused, the air felt different, full of electricity. A static shock burned her fingers as she flipped the latch and stepped into the passageway. As she massaged her fingertips a movement at the end of the alley caught her eye, she blinked and squinted into the dingy gloom of the early morning, then shook her head, there was no way she had just seen a man in a toga cross the end of the narrow street.

'Is it just me, or does it feel like time is holding its breath?' Jerry's voice was unexpected in the darkness and Suze jumped as his tall shadow followed her out of the gate.

She shook her head. 'It's not holding its breath Jerry; did you see the dome of St. Peter's earlier? The Vatican's a mosque.'

'So, maybe the Hagia Sophia is still a church, big deal,' Jerry replied with a shrug. 'Besides I doubt it's called St. Peter's any more, what if it's St. Judas's and they all worship a woman called Mary who brought down this nightmare of a bloke called Jesus?'

Suze stared at him and shrugged. 'Jerry everything could change, may have already changed. Our families, hell us, may not even exist in a future where Remus is the past. Did you never watch Doctor Who? You can't mess with the fixed points of time.'

'Well something happened,' Jerry said. 'Did you look at the skyline earlier, I mean really look, as hard as Simon did. It was obvious that the Pantheon was missing, and that St. Peter's had changed but did you notice the other two really striking things missing?' Suze stared blankly back at him. 'Figured, come on,' Jerry grabbed her hand and dragged her up the fire escape at the back of the building. 'There look, the Castel St. Angelo, Hadrian's tomb, it's missing.' He dragged a small pair of "borrowed" binoculars from his back pocket and passed them to her, the embossed SJM initials on the side glinting in the glow of a street light.

Suze laughed, giving Jerry a knowing look and, shaking her head, raised the glasses to her eyes, sighting first on the Vatican, then traversing the landscape to the end of the bridge where the round structure of the papal arsenal, the Castel St. Angelo, should be. 'Definitely gone,' she agreed, sweeping her gaze over the rest of Rome. 'Trajan's column too I think, and the Colosseum was still there earlier, and the forum… at least a version of it, so some things haven't changed. It looks like only Trajan and Hadrian's stuff is gone, why them?

'Goodbye Spanish Emperors,' said Jerry waving his hand at the sky, 'don't look at me like that, I know stuff. Not as much as Simon. I'm still working on the idea that he's a cyborg sent from the future.'

'If you know so much stuff, how come you're always acting the idiot?' Suze said, regarding the tall Welshman with a sceptical look.

'Better to be thought the fool, than be proved one,' he replied, deliberately mangling the famous quote. 'Middle child syndrome, well second of eight,' he shrugged and began counting his fingers. 'How many stepsisters do I have?' Without waiting for a reply, he began backtracking down the fire escape. 'Hey look, mopeds.'

Following him, Suze spotted what he'd seen. Three Vespas, relatively modern ones, sat just inside a car port, clearly belonging to the hotel. Once on the ground again they headed over, reaching the red, white and green scooters just as Mell and Sarah wandered out to meet them.

'Awesome!' Suze breathed, inching closer to check the tyres, lights and other moving parts. Suze loved bikes, she'd "borrowed" her brother's several times over the summer, only dropping it once. Andy had not been amused, he'd chased his little sister round the garden with a bit of wood, making her do push ups until she collapsed, before he banned her from ever touching it again.

'Scooters?' said Sarah, her face breaking into an amused smile. 'You're not serious are you Suze? I mean, I'm up for it, but you will never get Simon on one. I think he'd rather walk to the Alban Mountains than get on a scooter.'

Suze ignored Sarah, she'd spotted the keys dangling tantalisingly from the red Vespa's ignition. 'Thanks be to whomever the Roman God of Keys is,' Suze muttered. 'Now if the Roman God of Petrol and Two-stroke is willing…' she squeezed the front brake and, giving the throttle a little twist, turned the key. The Vespa coughed, spluttered, almost stalled and then idled peacefully into life; a supercharged hairdryer, buzzing like an angry hornet. Perfect.

'Coolio!' said Jerry, 'I call dibs on the green one.' He threw a leg over the seat and laughed realising how stupid someone his height was going to look riding it with his knees above his elbows. 'So, we have to scoot through Rome to an ancient volcano to stop a crazy nutjob changing history? This is gonna be all kinds'a epic!' he revved the engine.

'You know Sarah, sometimes I genuinely wonder how Jerry is still alive,' said Mell folding her arms and staring at him. 'What exactly did you guys have to do in Dover?'

'Oh, believe me, alone he would have lost his head,' Sarah sighed, as Simon joined them, sporting a clean white polo shirt. He'd changed his jeans too and his hair looked damp, suggesting that he'd tried rinsing the crispy blood flakes away.

He took one look at Suze and Jerry sat astride two of the Vespas and took a step back, eyeing the buzzing two wheelers with a mixture of apprehension and revulsion. 'Oh no, no way. If you think for one moment that I am riding one of those death traps you are very much mistaken.'

'Do they all work?' asked Mell, reaching for the handlebars of the white one.

'Seem to,' Suze replied, grinning excitedly, bikes and Romans were two of her most favourite things. 'They're easy as anything to ride, twist the throttle and go. Brakes are like a bicycle. Easy peasy.' She threw the little bike around in a tight U-turn to prove her point.

'There is no way on earth I am riding that!' Claire screeched, finally joining everyone. She'd changed into more figure hugging clothes than usual and her normally straight hair was freshly curled, reeking of hairspray, but still green. Mell shot her a curious glance, before exchanging an exasperated look with Sarah as they both wondered what she was up to now. Surely, she wasn't thinking of flirting with Simon again.

'Dearest sweet damsel, wilt thou not climbest on mine humble steed?' Jerry grinned, clasping one hand to his chest and offering Claire the other, in the overly dramatic fashion he usually reserved for Sarah. 'His name is Scootius Minimmus Speedius,' he patted the Vespa's metal frame as if it were a horse.

Claire giggled, unused to being the object of Jerry's faux knightly affection, and with an elegance imitating Lisa, slipped her hand demurely into his. 'Noble sir, you flatter me. Perhaps I could take a ride,' she slipped easily onto the pillion seat, wrapping her arms around Jerry's chest.

'Come on Sarah, you can ride with me,' Mell said quietly, spotting the hurt look on the other girl's face as Jerry continued his knightly courtship of Claire. 'I'll drive if you navigate?'

Sarah nodded, unable to speak. It hurt so much that Jerry would use his fake courtly act with anyone else. She'd assumed that because of what they'd been through together, that it was a special act, just for her. Their own little in joke at the expense of the others. With a sigh, she pulled her phone from her pocket and began loading a route, so that she could at least guide Mell, although she'd probably end up navigating for everyone.

'There has to be something else,' Simon muttered, moving further into the covered car port, desperately seeking something with four wheels. 'There is no way I am getting on a scooter.'

'Suit yourself,' Suze said revving the tiny engine on the red machine before opening the throttle and zipping forwards. It was a nifty little thing and she was ready to enjoy herself. 'The rest of us are leaving. Come on guys.' She popped a fast U-turn and sped out of the alley onto the roads of Rome, followed by the light buzzing drone of the other two bikes carrying Jerry and Claire, and Mell and Sarah.

Left alone in the car port, listening to the diminishing waspish drone of the scooters, Simon shook his head. He was uncertain whether to be annoyed that Suze had shot off without him, or admire her tenacity. The headstrong girl confused and frustrated him, she was young and intensely naïve, the complete opposite of Lisa in everything that she did, yet, there was something about her that he found almost captivating. Shaking his head, warding off any further thoughts in that direction, he moved further into the car port, eyes fixed on a large shape under a blue tarpaulin.

Cautiously he took hold of a corner and gently lifted it, revealing a vivid red metal and a well cleaned radial wheel with shiny central nut. '*Hola preciosa,*' he breathed, realising instantly what it was, and dragging the tarp further away. '*Es amor.*'

It was a car, a beautiful red car, so well-polished and loved he was afraid of touching her and leaving a fingerprint in the gloss. She was magnificent, low nose, curving chassis, gleaming chrome. A car to fall deeply in love with, sleek and soft, but exuding the power hidden in her V6 engine. A real treasure, hidden from the world.

A waspish buzz preceded Suze's impatient yell as she returned to pick him up. 'Hey Simon, come on! You are never gonna believe what's happened to Rome!' she slowed the bike and yelled again as Simon barely glanced up from examining the flashy red sports car he'd found. 'It's a car,' she said disapprovingly, cutting the engine of the bike, and kicking the stand down.

He spared her a condescending glance. 'More than just a car Suze, this is a Ferrari Dino 246GT, one of the greatest Ferraris of all time.' There was genuine awe in his voice, as though in the presence of a god.

She shrugged. 'Looks like a Porsche. Besides I thought you were madly in love with your own scrap heap?' she said, recalling the insane amount of affection he held for the clapped out, ancient Ford Escort that he drove.

'Esperanza is fine for every day driving, but this is,' Simon's hand hovered over the glossy bonnet, 'this is Venus rendered in metal.'

'Great, can't wait to see what it looks like after a trip down the cobbled streets of ancient Rome,' Suze grinned and began to tick of a list of destructive elements in the city. 'Through the dirt, the grime, the uneven cobbles, horse carts, the crossing stones placed randomly in the middle of the road.'

'Ancient Rome?' Simon finally dragged his attention away from the swanky car and looked at Suze. Her face was flushed and she was grinning as though it was the best day of her life. 'Suze, what do you mean ancient Rome?'

Her grin cracked even wider. 'You know how Rome has everything, like all its history is still there, just hidden behind the veil of time?' he gave her a sceptical look but gestured for her to continue. 'Someone moved the veil.'

Simon shook his head. 'What are you talking about?'

'Get on the bike, I'll show you, it's way too weird to explain,' Suze patted the pillion seat, her glee undiminished by the look of dread on her friend's face.

Simon let out a pained sigh and with a grimace of distaste took a step towards the scooter as Suze fired up the engine again. 'Fine, you win. Move back, if I have to ride it I am sure as hell not being a passenger.'

Suze snorted a laugh. 'You even know how this works?' She revved the throttle, making the little bike leap forwards.

'Do you have a licence?' he shot back, folding his arms, convinced that he'd won.

Straightening herself up Suze looked him dead in the eye and delivered her winning hit. 'As a matter of fact, I do. CBT 50cc motorbikes. Andy made me get it after I kinda stole his bike several times. Quit being a wimp and get on the damn back,' she grinned, and patted the pillion seat again. 'My turn to drive.'

With a final shake of his head, and many reservations about his life choices, Simon climbed on behind her and, wishing furiously that the scooter had some kind of seatbelt, clamped his fingers around the pillion bars.

The sudden warmth of his body so close to hers made Suze catch her breath, she'd not considered how close they would have to be. She squeezed the throttle, making the little bike roar in an attempt to clear her head, and buzzed out to join the others on the streets of Rome.

As soon as they left the alley everything changed. Three a.m. was suddenly much darker but warmer, the deserted street, wide and cobbled, the buildings bright and colourful, constructed in wood and plaster. As they zipped along the air rippled, and the street changed, the plaster buildings replaced briefly in stone, and reverting back to plaster as they passed along the street.

The others had stopped and were stood beside one of the old buildings. 'How is this possible?' said Sarah, reaching out to touch the plaster wall. It was hard and slightly warm to the touch.

'It mutates between stone and plaster,' Mell said thoughtfully, stepping backwards and forwards across the street. 'Almost as if we can see two different time periods. But that's impossible. Time travel itself is a paradox. It can't be done.'

'It must be something to do with Remus,' Sarah ventured, thinking aloud. 'If he has been resurrected to take, what Messalina believes is, his rightful place in history, then the Romulan version of history is in danger.'

'So, it's not just modern Rome in flux, it is the entire history of Europe and most of the Mediterranean,' said Jerry watching as a man in a toga walked across the end of the street, a second man behind him hurrying to catch up.

Curious, Suze buzzed her bike to the end of the street where the toga clad man had been walking, and peered around the corner. A narrow curving street led away up a slope, ramshackle three storey tenement blocks rising along the whole street, some with stalls selling food and pottery. And people, people everywhere, dressed in simple yet colourful tunics. 'Wow,' she hissed, smiling as she noticed a patch of phallic graffiti on the opposite wall. 'Simon are you seeing this?'

'*Si. Impossibile,*' he breathed, keeping his grip tight on the scooter. As they sat watching, the air shimmered again and the street was filled briefly with people in colourful Renaissance clothing, spilling out of a tavern.

'Do you think they can see us?' said Sarah, as Mell halted their bike alongside Simon and Suze, and stared in wonder at the constantly changing vista of the Eternal City in all her splendour.

XXXI

'Oh my god, this is so much fun!' Claire shrieked in delight from the back of Jerry's Vespa, as they raced through the narrow, cobbled, twisty and constantly changing streets of ancient Rome.

'Speak for yourself.' Simon groaned quietly. His eyes were closed and his hands clenched in a death grip on the pillion bars on the back of the Vespa, as Suze slalomed the little scooter between some raised crossing stones.

'Come on Simon, we are doing barely twenty miles an hour through the almost empty streets of ancient and medieval Rome, we're practically walking. You on the other hand threw us through a hedge at sixty miles an hour, in Wales, in the middle of the night,' she chided, twisting to look over her shoulder.

'In a car and it was an open gate, not a hedge,' he retaliated, opening his eyes very briefly to admonish her. 'I knew what I was doing. And keep your eyes on the road.'

'Oh hell, I hope we don't run anyone important over,' said Mell, as a particularly fat man in senatorial robes threw himself out of their way across a merchant's stall. His action shattered a large amphora, containing a particularly nasty smelling substance that all suspected was the legendary garum sauce, made from fermenting fish. Ancient Rome, closed to wheeled traffic through the day, was a busy place at three thirty a.m.

By contrast the medieval streets that they occasionally found themselves driving through were all but abandoned at this hour, with only the odd pair of skulking lovers making use of the shadows. All around the teenagers, Rome came to life. It was as though the city was rising from a long slumber and was shaking away its modernity to reveal the true phases of itself.

Anxious about how their actions might affect the past, and unsure as to how they appeared to be able to transcend time, the three little mopeds and their riders buzzed through the streets trying to avoid people. To reach the Appian Way and from there head to the Alban Mountains, they had to cross the centre of Rome, a task no easier in Roman times than it is on the busy streets today.

Scattering senators and merchants alike, they rattled past buildings of plaster and stone. For a long time the Colosseum stood majestic and imposing before them. Then, they were forced to swerve as a vast, glittering eyesore of a building materialised in the road, the glimmer of fire on water indicating the presence of the vast boating lake contained within Nero's golden palace.

From there they sped onwards towards what they hoped was the *Via Triumphalia,* which would lead them to the *Appian Way.* Sarah was still navigating, although detailed plans of the exact road layout of ancient Rome were hard to find. Fortunately, Rome had been a popular city for so long that most of the major roadways and thoroughfares had remained largely unchanged through the centuries.

Passing a huge bathhouse, they could hear the babble of voices and the slapping sound of the masseurs at work, and feel the heat emanating from the heated rooms. Clearly business never stopped in ancient Rome. As they sped past, the sounds faded and the magnificent bathhouse became a vast ruin, and the rambling words of a restless poet, wandering the skeletal structure, faded into the distance behind them. As time shifted again, they were forced to swerve around a wall and through one of the arches of an aqueduct, water spilled from the top, drenching them as they passed beneath.

As they drew closer to the edge of the ancient city, the road briefly became a dirt track, flanked by small huts of wattle and daub. A substantial cobble paving and the horrific view of a long straight road, flanked on both sides by an endless parade of crucified men, announced their arrival on the famed Appian Way.

Suze stalled the bike with a jerk. 'He really did it then,' she muttered, staring at the terrible scene. 'So many people, I wonder which one he is?'

Simon forced his eyes open, and immediately wished he hadn't. The pained figure of Christ on the cross, that he occasionally wore, was scant preparation for the sight of the real thing. 'Keep moving Suze,' he muttered, 'It happened a long time ago, there is nothing that any of us can do for anyone here. Besides, the one you are looking for most likely died on the battlefield. Drive on Suze, if you move on, this will all turn into cemeteries.'

She gave a long sigh and, composing herself, she took a final look at the condemned slaves of the Spartacus Revolt and pushed the bike onwards. Simon had been right of course, Roman law forbade the burial of the dead within the city and so for miles along the road out of Rome, lay the tombstones of her citizens, wealthy and poor. For the most part, it was just upright markers, but occasionally there was a real monumental cenotaph structure or sarcophagus, at least there was for those that could afford it. Elsewhere lay large pits, some closed by a mound, others partially open and reeking of decay. The common burial pits of the slave class. Or if time happened to slip into the medieval or modern periods, housing and farmer's fields, a much prettier sight. Until they reached the plague pits.

'That is foul,' hissed Claire pulling her shirt up over her nose in disgust as they buzzed past a particularly pungent burial pit with a horse's leg poking out of it.

'Gotta bury em somewhere,' Jerry replied, swerving around a body in the middle of the road outside a tavern. Drunk or dead, no one was stopping to find out. 'Hey Suze, there's a ramp up that crossing stone ahead. Bet you can't jump it,' Jerry yelled gleefully, revving the little engine harder.

'You're on,' she called back switching the line of the little bike and ignoring a yell of protest from Simon. They flew up the ramp and gained a little air over the crossing stone before hitting the ground gain with a thump. Simon swore in Spanish. A moment later Jerry and Claire's scooter hit the ground behind, Claire shrieking in excitement and egging Jerry on.

Mell and Sarah sensibly avoided it, although Mell was getting good at swinging the bike through narrow gaps and easily beat Jerry and Claire's bike through the next set of crossing stones in the road.

Their journey was fairly short and, tempting as it was to explore Rome's living, breathing history, they were all aware of the need to stop whatever madness Messalina had started by raising Remus. The destruction of the history of the Roman Empire would affect a huge portion of the world. If Remus succeeded, it was possible that the six teens themselves would be erased from time itself.

And so, within half an hour they reached the Alban Mountain range, weaving the scooters around rocky outcrops and petrified lava flows. Motoring as far up the mountain as they could until the terrain became impassable for the scooters. Out in the countryside on the slopes of the mountain, it was impossible to tell if time was still in flux so far from the city.

'Guess we walk from here,' Suze said easing the little bike to a halt among a copse of trees ankle deep in ferns.

'You okay Si?' asked Jerry with a grin. 'You look kinda ill.'

Simon staggered off the bike and sank down on a rock resting his elbows on his knees and burying his face in his hands with a groan. 'Please never do that to me again.'

'I thought it was great fun,' Claire said rewarding Jerry with a particularly sexy smile and flutter of her eyelashes. Which earned her a grin and a cheeky wink in response.

'Long way to go yet,' said Mell resting the bike on the kick stand and stretching her back out as Sarah disembarked.

'Do you think we have to go to the top?' she asked, looking up towards the forbidding peak of the mountain.

'Simon's idea,' Suze shrugged. 'I'm not sure what he was thinking exactly.'

'I was wondering if Remus was buried inside the volcano, but I have no idea where to start looking. There was a temple to Jupiter at the summit and the triumphal procession started from there, but I do not know if there was ever access to the caldera.' Simon's voice was muffled, his hands still over his face.

'So, we have no plan?' said Jerry.

'Sure we do!' replied Mell. 'We hike up the mountain, come on.' She strode off through the calf-deep foliage heading further up the slope, expecting the rest to follow her.

XXXII

As they marched onwards up the mountain the terrain subtly changed. The dense green foliage that they had abandoned the scooters in was gone, replaced by scrubby brush plants struggling for life in a harsh, dusty, environment. The air was hot and humid, and a thick, warm but foul-smelling mist was creeping in through the darkness of early morning.

'Urgh, smells like rotten eggs,' Claire gagged, pulling her shirt over her nose again.

'Sulphur,' Simon agreed. 'We must be close to a vent,' his eyes scanned the terrain but no part of the mountain was obviously venting gas.

'Wait, is this a smoking mountain?' Jerry's eyes widened slightly, and he stopped, staring towards the summit, just visible as a darker shadow against the dark sky. 'Could this sucker blow?'

'There is no recorded eruption during Rome's period of empirical expansion.' Simon replied, still moving forwards. 'It probably last blew around five thousand BC, it should be safe.'

'But Rome was fluctuating in time,' Sarah said quietly. 'What if we are still within the time flux, what if we walk through an eruption date?'

'Guess we're toast,' Suze replied. She was staring at the ground concentrating hard on putting one foot in front of the other, in the tiny pool of light cast by her rapidly draining phone torch. 'At least it will probably be fast.'

'Forget an eruption,' said Mell, glancing around, looking for indications of animal life. 'We probably should have thought of that one before we got here. Anyway, I think carbon dioxide levels may be more of a problem. We need to avoid any low pockets, there's not much wind.'

They tramped warily onwards, the sulphuric smell getting worse and then dissipating before wafting over them again. Everyone felt light-headed and sick, due to the noxious gases venting from unseen cracks in the dry earth. All around there was silence, not a single bird twittering from a branch, just an unrelenting, oppressive silence. And it was still three hours until sunrise. The ground kicked up suddenly as they reached the final rise of the mountain. Scrambling up a lose scree curve the teenagers found themselves at the mouth of a cave. A secondary vent to the main crater. Their phone torches illuminated walls scored with ripples where scalding lava had melted the rock in the violence of the last eruption. As they watched, the cave sealed itself. Time was still in flux, even this far outside of Rome, they would have to time it right to get inside. Noted by all, but unsaid, was the realisation that they could be engulfed in the lava flow that had created the vent at any moment.

Jerry shrugged and stepped forward into the mouth of the cave fumbling in his pocket for something. 'Aww shit,' he groaned, turning towards Simon. 'Your bloody girlfriend has my dad's lighter. At least she damned well better. It's all I got left of the old man.'

'You should really buy a torch, or at least bring your phone,' said Mell, stepping past him. Although, checking her battery she figured that if they were going to make a habit of getting into tombs and volcanoes she should probably invest in a real torch herself.

The cave mouth remained open, perhaps by going in Mell and Jerry had managed to halt the timeslip, or perhaps, like the hotel, the interior of the mountain was immune to the strange phenomenon? None of them understood how it worked, nor did they particularly want to know. Although each understood that the basic rule of time travel had to be; don't touch anything.

The brilliant beam of Simon's metal penlight swept through the cavern piercing the darkness beyond. 'How much light time do we have left?' he asked, eyes following his beam through the space.

'Half battery,' Claire replied squinting at her phone, moving slowly forwards, as Mell and Sarah mumbled something along the same lines. 'Do you think the passage goes all the way to the centaargh!' her words vanished in a scream of terror.

'Claire, what is it?' asked Jerry, catching her shoulders as she stumbled backwards away from whatever horror she'd seen.

The harsh beam of Simon's penlight illuminated a twisted shape on the floor. Curious he bent closer. 'Looks like a Roman soldier.' Tentatively he shifted a piece of broken metal aside to reveal the grinning skull and rotting bleached bones of a second century legionary.

'What happened to him?' Suze asked uneasily, her eyes scanning the cavernous hole in the rock as though expecting lava to be dripping from the ceiling.

'Something he definitely didn't live through,' said Mell, grimly inspecting the shattered metal around the torso of the skeleton. 'Simon look. His armour is melted. Nothing the Romans had could have done this.'

'The curse of Remus?' suggested Sarah.

'Not a pretty thought,' said Jerry, stooping to retrieve the fallen warrior's sword. It rasped on the stony floor of the cavern, crumbling and rusty like the broken armour. 'Aww yuck! There's blood on everything, this poor geezer had a seriously terrible death.'

'So will we and the rest of the world if we don't get moving and stop Remus,' said Mell softly.

'Ray of bloody sunshine you are,' Jerry replied cheerfully. 'Right then, onwards to certain doom it is.' He brandished the rust flaking sword in the air, covering himself with tiny red flecks.

Aiming their limited torchlight further into the darkness ahead, the group cautiously moved deeper into the volcanic vent. Ahead of them the passage curved around to the right and the gradient began to slope gently downwards. Simon, in his usual place, at the head of the group, edged around the corner first and let out a groan of distaste.

'What is it?' Mell hissed, as he retreated slowly back around the corner re-joining the group.

'There is more than one dead Roman ahead of us,' he swallowed. 'Considerably more. In fact, the only way to describe it would be a massacre.'

'What?' Jerry abandoned his place as rear-guard and peered around the corner. 'Yeesh! Guess we know what happened to that lost legion Tiberius mentioned. This was an annihilation!'

Slowly, one at a time the rest followed him around the corner, staying close to the wall, each now knowing and dreading the scene on the other side. The tunnel of the volcanic vent opened up into a chamber, revealing an underground battlefield littered with the bodies of, what looked like, an entire legion. The military standard lay discarded by the entrance to the tunnel where the teenagers stood, the once shining bronze eagle coated in a skin of mud, its wings paralysed mid-flight, unable to conquer the enemy.

Sarah picked up the rotten staff and brushed the mud from the eagle's silent beak, its stony eyes glared defiantly back as if displeased by its absolute defeat.

'What do you think attacked them?' asked Claire looking around, taking in the rotting bodies, some with facial features still visible.

'Messalina can control Lisa with poison, and we saw Remus bring statues to life,' Suze said. Realising as she did so, that if an army of stone soldiers or people like Lisa, possessed by feral speed and strength had once existed, then they may have been capable of this kind of carnage.

'Come on,' said Simon, giving himself a mental shake and attempting to reassume his leadership of the group. 'We have no time to loiter here, with every hour Remus grows stronger.' As an afterthought, he stepped closer to one of the felled legionaries and slipped the soldier's sword free of the lifeless hand that held it. Considering it a smart move Suze quietly did the same.

In an attempt to keep her mind occupied and shut out the horror of what she saw, Suze tried to work out the likely identity of the felled Legion. The rowdy and mutinous *Legio IX Hispana*, Simon had referred to back at the hotel, thought for centuries to have marched off into the mists of Scotland, were actually later recorded as wiped out in the East somewhere. Likewise, it couldn't be one of the three lost with Varus in Germany, nor one of those lost with Crassus in Parthia. She had a vague recollection of one of the tenth legions being decimated and sent somewhere, but nothing she could pinpoint.

The sweaty, warm drips from the ceiling were relentless, like rainfall, as if the cavern was striving to wash itself clean. In every direction lay defeated Romans, destroyed by an unknown force. Some soldiers had not even had time to draw their swords against their invisible foe. The dead were all clearly Romans, and unless the legion had been fighting one another, there was no indication of the identity of their victorious foe. But whatever had destroyed them had been powerful and, for the first time since making the tenuous connection between Romulus, Remus and Vulcan, the teens really began to suspect that they were on the right path.

Mell stumbled, catching her foot on a protruding arm clawing out of the debris, and Claire let out a deafening scream as the disturbed soldier's stricken face turned to stare sightlessly at her. Then he lay still, knocked into his new position by Mell's stumble.

'Let's get the hell out of here,' shivered Sarah, moving ahead faster as she spoke.

As Suze turned to follow she saw Simon stop to look at something. 'What is it?' she asked walking slowly back towards him.

'What does that look like to you?' he asked, digging in his pocket with one hand using the other to indicate what he was looking at.

Entwined around the clawing fingers of a centurion's outreached arm was a silver chain, and hanging from it, an oddly shaped pendant. 'Like a feather from the silver eagle,' Suze replied, staring it.

'Exactly,' he said laying a similar item across his palm. 'The old man gave me this at the museum. He kept saying that the "Eagle is the key", I confess I never gave it a second thought, but I think I see what he was getting at.' The artefact in Simon's hand was bright silver, the end sculptured as the eagle's tail feather. A perfect disguise. 'We may need this,' he continued, slowly disentangling the chain from the cold stiff fingers of the soldier and passed it to Suze. 'You look after it, then we have another if anything goes wrong.'

The two of them hurried along, doing their best not to look at the grisly spectacle any more than they had too, in order to catch up with the others who had already ducked into the shelter of another lava tunnel, out of sight of the killing field.

'How far into the mountain do you think this vent goes?' said Claire, nervously twisting her rings around her fingers. It was the first sign of her claustrophobia, and noticing her own actions she forced herself to stop fiddling and took a deep breath.

'No idea,' Simon replied, shining his torch beam further down the tunnel. 'I guess we just keep following it. The legion back there at least suggests that we may be in the right place.'

'That, or the legion was killed when the volcano erupted,' said Mell pointedly. Although, she very much doubted anything would have remained of the legion had they been caught in a lava flow.

'I am still open to suggestions if you have a better one,' Simon retaliated through gritted teeth. He was tired, they all were, but the strain of his worry for Lisa's safety was becoming more apparent. He was just hoping that she was still alive, it was all that was keeping him moving.

'We'll keep going,' Suze said attempting to keep the peace, and pushing herself off the wall ready to continue the hike through the volcanic vent. The others reluctantly followed suit.

A few hundred yards further on the passage stopped and in its place yawned a wide vertical shaft, the remains of the main vent. Simon leaned out over the void flashing his torch beam upwards. At the very limit of the light's penetration they could just make out the suspended backfill of rock and dirt that had closed the crater in the centuries since the last eruption. Exhaling loudly, Simon angled the beam downwards into the nothingness below.

'Please don't say what I think you're going to,' Sarah said, glancing at the illuminated rock face below. 'There is a magma chamber somewhere down there.'

'Anyone has a better idea, now is the time,' said Jerry, taking a step back from the hole. Gods he hoped someone had a better idea, because he really didn't like the look on Simon's face.

'Turn the light off,' said Claire softly. 'I saw something when you moved, turn it off.' Simon did as he was told, plunging the vent into near total darkness. Far away, low down in the mountain a shape glowed red, smouldering in the gloom.

'That is frigging lava!' Jerry exclaimed taking several paces further back and knotting his hands in his long corkscrew curls. 'I mean seriously, lava!'

'It's an eagle,' Suze said, suddenly seeing what Claire had. The shape of a Roman eagle carved through the rock, illuminated red by the boiling liquid magma far below.

'No, no way,' Mell said grabbing Simon's arm, he shrugged her off and she immediately grabbed him again, keeping her grip tight. 'Simon think! I know you love her, at least you think you do. I know you intend to propose to her,' she dropped her voice and spoke so that the others couldn't hear. His response was equally low although, the expression on his face told the others that whatever Mell had said she'd managed to shock him. 'Simon,' she continued in a normal tone. 'We are not risking our lives inside an active volcano for her. There has to be a line.'

'Like it or not, we are already inside an active volcano,' Suze offered quietly. She dared not look at the others. It was taking all her effort to control the sheer terror building within her.

'I wish there was a better way,' Simon said, more to himself than to his friends.

'Dude don't you go thinking about doing something stupid. There is lava down there, we ain't doing that shit, right Si?' Jerry bit his tongue waiting for a response. 'Simon?' he grabbed his friend's shoulder.

'Sarah!' Simon called softly, shrugging off Jerry and Mell, and crouching by the gaping void. 'You are the best climber among us, what do you think?' He played his torch beam over what could be seen of the rippled, lava coated rock face.

She crouched beside him, an expression of intense concentration on her face. 'The exiting blast has left a number of protrusions and ripples in the surface,' she gestured at the wall, indicating how she was reading it. 'So, there are good hand and toe holds. It is climbable,' she looked up and met his intense dark eyes, fixing him with a hard stare. 'If you happen to be insane enough to try it.'

Simon nodded, considering it for a second. 'Then I plead insanity,' he said, slithering off the edge and onto the undulating rock face.

'No!' Five voices spoke as one.

'Simon, what the hell are you doing!' Mell demanded. 'Get back here now.'

He paused for a moment, hands still on the edge. 'Remus has awoken and is changing the history of Rome, of Europe. He has Lisa and I cannot pretend that my actions are in any way selfless, but there are more lives than hers at stake here. The five of you can do as you wish, but I am going down there.' And, with that he slithered downwards out of sight.

'Well shit,' said Jerry, kicking a pebble, and pacing around in a circle scratching at the back of his neck.

XXXIII

Lisa felt dreadful. Her head throbbed, her back ached and her stomach churned with a nausea that was becoming frighteningly common. The world appeared to have fallen down a rabbit hole, or slipped into a parallel dimension or some other unfathomable thing; she absolutely refused to believe that they had travelled through time, such things were impossible. She realised that she could be dreaming, or more likely drugged, there was definitely something in her system that forced her to obey the Italian woman's command.

Dreaming or drugged, she pinched the soft skin on the inside of her elbow, hard enough to bring tears to her eyes. Not a dream then, but reality didn't feel right for the situation in which she found herself either. Hotel managers did not trap people in their basements and then bring the dead to life, nor could they change the fabric of the universe. Her head hurt from trying to contemplate the unreal situation.

Instead, Lisa put her energy into trying to work out where she might be. Simon had promised that he would find her, the least she could do was work out where in Rome she was. Clearly a poor area, remote from tourist hotspots, somewhere on the outskirts of the city. She was curled up on a bench in the corner of a dark and dingy old building, which, judging by the disgusting stale stink of old booze, the puddles of dried vomit, and another sickly-sweet scent that she couldn't name, must be a tavern of somewhat ill repute. Lisa wrinkled her nose in disgust, even the boys' locker room at St. Peters after a rugby match was nicer than this place.

The three of them, Lisa, Remus and Messalina, had left the hotel in a rush, running on foot through unfamiliar cobbled streets. They paused by the towering and still dripping edifice of the Colosseum, where Messalina had raised her hands skyward and called on whatever ancient powers she was beholden too. Slashing cuts into both her own hand and Remus's, she had merged their blood. Hers representing the present, his; the past, and before Lisa's wide terrified eyes the modern city of Rome had faded away. The streets turning to cobble, the Colosseum complete, then replaced by a palace and a lake. The transition had made her dizzy and she had almost fainted, then Remus had hefted her over his shoulder like a caveman, and dragged her back to this wretched little hovel.

Once inside though, Lisa found herself largely forgotten as Remus opened, what looked to be, a huge amphora of wine and proceeded to drink all of it before starting on a second, whilst eyeing up several others. Messalina though, seemed agitated. Leaving the silver eagle with Remus, she had paced through the building searching everywhere for intruders, all the while throwing filthy looks at the progressively more drunk Remus. After two thousand five hundred years, apparently all her promised saviour wanted to do was get wasted.

Lisa found herself strangely grateful for his actions, it meant that the pair of them seemed to have forgotten her existence. It was a new experience to her to be ignored, usually, whether at home, with her friends or riding horses with her boyfriend she was the centre of everyone's attention, and she liked it that way. Although in this case she had no desire to be noticed. Messalina was clearly deranged, she had been speaking in two voices, one harsh and grating, the other softer, like she had sounded when they first met in the hotel. But the second voice wasn't strong, and Lisa hadn't heard it for a while. Remus on the other hand had the kind of heavy brow, square jawed, flat faced appearance that suggested if he weren't drinking, he'd be assaulting, raping and killing, in whichever direction someone pointed him until he found a drink again. Without drawing attention to herself she began to scan the room for a potential way out.

'Remus!' Messalina's voice was like a whip crack across the rotting room. 'You must call your army.' Remus glanced at her and drained another cup of wine, before reaching for another. He'd laid several out along the table like a modern shots challenge. Messalina tried again. 'There will be wine later Remus. When you have subjugated Roma, claiming your title as father of the Eternal City.'

'Peace woman!' Remus growled, draining another cup. 'The city has waited more than two millennia, it can wait a little longer. Besides, my brother is not a threat. I do not see his slaves, his men or his standard. My men will rouse and flock to my banner when called. We control the army of shadows, why should we fear the echo of my brother's name?'

Seeing that aggression was getting her nowhere, Messalina tried a different track. Sashaying over to Remus she leaned across him removing his cup from his hand before settling herself on his lap. 'But Remus,' she purred, her index finger drawing small circles on his chest, as she tried not to choke on his alcohol soaked breath. 'What if someone should discover your brother's lost eagle, what if his standard rises above the Palatine?'

A deep rumbling laugh escaped Remus. 'My brother lies dead. Romulus cannot be raised, he never had the foresight to bind his soul to power. Besides, priestess, I dealt with his eagle,' he grinned and slid a hand up Messalina's leg. 'I left my slave, Meredius, orders to steal it on my brother's death and place it in my own tomb.' He took another swig from his cup and laughed, spraying her with wine.

Messalina froze as the white-hot rage of the ancient priestess filled her head. 'Your tomb?' Colour drained from her face. 'We have searched for centuries for his golden eagle, we thought it destroyed.' She slapped Remus, twice. And stood up so rapidly that she threw the table, and his carefully arranged wine cups to the floor. 'You idiot!' she paced the room again, tearing at her hair. 'Do you realise what you have done? His eagle can destroy you. Destroy us!'

Remus belched loudly. 'His tomb was flooded priestess. You saw to that. We need not fear my brother. His body is drowned, his allies are gone.' He unstopped another wine amphora. 'If my tomb was disturbed, Meredius would be here, but there are none on earth can find it, he hid my remains well.' He drank deeply. 'Tiberius would warn me if there was danger from Romulus, he was charged with keeping my eagle safe.'

Messalina was unconvinced. 'True, time in Roma fluctuates but your slaves will be long dead, and they may have betrayed you.'

Remus shook his head. 'Priestess, slaves belong to their master for eternity, death is nothing.' He raised his voice shouting drunkenly at the ceiling. 'Tiberius! Tiberius! Your master calls!' 'See,' he leered at Messalina, 'there is no danger, time floats, no longer anchored to the point of my death, so there is no rush.' He tipped his cup and finding it empty hurled it to the floor, shattering the fragile red ceramic. 'I need a woman.' He glanced in Lisa's direction and she shrank back against the wall as he staggered two steps towards her. 'Pretty little thing for a barbarian, isn't she?' he swung back around to look at Messalina. 'Take her to the Temple of the Vestals, she shall bear my heirs when I am victorious.' He belched again and collapsed onto a bench, his head hitting the table with a thump. Almost immediately he began to snore.

Simmering with rage Messalina, snapped her fingers at Lisa. 'You, come.'

Slowly Lisa uncurled herself from the bench. She felt stiff and cold, beneath the tall boy's borrowed jumper she was still wearing her dress, which felt damp but was becoming stiff with mud and blood as it dried. Low on patience, Messalina grabbed her wrist and dragged her from the room. 'Your liberator of history appears to be nothing more than a drunken lout,' Lisa observed as Remus, oblivious to their leaving, snored into a pool of his own drool.

'Yours is dead,' Messalina snapped in response, yanking her arm as inside her mind she felt the priestess's attentions begin to turn towards the younger prettier girl.

'Oh, he is not dead,' Lisa smiled to herself. 'Simon will come for me, he promised. But yours will never be anything more than a drunken thug.'

Messalina pulled Lisa roughly around and held her face painfully tight with her right hand, the Italian's eyes were too bright, the pupils too wide and there was a measure of glee in her papery voice as she spoke. 'Do you know the penalty for being an unvirginal Vestal? Those who lose their innocence through desire or force are taken from the temple and buried alive. See how much Remus wants you when he discovers that he is not the first to taste the fruit.' She watched Lisa's eyes widen in fear, and released her hold on the girl's face, brushing a strand of matted blond hair away in a tender gesture as she did so. 'Well my sweet deflowered one, what are you going to do now?'

Lisa said nothing, but her defiant stare dropped to the floor and she allowed Messalina to lead her along to another room in the stinking tavern. It was a small spartan room, four plain walls and a bed, no windows. A new prison, only slightly better than the dungeon in which she had been kept earlier. Messalina pushed her roughly inside and stood blocking the doorway.

'Do not look so fearful girl. Remus will forget you, after all you are nothing. I raised him from the shadows. I will lead him to his rightful place in history and I will rule his empire. You will rot in the Temple of the Vestals, if they don't have you killed first for your unchaste ways.' Messalina leaned on the doorframe and combed her fingers through her dark hair, she was exhausted. The longer Remus was active, the stronger the will of the priestess became and the less control Messalina had over her own actions. Since getting the girl back to the hotel the priestess had been in full control and she was fighting hard for her own mind now. And, potentially for her life if the new feeling that was surfacing in her thoughts was truly the ancient priestess yearning for Lisa's youth and beauty.

'Simon will come for me,' Lisa insisted, standing defiantly in the centre of her new prison room. 'He will come and rescue me from you, and I would bet he can figure out how to best your army too! He is the smartest man I know.'

Messalina let out and indulgent laugh. 'Naïve fool. Only Romulus himself or a direct descendent can control his army and defeat Remus, and they need the standard. We are unopposed. And you should not rely so much on a man to save you,' she stepped closer to Lisa, her face softening, her voice almost normal. 'You have a mind, you have all your limbs. A woman's worth does not rest on a man's decision to save her, she is perfectly capable of saving herself.' She reached out and twisted a lock of Lisa's filthy hair around her fingers. 'See where waiting for a man has got you. Darling,' she held Lisa's shoulders and met her gaze, her eyes soft and natural. 'To get what you want from this world, you have to take it yourself.' She let go and stalked out of the room, closing and locking the heavy door with a loud click.

Alone, Lisa sank down on the narrow bed and stared at the barren plastered room, her hands pushing deep into the pocket of the loaned hoodie, fingers searching out the comforting leather of Simon's wallet which she'd managed to keep hold of. But instead she found something else. A cool square of metal. Frowning she pulled out her find. A narrow square box with a lid. She flipped it open and a flame burst brightly into life. A lighter. Not hers, definitely not Simon's, it had to belong to the tall boy. Although she'd not seen him smoke.

Absently she closed the top and then flicked it open again, watching the instant catch of the flame. The building was plaster over a wattle frame. She'd noticed as Messalina, or whoever she thought she was now, had tugged her down the corridor. She was definitely in the poorer area of Rome, probably a long way from the centre. Everything she'd seen had appeared ancient and horrible. But also, flammable, she thought palming the lighter again. If only she could get out.

A movement caught her eye, and she screamed as a creature with a long tail scurried out from under the bed. Immediately angry with herself, although still afraid of the scurrying creature, Lisa clamped her hand over her mouth, keeping the scream of terror in, but allowing whimpers of fright to escape. She pulled her feet up onto the bed, wrapped her arms around her knees and stared at the enormous rat sitting in the centre of the room, staring back at her from large dark eyes.

The rat's nose twitched in the silence, smelling her fear, then deciding that she wasn't a threat, it dropped back on all fours and ambled, unhurried to the opposing side of the room, where it vanished into a hole in the plaster. Letting her breath out slowly Lisa stared at the hole, knowing what she had to do but needing time to think about it.

XXXIV

Sarah was still crouched on the edge of the void, an expression of disbelief on her face. 'Damnit!' she shook her head. 'Simon, wait!' she slipped herself over the edge, kicking in a decent toe hold, and wordlessly glanced up at the others before exhaling deeply and following him down.

'Aww balls, now I have to go,' Jerry groaned, screwing his eyes shut.

'Why?' asked Claire moving further away from the edge, clearly hoping that she wasn't going to have to participate in the decent into hell.

'She and I ... we ... sorta,' he gesticulated aimlessly searching for a word, 'kinda ... thing. Bollocks,' he knotted his hands in his corkscrew curls and looked out over the void. 'Can't have her falling off a wall thinking I'm still pissed off at her.'

'Mell?' Suze said, watching the other girl chew her lip as she thought through the situation.

'Guess we bloody well have to, don't we?' Mell replied. 'We've come through too much together to abandon one another now,' she closed her eyes. 'Come on let's go.'

Shooting anxious looks at one another, the four slipped slowly over the edge and began their uncertain, inexperienced free climb down the inside of a main volcanic vent. None felt particularly good about it, especially when a bout of distinctly warm, sulphuric smelling air wafted up the vent. The rock was rippled, formed into solid nodules and ridges under their hands, surprisingly easy to climb but disturbingly warm and almost soft to the touch. But the whole concept of free climbing inside a potentially active volcano was nerve wracking and they made slow progress.

From somewhere below the group came a yell of surprise followed by Sarah screaming Simon's name and a loud thump from further below. Suze glanced down to see Sarah leaning out from the rock face, one hand holding her weight the other flung well out into the void, brandishing a light as she leaned out and tried to see further down the vent. 'Simon!' Sarah yelled his name again.

'¡Estoy bien!' he responded with a groan.

'Sarah what's happening?' Mell called, leaning out as far as she dared, attempting to see the other girl further below.

'Simon slipped,' she called back. 'He fell a fair few feet, but I think he's okay. I'm going down. You guys please take your time. Secure every foothold, and rest your weight on three points before moving the fourth,' she pleaded, turning back to the rock face and scrambling downwards as quickly as she could.

'This is hell,' Claire said quietly from her spot beside Suze, where she clung tightly to the wall. There was a catch in her voice and Suze suspected that she might be crying.

'S'okay, pumpkin,' Jerry said, slithering down beside her and giving her green hair an affectionate tug. 'We'll get there, I could try piggybacking you down if that would help.'

'God no,' Claire croaked, and pressed tighter to the wall.

'Well babe you can't stay here,' he said, stating the obvious. 'I'll stay next to you until we reach the bottom,' he offered, and was rewarded with a nod. 'Besides,' he grinned, I bet Lisa couldn't do this.' Terrified as she was Claire managed a small smile at that one.

Gritting her teeth Suze scrambled down ahead of them, trying desperately hard not to rush and make a mistake but equally worried about the situation that might await at the bottom of the climb. There were muted sounds from below suggesting that Sarah may have at least made it down, but that didn't help Suze's anxiously racing mind. Taking a deep breath, she forced herself to concentrate on the climb and stared straight ahead at the rock face.

It was as Mell and Suze reached the bottom that Claire fell. She'd been struggling with the climb and Jerry had remained close to her, but they were roughly ten meters from the bottom when Claire lost her grip. She screamed as her hand slipped and Jerry lunged for her, almost dislodging his own precarious hand hold.

'Hold her Jerry, I'm on my way up!' yelled Sarah, practically leaping up the rock face towards Claire. But Jerry was struggling, he was only holding Claire's wrist and his hands were slick with sweat in the humidity of the vent. He let out a groan as Claire slipped in his grip.

'Jerry! Don't let go!' Claire screamed, wide-eyed with terror as she stared up at him.

'Claire sweetie, you gotta help me out here,' he groaned, as she twisted and shrieked, clawing her other hand at his arm. 'Grab the god damn rock, I can't hold you.' She slipped a little more in his grip.

'I'm almost there,' Sarah called. But she was too late. Jerry made a final valiant effort to hold on, but Claire was squirming too much and with an anguished squeal, she slid from his grip.

Sarah made a grab for her as she fell past but was unable to do more than snag her jacket, briefly slowing, but not halting Claire's descent. She hit the ground with an ugly sounding thump followed immediately by a scream of pain.

'Claire,' Mell moved the fastest, crouching instantly by Claire's side as Jerry and Sarah climbed down to join everyone. Claire let out a moan of pain as Mell helped her to sit up, leaning her back against the wall. 'Did you hit your head? How many fingers am I holding up?'

'No, three, you always hold three,' Claire groaned in response. 'My shoulder,' she whispered looking to her left, towards Jerry. 'You let go of me.'

He looked shamefaced. 'I'm sorry Claire, I tried.'

'There really wasn't anything else he could have done,' Sarah said, laying a reassuring hand on Jerry's arm and looking relieved when he didn't immediately shrug her off. 'He did well to catch you in the first place.'

'Can we get your jacket off? I need to see,' Mell asked gently, sparing Jerry from Claire's betrayed look.

'Leave her jacket on, her shoulder is dislocated,' Simon said, moving to stand beside Mell. Both Sarah and Mell shot him a curious look, he stared back, folding his arms across his chest. 'I play rugby, a dislocated shoulder is a ridiculously common injury on the field. One or other of us is always out with a dislocation. See how her left shoulder is squared and that little nub is sticking out? Her arm has dropped forward out of the socket.' Claire let out a gasp that could have been pain or fright.

'Thank you Dr Matherson,' Mell hissed sarcastically, gently helping Claire lean back against the rock wall.

'If it's dislocated you can put it back, right?' Suze said hesitantly.

'Well I know how, but I shouldn't,' Mell replied. 'It should be done in a hospital, what if it's broken? What if I trap a nerve or something when I put it back?'

'Well she can't climb back up with it busted,' Jerry said. 'Probably worth attempting to put it back.' Claire had gone very pale, and seemed to grow paler still at Jerry's comment.

'There's no guarantee that she'll be able to climb after I've messed with it either. It'll hurt,' Mell replied speaking directly to Claire. 'I mean really hurt, and I've never done it before. And if I really get it wrong you could go into shock.'

'Way to instil confidence Mell,' said Sarah, shaking her head. Knowing that Mell was doing the best she could under the circumstances, but all the same hating that there seemed to be nothing they could do to help Claire short of potentially making things worse.

'Just do it,' Claire hissed through gritted teeth. 'It'll either fix it or it won't. Can't be worse, right?' Mell twisted a strand of her long red hair around her fingers but said nothing, the expression on her face making her reluctance clear.

'Here,' Jerry crouched beside Claire, 'hold my hand.' He threaded his fingers through hers, as Mell probed the dislocated joint. 'Not so tight … Claire sweetie, ouch, babe that hurts!' Jerry pressed his free hand against the rock face for support, dropping to his knees, as Claire crushed all the feeling out of his right hand before Mell even began.

'Simon, I'll need your help. You hold her shoulder steady, I'll rotate her arm,' Mell chewed her lip as she thought her way through the procedure.

'If I may,' Simon countered. 'I am probably stronger than you, and I knocked Edmund's shoulder back in two weeks ago. Perhaps I should do the rotation?'

A flicker of relief crossed Mell's face and she nodded, switching places with him so that she could keep Claire's shoulder steady. 'Ready Claire?' she asked. Claire closed her eyes and nodded squeezing Jerry's hand even tighter. 'Okay, here goes. On three, Simon?' he nodded and she began to count. 'One, Two …'

Simon didn't let her finish and with a loud crack followed by a scream of pain he roughly popped Claire's shoulder back into place. Claire blinked rapidly several times and then fainted dead away into Jerry's arms, as Mell shot a dangerous look in Simon's direction. He shrugged. 'It works better if they are not expecting it, less resistance.'

Eager to push on, Simon led the way along the wide ledge at the base of the wall, towards the dully glowing red eagle that had been visible from above. The air was hot and stale with a distinct tang and breathing was becoming more difficult than it should have been. Nobody fancied remaining deep inside the volcano for long. Jerry, once again bare chested, having sacrificed his shirt for

Mell to make a sling, carrying the still unconscious Claire, ambled along in the middle of the line, Suze taking the job of rear-guard for once.

Drawing closer to it the reluctant explorers could see that the glowing eagle was man made and had been cut through the rock. Rough nicks left by the tools gave the impression of feathers along the base of the silhouetted wings, and the whole eagle shape glowed red in the strange light emitted from the magma chamber. Which everyone hoped lay far below on the opposite side of the rock partition. To their right was another tunnel.

'I guess we go this way,' Simon said, raking a hand through his sweat damp hair and scowling as a drip rolled down his nose.

'I hope it doesn't get any hotter,' Sarah replied, massaging her shoulders. 'It's like an oven in here. I can barely breathe.'

The others muttered their agreement, all were sweat soaked, with glistening faces and soaking clothes. It was like hiking through a steam room, the air so hot and dense, it burned their throats and lungs. Ahead, in the tunnel there was a dull hiss and along the walls, mounted torches erupted into flame illuminating the way forward.

Mell coughed and blinked in the flickering light. 'We're lucky the whole place doesn't ignite,' she gasped. 'The air is terrible down here.' She pulled her T-shirt up over her nose as a makeshift respirator but let it drop again almost immediately.

'We must be close now though,' Suze ventured, creeping forwards into the tunnel.

'Ewww! God! Man sweat!' Claire screeched waking up and finding her face resting against Jerry's sweat slicked chest. 'So gross! Put me down.' Her green hair stuck to his damp chest as he lowered her gently to the ground, taking care not to jostle her arm in the makeshift sling. 'So, so gross,' she repeated, pawing single handed through her ever-present bag for a cleansing wipe to wash her face. 'Urgh, that is disgusting,' she shuddered.

'Not a fan of eau de Jerry then?' he grinned pushing his long damp curls out of his face.

Claire wrinkled her nose in distaste and deigned not to answer, glancing instead at the sling around her arm. 'Mell! Is it supposed to hurt like this?'

'You have to rest the joint. It went back in and everything seems okay, but you should at least rest it a while whilst you can, and when all this is over we are getting a doctor to check it.' Mell replied, looking at the floor. 'You should at least get it x-rayed.'

'But what if we have to climb back up there?' Claire's face was a picture of dismay.

'Relax,' said Jerry draping a bare and decidedly damp arm across Suze's shoulders, 'If computer games have taught me anything, it's that tombs always have a back door. A nice easy exit that would have made life a whole lot simpler if you'd have just come in that way.'

'Name one tomb you've been in with a back door?' Simon demanded, turning to face him, a rogue comma of dark damp hair falling over his left eye as he did so.

'Gawain's,' Jerry and Sarah answered in the same breath.

'Hmm,' Simon raised his eyebrows in surprise but said nothing, before turning and leading the team onwards into the tunnel now lit by the flickering torches.

This second tunnel was like the first, formed by the passage of molten materials. It meandered along, descending at a barely noticeable gradient deeper into the mountain, bringing them closer to the heat of the volcano. Their steps were becoming torturous and Mell was seriously contemplating enlisting Jerry and Suze's help to overpower Simon, and force him back to the surface without finding the tomb. As she opened her mouth to call out, the group stopped. Before them the tunnel ended abruptly at a huge wooden door, scorched and warped, leaning drunkenly off its hinges.

'Well, that should be easy enough to get through,' said Jerry. 'A little help Si?' Scowling at Jerry's insistence on shortening his name, Simon flexed his shoulders and nodded.

Jerry counted them in and together they slammed into the door, which collapsed taking them both to the floor with it. 'Any more wise ideas, oh great sage?' said Simon, pushing himself quickly up, well used to recovering from similar manoeuvres on the rugby field. Jerry took a little longer.

'You didn't have to do it,' Jerry replied with a groan, obviously winded. 'Thought you were the smart one.' Simon smiled in response and offered him a hand easily pulling the taller boy to his feet.

'So,' Suze said quietly, 'the tomb of Remus. Love what he's done with the place.'

The chamber beyond the door was small and dark. Twisted blackened pillars of volcanic rock, formed over centuries by slow dripping and solidifying magma, joined the floor to the ceiling. The rock was black and scorched, the stone melted and fused, and here and there, patches glowed red with heat. The dark vision of Hell was completed when one of the red glowing patches of wall exploded outwards, emitting a hiss of deadly gas that shimmered in the air, making the whole room ripple. A dark sense of menace hung in the atmosphere, so oppressive it was like another person in the room, and the smell, the deep rotten egg stench of sulphur.

'We can't stay here long, we'll suffocate before we find the eagle,' Mell coughed, hanging back.

'Ewwww,' said Sarah in disgust, spotting something on the further side of the room.'

'You said it Sarah,' Suze agreed as they moved closer and gazed at the body of Remus.

'Not quite as good looking as his brother, is he?' Claire remarked, wiping a streak of green dye from her face. The sweaty heat was so intense it was actually drawing the dye out.

The twins' bodies were very different. Where Romulus had looked fresh and as though he were merely sleeping the centuries away. Remus was in the worst stages of decomposition. The skin left on his cracked and battered bones was green and blotchy, oozing yellow puss, shrunken and stretched tight over the skull. His toothless mouth was frozen in a twisted smile and one pupil-less eyeball dangled from the gaping socket, held by a single rotten string. His leather armour, cracked, shrunken and bloody seemed to be the only thing holding him together. Scored deep into the leather were Latin words, quickly and crudely fashioned.

'Simon what does it say?' Suze asked curiously, unable to make it out with her own rudimentary Latin.

'Curses,' he replied uncertainly. 'Bad curses, not anything I am willing to translate.'

'Superstitious?' asked Mell, noticing that Simon's left hand had moved automatically towards his chest where his cross should lie, having forgotten that he'd removed it earlier.

He curled his hand into a fist. 'No, just, trust me, if you could read them you would not wish to speak them either.'

'Where's the eagle?' said Jerry, getting straight to the heart of the problem. Other than the grotesque body of Remus, the tomb was empty.

XXXV

Silence hung heavy in the small foetid chamber, the sulphuric stink growing worse as the teenagers stood there helplessly. The eagle was nowhere to be seen, and worse, there was no indication that it had ever been in the room. The only thing in sight that had not been formed by the passage of molten rock was the decaying remains of Remus, abandoned and forgotten inside the mouth of Hell.

'*No, esto no puede ser correcto, tiene que estar aquí ...*' said Simon dragging his hands through his sweat soaked hair and staring frantically around the small space. 'It has to be here.'

'Dude it ain't,' Jerry replied. 'It's sweatier than Satan's armpit in here and stinkier than his ...'

'Jerry!' Mell's tone was sharp, matching the dagger eyes that she stared him down with and he obediently shut up. 'We can't afford to stay down here Simon,' she insisted, feeling her body convulse as she tried to suppress a cough.

'I know, I know. Just, let me think,' he paced the room an intense frown of concentration lining his face.

'The legion up in the other cavern,' Suze said, thinking aloud. 'What if they got here before us? What if we already passed the eagle and it's up there somewhere ...'

'In the killing field?' Sarah replied. 'I don't think so. The legion was destroyed by something, that would either have destroyed the eagle too, or taken it,' she coughed and wiped her eyes. 'Although I was only really looking at my feet. It was just too horrible to do anything else.'

'There is a keyhole here,' Claire slurred her words slightly as she indicated something on the stone slab below the corpse, and Mell snapped her gaze up to the other girl's face, concerned.

'We need to get Claire out of here,' she said, as Simon swept the mouldering head of Remus aside to see what she had spotted.

'There is a keyhole,' he said almost breathless with relief. 'Jerry, give me a hand, we need to move the body.'

'Dude! The guy is practically liquid! There is no way I'm touching that,' Jerry reeled backwards two steps and made a retching sound that turned into a cough as he struggled to catch his breath.

'Will you grow a bloody spine.' Simon's attention was focussed on the rotting corpse, all his energy focussed on the keyhole and the possibility that it might grant access to the eagle of Romulus. Which, in turn, might allow him to track down and rescue Lisa from any one of several nightmarish scenarios that were persistently running through his mind.

'I'm not your slave, you can't order me around!' Jerry retorted, taking a stand.

Simon closed his eyes and pinched the bridge of his nose in frustration. 'Jerry will you stop wasting time and just do it!'

There was a heartbeat's pause as the boys considered each other. Jerry taller, and street smart, Simon sport honed and intelligent. If they were going to fight it out, it was difficult to suggest which way it would go. Jerry muttered something under his breath but relented and they both began distastefully shoving the gangrenous and bloated body off its eternal bed.

'Christ, that stinks,' Claire said gagging, and immediately dry heaving as a putrid stench rose from the corpse.

'Oh, Claire don't,' Mell clapped a hand over her own mouth, trying to stifle the heave in her throat.

The body rolled off the block with a squelchy sounding thump, leaving an opaque greasy smear across the stone where it had lain. Suze forced down her own urge to puke, and stepped a little closer to the now vacated slab of stone. The small keyhole that Claire had spotted was not the only thing now visible in the stone. A second keyhole, lay where the corpse's feet had been. Both were outlined in silver metal, tarnished and blackened by years spent below the putrid body.

'*Aquila es clavis*,' Simon muttered, finally understanding what the old man had been trying to tell him. 'Suze do you still have that other key?'

Nodding, Suze dug the silver feather shaped key out of her pocket and passed it to Jerry, and the four girls crowded around to watch as the boys carefully inserted the keys into the stone and slowly turned them, unlocking the slab. A soft click was the only sound and they both immediately grabbed at a ridge in the slab hoping to lift or twist it, but nothing happened.

'We did unlock it right?' Jerry said. 'I mean, it wasn't open already and like idiots we just locked it?'

Simon pulled a face and shook his head, before coughing loudly, he was certain that they had opened the lock. 'Try again,' he stuttered between coughing fits.

'We should leave. Now! We have already been down here for too long,' Mell insisted, wrapping an arm around Claire's shoulders and heading for the door to the chamber. She clearly intended to start climbing back up to the surface.

Jerry groaned but ignored Mell and bent to the task, and with a little extra effort this time the slab moved. The huge piece of stone splitting, the surface on which Remus had lain swinging upwards on a hinge along the back edge, finally obscuring the putrid body from sight. Suze and Sarah moved closer eager to see what was inside the stone.

It was empty.

'Jupiter's balls,' Jerry swore and thumped the empty casket. His words covered everything the rest of the group were thinking, and they simply remained silent, staring in dismay at the empty stone.

'Guys we have to leave. Now!' Mell demanded, from the entrance to the room. At her side Claire was coughing, tears streaming down her face. 'We will never be able to climb the wall, and if we can't climb we can't leave!' she strode back into the room, intending to forcibly drag some of the others away from the empty hinged stone.

Simon made a noise in his throat and staggered backwards sinking to his knees on the floor, hands knotted in his short dark hair, eyes closed in defeat. His one potential chance to save his girlfriend, gone. He was out of ideas, he had a headache and the edges of his vision were beginning to blur. It was game over.

'Someone was here first,' Sarah said in dismay. 'But who? Surely if it were the followers of Remus they would have kept it, perhaps it's still in Rome.'

'They could have melted it,' Simon groaned from the floor. 'Ensured no one could ever use it. That Remus could never be stopped. They have clearly been searching for his eagle for years, they could have easily come across this one and destroyed it.

'Wait, it's not totally empty,' said Mell, catching sight of something and temporarily forgetting her desperation to leave. Reaching into the stone chest she brushed a layer of dust aside. 'Look,' she blew gently into the open stone, her breath dislodging the finer particles of dust and revealing carved words above a tiny oval depression.

'Simon,' Suze grabbed his shoulder, hauling him reluctantly to his feet, the effort making her head swim. 'Come on we need a Latin dictionary.'

The lettering was poor, scratched in by a barely literate individual rather than a master stonemason, and as the chamber continued to grow warmer, Simon spent precious moments they didn't have, puzzling over the translation. The words were not properly formed into a sentence but rather comprised a series of basic Latin words strung together in a phrase without thought as to verb placings or denominatives. But it made the point. '*Cum Caesare recurrit, et aquilae volat.*' He announced finally. 'When Caesar returns, the eagles will fly.'

'The hell does that mean?' Said Jerry suppressing a cough though his body shuddered with the effort.

'Damned if I know.' Simon replied, flicking sweat from his face. 'But I think the legion left this, the inscription is in a military style.'

'What is that for?' Mell asked, indicating the oval depression below the etched script.

The tiny shallow cut was green in colour, probably bronze, or brass, inlaid into the stone. Inside was a small image, almost impossible to make out. Mell leaned in and ran her damp finger over the metal, rubbing off some of the rusted muck, revealing a recessed image within the plate. A very tiny eagle.

'Give me your hand.' she asked Simon. He gave her a puzzled look and extended his right hand towards her. 'No, the other one,' she requested, 'with your stupid ring.'

'Mell,' he replied tiredly, but seeing where she was going with her thought. 'I really do not care what Romulinus said at the museum or Tiberius said at the hotel, they were both clearly insane. Caesar had no surviving heirs.'

'Stop being so bloody logical, after some of the stuff we've seen, what we've been through I'm surprised you can't open your well-educated mind just a tiny bit more.' Frowning, she grabbed his wrist and squeezed hard as he resisted.

'Melody, this is ridiculous. The eagle on the ring is the symbol of the de Valentia family, a crest of Spain, nothing more,' Simon pulled his hand away. 'We should leave, there is nothing here.'

'Then what is there to lose!' she yelled back, staring defiantly at him, before breaking into another fit of coughing. Closing her eyes, she realised that it was far too late for them all to attempt the climb back out. There really was nothing to lose. Losing her patience, she grabbed Simon's sweat slicked left hand and manipulated the signet ring free. Holding it carefully she reached into the hollowed-out stone, carefully lining up the embossed intaglio with the shallow bronze depression in the stone. She settled it in securely and twisted it like a key in a lock. A brief look of concern flickered over her face and she grabbed the side of the stone as the whole base dropped down and began to slide backwards.

'So, it's a Spanish eagle, is it?' Mell said smugly handing the signet ring back to Simon.

'Has to be a coincidence,' he muttered turning it over, examining the intaglio, the spread eagle of the de Valentia crest. He slipped it back onto the little finger of his left hand, a part of him hating how naturally it sat there.

'Sssssuze!' Jerry grabbed at her arm, his eyes on the inside of the box. Being taller than the rest he could see something. 'Shiny, very shiny,' he stuttered. 'Shiny and yellow, and … and Yes!' he hollered in triumph. 'Fortune and glory.' Throwing his arms wide he let out a whoop of delight and then dived headfirst into the stone box before any of the others could get a better look.

'Tah-dah! Richer than pirates,' he crowed emerging from the box with a glittering, golden eagle. With visible effort, he raised it above his head like a trophy, the golden wings spreading wide above him.

'Wow,' Claire breathed, limping back into the chamber to join them. 'It's beautiful.'

Like the silver eagle of Remus, it was magnificently carved, curving beak, elegant head, each feather rendered individually down the throat and chest. Scales on the feet down to the curved and deadly looking talons clutching two jagged lightning bolts. The bird stood almost half a meter in height with an impressive wingspan, almost a meter across. It was twice the size of the silver eagle of Remus and from the way Jerry was now staggering under its weight, it was probably solid gold.

A low hissing groan came from somewhere and the group fell silent.

'Could be a vent,' gasped Sarah, reminding them of their current location inside an active volcano. She massaged her throat and coughed.

'If it is, we do not want to be here when it blows,' Mell replied eyeing the eagle. 'How the hell are we getting that out of here?'

'Back door,' said Jerry with a grin, 'I told you there is always one. The eagle wasn't the only thing in the fake stone, look!'

He was right, carved into the base of the hinged stone, a series of steps descended away into a dark, but judging from the visible tool marks in the walls, man-made tunnel.

'How the hell is going further down going to help?' Claire coughed. 'Surely that just puts us closer to the danger?'

The sudden rasping scrape of metal on stone caught their attention. After summer, it was a sound they all recognised with dread, something else was down here. A shadow loomed around the side of the stone box and a rusty blade slammed into the floor, as the festering corpse of Remus lurched forward. As he stepped awkwardly around the yawning exit, a huge chunk of flesh detached itself from one of his legs, leaving a yellowed bone protruding from the greying flesh above the knee.

'Tiberius?' Sarah asked uncertainly.

'I don't think so. He's too afraid of dying to come down here,' said Jerry taking a step back and hugging the eagle to his bare chest.

'Meredius,' Simon said, recalling the name from somewhere or someone he couldn't place.

The obscene being turned its purple, gaunt face in his direction. The single eyeball dangling down its cheek like a broken yo-yo. Meredius, if that's who he was, raised a skinny finger and delicately guided the hanging eye back into the yawning socket.

'Okay, why do dead guys keep waking up around us?' said Claire. Eyeing the stairs with desire, afraid that their exit strategy was about to vanish as the rusty sword in the corpse's hand rasped against the stone again.

'Jerry, take the girls and the eagle, see where those stairs go. Get Romulus's eagle back to Rome,' Simon called snatching up the sword that he had taken from a fallen legionary earlier. 'I have this.'

As the others made for the hidden stairway, Suze reached behind her for the gladius that she had stuck through her belt loops during the climb. It wasn't Arondight but it felt good to have a real blade in her hand again.

From the stone box, having ushered the other girls down the steps, Jerry shot her an anxious look. 'Suze?'

She twirled the blade around her hand, and flashed him a smile. 'Go.'

XXXVI

Jerry clasped the heavy golden eagle against his chest, feeling the chill of the metal against his bare skin, a contrast to the heat inside the volcano. It was getting hotter and the staircase that had been concealed inside the stone seemed to descend steeply away into the heart of the mountain. Nope, Jerry was not sure he liked this at all, but there was no way he was going back up to face the sword wielding corpse either.

Up ahead Mell came to a sudden halt. 'Where's Suze?'

'Where do you think?' Jerry replied from his place at the back. 'She ain't gonna let Si have all the fun.'

'She stayed?' Claire exclaimed in horror.

'Suze is pretty damn good with a sword,' Sarah offered. 'She'll be fine. They both will. We should concentrate on getting out of here and back to Rome.'

'Sooner the better, treasure is heavy,' groaned Jerry, shifting the eagle's weight in his arms.

Mell frowned but said nothing. She strongly disapproved of the group splitting up after the trouble they'd run into over the summer, and again in the Colosseum earlier. As a group, they seemed to attract an amount of trouble but separated it tended to multiply, and people got hurt. Or killed, her mind forcibly reminded her. She shook her head, now was not the time to dwell on what she'd done and the terrible what-ifs that plagued her about the death of Richards.

The steps continued to descend, becoming steeper and narrower. Unlike the passages that they had followed into the volcano, this one was obviously man made. The steps were flat and squared, the walls showing notches left by the tools used to carve out the stone. A breath of fresh air wafted down the tunnel. The early morning was still dark, but up ahead a small patch of the darkness seemed less dense, they were almost out.

Alongside the group a loud hissing, like gas escaping a canister, could be heard in the wall, and wordlessly they increased their pace. Moments later the hiss became louder and behind Jerry, a portion of the passage was forcibly blown out as the volcano vented a jet of deadly gas.

'Move, Move, Move!' he yelled, his long legs eating up the ground. He rushed the girls along in front of him as the seething gas cloud behind expanded and raced down the passage after them.

Claire, her arm still strapped into the makeshift sling, was struggling and she cried out as she banged her injured shoulder on the wall. And again, as Jerry slammed into her from behind, jarring her shoulder and crushing the hard eagle between them.

'Sorry,' he gasped out as she struggled to regain her feet. 'Come on Claire!' He tucked the eagle awkwardly under one arm and grabbed her hand, pulling her along the passage as quickly as he could.

The air was growing stale and sulphurous, but the tantalising taste of fresh air was growing stronger. At the head of the group Mell was flat out sprinting towards it, her long red hair streaming out behind her. Sarah hot on her heels. Hearts pounding and limbs pumping they forced their way ahead, powering out of the mountain below the still, star spattered sky.

Outside surrounded by trees they stopped for a second, hands on their knees, heads down, breathing deeply. Breath did not come easily and both girls felt light headed. Sarah staggered a few paces, hands still on her knees, she felt sick, more so when she saw the dead bird by her foot.

'Eww,' she gasped, and then looking sideways saw another, and a third, a fourth. 'Shit!' she hissed. The passage had dumped them out on the lower slopes of the volcano, but in a deep pocket of the landscape surrounded by trees. Dead birds covered the copse, and the air was still and silent. 'Mell, we're in a gas pocket.'

'Bollocks!' Mell swore, and, staggering and dizzy, they scrambled for higher ground as Jerry and Claire finally emerged from the tunnel, the opaque cloud of toxic vapour just behind them.

'Come on, move,' Sarah tried to scream at them, but her throat hurt and she could barely draw breath enough to move herself. Clawing through the undergrowth on her knees she forced herself onwards.

Jerry was aware of the danger and despite Claire's protests to stop and rest a moment, he continued to drag her through the foliage. The priceless eagle still jammed awkwardly under his arm.

Claire stumbled again and sank to her knees. She knew that she was physically the weakest of the girls, but she tried. With a pained and distinctly unladylike grunt of effort she tried to push herself back to her feet and failed, her knees folding beneath her, she sprawled to the ground, ready to give up.

'Come on Claire,' Jerry urged, still holding her hand. 'You can do this, I know you can.'

'I can't,' she gasped, her right-hand clawing at her throat. 'I can't.'

Jerry dropped her hand and she let out a painful scream of fright thinking he was going to leave her there. 'Not going anywhere,' he promised. He took the heavy eagle in both hands and lobbed it as far up through the bushes past Mell and Sarah as he could. Then, leaving them to search through the undergrowth for it, he crouched down low enough for Claire to wrap her free arm around him, so that he could piggyback her up out of the gas filled hollow.

He was swaying, and his eyes were streaming as he finally staggered over the lip of the depression and into clear, sweet, natural air. He sank to his knees, allowing Claire to disembark before collapsing onto his back, wracked with coughing and searing pain in his chest. To his left Mell was crouched on all fours sobbing and hacking up her lungs, whilst to the right Sarah seemed less affected and was probing through the dense foliage looking for the golden eagle.

Catching their breath, the four teenagers kept their eyes glued to the passage that they had recently emerged from, hoping for a sign that Simon and Suze were following them. Thunder rumbled across the sky, close enough to make the ground tremble and the sulphuric stink of the mountain intensified.

Mell glanced up as the ground shuddered again. The sky was still dark, but above them, a darker streak blotted out the stars. The mountain was smoking. As thunder rumbled across the landscape again she realised that the sound came from the mountain rather than the sky. Steeling her nerves, she stared one last time at the empty tunnel leading from the tomb of Remus. 'Come on Simon,' she muttered giving them a precious few more seconds to appear before she was forced to unwillingly make her next move. 'Guys come on, we're going.'

'The hell we are,' Jerry objected. 'Si and Suze are still in there, they might need help.'

Instead of answering, Mell simply turned and walked away, keeping her phone light on the ground, they would have to follow her. Whatever happened now, they had to get the eagle back to Rome. She hated to abandon her friends, but both of them knew what they were doing and had been aware of the risks in staying.

'Mell,' Sarah caught up with her. She held the golden eagle, now looking a bit battered after its rough flight through the undergrowth. 'Mell, we can't leave them.'

Spotting the scooters still parked exactly where they had been left, Mell gestured back towards the mountain. 'He said get the eagle to Rome, so let's do that.' She watched as Jerry helped Claire towards them. Claire was in a bad way but still struggling gamely onwards. 'Listen,' Mell said addressing all of them. 'I don't know what we do with that eagle when we get to Rome, but I do know that the damn thing is far more useful to us there than it is here. We'll leave them a scooter, they know where they're going. Now let's get out of here before this mountain blows.'

*

Lisa was exhausted, grubby and sweating. Her hands were raw, already damaged from the Colosseum, her beautiful French manicure was ripped to shreds. Most of the false nails were missing and her fingers bled. Ignoring the stinging sensation in her palms she surveyed the enlarged rat hole with some satisfaction. It had taken a long time but, she had done it. The opening was just about big enough to crawl through and thankfully, she had not seen the rat again.

Cautiously she peered through the hole, only now wondering where her escape route would take her. Through the broken plaster and wattle work she could see the cobblestones of a street and, further away, the dirty plaster wall of another building. But no people, the alleyway outside was silent.

Lisa felt the rising of an internal conflict again. Staying in the room was a bad idea, staying in the room meant captivity and enrolment into some strange Roman cult, or worse, becoming Remus's mistress. But a deserted alleyway could be even worse. Alleyways were where pretty girls were attacked, raped and killed. She sat back cross legged on the floor, the tall boy's jumper stretched over her knees. What she wanted was for her boyfriend to appear outside and pull her to freedom. What she had was an empty street and two poor choices. She shook herself, mentally hearing her friend Louisa's voice in her head; *Lisa it's the twenty-first century, no one needs a man to rescue them. We are all strong independent women, who needs prince charming. We can do it ourselves.'* The words, she realised, were strangely similar to what Messalina had said earlier. Of course, it was Louisa who had gotten her into this mess in the first place by suggesting she be a modern, independent woman and come to Rome alone to surprise Simon. There was a time and a place for feminism, and right now Lisa wanted her man to rescue her.

Staring through the hole she had made, she found herself contemplating Simon's unsuitable female friends. They seemed to really be the free, independent, able to do-anything-they-wanted-to types, something that Louisa only thought she was. The reality of course was that Louisa still used daddy's credit card to buy things and expected Tobey to take her out for dinner. Lisa frowned, Simon's friends would probably all have already left the room by now, without sitting here contemplating their options, especially the short cocky one. Suze, Simon had called her, she was a trouble maker, act first think never. The one with the terrible green dye job though, she seemed softer, more feminine. Lisa clenched her teeth recalling the first sight of her; elegant make up, enviably stylish orange crop top and tight jeans, arm in arm with Simon. Yes, she seemed more feminine all right. Perhaps the rat and the empty alley would have stopped her too.

Weighing herself against her perceived rival, Lisa made her decision. There was no way she could let that jumped up green-haired little tart beat her and steal her man. Lisa had made it to Rome on her own, she could damned well crawl through a hole into a deserted street. Finally resolved, and before she could change her mind, Lisa flattened herself against the floor to wriggle through the opening and stopped, feeling something hard in the pocket of the oversized hooded jumper she still wore.

She had forgotten about the lighter. She debated simply throwing it behind her as she left, but immediately reasoned that the light could be of use if the alley was really dark, or as a weapon if she really needed one. But there was something else that she could do. It may not stop Remus and Messalina, but it would cause trouble and may even prevent them from looking for her.

With a smile, she carefully clicked the flame and sought out the only flammable looking thing in the room. Crinkling her nose in distaste she touched the fire to the disgusting looking blanket on the bed. It caught immediately and Lisa raced back to her hole in the wall, threw herself down and in a state of blind panic wriggled her way through the gap.

For a heart wrenching moment, she thought that she would be stuck as the plaster scraped along her back and derrière. Suppressing a scream, she pressed herself harder into the ground and dragged herself forward, feeling the jumper snag twice on the ragged plaster. Then she was free, sprawled on her stomach in a distinctly grotty alley smelling of urine, but free.

She stumbled to her feet, wishing desperately that she had shoes and glanced up and down the street. It was empty and, trying to be more like Simon's friends, she made the snap decision to run to the end of the street furthest from her escape hole. She fled, as fast as she could and stopped, heart hammering in her chest as she rounded the corner into a bustling market. Everywhere she looked were people, dressed in funny old clothing, tunics and shawls, there even seemed to be one man in a toga. Then the scene faded from her view and she just managed to dash out of the way as a man in medieval looking garb clattered through the streets on a horse. Utterly lost, she ran.

XXXVII

Once the others were gone Simon slowly transferred his sword to his left hand, his dominant hand. Standing behind him Suze couldn't help but smile at his action, he still kept it a secret. At least holding the blade in his left meant that there would be no messing about. She tightened her grip on her own sword and stepped up beside him, standing on his right, the blades defending their flanks. Simon acknowledged her presence with a tight smile.

The decaying creature, Meredius, continued to stagger slowly towards them, blade point scraping along the floor with a raspy squeal. It moved slowly, the extent of its own decay clearly a hindrance. A muted hissing sound, escaping gas, came from somewhere inside the mountain and a wave of heat rolled across the chamber, followed by a barely perceptible vibration beneath their feet.

'Circle to the right,' Simon ordered, already moving slowly to his left.

Both teens moved cautiously, slow cross steps, eyes always on the target as they moved to flank the swaying, leering corpse. It twisted its grotesque head, tracking Simon. Clearly it perceived him as the greater threat, that was its first mistake. It pivoted, remaining in the centre of the circle that the pair were walking, always facing Simon, allowing Suze to get behind it.

Standing behind the creature she could see the mottled shading of decay on its back. The armour covered much of the torso, but the back of the one fully remaining leg was a lurid purple, indicating where blood had pooled in the body. The hanging left arm indicated the same blotchy purple pattern. But Suze could see something else. In the left shoulder of the leather armour, where it hung at an angle on the decaying bones, a cut mark, the width of a Roman gladius. The mark of Remus's death, the place where Romulus had sunk his blade and removed his brother from history. Not a wound sustained in battle, but the merciless execution of a defeated enemy.

Suze flexed her hand around the handle of the sword, eyes flicking between Simon and the ghoul standing between them. In an ideal world, she would rather not stab it in the back, but needs must. She caught the subtle nod Simon threw her way and lunged forwards in a simple, but elegant, attack. The demonic creature whirled around, parried instantly and raised the pointed tip of its own sword towards her throat. Suze had been cocky.

Simon moved then, forcing Meredius to turn around and face him. The blade in his left hand momentarily giving him the advantage as it confused his undead adversary. But the creature was faster than initial impressions would suggest and well skilled in Roman sword play.

The humble Roman gladius was not an edged sword, but a point weapon. Designed for close combat and delivering a deadly stab to the victim, usually with a twist of the blade for good measure. The gladius though was shorter than their usual fencing blades and considerably smaller than Suze's precious Arondight, leaving them closer to the creature than either warrior had any desire to be.

Simon parried an attack from Meredius, the blades contacting with a solid clatter, and made a thrust towards his exposed shoulder, but the creature retreated fast.

Suze slipped in again, forcing Meredius around, taking his focus away from Simon. Between them, they hoped to wear him down, if such a thing could be done, forcing him to change direction fighting an attack on two fronts. Sooner or later he would make a mistake.

Moving, fast as a lightning bolt, Meredius took his third option and threw himself towards the wall, breaking free of the circular trap. This was a little more dangerous, with his back to the wall he could see both teenagers. The mouldering face grinned widely, displaying rotten, toothless gums as the almost fleshless hands came together on the handle of his sword. And with a twist, split the blade down the centre, creating two narrow, rapier like swords. The single eye glinted in triumph as Meredius held his weapons ready.

'Shit,' hissed Suze. 'I didn't know they could do that!' she coughed, the air in the room was thick and the battle was taking its toll.

'This is new,' Simon agreed, wiping sweat from his face, feeling how shallow his own breathing was. They would not be able to keep this up much longer.

Another wave of heat rolled through the room accompanied by a low growling rumble from deep inside the mountain. Suze felt the ground tremble below her feet and shot an anxious look at Simon, who frowned and tried to stifle a cough. The air, which had been thick and heavy to begin with, was noticeably hotter and getting more and more dense. Suze sucked in a breath feeling the heat sear down her throat. Something was wrong. Keeping her eyes on the duel wielding Meredius she pushed a hank of sweat drenched hair out of her face with her left wrist.

Meredius leapt forward attacking with both arms, engaging Simon with his right and Suze with his left. The blades clattered dully together, alternately meeting high and low as they vied for a gap in defence. Meredius stepped back briefly and punched both arms forward, dragging them back and punching outwards again in a piston like stabbing movement. His left arm was weaker Suze noticed. The thrusts tended to drop low and the defence was sluggish, although as the heat increased in the room her own movements were becoming slower.

The flailing corpse lurched around the cavernous tomb, swinging both blades in wild arcs. The flat of one landed a solid hit on Suze's arm, and she cried out in pain, almost dropping her own blade as a bruise blossomed into life almost immediately. Watching for his next upward swing she stepped in, blocked his downward swing with her left arm, and moved in under his defence forcing him to drop his guard against Simon and engage her blade with his right hand.

Simon jumped on the opportunity that Suze had presented him with, and rammed his blade home between the exposed ribs of Meredius's right side. The corpse bellowed in surprise, engulfing Suze in its foetid, decaying breath, and she staggered backwards away from it. Meredius immediately swung his left arm around to attack Simon, who jumped back leaving his own sword embedded in Meredius's side.

'¡Mierda!' he swore staring at the trapped sword. 'Suze throw me your blade.'

Reluctantly she tossed it over, watching as Meredius flailed ineffectively with his left hand. The blade sticking out of his right side restricted his movement with his dominant hand. Simon had punched upwards with the sword, sliding it between the reanimated corpse's ribs, the point of the weapon stuck out of Meredius's back chipping through the shoulder blade, but almost half the blade and the handle protruded at an angle from his right side.

Simon tossed the one remaining blade between his hands watching for Meredius's next move, looking for the inevitable gap in his defence that would allow the second blade through. Suze backed off towards the stairs and their way out of the mountain. There was another low rumble and a fragment of rock from the roof of the cavern landed on the floor in front of her. Another quickly followed and the ground heaved, causing all three participants to lose their footing. A jet of foul smelling steam escaped from a crack in the wall and the temperature skyrocketed.

'Simon?' Suze called, hating the tightness in her voice.

'I know,' he replied, his eyes never leaving Meredius.

Meredius had other ideas though. Why fight the armed adversary when there is an unarmed one? With a monstrous hiss, he dropped his guard towards Simon and sped towards Suze. Limbs feeling like iron weights she dodged out of the way of the outstretched blade in his left hand, but missed his follow up sideswipe. He caught her shoulder knocking her to the floor.

Thinking quickly, Suze dragged herself forwards and made to rise but felt the press of a hobnailed boot on her back. The pressure was lifted almost immediately as Simon slammed into Meredius from the side. He missed his attack with the sword but succeeded in shifting the weight from Suze long enough for her to scramble free. One of the rapier blades clattered to the floor and she snatched for it, rolling onto her back thrusting the blade upwards towards Meredius, dimly aware of heat radiating through the stone below.

Meredius reeled backwards from the point allowing Simon to finally catch him with a glancing blow of the borrowed gladius. The corpse swung around flailing and Simon dodged under his arms and hauled Suze to her feet as another rumble echoed from deep within the mountain.

'Come on,' he pulled her with him as fragments of the ceiling began to fall. Tendrils of toxic vapours were visibly seeping into the room through freshly opened vents. The cavern was beginning to collapse.

Together they hurled themselves down the hidden stairs. The corridor was dark and swelteringly hot, and even worse, the scrape of metal on stone indicated that Meredius was following. Suze fumbled for her light, as Simon shoved her ahead of him, he kept an eye to the rear, sword raised in his left hand anticipating that Meredius would catch up. Both teens were struggling to breathe in the noxious atmosphere and were moving noticeably slower. Already long dead, however, Meredius was still moving at speed.

'Keep moving Suze,' Simon gasped out, shoving her further ahead of him and turning to fully face the ghoul behind.

Unwilling to leave him but unarmed and unable to help, Suze staggered onwards through the hot tunnel still attempting to fumble her phone free of her pocket. From behind came a muted metallic clang followed by the thump of metal on stone and the intimidating hiss of another vent somewhere in the mountain.

Forcing herself to remain upright Suze staggered on, movement becoming slower and harder until she felt a hand on her back again and let out a squeak of fright.

'*Solo yo*,' Simon's voice was hoarse and he was gasping for breath.

'There's something … ahead,' Suze gasped between snatched gulps of stale air. Simon pushed harder against her back and she staggered forwards a little faster, hearing the scrape of metal still behind.

'Can not … hold him … off,' Simon panted struggling to move, talk and breathe at the same time. He twisted again in the narrow space and Suze heard a fleshy thump and a grunt of pain in the darkness, then the hollow clang of metal again, and felt Simon's elbow in her back, still forcing her to move.

All Suze wanted to do was sink to her knees. To stop. To give in to the asphyxiating pain in her lungs, dark spots clouded her vision. There was another hiss from behind and a horrific scream. Light flared in the darkness casting shadows ahead of them. The scream continued, a tormented howl becoming a keening wail and Suze chanced a look under her arm. There were flames in the tunnel behind and a wall of white vapour.

Suddenly there was space all around and Suze felt, rather than saw Simon grab her wrist, dragging her through the thick foliage outside the tunnel. There was opaque vapour swirling around their knees and she still couldn't breathe. 'Move Suzannah,' he hissed through gritted teeth as she tried to stop.

With a final heave, Simon dragged them both up out of the undergrowth and leaned heavily against a tree, one arm around Suze's waist keeping her upright. Clouds of vapour billowed out of the passage behind them, and within it a lurching shadow. Meredius. He was still coming.

The ground trembled, the tree branches were shaking above. The air reverberating with a loud roar like a plane taking off. The shaking grew more violent, hurling the teens to the ground. The tunnel through which the pair had escaped collapsed, crushing the lurching drunken shadow that was Meredius and, sprawled on the floor, Simon's left hand found Suze's right, threading their fingers together as with an earth-shattering roar, the top of the mountain exploded in a rush of fire and hot ash.

XXXVIII

Sarah sat on the pillion seat behind Jerry, the enormous eagle under one arm, her other wrapped around Jerry's bare chest, as they sped back towards Rome. The tension was killing her, although it was Jerry suggested that Claire rode with Mell. She wondered if he too was feeling the wrench of their destroyed friendship. It was her fault, she should never have accused him. Since that argument in Messalina's basement he'd become so closed off to her and she desperately hoped that the damage wasn't permanent. 'Jerry, I'm sorry,' she muttered, leaning her forehead against his back.

'You should be,' he replied, as the little bike zoomed onwards with a waspish whine. 'Contrary to popular opinion I am not an asshole.'

'I know, it's just,' Sarah struggled with the words. She knew what she wanted to say, just not how. She'd been so jealous when she'd seen him flirt with Claire earlier, especially in his faux chivalric way.

'Just what!' Jerry gunned the little bike over a break in the road jolting them so roughly, that Sarah almost lost the eagle and had to snatch it back from the air.

Sarah closed her eyes. 'Do you remember the tunnel filling with water?' she asked, unsure what his reply might be.

'How could I forget?' his voice had softened. 'First time I kissed ya.' Although Sarah couldn't see it, the smile on Jerry's face was evident in his tone, as he slalomed the Vespa between a pair of large stones that suddenly appeared in the road.

Sarah took a deep breath and closed her eyes. 'First time I kissed anyone.'

They both almost fell off as Jerry stalled the bike. 'For real?' he kept his eyes on the road, watching Mell and Claire zooming off into the distance.

A distant rumble of thunder almost drowned out her response. 'Yeah,' she replied, barely able to force the word past her lips.

Still staring ahead, eyes fixed on the road, Jerry had the uncomfortable realisation that Sarah was trying hard not to cry. He ran his tongue over his upper lip and, balancing the little bike between his long legs, twisted in the seat finally looking at her. 'You could have done worse.' he grinned. Her face crumpled.

'Hey, I'm serious,' he continued. 'Could have been some idiot whose name you didn't even know. Least we didn't go the whole way and have sex. Now that would make things weird.' He turned back to the road, already mentally cursing himself, but she'd caught him off guard with that first kiss comment.

'You're making fun of me!' she punched his shoulder in frustration, already wishing she'd not said anything, now he just had something else to tease her with.

'Not, I promise. And for the record,' he turned the engine on. 'If I'd known it was your first, I'd have done a better job.'

'You are making fun of me,' Sarah hissed. 'You know what Jerry, just forget it! Forget I said anything. I try to talk to you seriously for a second and you just make fun of me.'

He turned back to her, hurt written all over his face. 'Sarah come on, you're not being fair. What am I supposed to say?' he replied. 'I don't know what you want.' He turned back to the road and twisted the throttle moving the bike forwards again. 'Not sure you know what you want either.'

Behind him Sarah closed her eyes, her face was hot, she felt humiliated, what had she expected him to say? He was Jerry. He was hardly going to throw down the bike and tell her she was the only girl in the world he wanted. That wasn't what she wanted from him, she just missed their closeness. He'd probably lied about remembering it anyway.

It didn't take them long to catch up with the other two, they seemed to have stopped too. Mell had pulled over to the side of the wide Roman road and was sat on a mile stone, face buried in her arms, whilst Claire remained on the back of the Vespa staring absently at the smudge on the hazy horizon that marked Rome.

'Something wrong?' asked Jerry, skidding the bike to a halt.

Mell shook her head and looked up. 'Just tired, and when I get tired I see …' she shook her head, 'him, Richards everywhere.

Jerry glanced back at Sarah still sat on the pillion seat of their bike. 'Well dearest damsel looks like you get your wish. Mell can't drive like that. Take that bike and go with Claire,' he glanced up at the sky as a low growl of thunder interrupted him. 'We'll meet you in Rome.'

'Where?' Sarah demanded, deliberately avoiding meeting his eye as she passed the eagle to Mell and slipped into the seat of the other Vespa, trying to keep hold of her storm swept emotions.

'How the friggin' hell do I know,' Jerry swept his hands back through his long corkscrew curls, creating a small ponytail and shaking it loose again. 'Tiberius may be at the hotel, although going there seems a daft idea,' he scratched his nose. 'Where is smart? And what do we do when we get there?'

'We have the eagle of Romulus, and his body was in the Colosseum, perhaps we can resurrect him?' Sarah offered as another thunderclap rolled across the sky.

'Simon would know what to do,' said Claire quietly. 'He's good at making decisions.'

'No,' Mell replied, with a frown. 'Simon is simply good at making you think that he knows what he's doing. The man is a pathological liar. We know barely anything about him really and I'm not sure if even he knows who he is right now, he's hiding so much from so many. His mask will slip one day.' She climbed onto the back of Jerry's scooter.

'He'll lose Lisa if he lies to her though,' Claire argued. 'Gary and I split up because I couldn't tell him straight what happened over the summer.'

'No offense Claire, but I think he's smarter than you,' Jerry said. 'He doesn't lie to Lisa, just doesn't tell her the bits that she doesn't need to know, like how he broke his nose or that he stayed in a hotel with …' he trailed off and stared at the mountains, his mouth opening and closing like a fish.

Behind them smoke billowed up into the sky, a towering column of ash, flaring red at the base, strangely silent, then noise, like a low flying plane rolled over them. Relentless crashing noise.

'It's erupting!' Claire's hands flew to her face, and then frantically patted Sarah on the back. 'We gotta go.'

'Yeah, we do,' said Jerry, his eyes frantically scanning the road for any sign of the third Vespa. 'Ash travels fast, and if the wind collapses the column this way,' he glanced back over his shoulder, 'then Rome is directly in its path.' Urging the girls to go, he took one last look back at the growing ash cloud and shook his head. There was nothing they could do for Simon and Suze. 'Good luck guys,' he hissed under his breath, revving the tiny engine and urging the Vespa along the battered cobble paved streets of ancient Rome.

*

Simon and Suze stared up at the immense column of ash and rock billowing upwards into the sky. At the top of the dark pillar, miles above them, the cloud began to spread, mushrooming outward, blotting out what thin shreds of light had managed to break the dawn horizon. The column speckled light and dark, glowing with orange flame at the base, hurled ash and rock from the bowels of the earth into the sky with a deafening roar. From where they stood at the base of the mountain it looked like the end of the world.

'We are screwed.'

Suze glanced at Simon unsure, over the roar of the volcano, if she'd really heard him say "screwed", it sounded too colloquial and somehow wrong in his accented voice. Although it had the desired effect of freeing her feet from the ground, she'd not even realised that she'd been rooted to the spot in terror.

Simon gave her hand a squeeze, distracting her from the noxious shadow which now covered the sky. 'Come on,' he said, 'the ash is not falling yet.' Still holding Suze's hand, he began to run through the undergrowth, pulling them away from the ash spewing mountain.

Suze couldn't take her eyes off the deadly spectacle behind. 'What about the heat? Pompeii got the pumice and ash shower followed by the plastic flow ...'

'Pyroclastic flow,' Simon corrected her without thinking, or checking his stride.

'Yeah that, but on the other side, Herculaneum,' Suze insisted, tightening her grip on his hand and slowing her pace.

Simon swallowed, but didn't stop moving. 'Best not thought about.'

Suze wrenched her hand free and stared at him, wide-eyed and trembling. 'Simon! Their brains boiled in their skulls, their flesh melted!' She was aware of a rising hysteria inside and breathed deeply, trying to suppress it. Terror would do neither of them any good.

Mastering his own fear, Simon forced himself to stop and look at her. 'I know, believe me, I know,' Simon's hand touched her face, gently cupping her cheek, his eyes fixed firmly on hers forcing her to make eye contact. When he spoke again he was calmer, quieter, speaking as if to settle a skittish horse. 'I also know that it took twelve hours for the Vesuvius column to collapse. We. Have. Time.' The final three words were enunciated with careful diligence.

They wasted a few precious moments, staring at each other, both forcing themselves to swallow Simon's lie. The air shimmered in the heat, making the world a horrific mirage, another rumble came from deep in the ground. Suze touched Simon's hand, moving it from where it still rested against her cheek, slipping her fingers between his. Simon's grip tightened on her hand betraying his own fear but outwardly he looked calm, in control, and Suze did her best imitate his actions.

Together they raced through the undergrowth, noting that some of the leaves were beginning to smoulder. The sky was dark and with no idea of where they had come out of the mountain, neither could work out where they had left the scooters earlier. There was likewise no sign of the others, they could only hope that the four of them had gotten away with the eagle and that they may be able to meet up again in Rome.

Breathing was hard, after their extended stay in the noxious tomb and with the eruption spewing tonnes of toxic gas into the air, Suze's lungs burned and her eyes streamed, blurring her vision. The lessons of her new Latin class kept pounding through her head. The final chapter of the textbook, the annihilation of Pompeii. She tripped on a root, landing heavily on her knees and dragging Simon down with her.

'Are you all right?' he asked, scrabbling one handed for the sword which he'd dropped.

'Fine,' Suze lied forcing herself to her feet. Pain flared through her right leg, and she stumbled, leaning heavily on a tree to correct her balance.

'¡Mierda!' Simon coughed, struggling to breathe himself. 'Suze, I cannot carry you through this. I do not have the strength left.'

'Then go,' she gestured, making a real effort to keep the fear of being left alone in this horror off her face. She wouldn't be responsible for his death if there was a chance he could escape without her. 'You can move faster without me. I'll limp along, get as far as I can.'

He shook his head and fixed his dark eyes on her face again. 'You know I could never do that.'

'Why the hell not? Go! Get out of here!' she flapped her hands, shooing him away. 'Go, defeat the bad guy, rescue the girl. That's your job, right?' her panic was rising with every passing second.

'You know why Suze. The same reason you chose to remain with me earlier.'

Suze regarded him suspiciously, but Simon's face was completely open, earnest, his gratitude for her action obvious. A tired grin spread over her face. 'I had no choice, I've seen you duel before. I had to stay to make sure you didn't get skewered by a rotting meat bag.'

He laughed and glanced down at the gladius in his left hand. 'Really?'

'Course,' she gasped. 'I can kick your posh butt in a sword fight any day.'

They fell silent as the first charcoaled cinders began to fall from the darkened sky. A wave of burning heat rolled over them and Simon chanced a look up at the towering column. A vague but brief look of relief crossed his face and Suze judged that the heat wave had not signified the collapse of the ash pillar. There was a rattling clunk to her left, and another to the right, followed by a third and a fourth.

'Pumice,' said Simon, noting her frightened look. She was hiding her terror almost as well as he was, her actions provoking a rush of affection within him. Suze, two years his junior, had guts, real guts, and she never gave up. Simon had never known anyone like her, he genuinely admired her, and her resolve fuelled his own. Their chances were low, he knew, but he wouldn't have wanted anyone else beside him in this maelstrom.

In obvious pain Suze forced herself off the tree and limped towards him. 'We can still make it, right?' she asked.

He remained impassively poker-faced. 'Sure,' he lied, and slipped his left arm, holding the sword, around Suze's waist, draping her right across his shoulders. And they shambled forwards through the burning rain together.

XXXIX

In a temple on the burning Aventine Hill, Messalina stared at the blurred reflection in the blue tinted glass. The first time she'd seen her real self all night. She looked terrible, exhausted, but her eyes still shone with a terrifying brightness. Things were not going well. Remus was a useless cretin and she seemed to be losing her inner fight for control with the priestess. She raised a hand to her head allowing herself to groan at the pain behind her eyes. The priestess was becoming more powerful, taking over. In the past few hours Messalina, as the priestess, had achieved the impossible. She had raised the long dead twin, brought to fruition the cause of the ancient cult, that had controlled so much of her life. She had also understood something that the other *Lupa Cultum* members had not. They had never controlled the priestess, it had always been her directing them.

The cult had been ecstatic the first time the teenaged Messalina had emerged from a trance, speaking as the priestess, giving voice to her ancient commands. But it had never been Messalina's power, the priestess had chosen her as a vessel and unless she could force the priestess from her mind, then the ancient old crone would take her soul permanently.

'Why the delay?' the words came from Messalina's lips, but they were not her own.

Messalina gripped the table, pushing her mind back against the priestess. 'She's just a girl.'

'Remus has chosen her and until the time is right we are bound to obey,' the ancient papery voice forced past her lips. 'Prepare her for his victory.' There was a pause and for a horrifying moment Messalina could see the reflection of the ancient crone in the blurred glass as she spoke. A cruel face, rendered cragged and mouldy by time in the earth, but the eyes, those bright wolfish eyes that haunted the soul. 'And for mine,' the crone cackled. 'She is more youthful than you are Messalina, High Priestess of Remus. Perhaps you have done your time as my vessel.'

'No,' Messalina tried to resist but she was weak, exhausted by almost thirty years of unquestioning obedience to the cult and the priestess. She could feel her hold on sanity slipping away, feel the presence of the priestess in her body getting

242

stronger. She had left it far too late to fight against her mental chains, but she needed to try. 'She is just a girl, as I once was.'

'She will be more,' the priestess laughed, her thin voice high and scratching like nails on a chalkboard. 'She will never make it to the temple of the Vestals, what good is she there? Her body and Remus's empire will be mine.' In the mirror Messalina's face returned, but the eyes that stared steady and unblinking from her face belonged wholly to the priestess, as Messalina finally succumbed to her complete control.

*

Lisa fled. The city looked dilapidated, it was dark, she had no idea where she was, it was certainly a part of Rome that she had never been too and unlike anywhere she had ever had to take a car through. The streets were narrow and without exception they all smelled unpleasant. The last one she'd run through had even had a mouldering animal corpse just lying in the street. It had taken all her will power not to throw up. Even in her current state, she was far too dignified to be vomiting in the street like one of Simon's rugby team mates.

Gasping for breath she finally gave in to the gnawing stitch in her side and the pain in her bare feet and leaned on a wall, dropping her head and breathing in huge gulps of foetid street air. Dots of colour danced fleetingly before her eyes and she felt a swoon coming on. Knotting her fingers in the fabric of the borrowed hoodie she breathed deeper, willing herself to stay upright and conscious. It would not do to pass out alone in a dirty narrow street in an unfamiliar place, and certainly not in the attire she was currently wearing.

A roar of sound came from behind her. A combination of many pounding feet and loud shouts. Still trying to hold on to her consciousness, Lisa was unable to tell exactly what they were shouting and whether it was something to welcome or fear. But there was light in the direction of the noise.

Finally, she was able to discern a single word shouted over and over again in many panicking voices. '*Ignis! Ignis!*' Her Italian was good, but in the panic of the moment she did not recognise the word. Simon was better at languages and she tended to rely on him to translate things for her. Frightened by the panic she could hear in the crowd's voices though, she thrust herself away from the wall and hurried onwards down the narrow street, away from the flickering light and the noise, rounding the corner and finding herself suddenly ice cold, as though she'd run into an industrial freezer.

Slowly she stepped backwards towards the street she had just left and felt the prickle of warmth instantly return to her skin. Curious now, she stuck her hand out in front of her and felt the tips of her fingers grow icy cold. Confused she waggled her fingers trying to think of a reason for there being such a blast of cold air right there, the building she was stood by didn't look industrial enough to have a huge freezer. Someone giggled.

Lisa snatched her hand back and stared around the street, but she was alone. 'Is, is someone there?' She asked, still searching the empty street for life. Silence. She reached her hand forward again, but the cold patch had moved. Then she felt an icy hand on her shoulder.

With a scream she threw herself forwards, twisting to press her back against the wall of a building, eyes desperately scanning the street. Still empty. But something had touched her, she had felt it. Perhaps Messalina had sent something else after her. Twisting her hair around her fingers she stared a moment longer at the street, then resolved that nothing was there, stepped forwards.

Another giggle and that icy chill in the air stopped her again. Followed by a voice. 'Please, stop that. It tickles.'

Clamping both hands over her mouth, preventing the scream that was bubbling in her throat, Lisa pressed her back against the wall again and stared, with transfixed horror, as a bluish glow appeared in the street. The glow grew stronger, resolving its form into that of a man. A strangely dressed man that she could see right through. She closed her eyes and screamed, no longer caring who heard her. Icy hands grabbed at her wrists, causing her to shriek even louder.

'Shhh, *Lupa. Quid agis hic solus,*' the voice was quiet, secretive but recognisable in its authority.

Thrashing against his cold touch, Lisa had no idea what he was talking about, only that it must be bad. She clawed at the blue tinted figure, and then dissolved into shrieking again as her fingers passed through his face.

'*Lupa*, please,' the figure tried again. 'I am not your enemy, the young Caesar, the Spaniard, is my master.'

'I do not care who your master is. Let me go!' she screamed again, desperately hoping that someone would hear her.

The blue transparent figure looked up. 'She is coming, hurry *Lupa*. There is still time to escape. But you must come with me.'

The icy hands touched her wrists again, and Lisa screamed, hoping to attract attention from someone, anyone. She knew what happened to pretty girls who were caught alone in dark alleyways.

'Please,' the figure insisted, a note of sadness in his voice. 'I am Gaius Tiberius Decimus, guardian of Romulus, and I serve Caesar,' Tiberius insisted, floating beside her and holding his hands up in supplication. 'I am trying to help you, I work for the *Dominus*. He will return and overthrow Rem...' his words were cut off as Lisa's scrabbling hands wrenched a piece of glass from a broken window and in desperation she twisted and slammed it into his throat.

Or she would have done, had Tiberius been alive. As it was her efforts were in vain and the glass passed harmlessly through the ghost, who let out a shriek of his own and vanished. Lisa ended up on her knees in the street, alone.

'You, you tried to kill me!' the little ghost gasped, reappearing a few feet away, confused by the girl's vicious attack. 'Why would you do that? I am not a Reman,' Lisa screamed again as she saw him, but what she saw through him chilled her even more.

The drunken form of Remus stumbled out of a tavern further along the street. 'Can't you pleb bastards keep your women quiet! Some of us are trying to drink!' his head lolled slightly as he took a shambling look around the street. 'Ah-ha!' he said, a broad grin breaking across his alcohol flushed face. 'Tiberius!' he glanced down at Lisa. 'You found my wench,' he began laughing and raised his drink. 'You found my wench. Good slave. Now where's the bloody priestess? We have conquest to undertake.'

Tiberius breathed out, relieved as Remus turned away, then stifled a squeak as she appeared. The one that he dreaded seeing. New body, but the same old cunning crone's eyes. The priestess. He recognised her instantly, she had been there when Remus was executed. She had caused everything.

'Well, what have we here?' Her newly sensuous female voice came from the corner of the street and the priestess, in full control of the woman, Messalina, glided closer. 'Ah, *fortunato!* Well done slave. You found my wolf-girl. I had thought her burned to death,' she fixed Lisa's slowly reviving form with a piercing gaze, ignoring Tiberius completely. His one saving grace, he was a slave, she'd not looked at him in life, she wouldn't look at him in death. She would never recognise him as the one who betrayed her to Romulus.

Hearing the woman's voice, Lisa kept her eyes closed. It had all been for nothing, ruining her hands, fleeing through dark and smelly alleyways. All for nothing. She wanted to cry. Tiberius, whoever he was, may have been a friend and she had ruined her chance of real escape by fighting with him. Below her she felt a tremor shudder through the ground.

'All together at last!' Remus proclaimed. 'The promised leader of the seven hills, the priestess, a slave and my reward for conquest. Now we may begin removing Romulus from time,' he looked triumphantly at the priestess. 'I told you we had nothing to worry about, that Tiberius and Meredius would obey me to the last. Slaves know their masters.' he turned his attention back to Tiberius. 'Meredius guards my body as agreed? None have discovered my tomb? All was as she promised?' he shot a look at his priestess as he spoke.

Thunder growled in the distance and through almost closed eyes, Lisa noticed Tiberius glance down at the floor, before he responded. 'Yes *Dominus.*' That word again, perhaps he had lied to her, perhaps he did belong to Remus, but he'd seemed so vehemently against him.

'We colonize the Aventine,' Remus roared. 'I will have my seat.'

Unseen by Remus, the priestess rolled her eyes. 'Remus, my divine one. The Aventine is on fire, perhaps we should consider the Palatine?'

Remus moved quickly, far faster than any of his onlookers were expecting and grabbed the priestess by the throat. 'You dare to suggest my brother's hill to me? If I did not need your power, I would kill you where you stand,' he released her and turned away.

Outwardly unruffled, but internally, swearing bloody revenge, the priestess changed track. 'So, the Palatine reeks too much of success for your taste. No matter, there are five other hills.' She swept an arm around intending to encompass the city in a dramatic gesture, but in the narrow street her action lacked flare. 'Pick one.' Remus glowered at her and rubbed his chest, he wanted the Aventine.

'*Dominus?*' Tiberius ventured. He was floating in the street between the arguing pair and Lisa, trying to keep the blonde girl safe and hoping that they may forget about her. 'What about the Capitoline? It was the seat of the gods, Great Jupiter himself lived there under your brother's rule. What could be better for your own seat?' he looked nervously at the priestess as he finished speaking.

A broad grin cracked Remus's face. 'Tiberius makes a point. Very well, we shall burn the Aventine, and build a palace fit for a living god on the Capitoline Hill.' Delighted with himself, he went to slap the slave on the back and was disturbed when his hand passed straight through Tiberius's ghostly form. 'Bloody slave, where did you go?'

The priestess rewarded Remus with an indulgent smile, but her eyes were cold, calculating. Something troubled her. The slave, Tiberius had been caught with the girl, which meant that the girl had escaped from the locked room. Had the slave helped? She had been betrayed once before by one of Remus's slaves, although, much to her annoyance she couldn't be sure which of them it had been. She would have to be watchful, Remus had not foreseen this, he was blind to the danger, but she, the priestess, would not be.

On the horizon, observed only by Tiberius, a dark smeary column was rising into the sky, unclear in the hazy light of the morning unless one was looking for it, its upper column distorted by a breeze blocking the morning star. Moments later came another rumble like distant thunder. The little ghost smiled to himself, his capture was unfortunate but all was not lost, he would simply have to tread carefully.

XL

Pumice stone, ash and rock all fell from the heavy black sky, with burning cinders twirling among them like dancing fireflies. The heat was still rising and behind the two stumbling figures, brilliant red-orange flames marked the location of the mountain, lost in the darkness below the ash cloud. A fine grey powder coated the floor, lifting in little puffs as they shuffled onwards, exhausted. Suze had been leaning heavily on Simon for a while now, and the air was growing close and steadily more toxic. Both teenagers were failing, on the point of suffocation and fatigue, unable to walk another step.

The pain in Suze's leg had eased but risking a glance down at her feet she saw that her ankle was swollen, trapped within the confines of her boot. But she dared not stop to rest or look at the damage. Beside her Simon coughed harshly and she felt his body shudder with the effort.

'I have to stop,' he wheezed dropping his head to his chest, stumbling under her weight.

'Okay,' Suze agreed, slipping her arm from his neck and limping back to give him some space. She glanced up at the darkened sky. With sunrise still over an hour away and the ash now falling heavily from the sky, it was impossible to work out if they were even moving in the right direction. Either way, they were finally clear of the dense foliage that marked the slopes of the volcano. There was no sign of the scooter. They had either gone the wrong way and lost it, or the others had taken all three.

A flash caught her eye and she squinted harder into the darkness seeking it out again. There, in the darkness ahead, distant but definitely there. Light on metal, probably the flames of the eruption catching something metallic in a field. She looked around to point it out to Simon, but he was sat on the floor, elbows on his knees, fingers in his hair, staring at the ash between his feet lost in thought.

Knowing that his thoughts must be on Lisa, where she was, if she was still alive, Suze turned away, unwilling to interrupt. Instead she watched the periodic flash, staring at it almost hypnotised. Then she noticed another, lower down but in the same place, and another close by. 'Simon?'

His response was a barely perceptible grunt. He'd almost forgotten that Suze was there, busy beating himself up about how badly he'd failed in protecting Lisa.

'Simon look, there's something moving over there,' she tried again, raising her voice forcing Simon's concentration back to their real predicament.

He looked up following the direction that she was indicating and stood, brushing ash out of his hair. 'What is it?' he asked, staring intently into the murky gloom.

Suze shrugged and continued to watch as more and more flashes of light on metal became apparent, and, barely discernible beneath the constant jet like roar of the eruption, a familiar rhythmic metallic clatter. Simon reached for their discarded gladius as the mournful call of a brass instrument broke through the sound of the eruption.

'Soldiers,' the weary pair spoke as one, both recognising the sound as a Roman legion on the march. At least according to the movies.

'How many?' Suze said, still staring into the darkness ahead.

Simon shook his head, 'Impossible to tell. But it sounds like a lot. A cohort maybe?'

'Can we fight our way out?'

Her question took him by surprise and Simon laughed, a real proper sincere laugh. The first time Suze had heard him laugh like that in ages. 'Two of us, with one sword against a whole cohort? You know that is four hundred men? Eight hundred if it happens to be the first cohort.'

'Only if it's at full strength,' Suze retorted, as the first human shadows began to loom out of the darkness.

'So, the plan is to hack our way through four hundred fully armed, fully trained Roman soldiers, with one sword between us, before the ash column back there collapses? I do love your optimism Suze,' Simon shook his head but was unable to keep the smile from his face.

Another trumpet blast came from their right, revealing more troops and a hurried glance to the left suggested that yet more soldiers were flanking from that direction. As they advanced their rectangular shields and segmented armour became clearer. These were legionaries, crack troops, the Roman army at its finest. Whatever had stopped the strange time fluctuation inside the volcano seemed to have shifted. Simon and Suze, still no wiser as to how or why the time fluctuations were happening, now appeared to be trapped in a time period around the second century AD, and at the mercy of the professional Roman army.

'It's a whole legion,' Suze hissed through clenched teeth, watching with a mixture of fear and fascination as the troops were deployed. She knew there was no way out. They were trapped with five and a half thousand armed soldiers surrounding them. A front row seat to a full display of Roman military might.

Simon swallowed and weighed his sword in his hand, resting his back against Suze's as they tried to see everything. 'See the standard anywhere?' he asked, trying to hold his nerve, as the army advanced on them in total silence. Or as total as silence could be when bits of armour clanked. Their silence was unnerving, movies and books suggested that armies roared and jeered at each other or banged swords against shields. The unnatural silence with which the Romans surrounded them was a powerful display of discipline, inducing fear to the point of paralysis.

Suze snorted. 'Jesus Simon, priorities. We're at the end of the road and you wanna know which legion is killing us?' she scanned the mass of armoured bodies, narrowing her eyes against the falling ash and finally spotted the banner. 'X. The Tenth.'

'Tenth?' Simon's head came up, and he twisted, trying to look back over his shoulder. 'Which tenth? What is their symbol?'

'How the hell do I know,' Suze squinted trying to make it out. 'Standing female deity maybe.'

'Venus?' Simon was clutching at straws, unsure of what he was aiming for.

'I don't know, maybe, wait, no. It's the constellation of Gemini,' Suze shook her head. 'It keeps changing. Must be something to do with Remus changing history.'

'But it is always the tenth?' Simon was thinking, Suze could practically hear the gears in his brain working.

She shrugged. 'Seems to be.'

Simon thought for a moment, screwing his eyes shut, desperately willing himself to think of something useful. 'The Tenth Equestris - Veneria, later the Tenth Gemina … Caesar's Legion.' Suze said nothing, eyes fixed on the three moving squads of armoured men, still relentlessly marching silently towards where the two of them stood.

'I wonder if …' Simon's thought process was cut off as a single trumpet note rang out and, with a deafening roar, a clank of armour and rasp of drawn blades, the three units of the Legion finally broke formation and surged forward, closing the open space between their units and the teenagers with an alarming speed. 'Come here!' he demanded and pulled Suze tight against his chest, curving his body over hers, protecting her, throwing his sword wielding left arm up to shield his head. It was his final action that saved them.

'*Teneo!*' a voice boomed. The first spear centurion called halt. '*Tu habet jus annulorum? Quis es?*'

He spoke in Latin, but Suze caught the general gist. He'd spotted Simon's signet ring and wanted to know how he came by it. Simon replied, in Latin, that it was his, a symbol of his Spanish inheritance.

'*Hispana, Iberia? Valentia Edetanorum?*' the officer spoke sharply, studying Simon's face.

Simon stared at the soldier, as he named the ancient settlement of Valencia. '*Sí,*' he replied warily, twisting the signet ring around his finger, keeping Suze pressed tight against his chest.

The centurion stepped back and sank to one knee, bowing his head and opening his arms in a gesture of submission. He bellowed two words. '*Ave Caesare.*'

Hail Caesar.

Following his example, the entire legion, five and a half thousand men dropped to their knees before the teenagers and echoed the centurion's triumphant cry. '*Ave Caesare.*' They were proclaiming for Simon.

'Holy shit!' Suze breathed, still pressed tightly up against his chest, her fingers tangled in his shirt. 'They think you're Caesar! I have got to get me one of those rings.' Simon stared at the eagle signet ring on his left hand in disbelief shaking his head, before raising his gaze to take in the submissive legion, all kneeling, heads bowed, awaiting their orders.

The Centurion standing beside the pair bellowed an order, the only word of which Suze understood was, *equus*, horse.

As another officer scrambled to obey, Simon glanced down towards Suze, their eyes met. Suze could see the confusion and disbelief written in the dark depths of his gaze, and for a terrifying moment she thought he was about to kiss her. In that moment, her whole world dropped away, the volcano and the army distant memories. Then the moment was broken as the Centurion gripped Simon's shoulder and gestured towards a huge muscular white horse that was being led over. White to keep the commanding officer visible to both friends and enemies and already equipped with the small uncomfortable looking saddle of the ancient Romans. Stirrupless, it consisted of the seat and four pommels, the forward pair curved to hold the rider's leg in place.

Simon, familiar with horses from years of playing polo, vaulted easily into the saddle unassisted, surprising his officers. Although they were even more surprised when he leaned down and offered Suze his arm to lift her onto the horse too.

Suze stared up at him, trying to control the raging turmoil she felt inside. She'd always kept herself in check, promised herself that she'd never go simpering after someone. Especially not a friend. Jerry had teased her on and off since they met about having feelings for Simon, but she'd never given it the slightest consideration. Simon was just a teenage boy, like any other. So why had she forgotten to breathe when he held her against him, his dark eyes boring into hers. Even with a whole army surrounding them she'd felt safe. When Simon had broken eye contact, looked away, Suze knew she would have collapsed breathless if his arms had not still held her. 'I …' she struggled to speak. 'I've never ridden a horse in my life. I'll walk with the army.' She took a step back. Horses didn't scare her, but that didn't mean she wanted to ride one and right now, after the intensity of that locked eyes moment, she did not want to be pressed up close against Simon for any period of time, let alone a ride into Rome.

Simon withdrew his arm, turned the horse and moved it closer to her, effectively cutting them both off from the officers, who stood in loose formation nearby. 'Suze,' he said, his voice so low she could barely hear him. 'There are nearly six thousand soldiers here and their blood is up. Get on the horse.' He extended his arm towards her again, concern creasing his face. 'Come on.'

'My brother's a Royal Marine. I can handle a few soldiers,' Suze stepped away folding her arms, refusing to comply. Desperately trying to squash a feeling she didn't quite understand. The idea that he might have kissed her was terrifying, utterly undesirable, it would have ruined everything. Worse it would mean that Jerry was right. There was no way Suze could live in a world where Jerry was right, especially about something as complex as this. She took another step back.

A look of intense irritation crossed Simon's face and he moved the horse closer again. '*Carajo* Suze. For your own safety get on the god damned horse.

Now,' he leaned down offering her his arm again. She wasn't sure what the Spanish meant but the look of exasperation on his face suggested it probably translated in four letters.

She tried stalling again. 'I don't know how to ...' her back hit a tree, there was nowhere else to go.

He smiled and his tone softened. 'Suze, everything will be all right. I promise. Just sit behind me and hold on,' he leaned down and caught her elbow. Taking a deep breath Suze locked her fingers around his forearm. *'Bueno,'* he smiled. 'Ready? Jump.'

She was light, and he swung her up easily onto the horse's back behind the saddle. Feeling intensely uncomfortable and afraid of how high the horse seemed, Suze wrapped her arms around Simon's waist, pressing her face against his back.

'Hey not so tight,' he groaned prising one of her hands free and twisting to look over his shoulder. 'Are you scared?'

Suze's response was muffled in his shirt, 'No.'

'You are an interesting one Miss Jones,' Simon twisted on the horse trying to catch her eye, but she was pressed too tightly against his back. 'Willing to single handedly take on an army, but afraid of sitting on a horse.' His attention was distracted by the first spear Centurion.

'Your orders Commander?' the tone was sharp the accent grating, the grizzled soldier's face registering a mild curiosity about the girl on the horse, but otherwise expressionless.

Simon turned his attention to the army and took a deep breath. 'Rome,' he muttered softly, then cleared his throat, sat up straighter, smoothing his face into the impassive mask that he wore so well and announced his intentions in a stronger voice. 'Rome ... We march on Rome.'

XLI

Remus was passed out, face down in a pool of drying vomit and wine when the priestess found him. A scowl of disapproval crept across her face, he'd said he was going to raise the army, clearly wine had distracted him, again. Nothing had gone to plan since she had woken the lazy drunken excuse for a man. He now lay snoring bubbles into his own, or possibly someone else's bodily ejecta on the table. In the sleeve of her robes her hand closed on the hilt of her dagger. It would be easy, Remus was comatose, he wouldn't even feel the blade as she slit his throat. But then what would centuries of efforts have been for.

She stabbed the dagger down into the table between his fingers, but Remus simply snorted and continued to sleep. It was easy to see why Romulus had been the one to found Rome, she felt cheated. All her attempts, all those who had tried to restore the Reman faction to power. All failures; Sejanus, Galba, Elagabalus. Elagabalus had been close but ultimately assassinated just like the others. Throughout history the Reman line had tried and failed to take control. It's only relatively successful period under the Valencian Borgia family and their control of the Papacy, but that had been short lived. Unable to raise Remus the family had ultimately driven themselves to destruction. Then there was Mussolini, drunk on his own power, her own cult had been forced to remove him.

But then something glorious had happened. An unwanted child, Messalina, had been sold to the *Lupa Cultum* and grown up believing in the cause. Devoting her life to the prospect of raising the elder of the Trojan twins from the dead to take his rightful place. The priestess had chosen her, and so, of all her ancestors, she was the one who had succeeded, she had raised Remus. For all the good it had done, the priestess reflected ruefully as the brainless oaf let out a horrendous fart and snorted into the mess on the table. He was vile, and useless. If the Remans were going to change history, she would have to do it herself. As she should have done on that windy hillside two and a half thousand years ago.

Her robes swirling about her, the priestess paced the room considering her options. It would be important that, as long as he was conscious, Remus thought he was the one ruling. Given how long he'd been back from the dead and how long he'd been conscious that should not, she thought, be a problem. Her main problem was how to take the city. Time in the Eternal City was still in flux. As she'd wandered the streets looking for the blonde girl she had seen various changes. Buildings of stone appeared as wood and then flickered back again or vanished completely. As she'd passed through another part of town, men spattered with blood, screaming that the tyrant was dead had pushed past her in the streets, only to be replaced by a Renaissance sculpture workshop and then a car. All this in the space of seconds.

Although her actions had caused it, the timeslip was now causing problems. A reddish glow swept across the room and she glanced up. The fire the girl had somehow started on the Aventine was getting worse, but only in one time period. She, they, would have to move further up the Capitoline sooner or later though, or else the building they were in may be engulfed if the wind changed direction. As the glow died something else caught her eye. A dark smudge to the southeast, like a charcoal line drawn on dark paper. She'd not been able to see it earlier when the sky was dark, but as the horizon began to pale she could see the streak and above it, a spreading dark cloud. She continued to stare at it until the red glow of the Aventine fire bathed the room red again. Whatever the smudge was, it transcended the fluctuating time in Rome.

The timeslip was localised then. The rest of Italy still lay blissfully in the grip of the twenty-first century, or at least in theory anyway. The priestess frowned, considering something. The times in which she was currently passing through were not filled with screaming confused people, she saw no one else from the twenty-first century, nor did she spot ancient Romans in Medieval Rome, therefore each layer of Rome must still function, each overlapping period of history unaffected by the other's presence. Only she, Remus and the girl, and, that dark smudge, were transcending time. Perhaps Remus was right and there was nothing to fear. The teenage troublemakers were presumably still trapped in her basement in modern Rome. The Spaniard though? His absence more than anything else troubled her. It seemed unlikely that with so much happening that he could possibly have any way to stop her, but she didn't like loose ends.

And thinking of loose ends. She pushed open the door, pausing as the world around her flickered briefly into a busy office block and she heard a phone ring, then continuing as the corridor returned. Not bothering to knock she unlocked the door to the room where she'd left the blonde girl and barged in.

*

At the sound of the door banging open Lisa flinched. She had only just finished dressing and felt horribly exposed, although not as exposed as when she had first slipped on the sheer white Vestal robes that had been left for her. She had little choice but to wear them, her own dress was beyond ruined, but she had been horrified when she first slipped them on and realised that she could see her breasts clearly through the fabric. Fortunately, the new underwear that she had bought in preparation for a romantic night with her boyfriend was a pale coral pink. And, whilst the dress was still sheer, at least now her more intimate areas weren't on display to the world, and her bra was a convenient place to tuck the tall boy's lighter.

Something was happening now though. Messalina had barged into the room like a hurricane, the look on her face wild and deranged, nothing like the person she had been before. Beads of sweat stood out on her face and her voice was the creaking harsh voice that had been more usual since Remus's resurrection. Afraid to resist, afraid that something had taken over the Italian woman's body the way the wolf took over her own, Lisa followed her back to the main room of the small house in which they were squatting, the whole room lit a bright orange by the flames on the Aventine. They were closer than they had been when Messalina had dragged her back to this place, the fire was spreading.

*

'Remus,' the priestess's voice was sharp in the otherwise silent room. Astonishingly he lurched to his feet. Incoherent and babbling but standing nonetheless.

'The girl,' he growled, shaking his head in a vain attempt to get rid of his budding hangover.

'Robed and ready for your victory,' the priestess replied, shoving Lisa towards him. Remus barely noticed. Instead his slack-jawed gaze focussed through a window, on a smudged grey line on the horizon. Lisa risked a glance to see what held him in thrall, but all she could make out was a darker line, a little like a column, against the slowly lightening sky of the early morning. It didn't seem important.

'Meredius!' Remus bellowed, 'Meredius!' Before the priestess's eyes, he sank to his knees with a howl. 'Meredius!' his arms raised imploringly towards the smudge on the horizon, the form of which was becoming clearer with each passing moment. An eruption, a vast pillar of smoke and ash rising from the Alban Mountains. 'My tomb,' Remus groaned. 'They have destroyed my tomb.'

'What!' the priestess snapped, forgetting the blonde girl as the implications of his words hit her. Unthinking she strode across the room and delivered a stinging slap across Remus's face. 'You idiot, you swore none could find it!'

Remus ignored her, a look of dawning horror on his face. 'The legion, his legion,' he hissed, rising swiftly to his feet and squinting towards the column of smoke. 'My brother's legion comes, we must raise my troops now! I must not lose the seven hills a second time. We will march and meet them in pitched battle!' he glanced around the room. 'Tiberius! Where is that useless slave? He should be here. We shall form up on the *Via Appia*.'

'With what troops?' the priestess screeched, following him around the room. She was both terrified and delighted, finally she would have what she wanted. The battle for Rome, but Remus was woefully unprepared and, if there really was a rival legion marching towards them, she could not see how they would succeed.

Remus fixed her with a dark and powerful look, snatched up his standard and strode from the building into the smoke-filled streets, powering his way towards the temple of the divine triad on the peak of the Capitoline. The priestess followed, dragging Lisa with her, from now on she couldn't let the girl out of her sight. Not if she wanted to be the young, radiant empress of her eternal empire. Clutching the blonde girl to her, the priestess watched with a mounting mixture of hope and dread as Remus raised the silver eagle standard and brandished it at the sky, finally calling forth his rabble army from the infernal fires of the underworld.

The flames died on the neighbouring Aventine as time changed, and Remus tightened his grip on his standard, watching, waiting. Then, as the orange flames roared into life again it happened. The earth trembled and the priestess watched, with unconcealed delight, as demonic soldiers crawled from the ground, emerged from the walls, and marched from the flames. Clad in black segmentata, black and smouldering crests on their helmets, fire scorched limbs and soulless eyes, they clawed their way from the ground in all parts of the city. An army of the damned creatures of Rome, the unholy army of Remus.

The girl, Lisa, let out a cry of shock at the sight of the repulsive creatures, and shuffled behind the priestess, trembling and clearly afraid. Below her delight at Remus's army, in a small part of her mind the priestess felt Messalina recoil in horror at the creatures. She shook her head, Messalina was nothing to her now, and examined her army. Their scorched, blackened limbs encased in leather and metal. They had various types of Roman and medieval armour and one or two even carried rifles. The smell of roasted flesh carried on the air and an evil smile crossed her face as Remus began to address his troops.

Lisa swayed suddenly unsteady on her feet, as mercifully the Aventine roared into flames again, its billowing smoke crossing the Capitoline, obscuring the tormented army of sub-human souls hanging on Remus's every word. To her surprise the priestess's cold, clammy fingers closed on her wrist. When she spoke her voice was lighter, her lips barely moving. 'Stay with me girl, you and I are in great danger here. But see the line of smoke? It is his tomb. It could be his defeat.'

Lisa glanced up in time to see a look of intense pain cross the woman's face as she raised a hand to her head with a moan. 'Not yet,' she muttered, but with a gasp of pain her whole demeanour changed. 'We shall stand triumphant on the battlefield with Remus,' her voice was as it had been before, harsh, calculating and emotionless as if she had morphed into a different person.

'My brother's army comes this way,' Remus roared, 'leaderless! We shall march to intercept them before they reach the city and those we do not destroy we shall win to our side! Today is ours. Today we correct our lives. Today the seven hills fall to us! The city of Rema shall rise like the phoenix from the ashes of time itself. Victory is ours by right. Take her!'

At his words, the city of Rome vanished. Remus, his army, the priestess and her prisoner now stood on open ground on the side of the windswept Capitoline Hill. Dirt paths crossed the flanks of the seven hills and skirted the marsh in the valley, but there was no other sign of settlement or life beyond the soulless creatures that gathered before their leader. With a dark laugh Remus turned his lifeless eyes on the priestess. 'Would you deny my victory now witch? We are back at the start and this time, this land, with all its history shall be ours.'

XLII

The two small scooters and their four riders sped towards Rome. Behind them, black smoke continued to billow above the volcano, but they dared not look back. Ahead, a red glow flared into life and died again in the city. Moments later it flickered again, time was in flux in the capital and somewhere, sometime a substantial fire had broken out. Sarah slowed her bike intending to wait for Jerry and Mell to pull alongside. The city could be dangerous, she risked a glance back over her shoulder and saw Jerry frantically gesturing at her to check the road. Except, when she looked back, there was no road.

Rome, the city, the walls, the tombs and the road were gone, in their place empty fields. The seven hills, where the city should be rising into the gloom of early morning. And immediately in front of her, a tree. Shocked, Sarah pulled the brakes and halted the little scooter neatly in the grass.

Jerry had less luck, in the moments he'd spent yelling at Sarah to look back he'd not dropped their speed and now with no other option he hit the brakes hard, hauling the bars of the scooter to the left. The small tyres, not designed for off roading, slipped in the wet grass and the scooter went down, landing on its side, throwing Mell off the back and dragging Jerry several yards into a shady copse of trees.

'What the hell happened?' Claire said, climbing slowly and awkwardly off the scooter, her dislocated arm still in the sling of Jerry's T-shirt. She stared at the empty horizon where moments ago, Rome had been.

Mell sat up in the grass, the golden eagle lying a few feet away and closed her eyes, mentally checking herself over. She was fine. Opening her eyes, she looked around, noticing for the first time that everything; road, city, people, seemed to have vanished. 'I guess this is Rome, just before the Romans moved in,' she said, rising slowly, feeling a twinge in her wrist as she stood. 'Jerry, you still alive?' she called turning to look for his lanky frame.

'Fanfriggintastic,' Jerry groaned, peeling himself off the ground, lifting his left arm and grimacing with distaste at the large friction burn he found there. He winced again lowering his arm, realising that his back seemed to have taken most of the impact. 'Gonna sting in the morning!' Noticing the girls' frowns of concern he clarified. 'I'm good, Scootius is wrecked though.' The little Vespa lay on its side, handlebars twisted around, light smashed and one brake lever hanging loose. Whatever Jerry had hit, he'd hit hard.

'Can't use the scooters now anyway,' said Sarah. 'Guess we walk from here?'

'And do what?' Claire asked, looking back to where the volcano still belched fire and brimstone into the sky. 'Rome has gone, the mountain exploded, Remus is running around undead somewhere, Si and Suze are missing and we are quite literally stuck in the middle of nowhere with no plan.' She dragged the fingers of her free hand through her short hair wincing as they snagged in the tangles, then frowned as she realised that the green dye was staining her hand.

'There's something moving over there!' Jerry said pulling a pair of binoculars, miraculously still intact, from his trouser pocket and gesturing for the girls to come into the trees with him, out of sight of whatever it was. He stared silently for a long time at the space where Rome had been, then simply swore and lowered the glasses, hand covering his mouth as he debated what to say to his friends.

'Jerry?' hissed Sarah, gently touching his arm. Wordlessly he passed her the binoculars and retreated further into the trees, slumping down on a fallen one. Sarah raised the binoculars, noting Simon's embossed initials on the side with a sigh, and swept the horizon searching for what had rattled Jerry. With a sharp gasp she lowered them, then raised the glasses again unable to believe what she'd seen.

Black figures swarmed over the seven hills that marked the site of Rome. There were thousands of them. A creeping fear shuddered up her spine and she lowered the glasses again 'Looks like Remus has Rome. He's won,' she said quietly, passing Simon's binoculars to Mell.

'All is not lost *Amici.*'

Three shrieks pierced the air and Jerry fell backwards off the log as the disembodied voice spoke. The four stared anxiously around the clearing, the voice had sounded as though the speaker were right beside them, but in the grey morning light no one was visible but themselves.

Jerry clawed his way upright, mildly annoyed that the voice had scared him. 'Show yourself!' he demanded, eyes flicking around the empty space. Between him and the girls a faint bluish glow appeared, slowly taking the form of a man, a Roman slave.

'Tiberius,' Mell said, relaxing a little as she recognised the funny little ghost from the Colosseum. 'Where the hell have you been? You vanished as soon as Messalina left the hotel.'

The little ghost hung his head, a disturbing vision as he floated six inches off the ground below a tree. 'I had a plan,' he groaned. 'A plan to stop her. She went to find the wren, I would have been powerless there, but Romulus would know what to do. I went to get Romulus.' He gestured towards the golden eagle lying in the grass. 'With his standard, we could have raised my old master, he could have summoned his army, we could have defeated the priestess before she started.'

'So, what happened?' Claire asked. 'Where is Romulus?'

The little ghost faded out and then back in again as he hung his head. When he spoke, his voice was a whisper, as insubstantial as his body. 'The tomb was still flooded, I cannot swim. I didn't want to drown. I felt Remus's presence, so I ran away, hid myself in the streets. Which is where I saw the girl.'

'Which girl?' Sarah asked, although she was sure she already knew.

Tiberius perked up at once, eager to state his case and defend himself. 'The silver girl belonging to *Dominus*. She was alone in the street, escaped. I found her but she was afraid of me, fought against me.'

'Poor Lisa,' Claire murmured to Mell, surprising herself with the pang of sympathy she felt. She'd really hated the girl when she'd first appeared in the museum, interrupting the rapport she'd been building with Simon. It had physically hurt to see how fast his attention had been consumed by Lisa. Now though, she just felt pity, the poor girl must be going through hell.

'Where is she now? Is she alright?' Sarah demanded, the girl clearly wasn't with Tiberius, and she was nowhere in sight. With Simon currently absent from the group, having stayed behind to allow them a chance to escape she felt that she had to at least try and find out what had happened to his girlfriend.

Tiberius flushed a furious shade of red and stared fiercely at the floor. 'She stabbed me in the throat, tried to kill me!' he wailed, his ghostly hands clawing at his neck.

'Tiberius!' Jerry was laughing. 'Dude, you need to chill on the whole being killed thing. You're dead. No one can kill you. Did it even hurt?'

Tiberius halted his theatrics and frowned as if trying to recall. 'It frightened me. But then the priestess and Remus appeared. They have her now. Remus wants her as his … victory trophy,' he seemed to shrink visibly as if expecting a beating or some form of punishment for bringing bad news. 'But the priestess,' he turned huge saucer-like eyes on Mell. 'The priestess wants her life, Messalina fights her though. It was her who sent me to you. Remus …'

'Wait!' Jerry threw his hands up calling time out. 'Who the fuck is the priestess if it's not Messalina? Is there some third deranged woman up there?'

'Let him talk Jerry,' Mell said. 'We need as much information as we can get, if we are going to fix this.'

'How the hell are we gonna fix it?' Jerry yelled back, tripping over a tree root as he staggered towards the girls. 'We lost the friggin encyclopedia Latinus in the volcano.' He dragged his hands through his tangled curls and stared back at the ash column still powering its way into the sky. A soft glimmer was visible in his eye as he turned his face away.

Sarah detached herself from the others, she'd seen him like this before. 'Jerry, calm down.' She laid her hand gently against his bare chest, feeling the pound of his racing heart below the Welsh dragon. 'There are four of us,' she continued softly. 'Five if we count Tiberius. We can figure something out.'

Mell spared the pair a glance and gestured for Tiberius to carry on. 'Explain what you can,' she said.

Tiberius nodded. 'The priestess is the ancient one, the one with all the power, Messalina is merely her vessel, her body on earth. The old witch must have ensured that a relic of hers survived the ages, probably a bone, some element of herself anyway. As the priestess grows more powerful, Messalina loses control of herself,' he broke off to check that the group was following.

Sarah held up her hand, she was thinking, something he had said was jangling a memory. 'There was an ancient skull in Messalina's basement. It was on the altar, covered in dried blood and strange patterns,' she said watching him for a reaction.

Tiberius nodded. 'The barbarian peoples used to believe in the power of their enemies' skulls, perhaps the priestess did too, but that's not important. Remus wants the silver girl, he likes her, she is young, pretty and capable of bearing his heirs, whether she wants to or not,' he stopped again interrupted by the crack of Mell's knuckles as she flexed her hands. 'But the priestess wants her too. She sees Remus's infatuation and she wants to control him. Ultimately she wants to be rid of him and have the empire for herself to rule.'

'And she wants Lisa's body as her own,' Claire finished. 'A younger version of Messalina, better able to wield power over a man who thinks with his balls.'

'When she had a chance, before the priestess took her completely, Messalina sent me to find the *Dominus,* the Spaniard. She intends to get the girl to a safe place. But the priestess is powerful and jealous, and since the silver girl set fire to the Aventine she keeps her close.'

'Lisa set fire to the Aventine?' Mell asked quietly, the little ghost nodded his head. She smiled at the others. 'Good for her! Maybe she's not such a pampered princess after all.'

Jerry, in control of himself again, shoved his hands in his pockets and grinned. 'That'll give Simon a shock, he's convinced she has no idea how to make coffee. He can barely believe that she managed to get here in the first place.'

'Maybe he has as little idea about who she is, as she does about him,' said Claire thoughtfully. 'Although I guess they might both put up a front around other people.' She sighed and twisted a strand of green hair around her fingers. 'So where do we find Lisa, where is the safe place Messalina intended to get her to? Even if she is not there now, if we can reach it, we are there to grab her when we can.'

Tiberius nodded. 'Remus wanted her sent to the temple of the Vestals to remain a virgin until he triumphs. Messalina hoped that the girl may be safe there long enough for the *Dominus* to reach her. But I do not see the *Dominus,* where is he?'

Wordlessly Jerry jerked a thumb in the direction of the smoke spewing volcano, and as Tiberius stared at the ever-growing mass of smoke his form grew fainter until he almost vanished.

'Screw Simon!' hissed Mell, hands clenched into white knuckled fists at her sides. 'We cannot let Remus have her, no woman deserves that. We have to find the temple of the Vestals, perhaps we can rescue her from there. Come on,' she turned away intending to leave the tree lined space.

'Mell!' Jerry yelled chasing after her, stopping her just before she stepped back into the open space where the Appian Way had been. 'Mell. I get what you're saying, but think it through a little. Rome isn't even there anymore, no Rome, no temple. And the hills are crawling with bad dudes. We need a plan,' he rolled his eyes. 'In all honesty we probably need Simon, or at least Suze, they both seem to know Roman history.'

She turned back to him, tears glittering in her eyes. 'I can't do nothing Jerry. I can't, after Richards,' she paused. 'I can't let that happen to Lisa. Besides, we don't even know if Simon and Suze are alive.'

'Don't say that Mell,' hissed Claire, who had followed them, Sarah and Tiberius just behind her. 'They could have got out. But Jerry is right, we need a plan, we at least need to know where the temple is.'

'The temple of Vesta lies at the foot of the Capitoline,' Tiberius offered. 'There was a temple there even before Rome. That's why Messalina thought the girl would be safe.'

'Right,' said Mell. 'Let's go then, Tiberius can lead the way.' She pushed her way out of the little copse of trees and stopped. The Eternal City was still missing but in its place, crawling all over the hills, spreading rapidly across the fields were the blackened figures of a vast army. The army of Remus.

'Stuck between an erupting volcano and an army of the dead. Remind me never to go on holiday with you guys again,' said Jerry dragging the binoculars from his pocket again and scanning the scene. With a sigh, he swung his gaze around to the volcano and stopped. 'There's something else back there, a large dust cloud, lighter than the volcano with an occasional glint of metal showing through.'

Tiberius floated closer to him and raised a hand, staring off into the distance. A dazed and vacant look came over his face, and it seemed as though he was staring through time. From somewhere to the south, towards the hulking mass of the volcano, came the mournful bray of trumpets.

XLIII

Jerry could barely believe what he was seeing. Eyes glued to the binoculars he watched them march through the morning gloom. The rattle and clank of metal was muted in the dense atmosphere, but the nodding red crests of the centurions, the polished metal of armour and vivid red and yellow paint of shields was a sight to behold. They moved fast. Within seconds he could see their banners, the X of the tenth legion displaying proudly above the constellation of Gemini, but no eagle. Their legionary standard was missing. The girls and Tiberius hung on Jerry's words as he described what he was seeing, ignoring repeated demands to hand the binoculars over.

Soon they could hear the rhythmic trudge of boots, the hobnails grinding against the stony ground. And not a minute too soon. The sight of Remus's army of the dead forming up around the seven hills was nerve shattering, although there had been no sign of Remus himself. Finally, Jerry spotted what he was looking for. A wide grin plastered across his face, he lowered the binoculars and handed them to Sarah. Keeping his eyes fixed on what he had just seen. 'Take a close look at their general,' he advised, dragging a hand through his long curls and fidgeting.

'How will I know which one that is?' Sarah said, raising the binoculars to her eyes and letting out a gasp of surprise as she saw the legion marching forward.

'Cos he's the blindingly obvious dumbass on the white horse,' Jerry said still grinning. Sweeping Mell and Claire into an impromptu hug in his excitement as they tried to see what was happening.

'What is it?' Mell asked, shoving Jerry aside and holding out her hands for the binoculars. Although by this time the front ranks of the marching legion were visible without them.

'*Legio X Gemina*,' Tiberius sighed with relief, floating alongside them. 'Caesar's legion. I knew it would be.' He turned to Jerry, panic all over his pale form. 'Their commander?'

'Oh yeah, they have a commander all right,' Jerry was laughing, his excitement palpable. He couldn't keep still and was pacing around the stony path, a huge grin on his face laughing in disbelief.

'No bloody way!' Sarah still had the binoculars trained on the centre of the front unit of marching men, beside the standard rode a man on the white horse of a general. Unlike the rest of the army he wore jeans and a battered polo shirt. 'Simon,' she breathed in disbelief.

'Let me see,' Claire demanded, elbowing Mell aside and practically snatching the glasses to see for herself. 'And Suze is with him.' She lowered the binoculars amazed at the speed with which the legion was marching towards them. They would be upon their small group in moments. It was exciting, terrifying, impossible and adrenaline inducing all at once. She felt in serious danger of having a heart attack as the clattering army drew ever closer.

'*Legio Decem*, Hold!' the command was loud, imperious, accompanied by the raising of a fist from the general on horseback. One of the lower rankers beside him spoke in low tones and was dismissed. A command issued down the line for the legionaries to stand down and the orderly marching line became ragged as men stepped aside, or sat down where they stood, taking water from canteens and mopping brows, dropping helmets to the ground. But their eyes remained on the place where Rome should stand, and the army of Remus. They were battle ready.

The general moved the horse closer to the awestruck group standing on the verge and a second figure could now be seen behind him. Reining the horse in, Simon looked down at his friends, relief flooding through him. Everyone seemed to be safe, although, he noticed with a pang, Lisa was still absent. 'What have you done with my city?' he said, swinging his leg over the horse's neck to dismount, before turning and lifting Suze gently down. 'There you are Suze, solid ground.'

'Awesome,' she replied, with a weak smile, both disappointed and glad to push him away. She felt a huge sense of relief at not being alone with Simon anymore and was pleased to see her friends all in one piece. Now finally she'd be able to think about something else and straighten her head out. All the way to Rome her mind had been plaguing her with that almost kiss. She'd tried everything to quiet it, but confusion reigned supreme and now that she was free of him, her body felt like it was aching to feel his warmth again. She cursed inwardly and tried to stuff the thought into a locked mental box.

'Simon, where did the army come from? We left you two alone with Meredius, how did that become this?' asked Mell, gesturing to the soldiers, now standing idle along the route.

Simon's eyes fixed on the binoculars in her hand. 'Are those mine?' he asked, deliberately dodging the question.

'Is that yours?' countered Jerry, staring at the legion in the road and as curious as Mell to know what had happened.

Simon fixed him with a level and powerful stare. 'Apparently so,' he massaged his forehead. 'Although I could not begin to tell you how.' Spotting Tiberius he addressed the long dead slave. '*Salve*, Tiberius! I see Remus has colonised the city. Does he intend pitched battle or is he hoping to scare us?' his voice, with a hint of sarcasm, was loud enough to elicit a laugh from the soldiers closest to him.

'Careful Si, Tiberius has been in Remus's camp.' Jerry grabbed Simon's shoulder as he spoke, and suddenly the rasp of steel filled the air as five and a half thousand swords were drawn and the army gave a collective grunt.

'Stand Down!' Simon bellowed, raising a hand and casting an eye over his devoutly loyal troops, as the colour drained from Jerry's face. There was a heartbeat pause before the entire legion saluted in unison and returned their swords to scabbards. Simon watched them a moment longer before turning back to Jerry. 'What were you saying, Jerry?' he placed a hand on his friend's arm as they spoke, signifying their relationship to the legion.

Jerry glanced nervously at the army before he spoke trying to mask his fear with humour as usual. 'Jesus Si, you were intimidating enough without the army.' He scratched at the dragon on his chest then stopped, realising that his blond hair, bare chest and dragon tattoo probably made him look like a barbarian of legend. 'Uh, Ti … Tiberius, 'he stuttered. 'Was with Remus, in fact he almost rescued Lisa, then he lost her again.'

Tiberius looked at the floor, fading out so much he was barely visible. 'The silver girl you are so interested in *Dominus*, she had escaped,' Tiberius paused and Simon, his face betraying no emotion, gestured for him to carry on. 'I captured her, but she was afraid of me. Then Remus and the priestess arrived. There was nothing I could do for her.'

Simon held up his hand for silence. He looked more and more like a commander with every passing minute. 'Lisa! Where is she? How is she?'

It was Claire who answered, speaking for Tiberius who continued to fade out of sight under Simon's imperious stare. 'Apparently, she is to be taken to the temple of Vesta,' she paused, uncertain how best to phrase the rest. But with a groan of distress Simon sank down on one of the recently returned tombstones flanking the road, his hands covering his face.

'Simon, she'll be safe there, surely,' said Mell, moving behind him and giving his tight shoulders a reassuring squeeze. 'If Remus dumps her in the temple of Vesta no one can touch her. Surely the bigger concern is the priestess anyway? She's the one who wants to possess Lisa's body.'

'The penalty for being an impure Vestal is to be buried alive, she is no more safe there than she is with Remus and the priestess,' Simon replied, shrugging Mell off and standing, raking a hand through his dusty hair. He paced between the tombstones, his thoughts racing. Lisa was in danger whatever he did, but the history of Europe was at stake if he made the wrong decision. He twisted the signet ring on his finger cursing inwardly, weighing up duty and desire.

'Impure Vestal?' Sarah asked.

'She's not a bloody virgin.' Simon replied hotly, banging his hand against a tombstone.

Jerry raised an eyebrow with a lopsided grin. 'Are you sure?'

'No, I confused her with a pillow!' sarcasm was rare from Simon, but always delivered with pointed venom. 'What do you think?' he stared at the ground for a second, breathing heavily. Then turned on his heel and strode away from the group, plucking his binoculars from Mell's hand and bellowing at the army. 'Form up!'

Climbing onto a raised mausoleum he turned his gaze on the barren land before them and the massing Reman army. Remus had more men, that much was obvious, although they seemed disorganised and a quick sweep of the outlying regions of the disorganised mess did not pick him or Messalina out. Remus was not expecting resistance then. A cheer from his own troops caught his attention and, tossing the binoculars back towards Mell, he watched as Jerry handed the golden eagle to the lion skin clad *Aqulifer,* who attached it to the legion's laurel and medal draped main standard. Unnoticed by anyone the road slowly began to reappear.

'Officers to me!' Simon bellowed, and all along the line of fighting men, soldiers with red crested helmets scurried to obey. Another brought the white horse over to him. Keeping his fidgeting left hand behind his back, hiding a nervous twitch from the assembled officers, Simon beckoned his five friends and Tiberius to come a little closer. He was nervous but hiding it well, standing straight and seen in profile, if not for the jeans, he could easily have passed for a younger version of his famous ancestor.

Claire certainly seemed to think so, whispering to Mell under her breath. 'Caesar reincarnated,' Mell nodded her agreement and shushed her, allowing Simon to speak without having to command attention.

'Officers of the tenth,' Simon's voice was strong and carried over the officers to the front most ranks of his troops, drawn up in the returning road. 'My friends, you have overcome formidable enemies and are now to encounter the damned soldiers of Remus. This day will decide everything. Remember how you swore to each other in the presence of Caesar that you would never leave the battlefield, except as conquerors. These men of Remus are the same as you have faced before, the same as you have triumphed over before. We shall not prevail upon them by offering fair terms, nor win them by offering benefits,' Simon paused, both to let his words sink in and recall the rest of Caesar's civil war speech that he was bastardising. His mind was racing too fast and he could only clutch at a line in Spanish that he knew belonged to El Cid; the legendary liberator of Valencia.

Suze had understood what he was doing though, by the third line she'd realised that it was an edited version of Julius Caesar's Civil War speech. Ten seconds later she'd also realised that he needed the next line. Thinking on her feet, she slipped Claire's phone from the girl's pocket and desperately punched in a search. Jupiter only knew where the internet signal came from but it was there. She moved a little closer and hissed the opening of the next line. 'It is not difficult for hardy and veteran soldiers ...' It was all he needed, like a car with a jump start his brain kicked in and the rest of Caesar speech, with edits appropriate to what they faced rolled off his tongue.

'He's amazing,' said Sarah as the army too roared its approval. 'How does he remember all that stuff, and under so much pressure?' Suze just shrugged and slipped Claire's phone back to her as the green-haired girl stared at Simon, striding across his makeshift platform whipping his legion into a frenzy of bloodlust.

The final roar from the legion even roused a response from Remus's troops over half a mile away, clustered at the gates of Rome as the city began to reappear behind them. Simon glanced over and allowed a cold smile to grace his face before delivering his final words to the army. 'See how they fear us already. Our task is easy. Rome will be ours. Raise the eagle!' With a gesture, he dismissed the officers, returning them to their cheering troops and gave the order to deploy across the field between the road they stood on and the Appian Way visible to the west.

Simon managed to remain standing and in control until the last soldier had moved away, and he was no longer visible to the rank and file. Only then, under the impressed stares of his friends, did he stagger backwards, groping blindly for one of his horse's saddle pommels, just managing to drape his left arm over it before his legs gave way and he collapsed against the horse.

'Jesus Simon that was impressive,' said Jerry shaking his head. 'Almost as good as a Slash guitar solo.' Simon gave him a weak smile in response. His legs still felt like rubber and he was terrified that if the horse moved, he would fall.

'I cannot believe that we are actually attacking Rome,' said Claire quietly.

'There is no we,' said Simon pushing off the saddle, forcing himself to stand. 'The army, under my command is attacking Rome. You five are to stay well out of it.' He turned and hauled himself back into the saddle.

'Bollocks to that!' yelled Suze, her eyes flashing lightning as she strode forward, but Jerry grabbed her arm and pulled her aside. 'I can fight as well as any soldier.'

'The lady has a point Si,' Jerry hissed, struggling to keep hold of Suze as she wriggled in his grip. 'You can't just order us all out of it. We …'

'Cállate Jerry!' Simon held up a hand cutting him off. His face had gone a deathly shade of white and he was really struggling to keep his composure. 'This is not a game, people will die,' He shook his head correcting himself. 'There is no way I can reach Lisa before the army. My actions may have just killed her. Do not allow me to lose the five of you too,' without waiting for an answer, he turned the horse and raced away, back to the front of his army.

Jerry scuffed a stone along the ground and glanced towards the small knot of men clustering around the golden eagle and the general. 'Pompous git, but you can't say the man ain't got balls,' he said, looking back towards the group. 'Takes real nuts to stand up in front of a whole army and give them something to fight for. It was a good speech.'

'Oh, the man has balls,' said Mell folding her arms and staring across at Simon. 'But he has no idea what's good for him. Come on, I play Total War all the time, we can take care of the army, he can go rescue the girl.'

*

Having carefully chosen a vantage point on a part of the city wall that she knew would remain in existence through the time fluctuations, the priestess stared at the opposing army with mounting dread as they deployed on the field.

Movement in the sky caught her eye and she glanced upwards to see a large owl fly across the army's path, left to right. A terrible omen. The owl was a symbol of death to come and in the first light of morning too. Quickly, following an old superstition she licked her finger and dabbed it behind her ear, warding off bad thoughts, she had not come this far to fail. The entrails of a rat she had slaughtered earlier, had promised a great victory, and as Remus had said, his brother's army was leaderless. It would be a bloodless battle. The owl merely reflected the death embodied in the demons that comprised Remus's army. Satisfied at her reading, she tossed her hair and turned her attention to the opposing army.

The legion was well organised, true it was a tiny army by comparison to the hordes of Remus, but they were organised. Then she spotted what Remus had not considered possible. A tall figure on a white horse, easy to pick out as he rode the battle lines. A general. She leaned over the wall. 'Remus! You fool, fall back they have a commander.'

Remus, standing at the back of the army, below her, roared with laughter. 'He's just a boy, not my brother. He is no threat to us. Mars, God of War is my father.' He gestured to the creature beside him and his silver eagle standard rose into the air, the hitchhiking wren, cheating king of the birds, crowning it.

By the priestess's side Lisa let out a gasp of delight, as she recognised the man on the horse leading the opposing army. 'Simon,' she breathed, pressing her hands to her heart. She straightened up and turned an icy gaze on the woman. 'I told you he would come for me.'

'It is a small army,' the priestess retaliated. 'Remus outnumbers him ten to one. Your man will be defeated, his body broken and inhabited by Remus.' She leaned on the wall, gripping the stone, her knuckles white with tension.

Inside the priestess's head Messalina was desperate, a caged tigress. A damned creature at her most dangerous. She had a plan to save the girl but it all depended on the Spaniard. The priestess let out a low chuckle. 'I hear your thoughts Messalina,' she muttered, briefly attracting Lisa's attention. 'I know your plan and if Remus fails and your plan works, then I can escape the rout of Remus's troops and still have everything I want.' She shook her head, silencing Messalina's voice and settled to watch the carnage of her victory.

A movement by her side distracted her, the girl was trying to run again. The priestess snapped her fingers and two of Remus's creatures appeared. They grabbed Lisa's arms and dragged her back. Keeping her eyes on the unfolding drama on the field the priestess spoke slowly. 'Try escaping again, and I will throw you from the walls and let the soldiers have you. I don't need your virtue, just your youth.' Several trumpet blasts split the air, and the demonic troops began to move forward. The priestess smiled, an almost lipless slash of movement on her parchment like face. 'Now, let's watch your precious Spaniard and his friends die.'

XLIV

The legion had deployed, they were battle ready. First, fourth and tenth cohorts on the more vulnerable left flank, second and third to the right, with cohorts five, six and seven forming the central part of the line and eight and nine held back in reserve. With no auxiliaries to draw on, Simon had little choice to do much else. The sun was finally rising, bathing the scene in weak morning light. Moments ago, a horn had blared from Remus's side and he had been forced to deploy his first troops in response.

Now he sat, still mounted beside the golden eagle standard, clearly visible to the whole legion, and the enemy battalions. His face was an unmoving mask. A part of him wanted to be like Julius Caesar and lead from the front, be the first man into the city, but he was no trained legionary and would probably only hinder the army and succeed in getting himself killed. He would have to command from the rear, which, although giving him the advantage of being able to see what was happening, meant that he would never be able to reach Rome in time to save Lisa from her fate.

His eyes fixed on the troops that he had just sent forward, Simon didn't notice that the others had followed him until Claire tapped his leg. Her touch was so unexpected that he jumped, startling the horse and he found himself having to fight for control of the beast. 'No preocuparse.' He muttered patting the horse's neck and walking him in a tight circle to settle. Satisfied that the horse wouldn't bolt he finally looked up. A surprised but tight smile creasing his face, as he realised that all five of his friends stood before him.

A shouted order came from the front ranks of the engaging troops, momentarily distracting Simon's attention. The heavy rectangular shields of the front ranks thumped together and the row behind raised their throwing spears. Their movement was fluid, natural and conducted without any loss of speed as the front ranks continued forwards to meet Remus.

'What are you guys doing here?' said Simon, tearing his eyes from the battlefield and looking down at his friends, as another shouted order carried back from the front ranks. The group glanced up to see the pilum spears of the front ranks arcing through the air, cutting swathes through Remus's unruly mob as it continued its suicidal race towards the disciplined Roman army.

Simon turned and barked a sharp order at the bugle player. 'First three centuries cohorts one, two, three and four. Forward and engage.' The bugle player nodded and issued several sharp blasts on his instrument. Almost immediately detachments began moving on the right and left wings of the army. He turned back to his friends. 'I cannot run this battle if I am worried about your safety,' he said looking at their indignant faces. 'If you stay behind the reserves you should be safe, if at any point it looks that we may be routed, get the scooters and go.'

'Bollocks!' said Jerry, folding his arms and staring up at Simon. 'We're staying and there ain't nothing your generalship can do about it. Besides, Mell's like a secret friggin expert at Total War, her Romans always beat my barbarian horde. You need her.'

'I have no idea what you are talking about, but this is not a game!' hissed Simon, as a huge roar from the battlefield, followed by the clatter, thump and screams of battle indicated that the two armies had engaged face to face. The bugle sounded again and a second wave of Romans marched to the aid of the first. Simon closed his eyes and dragged his attention back to the group. 'Melody, is he right? Can you command an army?' Simon dismounted and gestured for someone to take his horse.

'On a computer game, online, against Jerry, sure,' she replied tentatively, but her eyes were scanning the surrounding legion. 'You might want to move a detachment of cohort ten forward. When you moved one through four you forgot about ten on your left flank. That is where you think your weakness lies, but you need to bring your troops in.'

'Good enough,' Simon muttered. He raised his voice so that the knot of officials around him could hear him clearly. 'First and second century, cohort ten to front line.' He took a breath and placed his hand on Mell's shoulder, singling her out in front of his assembled officers. 'Melody Knight, you are second in command here, your orders bear equal weight to my own and let no man among us disobey,' he glared at the officers, daring any to challenge and was met with a stony silence. A light shuffling of feet and some guarded looks indicated that there was some disapproval but no one challenged her appointment.

'What do you want us to do?' asked Suze, staring at the carnage on the battlefield. She was pale and trying to control a trembling that she wasn't certain was fear, or a strange desire for combat.

'Be our eyes and ears,' Simon replied. 'Locate Remus on the field and keep watch on him. If we can break his army hard, he may run, and we shall have to chase.'

'What about Lisa?' said Claire, pointing at the city walls. She had been sweeping the walls of Rome with Simon's binoculars and had located his girlfriend. She stood beside Messalina, the priestess in black, Lisa in white. Two smudgy figures viewing the battlefield from a place of relative safety.

For a moment Simon looked haggard, the last day's events forcing through to the surface. Then taking a slow breath he straightened, his composure returning. 'Right now, we can do nothing for her except hope that she makes it through. Messalina is too close to her, she would be dead the moment any of us moved towards her,' he gestured at the bugle player who sounded a call and the second wave of men from the wings began to move forward.

*

The priestess watched the carnage with a growing sense of dread. Remus may have more troops but the boy general had been clever. He clearly knew something of Roman battle, or there were good officers with him that he was willing to listen to. Remus by contrast, was just throwing men forward. There was no order, just an unruly charge. She'd watched as the line was decimated twice by the throwing pilum of the legionaries, and heard the rattle and clatter as the two opposing sides slammed into one another.

Cries and screams of pain echoed up from the battlefield, but the carnage was mercifully far enough away that Lisa could not see the damage being wrought clearly. Trying to block out the sound of battle she remained focussed on one figure in the opposing army. She had almost lost him when he'd dismounted from the horse and she'd watched with her heart in her mouth, thinking that he was about to do something stupid like join the next wave of fighting men. Unable to stop herself she leaned on the wall, unconsciously mirroring the priestess's stance as she watched the chaos unfold beneath the rising sun.

A second wave of Romans moved from the wings of the opposing army, and suddenly Remus's force seemed to lose all substance. Men began moving differently; the rear ranks of his messy attack surged forward but the front ones turned tail and fled from the Romans. It was chaos.

'No,' the priestess banged a fist against the wall. It was a reverse. 'Remus! Call retreat, refortify and attack again as they move back,' she yelled. The drunk man at the base of the wall ignored her and sent more men forward. But the fear emanating from those streaming back towards the city walls was infectious, and less than half of the new wave made it to the centre of the field. 'Idiot,' the priestess muttered. She watched just long enough to hear Remus finally sound a retreat.

'Bring the girl,' she hissed to the two soldiers on the wall, and without waiting to see if they obeyed, she hurried down the stairs to the Appian gate and out onto the battlefield. True, she had hoped to use the girl's body as a replacement for the one she currently inhabited, but winning the battle for Rome was more important. Fighting her way through the troops, keeping the silver eagle in sight she finally reached Remus. 'You will attack again?' she demanded breathlessly, casting a quick glance towards the Romans who were also retreating, in careful formation.

'Of course,' Remus replied. 'I can throw men at them all day, they will die exhausted and unable to stand. I have plenty of fresh troops.' He turned and bellowed an order to someone further down the line and a trumpet sounded mournfully across the field, answered by a blast from the other side.

'You need to inspire your men,' the priestess insisted grabbing Remus's arm. 'Clear a space, and sacrifice the girl. Their general will lose his mind, he will be unable to command, you can take his army.' The guards following the priestess pushed Lisa forwards, each held one of her arms and one held a sword in her back forcing her to push her chest out.

The priestess drew a black bladed dagger from her robes and placed it against the trembling girl's throat. 'It will be quick and easy. His resolve will fail and your army will be victorious,' she smiled, pressing the tip of the blade into Lisa's neck. She was painfully surprised when Remus struck her, hurling her to the floor, she'd not expected him to resist.

Remus fixed a leering gaze on his prize. 'I told you priestess, the girl is to produce my heirs.' He wrapped a meaty hand around Lisa's throat forcing her to look up. 'I am looking forward to my victory celebrations,' he dropped Lisa. 'Take her away.'

The priestess bowed her head. 'As you wish, *Dominus*,' she replied, but her mind was made up. She would stay on this battlefield no longer, Remus would lose, it was inevitable. She had to look out for herself. Dismissing her guards and grabbing Lisa's wrist, she began marching back towards the Appian gate. Behind her Remus called for the second assault to begin.

*

'Did we win?' asked Claire as both sides retreated from the battlefield. Between them Mell, Simon and the officers had managed to force Remus into a retreat. The first wave of his demonic troops lay defeated and the detached Roman centuries retreated slowly backwards, eyes on the enemy, into the ranks. They were swiftly swallowed and rearranged at the back, leaving fresh troops to face any new assault.

'A well-oiled fighting machine,' Suze muttered, watching the army manoeuvre, entranced. They were quicker and cleaner than anything on the Hollywood screen. The bugle sounded, men moved, it was mechanical, unstoppable. Amazing.

'If he's smart Remus will come again,' said Sarah. 'He has the men to keep going. Could be ten times our numbers.'

'Something's happening on the walls,' hissed Jerry, holding his hand out for the binoculars. Once Claire had pointed them out he'd been keeping an eye on Lisa and the dark shrouded priestess. 'Give me the damn binos or I'm never gonna see where she goes.'

'I think she's going to Remus,' said Sarah, spotting Messalina's black clad form emerging from the Appian gate as she handed the binoculars over. 'Can you make anything out?' she asked him, glancing towards Simon and Mell, deep in strategy conversation with the officers under the standard. 'If we have the chance to rescue her, we really should try.'

'Messalina looks pretty pissed off,' Jerry replied, watching events unfold. 'But you heard what Simon said about going after her. We'd never reach her in time. He'd be after her himself if there was a way.' He lowered the binoculars and watched the fresh ranks of Simon's army forming up ready to march again.

'Jerry!' Mell's yell distracted the rest of the group. 'Binoculars, now!' she demanded racing towards him. Jerry obediently passed them over as she arrived and Mell raised them to her eyes muttering. 'Where is she, where is she?'

'By the standard,' said Claire, gently taking hold of the binoculars and guiding Mell's gaze towards the silver eagle. 'Messalina dragged her down to Remus. The three of them are together.'

'Shit!' hissed Mell, as Simon, flanked by two centurions, re-joined the group.

'Remus has suffered a retreat, if we can force another on him, then he may run.' Simon bit his lip trying to ignore Mell, although it was clear that he knew what she was looking at. He turned his attention to Suze, doing his best not to let his gaze wander towards the figure in the white dress on the other side of the battlefield. 'Keep your eyes on him, we defeat him and we end all this. If he moves, tell me immediately.'

'Simon,' said Mell quietly, brandishing the binoculars at him. 'You might want to look.' He glanced down at the binoculars and shook his head turning his attention back to the army, as the bugle sounded the order to march again. There was a wall of noise as the fresh centuries of the middle cohorts, five, six and seven, picked up their shields and moved forwards. Not taking no for an answer Mell crushed the binoculars against his chest. 'By the standard,' Mell said, her voice cracking, as he slowly took hold of the glasses.

Reluctantly he raised the binoculars to his eyes, dreading what he might see. His heart almost stopped when he saw her. She was still beautiful. Lisa stood proud and defiant, almost radiant in the white robes that she wore. He stared at her, a pained groan escaping his lips as the black clad priestess pressed a knife to Lisa's throat. Panic gripped him, there was no way he could reach her in time, but he couldn't stay here.

'*Equus!*' he yelled, unthinking, shoving the binoculars back into Mell's hands. One of the legionaries brought the white horse around and, without a moment's hesitation Simon vaulted into the saddle, and urged the horse forwards.

'About bloody time,' Mell hissed to herself. Where Simon had been distracted, she could now be free to command without complications. She raised her voice. 'Second wave, centuries one to three, cohorts five six and seven, advance, cover the commander.'

Catching sight of Suze waving a sword at him, Simon reined the horse in, pausing long enough for her to hand him a gladius. As she turned to keep her eye on Remus he grabbed her arm, his fingers closing around her elbow. She responded automatically, clasping his forearm, glancing up towards his face. Time seemed to stand still for Suze again as the moment stretched into several more seconds of awkward silence before Simon finally spoke. 'Try not to get yourself killed, all right Jones?' he said, his dark eyes searching the depths of hers.

'I will if you will,' she replied awkwardly. She let go of his arm and giving his horse a hefty smack on the rump, sent him off, as Mell ordered more troops forward. She'd expected him to skirt the battlefield and leave discreetly, but instead he headed straight for the centre of the battle. 'Jesus Simon,' she hissed in admiration.

In a daring move Simon charged between the lines of his own ranks, his men cheering and whooping as he passed, galvanised to fight on. As he surged ahead of them into the loose ranks of the enemy, they began chanting, 'Caesar!' His bold move was working. It looked like Remus would be beaten back again.

'Hold the lines,' Mell screamed, knowing that without Simon, she would really have to prove her skills to the army. They had accepted her when he placed her as his second, but only grudgingly. 'Sarah, Claire, you both have phones, right?' she licked her lips, desperately aware that her hold on the army was tentative. 'Communication is key here, Sarah take the left flank, Claire the right, I want contact at all time.' She beckoned the *Aquilifer* over. 'Bring forward the eighth and ninth cohorts.'

The man stood silently, staring at the battlefield, his eyes following the commander as he surged across the field through the fray. The expression on his face was unreadable.

'Soldier?' Mell yelled, but was again met with silence. With an exasperated sigh, she moved closer to him, so close their noses almost touched, her hazel eyes boring into his. 'Do as I say, or get the hell out of my army and let Remus ruin Rome.' She held her ground, not wavering in her surprisingly imposing stare. He said nothing but held her gaze. 'What's it to be soldier boy? I've not got all day. I can and will replace you.'

He planted the eagle in the ground and knuckled his forehead. '*Praeceptorem*. Apologies Prefect,' a smile cracked his grizzled face. 'I've not seen a General join the fray like that since Caesar himself.' He raised his voice, bellowing her order to the rear ranks.

Mell grinned, relief flooding through her. She had control, power. The entire army was under her command. She took a deep breath. 'Let's take back Rome, and crush this usurping bastard.' The army roared its approval and she smiled, feeling almost like her old self.

XLV

Remus roared with laughter as he watched the young man on the white horse surge across the field and through the Appian Gate into the city. At first, he had been worried as the attacking Romans seemed to gain a second wind at their general's presence in the ranks. Then, as he'd watched, the fearless leader of the Romans had hurtled through the front ranks of his own army, into a loose section of Remus's own men and careened onwards towards the city gate, fleeing the battle.

'Behold their commander! A mere boy against all our might. See how he flees before us leaving his men without a leader. They are lost now. Push forward! Forward and end it. Rome will be ours within the hour!'

Chuckling with delight, he committed more of his unending troops to the fray before looking up to taunt the priestess. The wall above him was empty. Concern stabbed through his mind and he grabbed the soldier closest to him. 'Find the priestess, ensure she sees my brother's last stand.' Without waiting for a response, he threw the man away from him, and grinning widely, began to imagine his victory. A triumphant tour through his city, the elevation of his friends to power. The execution of that witch, the priestess, at his victory banquet, and finally, what he was looking forward to most of all. The temple dedication, to honour his divine father and ensure the fertile succession of his line, he would stain the altar with the blonde girl's virgin blood. For such an offering, the great God Mars would surely grant him anything he desired.

Lost in his depraved fantasy, Remus failed to wholly recognise both the absence of the priestess and the direction of the young general's flight for what it was. His reinforced army surged forwards, threatening to break the Roman line, and he laughed again.

*

The battle was carnage. From every angle came the thump and clatter of combat weapons, voices crying out in triumph, loss or pain. Trumpets blared, although making out their orders seemed impossible. Following Simon's heroic, although bordering on suicidal, charge through the ranks, the army of Romulus had cheered and surged forward. Even to the five teenagers and Tiberius, left behind on the hill, it looked as though victory may be within grasp. The army pushed forwards, another wave of men joining those who were beginning to tire, and the battle lines moved visibly closer to the city walls.

Mell was busy, run off her feet, listening to advice from the officers and issuing orders to the bugle player. The officers had taken to her command with delight, her orders were simple but inventive, as though she was a victor of a thousand battles. Her decisions were fast and relayed with a confidence that ensured no challenge or insubordination.

Realising that the battle looked nothing like the almost neat lines on her Total War game, Mell had sent Claire and Sarah to monitor the ebb and flow of the field movement on the left and right flanks. Both were managing to feed her a constant stream of information through a phone app, giving her the same information that she'd have on a heads-up display on the computer. Information that Roman commanders would have killed for in their day, and allowing her full control of the battle.

Suze and Jerry remained in the centre, close to the standing reserves of the eighth and ninth cohorts, keeping an eye on Remus. Jerry, looking for all the world like a bare chested, tattooed barbarian, stood over a foot taller most of the Romans. He had scanned what he could see of the city several times, but he'd been unable to spot Simon, or Lisa in the changing mass of buildings.

From Remus's position came the mournful howl of a bugle and more of his men surged onto the field. From where the teenagers and Tiberius stood in command of the tenth legion it appeared that Remus had just doubled the size of his offensive. Their opponent seemed to be throwing his whole army at them, keeping nothing back.

'Does he know something we don't?' Claire muttered to herself. She watched the new troops smash into the centre of the Roman line, as a collective groan came from the men of the tenth legion, both on the field and in reserve.

A frown creased Mell's brow as she watched the fresh slaughter unfold, and she glanced back at the two remaining cohorts. She wanted to hold fresh troops for as long as she could, but not risk having to retreat before she could use them. She needed a read on the morale of the troops, they had to believe in victory. She dragged her hands through her long red hair, unwittingly mirroring Simon's signature stressed gesture. 'Suze? You know the Roman army, right? What is the morale like? Will they break? In Total War, you get a heads-up display that tells you all this stuff.'

The younger girl handed the binoculars to Jerry and joined Mell, casting a critical eye over what she could see. She glanced up at the standard bearer before she spoke. 'It looks like our lines are holding, for the moment. The major problem is numbers, Remus has more men and he doesn't care how many he loses. His tactic will be to wear us down, flatten our resolve. When the time comes we'll most likely have to either swap out two cohorts or simply send our two reserves to join the fray.' The standard bearer nodded his agreement.

Mell cast her eye over the battle again, Suze's verdict agreed with her own. The tide seemed to be changing, they had lost ground. She breathed deeply, needing to concentrate. A wrong move now and the whole thing could collapse. She turned to the standard bearer. 'We can still win?' it was more a statement than a question but the man understood.

He snapped a salute and planted the eagle in the ground. 'We are the Tenth. We have a reputation. Our chances are slender, but we fight on,' he raised his voice to a battle cry. 'Tenth Gemina. Death or glory!' The cry was taken up by the reserve units, who banged their swords against their huge rectangular shields, the sound carrying to the battlefield where the fighting troops echoed it and pressed back against the enemy.

'Let's hope it doesn't come to that,' said Claire, hearing the roar and staring at the carnage on the left flank. She was not a fighter and her arm, still wrapped in the makeshift sling was beginning to throb. 'I dread to think what will happen to us should any of Remus's men break through.'

'If you're lucky it will be a fast death,' a nearby officer replied. 'But if they break through, we defend the eagle to the last man. The tenth has never run and never lost its standard. Even when General Antony surrendered us at Actium, and Octavian decimated the legion, we kept our eagle.'

'Well then, let's not start,' said Mell hearing the officer's words through the tinny three-way phone feed she had set up. 'Sarah, Claire, keep watching the flanks. Jerry, you have Simon's binoculars, get a fix on Remus, watch him. When he moves, we send the first century of the ninth cohort after him, the second century too if he leaves with a large bodyguard. We need that silver eagle.' The other four listened carefully to the instructions and fanned out, accepting their roles without question.

Sarah had barely returned her attention to the left flank when she noticed that something was wrong. The first cohort on the extreme left was a little forward of the fourth, who were forward of the left central fifth cohort. The problem was the thin line of the fifth cohort. Scanning along the battle line she realised that the remaining men of the fifth were being pushed back at an alarming rate. The sixth cohort in the absolute centre of the field was also ahead of the struggling fifth. The line was going to break. 'Mell!' she yelled into her phone, straining to be heard above the battle roar. 'Mell, our lines are going to collapse.' The wall of men was bowing in as she watched. It would be a matter of moments before the first of Remus's troops broke through and once that happened they would be able to turn and attack the small legion from both sides.

Noting the problem Mell balled her fists. 'Shit.' she glanced around trying not to panic. 'Claire, situation on the right?'

'Holding strong.' Claire replied, keeping her eyes on her fighting men. The second and third cohorts were fighting well, managing to cycle through their men and keep the front line as fresh as they could. Allowing those who were tired or wounded to slip back through. She was glad that her side seemed to be doing okay, although she wondered if she'd really know if they were in trouble.

'Sixth and seventh cohorts in the centre are strong too,' Jerry offered, handing Suze the binoculars, and taking a break from watching Remus sit and drink himself stupid in a litter under his standard.

Mell glanced once more at the groaning shield wall, where the fifth cohort struggled and made a decision. 'Send in the eighth cohort, left flank work it through to the front take over from the fifth, send the wounded and spent men back here. Any able bodied of the fifth to remain in the rear ranks of the flanking force. And move those of the tenth who are able, closer to the centre.'

The officers and bugle player acknowledged without argument and passed the order to the troops. The eighth cohort's leading officers raised their voices and as a whole, the unit of roughly four hundred and eighty men picked up their shields, drew their swords and moved as one down towards the failing fifth at a quick trot. As they moved, their blades hammered a rhythm against their shields, but they remained otherwise silent. A deadly force moving with intent. As they closed on the beleaguered front line of the left flank, their war cry went up and for a split second the whole battlefield seemed to pause. Then the nightmarish fray continued, although the odds were beginning to swing in favour of the smaller, but organised legion.

A small number of injured men from the fifth cohort began arriving and Mell sent them to the rear, praising them for their valour.

'It's worked they've plugged the gap. We're pushing through!' Sarah exclaimed with delight as she watched. The addition of the new troops injected a huge morale boost into the men already defending their lives, and the life of Rome on the front line of the battle. Remus's men appeared less inclined to throw their lives away for his cause and as the men of the fresh eighth cohort pushed forwards, Remus's army began to give ground.

Suze missed the change in control of the battle, she was busy watching Remus. Up until Mell had ordered the eighth cohort forward he had been lounging in a litter, a cup of wine in one hand. Now he sat up. Suze tightened her grip on the binoculars and nudged Jerry with her elbow.

Almost imperceptibly, Reman soldiers began leaving the battle. It was one or two at first, barely noticeable, then a steady trickle began to detach from the rear lines and head for the city. Suze kept her eyes on Remus, one of his officers was talking to him and the resurrected twin suddenly looked angry and concerned. 'Get ready,' she muttered to Jerry who passed the information on to Mell.

As Suze watched, Remus barked an unheard order at the men forming his bodyguard. Almost immediately they were moving, taking Remus and his silver eagle to a safe place, retreating rapidly towards the Appian gate. Mell was watching already, alert to Remus's movement.

'Ninth cohort, first century! Ready to march!' she yelled. The men lifted their shields and stepped forward with a roar. 'Follow the silver eagle! Cut Remus off before he reaches the city.' A roar of approval met her order and the eighty men and their centurion moved out, coming together as a tight wedge-shaped unit. The centurion bawled an order for double time march, and the unit began to skirt the battlefield heading for the Appian Gate.

Suze kept her eyes on Remus a few moments longer, then, thrusting Simon's binoculars into her pocket and ignoring the pain in her swollen ankle, she sprinted after the legion. They would never make it to the gate in time to block Remus and Simon would end up isolated and alone between the resurrected twin and the deranged priestess.

'Suze get back here!' Mell yelled, but the girl was already halfway to the detached century. 'Fuck.' Mell swore, raking her hands through her hair. 'Jerry get after her, try not to let her do something stupid.'

Jerry flashed her a wordless salute, for once unable to muster a quick quip, and raced after Suze. Behind, he could just hear Mell call the order to commit the rest of the ninth cohort to the battle. He ducked his head and doubled his speed.

*

Chasing the first century as they marched swiftly away from the battle, Suze, unable to help herself, darted quickly onto the field to grab an abandoned shield. She'd imagined herself effortlessly scooping it up and returning to the century at a run. Racing at a flat out pace she reached, left-handed, to hook her fingers through the exposed handle and found herself sprawling on the floor, as the heavy shield refused to lift.

Reaching her Jerry burst out laughing. 'Some Roman soldier you are!'

'Like to see you do better,' Suze muttered, picking herself up and trying to heft the heavy legionary shield again. It was much heavier than she'd thought it would be, and, now that she was holding it, much bigger too. Almost as big as her. Still at least it would be protection, provided she could carry it. Along with the blood-stained gladius she'd managed to acquire earlier, she was now fully equipped, and slipped easily into the ranks of the century. Earning a sharp look of disapproval from the centurion, who did not appreciate the last-minute additions to his detachment.

Jerry also managed to snag a shield as they moved closer to the gate. 'Least I can lift it,' he said, jabbing Suze in the back as he struggled to remove a broken pilum head protruding from it.

The centurion slowed the pace as the unit drew into the city proper. Around them Rome fluctuated, buildings changing from wooden, high rise slum tenements of ancient Rome, to stone houses, to chic modern glass and chrome, and the empty space of pre-Roman Rome. The century was instantly on guard, shields up, swords drawn, anything that moved considered an enemy. With history in flux, time and the street plan were constantly changing. It was like a maze, and somewhere within the rat run, Remus was escaping.

'Suze, on the buildings.' Jerry hissed, looking up. She followed his gaze, trying not to trip over the cumbersome shield as she did so. Ahead, at the top of a rickety looking Roman tenement block, several of Remus's soldiers stood waiting, spears, slingshot and anything else they could find to pelt the Romans with, close at hand.

The centurion saw them too. The century was off the battlefield and in a tight enclosed space. Exposed. They needed a defensive tactic. 'Form *Testudo*,' he bawled.

285

The reaction was immediate. The ranks shifted a little, giving themselves room. As the front ranks lifted their shields to eye level, those behind, including Suze and Jerry, raised theirs over their heads, overlapping with the shield of the man in front to form the most famous Roman battle formation. The tortoise.

Spears and stones clattered down onto the curved shields protecting those beneath from injury as long as they kept formation. But it was slow going. Only the front rank could see ahead and with the immense weight of the shields overhead, the century's progress slowed to a crawl. Spotting what another legionary had done, Suze wedged her gladius in the handle of the shield and used both hands to keep the huge curved thing in place. All it took was one soldier to fail, and the Remans would pin the century down and destroy them in the narrow road.

XLVI

Simon crouched low over his horse's neck willing more speed from the animal, the stirrupless Roman saddle surprisingly comfortable. Charging through the battle lines had been terrifying, but worth it to galvanise his flagging troops. The worst bit had been cutting his way through Remus's rabble, but they'd mostly scattered before the pounding hooves of his horse. Only one that he could remember, had made a slash at him and then the blade had thumped into one of the saddle pommels, harming neither Simon nor the horse.

Orange light flared to his left as the Aventine burst into flames again and he felt a wave of heat roll over him, less intense than the volcano but almost as uncomfortably close. As the flames vanished, Rome flirted into its Renaissance era, ramshackle Roman houses for the poor giving way to beautiful merchants' houses.

Simon understood the timeslip, in theory. Since Remus had risen the history of the city was in a state of flux. If Romulus never defeated Remus the consequences of history were innumerable, and so everything that Rome had ever endured, created, and lost were no longer fixed. The fire on the Aventine belonged to a single day in the entire history or alternate history of Rome. It stood to reason therefore, that other days contained other hazards.

He reined in the horse sharply as a loaded wagon materialised in front of him, barely keeping his seat as the animal lashed its hooves in the air, startled by the indifferent man pushing the wagon, until time shifted and the road was clear again. Slapping the flat of his sword against the horse's hindquarters, Simon urged it forwards again, racing into the narrow, crowded streets of the central city where he was forced to slow down. Thanks to Tiberius, he knew where Messalina was most likely taking Lisa, and if the street layout remained broadly the same, he reckoned that he may be able to intercept them before they arrived at the temple of Vesta.

He pushed the horse as fast as he dared through the winding streets, wary of the animal's skittishness whenever the fire on the Aventine roared into life. Winding through part of the city that looked particularly medieval in period, he felt someone grab at his leg trying to drag him from the horse and slapped at them with the blade in his hand, hearing a pained yelp, as time shimmered into yet another phase. In the distance, he heard the blare of horns raised in triumphant joy. He paused a moment, trying to work out if the sound belonged to his army, or that of Remus, but in the noisy packed streets, it was too difficult to tell.

Finally, he reached the Circus Maximus, intending to charge across the empty parkland that he knew it to be in modern Rome, hoping to reach the temple on the other side before the priestess. He burst from the crowded streets and was rewarded with the sight of his quarry halfway along the scrubby parkland, and made to follow them when an ornate marble wall suddenly blocked his path. The Circus, as it had once been.

From inside the building came the loud trumpeting of horns and Simon's heart sank. Race day, the circus track was in use. Thinking on his feet he hauled his horse around and headed for the competitors' entrance at the south-western end. Cheers erupted from the stadium, before suddenly, the whole structure vanished again; revealing an open expanse of lush grassland. Taking his chance, Simon urged his mount down the spectator embankment and onto the track.

'LISA!' he yelled, his voice echoing back from the empty Circus as it restructured itself around the trio.

The priestess stopped and slowly turned to look at him, keeping a firm grip on Lisa, who immediately began to struggle. Even from where he was, over half the stadium away from her, Simon could see the smile creep across the Italian's face. She thought she'd won. 'Alone, young Caesar? Without a leader Remus shall crush your army and claim Rome for himself, and you would let him for the sake of an insignificant girl.' Pulling Lisa tightly against her, the priestess drew her dagger from her robes and held it to the girl's throat. 'Not one step closer, blood of Caesar, or I spill hers.'

Simon halted the horse, his eyes on the raven-haired priestess, ignoring Lisa for the moment. 'Let her go,' he demanded. The priestess shook her head. Gritting his teeth Simon tried again. 'Let her go, and I will halt the army before they kill you once Remus is defeated.'

'An ultimatum, how very male,' the priestess replied, edging towards the *spina* marking the centre of the circus. 'But you are in no position to bargain young Caesar. Look around you. Your remaining life can be measured in seconds.' She dragged Lisa roughly up onto the *spina* as the stadium exploded in a riot of colour and noise.

Simon had less than a second to react as several four-horse chariots, the pride of the Roman games, thundered towards him. Reacting without thinking, in an act of desperate self-preservation, he wheeled his horse around and with the roar of the Roman crowd deafening him to the chariots, charged ahead of the racing teams around the turning post and back along the other side of the *spina*. Time shifted and Simon slowed his tired mount to a halt on the now empty Circus track.

'You risk her life by keeping us here,' the priestess's voice rang out from above. 'All it takes is one little shove and goodbye blondie, mangled by horses and wheels, another broken wreck in the arena. They wouldn't even notice.'

'Simon!' Lisa screamed, twisting against the painful grip of the priestess. 'Simon get out of here, she'll kill you.' Tears glittered in her eyes and her heart was thumping wild, both delighted to see him and terrified for his life.

Simon checked himself. His position was dangerous he knew, especially with no idea of what was going on in the field. But all he had to do was avoid the chariot race, reach the other side of the stadium and lure the priestess out, leaving Lisa safe on the *spina*. Easy put that way, but in practice the whole thing was much more dangerous.

*

It was getting hot, and pretty grim under the *testudo*. Eighty men in full battle kit, shields raised, moving as fast as they could through the time flux that was the city of Rome. It was like the worst sauna in the world under the shields, like the boys changing room at the gym on a hot afternoon when the football team had just gone through it. But it was worse, the stink of sweat, unwashed bodies and clothing, the animal grease in the sword scabbards. The reek of effluence as Rome phased through a particularly nasty piece of her history, occasionally the tang of blood was in the air and always, always the charred, roasted meat smell of Remus's soldiers. Suze glanced over at Jerry, an expression of pure distaste on her face.

'You wanted to be a soldier,' he hissed back.' Besides it's actually no worse than the London tube at rush hour,' he grinned. 'Might even be marginally better. Least everyone knows which side they're on here.' He pushed his shoulder into his shield and let out a quiet groan as another stone rattled off it.

The front ranks halted and the whispered order to break was passed through the *testudo*. As one, the soldiers broke and formed a shield wall blockading the street in which they now stood. The unit had progressed through the heart of the city, across the base of the Palatine and now found themselves opposed by a wall of elite looking Reman troops blocking access to the Capitoline Hill. Remus's stronghold. From behind came a hearty roar and Suze and Jerry allowed their attention to drift, just long enough to notice the Colosseum and the Circus Maximus in their full glory. As they watched both structures crumbled to ruin like a time lapse video and the interiors became visible, there were figures moving around in the Circus, but they were too far away to see clearly. Besides the Reman barricade ahead was far more pressing.

Remus's men guarded the narrow entrance to the Capitoline. The century would have to fight their way through to him and his eagle. The sun on the bird's glossy silver wings gave away his position, Remus was heading for the temple of the Capitoline Triad, and the alleged location of the Tarpian Rock. The place where traitors to Rome were executed during the period of republic, and the sole reason that Tiberius had suggested Remus make his home on the Capitoline Hill.

Suze's throat was dry. She wanted to speak, feeling that the time had come to reinforce Simon's earlier speech to the troops, but she couldn't make the words come. She genuinely had no idea how Simon had managed it, to have the confidence to just stand there, before a whole army, men who were likely to die at his command, and speak words of encouragement. Sure, he'd borrowed heavily from Caesar, but that didn't diminish the achievement. Unable to speak for herself she glanced at Jerry and made a small noise in her throat. He just shrugged and indicated the centurion.

The centurion, a battle-scarred man missing two fingers from his sword hand raised his voice. 'Onwards lads, Remus digs his own grave, he heads for Terminus whom not even mighty Jupiter can move. Towards the Tarpian Rock, where all traitors to Rome die. We fight and die for the glory of the Tenth!'

The men answered with an inarticulate, howling battle cry and surged forwards, shields meeting shields as Jerry and Suze stepped back from the fray. Jerry without a weapon and Suze too exhausted from holding the heavy shield above her head to wield the clumsy gladius.

The eighty men of the century moved forward, step by step, their discipline outweighing the Reman desire for death. In bloody unison, the front rank of Romans punched with their shields, moved the cumbersome defence to the left, stabbed with their swords, twisting the blades before withdrawing and covering with their shields again, ready to repeat the move. The second rank dispatched any fallen Remans still alive with quick precise thrusts to exposed throats. Blood drenched the gutters as the Romans systematically hacked their way through the puny force of Remans. It was brutal, murderous butchery. The Romans were well drilled and relentless; shield punch, stab, twist, out, shield punch and so on, until every last man of the Reman guard lay dead. Jerry turned away unwilling to watch, but Suze found herself unable to look away, there was some bizarre beauty to the choreography of death orchestrated by the Roman soldiers. She was sickened, true, but grimly fascinated.

The changing temple of the Capitoline Triad was silent as the century clattered up the hill towards it. The small unit had been forced to leave three men too wounded to continue at the base of the hill, but otherwise the small force was complete. Under the direction of the centurion, the legionaries fanned out, covering the front and sides of the temple, standing silently shield to shield in a curving line. The rear was covered by the cliff. Remus had nowhere else to go.

'Surrender and die with some honour Remus,' the centurion bellowed, projecting his voice towards the temple where Remus was holed up.

'Shouldn't it be surrender or die?' hissed Jerry, hanging back with Suze well behind the legionaries out of the way. Suze hushed him as a swaying figure appeared weaving drunkenly between the columns of the temple.

It was Remus. He lurched forward, barely conscious, drawing his sword with one hand, throwing his arms open wide. 'Comeonthen,' he slurred. 'I'mnot, imnot afraid of you.' Behind him stood his standard bearer. Another of the charred denizens of hell dragged back to a bloodless life for his cause. The silver eagle and his standard bearer were all Remus had left now of his once vast force. From the top of the Capitoline Hill he could see the whole battlefield and parts of the city littered with the blackened bodies of his demonic creatures. To the south, by the Appian Gate, the golden eagle of Romulus was entering the city. Remus had lost.

'Meshalina!' Remus bellowed. 'Meshalinas!' Panic flared in his face when she did not appear and Jerry and Suze both realised that he'd never even considered that she may have left him. 'Prishtesh.' This last was almost a plea. Then he shook it off. The drunken lout shocked into sobriety. 'Rome is mine. The rabble of the Aventine will rise and fight for me.'

'You burned the Aventine mate,' said Jerry, gesturing to the conflagration behind as it flickered in and out of focus. The entire hill was alight now, the people mostly fled to other, safer parts of the city, save for the unfortunate few who had perished, burned alive in Lisa's accidental arson of half the ancient city.

'No,' Remus refused to see sense. 'I am their master, they fear me, but they will fight for me. No man of my city was ever killed by his people.' Behind the deranged twin his standard bearer shuffled back a few steps, planted the silver eagle's pole in the ground and melted away into the shadows, his loyalty finally exhausted.

Suze snorted with laughter. 'Wanna bet, Caligula was killed by his own body guard, Commodus and Caracalla too, and others, both proclaimed emperor and killed by their own praetorians. This city, the empire, was a brutal place, your brother's people, hard and unforgiving. But clever, very clever, diplomacy, trade, military might, infrastructure, architectural innovation. Your brother's descendants made the world. And you, in the mind of Rome you were never entirely forgotten.' Suze pointed at the Capitoline museum as it shimmered conveniently into view, the statue of the wolf and twins prominent from this angle.

'No,' Remus bellowed. 'I am the elder. Romulus is naught but dust in the wind, I am the city of Rema, I am the son of Mars!' He drew his sword and sliced the blade deep into the back of his hand making an offering to the God of War. Unsure of what was happening the century drew back a step. Remus's blood spattered the marble, vivid red spots on the pristine white steps. And Remus began to change.

He was suddenly bigger, much bigger, older, taller, more muscular; bare chested, with abs of chiselled steel, save for the single black strap of his sword belt. A short, armoured military kilt and calf length military boots, swirled about his legs, but it was the helmet and weapon that were most impressive and terrifying.

'Think he's compensating for something?' cracked Jerry, although he took a step back along with the rest of the century.

Remus now wore a large Corinthian styled helmet with a huge black plume, the tail of which brushed the floor behind him as he moved, and in his meaty hand, an enormous spear. He looked like Mars himself. Behind him two pairs of yellowed eyes glowed in the darkness of the temple. *Timor* and *Fuga*, Fear and Flight, the pet wolves of the God of War. Mars had answered his son.

Anticipating what was coming next Suze tightened her grip on the sword and shield in her hands, crouching lower, ready to fight. The rest of the century did the same. Jerry slipped quietly behind the ranks of fighting men and sincerely hoped that he wouldn't have to use the short sword he had acquired.

Unnoticed by all, ash began to fall from the sky.

XLVII

Simon was in the thick of the race this time, light wicker chariots ahead and to each side, with another, he was sure, behind. Thunderous noise rumbled all around him, the pounding of hooves, wheels, and the roar of the crowd. His horse was tiring, and it was all he could do to keep urging the poor beast onwards in the heat of the moment. A whip brandished by one of the racers lashed across his arm catching the horse too, and startled, it shied to one side. For an awful moment, Simon felt his left leg pinned between his own mount and one of the charioteer's horses. Reins and bits of harness from the racing horses flapped against him and his mount and he was all too aware that a rogue strap of leather could drag him from the saddle and below the wheels of the racing cart before he'd even realised it had happened. Then suddenly the pressure on his leg eased and silence hung in the air as the racers vanished back into history.

In the second it took Simon to catch his bearings the city heaved in time again and a huge piece of fallen statuary appeared right in front of his horse. They didn't have the space to jump it and the horse tripped, stumbling as it tried to stop. The momentum brought the poor creature down, throwing Simon over its shoulder and trapping his left leg beneath it, as both man and horse rolled in the shifting sand and hard earth. Winded, Simon dug his elbows into the sand and made a half-hearted attempt to drag himself free, but his leg was firmly pinned under the horse.

Angrily he swore at himself and tried again as the downed horse whinnied in pain. The fall had been hard, and Simon suspected, sadly, that the proud warhorse wouldn't be getting up again. He could hear Lisa screaming his name and, unable to see her, he raised one hand high enough that it could be seen over the bulk of the horse, letting her know that he was at least conscious.

Not three seconds later she sank to the ground beside him in a diaphanous waft of white material. 'Simon,' her eyes were wild with fright and her voice was barely a whisper as she grabbed his hand. 'Simon I'm sorry, I'm so sorry, she will make me...' whatever Lisa had been about to say was cut off as the priestess seized a handful of her hair and dragged her, screaming in pain, to her feet.

'Let her go!' Simon growled through clenched teeth as he tried again to drag himself out from beneath the horse, kicking at the saddle with his free right foot.

294

Then came a sound that froze his blood. The bray of trumpets. Knowing there was no way he'd be able to free himself before the chariots hurtled around the turn he glanced up, wanting one final look at Lisa, but it was the priestess who caught his eye.

The Italian suddenly looked terrified, her calculating demeanour gone, she looked just as terrified as Simon knew he was. Then she blinked, and it was gone, replaced by a much calmer façade, as if she were two different people. Catching his eye, the dark-haired woman blew him a kiss. '*Ciao, Senor,*' she said, grasping Lisa and dragging her away towards a lower part of the *spina*. Miraculously the chariots had not yet appeared, and Simon briefly wondered if it had been a military call in the city rather than the race trumpets that he had heard.

As she was pulled roughly up the central spine of the racetrack, Lisa grabbed the priestess's arm and sank to her knees. 'Please, we have to help him. The chariots will kill him,' she was desperate, appealing to the real Messalina, the terrified woman that she now knew was in there, under control of the priestess. But her time was up, the trumpets blared, the crowd roared, and the Circus was filled with the smell of horse sweat and the thundering rumble of the race. Her mind racing, Lisa wrenched her arm free of the priestess's grip with a strength she didn't know she had, and moved towards the edge of the *spina*, aiming for the racetrack.

'Lisa no! Do not even think about it,' Simon screamed at her, kicking his right foot against the horse's back, trying one last time to free his trapped leg before freezing as the chariots made the turn and charged towards his downed horse. Out of time and out of options, Simon pressed himself up against the bulk of his saddle, the body of his horse the only thing between him and the pounding hooves and wheels of the chariots. Keeping his head low and tucking himself in tight was his only possible chance, but it was not good. Above the din of the chariots and the roar of the crowd he could hear Lisa screaming. Then the world lurched as one of the chariots hit his poor horse, and the beast screamed, its body rocking with the violence of the impact. A flailing hoof from a fallen race horse came down close to Simon's head as the chariot overturned, drawing a huge roar of approval from the Roman crowd, but Simon had his eyes tight shut and didn't see. He felt the wind of a wheel passing over his back and heard the screaming chaos of the crowd, the loud snapping of wood or bone. He pressed tighter against the unmoving body of his horse and waited for it to be over.

*

The twin wolves attacked the century first. Made of smoke and mist they snapped and snarled, keeping the legionaries busy, diverting their attention from Remus. The men of the century were suspicious, wary of attacking a creature so tied into the founding of their city as to be considered sacred, and unwilling to further provoke the wrath of their God of War, Mars.

Standing on the steps of the Capitoline Temple, Remus contemplated his escape as the smoke wolves kept the soldiers busy. But he had not counted on Suze. He had noticed the teenagers, but considered them to be insignificant. Both looked younger than the youthful general on the white horse who had fled the battlefield. The tall bare-chested barbarian looked as though he didn't know one end of a sword from the other and the second was a girl and of no consequence at all, although amusingly she'd assumed the stance of a fighter.

Suze looked up at the huge man on the temple steps. Remus was twice her height following his transformation, higher still stood on the steps. She weighed the cumbersome shield in her left hand, wondering if she should just ditch it and bounced lightly on her toes, ready to fight him.

'Suze?' Jerry said, his voice creaking but making no move to stop her. 'Whatever you're thinking, don't. I am in big trouble if you kill yourself, like really big trouble. Like, Si will have my guts, and that's before your Royal Marine brother gets to me.'

Suze flashed him a grin and twirling the gladius around her right hand replied. 'Afraid that our posh boy might beat you up? C'mon Jerry even you could take Simon.' Without waiting for a response, she raised her sword and charged at Remus.

Remus had not been watching and as Suze raced forwards he almost missed her completely. It was a flutter in the corner of his eye that caught his attention and he raised his spear too late to intercept her, but enough to deflect her blade from his chest.

He drew the spear back and thrust forwards again, but the small warrior was too quick. Deflecting it up and over her head with the heavy shield, she ducked in underneath the spear shaft, to punch upwards towards his unprotected chest with the blade. She missed but was close enough now to render his huge spear useless.

Tossing the cumbersome shield aside Suze raced towards Remus's left side, noticing how slowly he moved. This would be nothing like her fight with Lancelot over the summer. It wouldn't even be like fighting Meredius with

Simon earlier. If Remus only had the spear as a weapon, this would be over much faster, except Roman swords were no good for cutting. She landed a flat slap to the back of his ankle, and cursed. She'd been aiming for an Achilles chop but the gladius, designed for stabbing, was blunted along the edge. Not unlike her fencing foil, she realised.

Bellowing in indignant shock rather than pain, Remus swept his long spear around and Suze leapt to the side, into the temple. She ducked as the shaft whistled over her back, the deadly pointed tip so far past her it was not a threat. She was still too close to him for it to be of any effective use. In the *piazza* before the temple, the legionaries had stopped watching the smoky wolves and were watching her. Without anyone paying attention to them, the wolves, sustained only by the feelings of fear and flight which gave them their names, faded away back into smoky nothingness.

The important thing that Suze, and by extension the legionaries, were learning, was that Remus was not Mars. He had been gifted the God of War's armour, but his fighting skills were his own and he was untrained and undisciplined, reeking of alcohol and barely able to stand. He swung the spear in a huge sweeping arc again and Suze ducked beneath it and stepped backwards, further into the temple, closer to his standard. Gesturing subtly to Jerry to creep round the side and join her, Suze kept her blade point high and continued to inch closer to the eagle, as behind Remus the century closed in, their rattling steps attracting his attention. With a final glance at the armed girl, Remus swung around and staggered down the temple steps into the falling ash to meet the soldiers, believing to the end in his ultimate invincibility.

As Remus turned his attention to the men of the century, Jerry joined Suze in the temple. He grabbed the standard intending to pull it free, but Remus's standard bearer had driven it deep, and he appealed to Suze for help. With Remus now engaged by the century, she dropped the sword and joined him. The legion roared their approval as the pair freed the standard and when Remus turned to see what was going on the legionaries closed the circle around him, locking their shields together, swords pointing inwards resting on the upper edges. It was over for Remus, there would be no escape now.

Suze recognised the century's actions and realised with a jolt that Remus was never going to be their prisoner, that they would kill him where he stood. She tightened her grip on the silver eagle standard and looked away. Jerry too looked away but kept an eye on Suze, he knew enough from talking with Simon over summer, that the girl was made of strong stuff, but he also knew she had a breaking point and Remus's death was going to be messy.

There was a thump as Remus threw himself against a shield, and another and another. Then the Romans all took another step forward shrinking the circle, and he nervously began to offer bribes and plead for his life. His voice quaking and high pitched as he tried, fruitlessly, to bargain with the soldiers. But these were soldiers who had fought for Caesar, for Marc Antony; survived decimation by Octavian Augustus, their loyalty was not for sale.

Both teenagers kept their eyes on the silver eagle as the first attack on Remus was made and the circle shrank again. Suze lowered the eagle and wedged her retrieved sword under the spread wings, whilst Jerry grasped the silver body, trying to prise them off, breaking the eagle apart. The blade gouged into the silver body shaving off tiny tendrils of silver as she struggled.

'Give it,' Jerry said offering his hand. Suze passed the blade over willingly, taking her turn to hold the bird, and then almost instantly regretting it as Jerry incorrectly wedged the blade and nearly took off her hand. Behind them Remus began to shriek, which turned almost instantly into a bubbling, guttural whimper as one of the soldiers stabbed him in the throat. The eagle's wings came free with a popping sound as Remus succumbed to death, as if his life force had been holding the standard together. And it may have been Suze's imagination, but she was sure that the silver metal dulled too.

Shouts of victory went up from the men of the century and several of them stepped back to allow three men to do the final job. The two teenagers, holding the fragmented remains of the silver eagle and wren, watched with a mix of fascination and horror as two soldiers pinned Remus's now lifeless body to the floor and a third stepped forward to sever the head of their enemy. There was a dull thump and a wet sucking sound as the first blow failed to decapitate Remus, the blunt edged gladius not fit for the task. The second blow rang against the floor and the head was unceremoniously kicked away, rolling to a stop face down beside the dismembered eagle.

'Don't look at it,' Jerry hissed, staring straight ahead and breathing deeply, before muttering. 'Why do I always get the decapitation to deal with? Least Gawain was fast.' Seeing her stagger a little, Jerry pulled Suze into a gentle hug as he kicked the head back towards the century. 'If you want to throw up or faint I promise I won't tell anyone,' he offered, watching as one of the legionaries ran over to grab the standard pole, whilst another retrieved the head. Within moments Remus's head was on the pole and waving above the knot of soldiers on the hill, blood dripping from his ragged neck. Several other soldiers under direction from the centurion hefted the body onto their shoulders and marched to the cliff edge where the centurion solemnly proclaimed Remus a traitor to Rome and, with a cheer of victory, the soldiers hurled the headless corpse from the cliff.

'So that's where the Tarpian Rock is, huh?' said Jerry. His arms still loosely around Suze's shoulders. 'Soooo,' he continued, 'we have eighty slightly crazed, bloodthirsty Romans here. What do we do now?'

Suze stared at their century, now stood loosely in formation awaiting their next order. 'They're still here. Remus is dead but it's not over,' she said in confusion and turned to look at the city. Time was still in flux. 'But Remus is dead! I don't understand.' A roar came from the Circus Maximus and as time fluctuated she caught sight of the colourful riot of a chariot race. And a figure in black robes, a dancing shadow amid the falling ash.

'Messalina, the priestess, must still be down there,' she muttered to herself. Then straightening up and forcing herself to look at the soldiers she gave an order. 'We need to get to the Circus!'

'Defeat the bad guy, save the city, rescue the girl,' Jerry translated. 'Got it.'

XLVIII

Lisa stared at the battered body of the white horse. The poor creature was dead, hit by two of the chariots as they had hurtled around the racetrack. The crash had been horrific, horses screaming, men flying through the air and then, wrapped in their reins, dragged behind their horses and beneath the hooves and wheels of another chariot. She'd blocked everything out, her eyes pinned to the white horse's saddle, where she knew Simon was trapped. Kneeling on the stone of the central spine of the racetrack she dug her fingernails into her palms and continued to stare, feeling her breath catch in her throat.

By her side the priestess was also watching, waiting. If she had managed to get rid of the young general then what remained of the Roman legion would be leaderless and Remus, if he lived, would be able to assume control. She could still take Rome and finally destroy the Eternal City, eradicating it from history once and for all.

Spotting movement Lisa let out a gasp, and immediately clapped a hand over her mouth to stifle the sound. She was too late; the priestess had heard and her eyes sought to confirm Lisa's thoughts. The white horse rocked slightly, and as both women looked closer they could see fingers, hands, extending into the sand, blooded but still strong. Simon had survived the chariots.

Lisa closed her eyes knowing what was coming. The priestess had detailed her whole plan earlier. She would be the wolf again, controlled by the demon in her blood. It would be her who was sent to kill Simon, whilst the priestess made her escape. Digging her fingernails into her palms as the Etruscan witch began to chant the words that would conjure the wolf, Lisa screamed out a warning, begging Simon to leave, to get out of the circus and re-join the army. Her screams ended in a guttural snarl as the wolf took control.

The priestess smiled, reaching out to pat the wolf-girl creature on the head, as if she were a beloved pet. 'A final task for you my sweet,' she said glancing down at the arena. 'Kill him,' she paused, thinking, 'and then finish yourself, I have no more use for you.' With a low growl the wolf creature leapt down into the sand. The priestess rubbed her forehead. 'No' she growled in the strange light voice that wasn't her own. 'The girl doesn't need to die,' she shook her head, losing her balance and almost fell, but the stronger force within her was still winning, and with a low chuckle she righted herself and turned to look up at the Capitoline Hill. Her empire awaited.

*

Simon could hear Lisa screaming, but couldn't make out the words. His head was pounding, his whole body felt like jelly, his leg was still pinned below the dead horse, and he suspected two of his fingers were broken, but he was alive. Tucked in tightly against his horse's body he'd managed to survive relatively intact, although there was no way he wanted to chance his luck again.

Sprawled full length in the sand, he turned and bracing his right foot against the dead horse, concentrating hard, slowly, inch by painful inch, began to pull his left leg free. A blur of movement in the corner of his vision alerted him to a new danger. He threw himself sideways as best he could, as Lisa plunged his discarded sword into the space where his head had been.

'Lisa?' lying on his back he held his hands up, noticing the odd angle of the first two fingers on his left hand. 'Sweetheart?' She was looking right at him, her face a snarling mask, and he groaned as he noticed the yellowed wolf eyes staring back at him. From far away came the blare of horns again and Simon braced himself for another lap of the chariots, but the circus remained quiet, the horns had come from the army outside. But from which army he was unable to tell.

Lisa raised the sword again and with a final kick to the horse and moan of anguished pain, Simon finally dragged himself free and out of her immediate range. He rose awkwardly to his feet, a bolt of pain in his left ankle driving him to his knees again as Lisa came closer.

The wind in the ruined arena caught her robes and hair, billowing them around her as she swung the heavy blade without skill. She was beautiful, the gauzy white material translucent against her skin, hiding nothing. Elegant almost to the point of divinity and Simon had to remind himself to breathe as he struggled to his feet again, staggering slowly backwards. 'Lisa, *mi amor*, come on. You know me,' he stretched out his right hand towards her, hoping to appeal to the girl he knew was held hostage by the wolf.

She held the blade in a two-handed grip and swung it towards his outstretched hand, teeth bared in a snarl, forcing him to snatch his arm back and retreat quickly, as she swung again for his chest. The point snagged his shirt and there was a tearing sound as the material ripped. As Simon glanced down at the ragged slash, Lisa let out an animalistic howl, the sound echoing around the near complete arena.

Simon backed away, keeping his eyes on his girlfriend's face. He felt helpless, she was clearly under direction to take him down. He would need to defeat the wolf, but had no wish to hurt Lisa. He took another step backwards and felt his boot scuff the stone of the *spina*. He had nowhere else to go. 'Lisa, please,' he entreated, holding both weapon-less hands out towards her. 'I know you can hear me.' The sword clattered against the marble beside him and he inched slowly sideways along the *spina*.

He watched as Lisa raised the sword again and, allowing his instincts from the rugby field to take over, Simon ducked and charged under her arm, sprinting a short distance away before turning to watch her reaction. He'd seen the wolf version of her move before, down in the lower chambers of the Colosseum, she had been fast. Not now though.

A wolf knowing her prey, Lisa turned slowly and stalked with a deliberate slowness towards him, the point of the sword drawing a line in the sand behind her. Still trying frantically to come up with a plan, Simon risked a glance up at Messalina. The black robed priestess still stood on her high vantage point on the *spina,* watching the drama unfold.

Simon ran his tongue over his lip. 'Call her off!' he yelled not expecting a response. A low chuckle was all he heard, the priestess would not do anything unless she felt that she was losing, and from where he stood, with no idea what was going on outside the walls of the Circus, Simon felt as though she may be winning. 'Come on Lisa,' he muttered, 'I really do not want to have to hurt you.'

Since she arrived unexpectedly in the museum less than twenty-four hours ago, all he had thought about was finding her. Now he had her in sight, within arm's reach, and he still couldn't save her. An anguished groan escaped his lips, he would never be able to forgive himself if he hurt her, or worse, if his actions got her killed.

Lisa swung the blade as she came towards him, looping it in a figure of eight, the blade so heavy that its motion twisted her body with it. With huge effort, she dragged it back up and swung again, twisting her body the other way and driving the point of the blade into the sand. Simon backed off another step. She had no skill it was true but she was still dangerous.

He watched, looking for a pattern in her movement. The blade was heavy and she needed a great deal of effort to move it, even in a double handed grip. The downswing was fine, the weight of the blade and gravity saw to that, but lifting it she was vulnerable, especially as she reached the apex of the swing and had to reverse the direction.

Simon kept watching, taking slow fencing cross-steps backwards, gauging the speed he would need. Years of fencing and rugby had left him with quick reactions, but he was exhausted, well beyond his limits, a sudden change in pattern and she would have him. He reminded himself that it was Lisa, not Suze who he was facing. Suze could lull him into a false sense of security on the fencing piste and she had a quick change of line that had caught him out more times than he'd like to admit. Lisa though, to the best of his knowledge had never held a sword in her life. Ultimately it had to be worth the risk.

As she lifted the blade he darted in, slamming his right hand into Lisa's wrists. His hand, bigger than hers, sought to catch both of hers in his grip but he missed her left. Stronger than Lisa, Simon kept enough pressure on her wrist to keep the sword above their heads. Her yellowed wolfish eyes fixed on his face, her lips peeled back in an ugly snarl. 'Lisa *mi amor*,' he began, and let out a gasp of surprise as he felt something punch between his ribs, forcing the air out of his chest.

It took all Simon's will power to remain on his feet. A part of him had always expected Lisa to come to her senses before she dealt him any harm. But the knife to his ribs had proved that she was utterly under the priestess's control. Unless he did something about it, Lisa would kill him.

There was a burning pain in his side where she'd withdrawn the small blade and he could feel a damp patch growing on his shirt as the wound bled. He sucked in another breath, his right hand still holding Lisa's wrist and the sword above them.

Ignoring the potentially broken fingers on his left hand, he lunged for the dagger. Letting out a moan of pain as he forced his broken digits to grip Lisa's hand he twisted her left wrist, forcing it back, sincerely hoping that she let go before he broke her hand. With a sharp gasp, she dropped the dagger and he managed to twist her body around, so that she faced away from him.

He pulled her against his chest, keeping her sword wielding hand above their heads. 'Lisa, please, I do not wish to hurt you.' His broken hand encircled her waist as trumpets blared again, although outside or inside he could no longer tell. '*Mierda*,' Simon hissed, expecting the chariots and glancing around as the priestess let out a shriek of frustration. Carefully, keeping the priestess in his sight, Simon slid his hand from Lisa's waist, up the side of her body until he touched her jawline and could turn her face. 'Lisa, I love you and I hope you can forgive me for this,' he whispered, and leaning close, ignoring her gleaming wolfish eyes, he kissed her.

XLIX

'Hold,' Mell yelled, bringing the first cohort to a stop just inside the competitors' entrance to the circus. She needed to wait for the rest of the legion to cover their access points before she could risk being seen. The military men obediently halted behind her and stood silently awaiting their next command. Tiberius was with the unit that was covering the opposite end of the Circus, the one that would be last into position, Sarah and Claire, with units on the sides. Only when she knew they were all in place could she make her move.

Having finally routed Remus's army and entered the city, Mell's unit had met with Suze and Jerry at the base of the Capitoline Hill, and their grizzly trophy, Remus's head dripped blood onto the ground behind her. It was horrific, but if they marched into the Circus with it, hopefully the priestess would see that she was out of options and give up. As they waited for confirmation that the other units were in place, the three teens stared at the scene within the Circus.

The priestess, clad in black was striding along the central spine of the racetrack, her movements jerky and agitated, her attention on two figures on the sand, oblivious to the gathering army outside. The figures on the sand were harder to work out.

'I think he's kissing her,' said Claire, her voice distorted through the small speaker of Mell's phone. From where she stood Simon was more visible than Lisa but both of them had a hand on the sword that pointed straight up into the air above them.

'He's bleeding,' Sarah added. The angle of her view on the scene allowing her to see the large red stain on Simon's shirt as Lisa let go of the sword relinquishing it into his grip, her fingers moving to tangle briefly in his dark hair. Then as the teenagers stood, waiting to make their move, Lisa seemed to collapse in Simon's arms, her weight pulling him to the ground with her.

'What the hell is the rest of the bloody legion doing?' hissed Suze moving forward. 'We need to get in there now!'

Mell grabbed the younger girl. 'They're not all in place yet, we can't let Messalina,' she shook her head. 'The priestess, escape. We have to wait for Tiberius.'

*

The second she returned to being herself, responding to his kiss, Simon felt the strength leave Lisa's body. She sagged heavily against his left arm with a sigh, ripping a groan of pain from him as the addition of her weight pulled his left arm down opening the wound in his side. His strength failed and he dropped her, landing heavily on his knees beside her.

'*Lo siento,*' he gasped out, pressing his broken hand against his left side in an attempt to stem the blood flow. Lisa didn't respond and he immediately ignored his own pain and focussed his attention on her. 'No, no, Lisa come on. Stay with me sweetheart.' Through the sheer fabric of her white robes he could see the rapid growth of black lines on her body. The toxic poison in her veins. He shook his head. They were back at the beginning again. 'No,' he said again disbelief, his gaze snapping up to the priestess on the *spina*. She caught his eye and began to laugh. 'Let her go!' he screamed, using the blade of Lisa's gladius to force himself back onto his feet. He was running on pure adrenaline now, unable to focus, to think to do anything but stagger after the priestess, intent on ending this nightmare.

'Simon, no,' Lisa's voice was barely a whisper as she struggled to speak. 'It's not … not her … fault. She …' Lisa coughed, her body trembling as she tried to snag the leg of Simon's jeans, to stop him. Pain ripped through her body and she tried, but was unable to scream. The world was fading to black at the edges and all she could see was the sky. 'Simon?' she whispered, and closed her eyes, as a blast of trumpets rocked the stadium.

*

At Mell's order the legion advanced, entering the Circus from every entrance, blocking any escape. Anticipating that at some point, if they were still time slipping, the Circus must have chariots thundering through it, she sent twenty men with Jerry to form a protective shield knot around the girl lying motionless on the floor. Jerry, eager to avoid being run over by chariots himself, raced them double time into the arena, scuffing to his knees beside Lisa, as the priestess let out a screech of laughter that halted everyone.

'Mighty Caesar does my job for me!' she cackled with glee as she spotted the head of Remus waving on its pole. 'Rome is almost mine.' She looked down at the blood-spattered boy marching his way, alone across the sand towards her. 'You could always join me Caesar,' she stepped carefully along the *spina* and climbed slowly down, keeping her eyes on Simon. 'Once her spirit is gone, I can live in her body if blonde is what you prefer.'

Simon raised his blade and stepped closer. 'Stay away from her.'

The priestess simply cackled and moved closer to him. The chariots would be through again soon. If she couldn't convince him to join her, she would at least be certain of his death.

Across the arena Mell opened her mouth to deliver the order for the legion to move, to take down the priestess. Then silenced herself as Simon, noticing the soldiers surrounding the space, raised his left hand in a ragged fist calling a halt. His command outweighed hers and the legion halted. Although Jerry had already managed to get the twenty men he had with him to surround Lisa with a shield wall.

Within that knot of men, ignoring whatever his friends were doing outside, Jerry slipped his hand into Lisa's. She was frozen, through the transparent material of her dress he could see that black veins covered her body and were rapidly spreading. 'Aww hell,' he muttered, before standing and moving one of the soldiers aside. 'Mell?' she was too far away. Turning he spotted Sarah closer and waved to catch her attention. 'Sarah, tell Mell I need her!' he bellowed, miming a phone. But he had no time to see if she understood as with a loud blare of trumpets the Circus exploded into a riot of colour and noise. He ducked back into the protective shield wall with a curse and threw himself on the ground beside Lisa.

'Oh my god,' Claire gasped, one hand flying to her face as she realised the danger faced by those on the arena floor. 'Guys are you seeing this?' she screamed into her phone. Directly across from her she could just see Sarah, who'd gone white and was staring towards the cluster of men protecting Jerry and Lisa, with her hands curled into fists at her sides. 'He'll make it Sarah, they have to do a whole lap before they reach them,' she said speaking gently into the phone, knowing that Sarah must be listening.

Mell stood with Suze at the competitors' entrance and both stared as the racers thundered around the turn immediately ahead of them. Two of the chariots touched wheels and the whole crowd, Suze and Mell included, held its breath waiting to see what happened but both drivers were in control and held steady, as the race hurtled into the open straight. Directly towards the priestess and Simon.

'What the hell is he doing?!' Suze screamed, staring in disbelief as Simon ran towards the chariots rather than away from them. She watched in rigid horror as he dodged between the black horses of the chariot on the left and the brown ones on the right. Then almost screamed again as Mell grabbed her arm to stop her going after him.

'Trust him Suze,' Mell said quietly. 'It doesn't look like it but I assume he knows what he's doing. We need to get to Jerry and Lisa.'

'I can't leave him,' Suze gasped back in horror, jabbing her gladius towards the racing chariots. 'I should have his back, we're sword partners.'

Mell dragged the younger girl closer. 'Suze, he has an entire legion at his back. I need you covering mine,' she held Suze's eyes for a moment, pushing her point home, willing sense to win over the unmistakable crush the girl had on her Spanish friend.

Suze turned back to watch Simon as he leapt forwards over the wheels of two chariots, hitting the ground and rolling to his left, and narrowly avoiding the hooves of the following horses. Her heart was hammering so hard she thought the whole legion must be able to hear it. She tightened her grip on the sword and shield that she still held, willing Simon to survive whatever crazy stunt he was pulling and with a sigh, followed Mell out onto the racetrack, running towards Jerry's knot of men.

Sarah and Claire took the chance to abandon their positions and join the others within the relative safety of the shield ring. As the four of them arrived together the soldiers wordlessly parted letting them through. Jerry barely gave them a glance. 'She's going fast,' he said, his huge hand still wrapped around her frozen fingers. 'But she's been trying to speak, I can't make it out though, something about Messalina and an ancient skull.'

A harsh cough from Lisa caught Mell's attention and she crouched by the stricken blonde girl as she tried to speak. Lisa was dying, that much was clear, the black veins were spreading rapidly across her body and affecting her ability to move, speak and breathe. She didn't have much time, and with the ash still falling from the sky, neither did anyone else in this game.

'Lisa, I know this is hard but help me out,' Mell spoke quietly, batting Jerry away and slipping her hand into Lisa's. 'Once for yes, twice for no, you follow?' Lisa squeezed her fingers feebly. 'Okay. You're trying to tell us that this is not Messalina's fault?' One squeeze. Mell bit her lip trying to think of another question but Sarah interrupted.

'Is a skull possessing Messalina the same way that the wolf possesses you?' Sarah asked thinking aloud. Mell felt Lisa's response and nodded encouragingly. 'So that's what she means by it not being Messalina's fault. The woman is being controlled?' Mell nodded as Lisa squeezed her hand again.

'There was a skull in the basement of the hotel,' Suze offered, standing close to the legionaries, hands still tightly gripping the sword and shield that she refused to let go of.

'Skull in the crazy basement or on Messalina?' Jerry said, casting an eye out over the circus, where the chariots and most of the structure had vanished. Simon and the priestess were miraculously both picking themselves up out of the dust.

'That's not a yes or no question Jerry,' said Claire. 'Lisa, is the skull still in the hotel basement?' Lisa squeezed Mell's hand in the affirmative.

'Right,' said Mell hoarsely. 'Jerry, take Sarah, get back to the hotel, find the skull and destroy it. I'd tell you to take a century of men but I think we may need all of them here,' she glanced up spotting the pale form of Tiberius floating close by and smiled. 'Take Tiberius, he knows Rome. Suze,' she paused as the younger girl glanced her way. 'Suze I'm really sorry but you're probably the only one of us who can do this. I need you to stop Simon.'

Suze stared at her, as Jerry and Sarah pushed their way through the soldiers and fled the Circus for the streets of Rome, Tiberius gliding silently along behind them. 'You're killing me, you know that, right?' Suze hefted her shield. 'The second I get between him and Messalina I become an enemy to the legion, more so if I pull a blade on him.'

Mell nodded. 'I'll do what I can and if I can't hold them they should listen to Simon, and hopefully he will listen to you.' Suze nodded, checked her grip on the heavy shield and ran out into the arena. Mell turned to Claire. 'Guess it's up to us to do what we can for Lisa and hope the others make it in time.'

*

Simon moved towards the priestess in a defensive crouch. He'd survived the last brush with the chariots better than her, but his previous injuries were bad and it was only his anger and desperation to save Lisa that was keeping him upright and moving. Holding her right arm tightly against her body the priestess moved away, keeping the distance between them equal, her eyes pinned to the sword in his hand.

Simon raised the blade. 'You have lost priestess, Remus is dead. Surrender and let her go.'

The priestess cackled. 'You think I need Remus to take this city?' she threw her arms wide, gesturing towards the collapsing ash column on the horizon, wincing at a stab of pain as she did so. 'Look around you heir of Caesar. Rome is doomed. Wiped from time itself, never to rise again. It is you who have lost. The girl has only minutes left to her, and should you save Rome, you will lose her,' she began to laugh.

'The hell with etiquette,' Simon muttered and threw himself at the priestess, hurling them both to the ground. She rolled beneath him still laughing, wrapping her legs around his waist and pulling his body tighter against hers. Behind them the legion began to advance.

He struggled against her, but she knew where he was injured and her fingers jabbed at the raw wound in his side, knocking the breath out of him as she rolled them over, reversing their positions and pinning Simon beneath her. 'Mmmm, I knew you would be a passionate lover, young Caesar,' she whispered, grinding her hips against him and throwing back her head, feigning ecstasy. 'Let the girl die, you can have me.'

Simon ignored her, forcing all his energy and thought into reaching for the discarded gladius that lay just beyond his grasping fingers. He clamped his broken left hand against the still bleeding wound between his ribs, and stretched his right arm as far as he could, his fingers just brushing the hilt of the sword. The priestess's hand landed on his chest tangling in the fabric of his shirt and with a strength he was unaware she possessed, she hauled him up to meet her and kissed him. Her teeth sinking into his lower lip, drawing blood.

'That'll be enough of that,' a harsh Mancunian accent yelled, as a Roman legionary shield punched into the priestess's side, throwing her off Simon. He looked up to see Suze standing over the priestess, huge shield in one hand, blade in the other, her stance threatening. She spoke without taking her eyes from the Italian woman. 'Simon, go to Lisa. I'll deal with Messalina.'

'Do you seriously think I will leave you on your own to do that,' he replied, clamping his left hand to his side again and struggling to his feet. Before bending to collect the discarded gladius that he'd been trying to reach.

'Simon, please go back to Lisa,' Suze hissed through gritted teeth, she knew exactly where this was going and really hoped he'd listen. 'Don't make me do something we might both regret. Go,' she kept her gaze on Messalina. The Italian woman had remained sprawled on the floor. Suze had given her a good bash with the shield hoping that if she was possessed, a crack on the head might go some way towards keeping her docile. Or reawakening the real Messalina held prisoner within the shell of the priestess.

'Suze, what are you talking about?' Simon asked, unable to follow her at all. His head was spinning and his vision was beginning to blur slightly. He raked broken fingers through his hair and winced. 'Just get out of the way and let me finish this.'

Suze sighed and shook her head. 'Can't do that,' she replied, pushing him back with the shield.

'Suze are you mad? Get out of the god damn way!' Simon lunged forwards.

With no choice Suze punched the shield out, catching him off balance, forcing him to his knees. Stepping back, she brought her hands together so that her large shield covered her body, and her blade, aimed at Simon's throat, rested on the shield rim. From every corner of the circus came the rasp of swords drawn from scabbards, and Suze closed her eyes as the legion moved forwards.

L

Alarm bells of pain were ringing through Simon's head and as he shook himself, trying to clear his thoughts, the message his body was trying to send him finally got through. Trying to keep pressure on a bleeding puncture wound with a hand sporting two broken fingers, was not working. With a groan he shifted position, clamping his right hand over the puncture wound and leaning his left forearm on the gladius, standing point down in the ground. When he looked up there was a wall of men in front of him and his brain struggled to recall why they were there. He heard a high-pitched scream, then caught Suze's challenge, issued in the broad Mancunian accent that only came out when she was being defensive or was truly afraid. Somewhere in his head it registered that she'd just challenged an entire legion to a fight and a snort of laughter escaped his lips, forcing him to wince in pain and press his hand more firmly against his side.

'Simon!' A shout from behind distracted him and he turned to see Claire and Mell, followed by a group of legionaries. At first, he couldn't make out what he was seeing, then suddenly his eyes focussed. Two of the legionaries carried a shield, on which lay a girl with long blonde hair.

'Lisa,' her name escaped his lips in a moan of pain and he forgot about Suze and the rest of the legion. Letting the gladius fall to the ground, Simon staggered three steps closer to the small unit as they shuffled closer and gently laid Lisa on the ground beside him.

'Simon I'm so sorry,' Mell said. 'I ... I tried everything. She ...' Mell's breath caught in her throat and she covered her mouth with one hand as she tried not to cry. Simon stared back at her a look of incomprehension on his handsome, but fatigued face.

'She's dying Simon,' Claire said gently, kneeling beside Lisa on the ground and taking the girl's hand. 'Jerry and Sarah went with Tiberius back to the hotel. Lisa was muttering something about Messalina being possessed by a skull. They went to find it. We hoped that ...'

'We hoped that destroying the skull would break whatever this curse is,' Mell interrupted, swiping her wrists across her eyes. 'But they've either not found it or it didn't work.'

'That explains Suze,' Simon muttered, looking back at the army. A muted series of thuds came from somewhere he couldn't see, followed by a loud clang as metal hit metal. He licked his lips, drawing in a deep breath to call halt, dimly aware that the thuds indicated fighting within the tight semicircle formed by the legion, when Lisa let out a rattling groan. It was like nothing he had ever heard before, a deep rattling wheeze from deep in her chest. A death rattle.

Claire and Mell could only watch as Simon fell to his knees beside Lisa, forgetting his own injuries to press her cold hand between his broken and bloody ones. Mell exchanged a horrified look with Claire, she'd heard that deep rattle before, it had been the last sound Richards made, a sound that woke her, sweating, in the middle of the night.

'There's nothing else you could have done Mell,' said Claire, noticing Mell wrap her arms around herself and shudder. She moved closer and folded her friend in a hug, feeling a damp patch appear on her shoulder as Mell began to cry quietly.

'Lisa?' Simon's voice cracked a little. 'Lisa, come on sweetheart, look at me. Please.' His blood caked right hand brushed a lock of her blonde hair back from her forehead, leaving a smear of red where he touched her, and her eyes flickered slightly in response.

'Where's Suze?' Claire hissed quietly to Mell, looking around the arena and realising that she couldn't see the youngest member of the group.

Swiping furiously at her eyes, Mell stepped away and swept her gaze around the arena. 'Shit,' she said, realising what the dull thumps and odd clangs of metal were. Claire's face transformed into a mask of horror as she followed Mell's thought train and she looked at the legion. 'Hold!' Mell called in a hoarse cracking voice but the soldier's paid her no attention. 'Hold damn it!' she yelled again, but there was nothing she could do. Suze had been right, the moment she put herself between Simon and Messalina, the second she stood in defence of the priestess, the legion moved to defend their commander. 'Simon,' she hissed, hating to drag him from Lisa in her dying moments but needing his authority.

He waved her away. 'Not now.' He leaned forward resting his burning forehead against Lisa's cold clammy brow. '*Lo siento, mi amor,*' he said softly, planting a tender kiss on her dry lips.

'Simon, you have to stand the legion down,' Claire said, grabbing his shoulder and almost screaming in his face as another clatter was followed by a yell.

Although whether a yell of pain or aggression it was hard to tell. He shook her off, Lisa was all he wanted right now. Nothing else mattered.

'*Teneo!*' Mell screamed trying again to halt the troops, and pulling the Latin word from the depths of her mind. But it was no good. 'Oh hells fire,' she gasped. 'Simon please pay attention to me. You need to halt the legion.' There was no reaction, he was completely devoted to Lisa. 'Right, sorry Si, but you asked for this.' She knelt beside him and with a grimace of distaste, pressed her fingers hard against the ragged wound in his side.

More shocked than in pain, Simon glanced around at her.

'Halt the god damn legion,' Mell demanded. 'Or you're gonna kill Suze.'

*

Sarah and Jerry flung themselves through the doors of the hotel, Tiberius right behind them. Without the obliging little ghost's help, they would have spent hours wandering the ever-changing streets of Rome without finding it, but Tiberius had led them straight there. And not a moment too soon.

'Jerry,' hissed Sarah, groping for his hand as she stared at the chaotic scene behind. 'Jerry look.'

He caught the note of panic in her voice and looked back. The ash column spewing out of the volcano was collapsing, folding in on itself, the grey material already visibly speeding towards the city. 'Aww shit.' He grabbed her hand and practically dragged her across the reception. 'Basement. Fast.'

Together they scrambled around the desk and into Messalina's private room. The basement door yawned open exactly as they'd left it a few short hours ago, and without pausing to look at the décor of the room they raced down the steps into the darkness below. Jerry pausing only long enough to locate the mechanism to close the door, sealing them in the subterranean darkness.

'What the hell did you do?' Sarah shrieked, dragging her phone from her pocket and tapping the torch into life, sweeping the pale beam around the small dark space. 'You idiot you've trapped us down here, and the volcano …' she trailed off.

Jerry shrugged in the white light of her torch. 'Better chance of survival if we're sealed in, but,' he moved slowly down the steps to join her, 'totally screwed if anything buries the door. But one problem at a time; let's find the skull.'

Holding her fear, Sarah swept her light around the room. It was eerily quiet, the table where the body had lain waiting to be inhabited by Remus stood empty before the altar, Lisa's leg chain snaked out across the floor and scraps of rope lay scattered, unmoved since their escape.

'There is evil here,' muttered Tiberius shuddering. He'd avoided the realm of the priestess earlier, her presence enough to keep him in hiding. But now her aura in the basement was faint, her power was fading, but she was not defeated yet. He could still feel her, could almost see her face as clearly as he had that night in the driving rain when Remus had bowed down to her on the Aventine, and let her take his immortal soul.

'Was this dead bird here earlier?' hissed Jerry, looking over the altar and spotting a small bird splayed out, wings pinned back, guts spilling over the table. When Sarah didn't respond he turned back to look at her. She was stood, frozen on the steps, eyes fixed on the closed cellar door. Slightly muted by the closed trapdoor they could hear a deep roaring rumble as the cataclysmic milkshake of ash, rock, and whatever else the volcanic flow was picking up, approached Rome.

'Guess we're out of time,' Sarah said finally looking away from the door, and wrapping her arms around herself. 'The world is ending and I'm stuck in an underground hovel with Jerry. Again.'

Unable to tell if she was joking or not, Jerry took his chance. 'But you wouldn't have it any other way, right?' She looked up at him with an unreadable expression, and he dropped his own gaze back to the altar as, above them, the pyroclastic flow hit the outskirts of the city, burying everything in its path.

'The skull should be on the altar Jerry, between the statues,' Sarah sighed, directing him. He'd clearly missed it when he spotted the dead bird.

'Ah-ha. Got it,' he said, returning his attention to the altar. 'Got distracted by the bird.' He picked it up, poking his fingers through the eye sockets and dumped the skull on the table, where the corpse that had become Remus had lain.

Tiberius took one look at it, shrieked and vanished.

'Guess that means it's the right one huh?' said Jerry, staring at the space where the little ghost had been. 'Tiberius? Buddy, you coming back?' There was no response. 'I think we're on our own,' he said, looking towards Sarah, still curled up on the stairs. 'Sarah?' She glanced over. 'You wanna do the honours?' he gestured to a gladius close to her foot, unable to recall if either of them had brought it with them or if it was just conveniently there for them to use.

Sarah allowed herself a half smile, destroying the skull, ending the whole thing. It sounded like a job for one of the others, Suze was aggressive, Simon was smart, Jerry worked things out by accident, whilst Mell could happily take control of situations. Slowly she moved down the steps and walked to the table, collecting the sword on the way.

She paused a moment, looking at the skull. It was brown and flaking, with cracks along the sutures, swirled charcoal patterns and a streak of what looked like dried blood running from each hollow eye socket. Yes, Sarah would be glad to finish this. With a glance at Jerry, who gave her an encouraging nod, she raised the sword, and taking a careful aim, slammed the point through the top of the skull.

Almost immediately the roar upstairs grew louder and the temperature in the basement increased. Sarah gave the shattered skull one last vicious swipe, before dropping the sword and staggering backwards. A loud thump came from above and she looked up at the closed basement door. The dust cloud, or lava flow or whatever it was from the volcano had reached them. She lowered her head and closed her eyes, they had been too late to stop it.

'Is this okay?' Jerry's voice whispered softly in her ear, as his arms gently circled her. Sarah nodded numbly and turned to bury her face in his bare chest, feeling his nose against her hair as he bent his head. 'I'll look after you I promise,' he said squeezing her tight. 'Neither of us has to die alone.'

LI

Suze was tiring. When Simon hadn't halted the legion, she'd pushed the dazed Messalina behind her, telling the Italian to stay there. From that point on though, things had spiralled rapidly out of control.

While Suze's focus had been on the encircling soldiers' weapons, Messalina had risen with a scream, distracting her attention and clawing for Suze's sword like a spitting cat. Suze had finally managed to slam the heavy shield into the desperate woman a second time. She had screeched out an almighty wail, before collapsing to the ground, allowing Suze to return her attention to the advancing legion.

Which is how she'd found herself trapped, back against the wall with no escape. She may have knocked the priestess out of the game but it had cost her the chance to evade several hundred battle ready Romans.

The first attacks had been slow, the soldiers were feeling her out, the same as with Remus earlier. One lunged forward from the right, then as he stepped back another would move either left or centre. Suze could deal with that easily enough, it was child's play; parrying each successive sword thrust and riposting fast enough to drive each opponent back. But she began to grow tired as the attacks continued and eventually they began to move in pairs or threes. The shield was heavy and cumbersome but she dared not drop it, even though each sword thrust that thudded into it jarred her arm and threatened to break her fingers loose.

She'd given ground, slowly at first but then more rapidly, trying to limit the number of attacks that could come at her. She thought she'd heard Mell's voice call a halt, but the legion didn't respond, so she fought on. Sweat running down her back and face, her movements slowing. Eventually, totally exhausted she sank to one knee behind the shield, still trying to protect Messalina but knowing that in moments a blade would punch through her defence.

She ducked her head behind the shield, bracing her legs below her for one final push, perhaps if she could spring up quick enough she could try to carve a way out through the soldiers. Then just before she moved came the sound she'd been waiting for.

'Hold!' Simon's voice filled the circus, strong and commanding and the onslaught stopped.

Suze dropped her sword wielding hand to the floor, and sucked in a deep breath of air, as the legion parted to allow the commanding officer through. Warily she poked her head up above the shield, Simon was moving between the rows of troops towards her, a strange glint in his eye and an enigmatic smile on his face.

'About bloody time!' She gasped, trying to control her trembling limbs, noticing Mell and Sarah beside a still unconscious Lisa behind him.

'You pulled a sword on me, whilst I was in command of a legion, what did you expect?' Simon replied unperturbed, although that mischievous glint was still in his eye and a smile twitched at the corner of his mouth. Reaching Suze's side, Simon leaned down and offered her his hand, closing his fingers around her wrist as she did the same to him. 'Consider it revenge for the scooter,' he said quietly, although Suze noticed his words slurred and there was a sheen of sweat across his brow. As he moved to pull her up a spasm of pain shot through his body and he stumbled, dropping to one knee beside her.

'Jesus Simon,' she hissed quietly, draping his arm over her shoulder and trying to haul him to his feet. 'Don't die on me.'

'*No lo haré si no lo haces*,' he mumbled back.

Suze gave him a tight smile. 'Sorry buddy, no idea what that means.' She balanced his weight against her and risked a glance back towards Messalina. The woman lay sprawled on the floor of the Circus, but she was breathing and her face appeared more relaxed. The priestess appeared to have gone. 'Come on Simon,' Suze muttered. 'You rescued the girl. Mission successful, Prince Charming.'

'Doncallmethat,' Simon slurred back, or at least that's what it sounded like to Suze.

'Mell!' she yelled, 'Mell, I think I'm losing him.' Suze could feel panic pounding through her, and Simon's weight was getting heavier as he leaned against her. It was obvious that he was going to black out, she could feel how wet his shirt was and it suddenly registered. Blood. There had been blood on his shirt earlier. Thinking quickly, she eased Simon down to the floor as best she could and without thinking, ripped his shirt free of the wound. Pressing her hand hard against him. He flinched a little at her touch and let out a groan of pain, raising a hand to swat her away. A hand with two obviously broken fingers. 'Christ Simon,' Suze muttered, gently taking his hand and placing it by his side.

A piercing shriek filled the Circus, as Lisa finally returned to the land of the living and the sight of her boyfriend with yet another of his female friends. 'SIMON JAMES MATHERSON!' She took a breath to continue whatever rant she was about to head off on, and stopped. Her eyes now fixed on the skyline. As she stared unwaveringly into the distance the blood drained from her face, and slowly the attention of everyone, teenager and grizzled soldier alike, turned to see what had terrified her so much.

On the horizon, the column of ash had collapsed and a great wall of black was rushing towards them. 'Oh no,' hissed Claire, her heart sinking. They had defeated Remus, destroyed his eagle and taken down the priestess. But there was no way to stop the eruption. Blindly, staring at the churning mass of ash and dust Claire groped for Mell's hand.

'Shields up. Protect your commander!' Mell yelled, practically screaming the words to be heard over the rising storm. The teens crowded closer huddling around Simon and Lisa, as Claire half dragged, half coaxed a dazed Messalina closer. The legionaries obeyed Mell's final order and drew a tight formation around the group. Locking their shields together around and above everyone, blocking out the light.

A wave of intense heat rolled over them, and Suze, recalling the inhabitants of Herculaneum, braved Lisa's wrath and reached for Simon's left hand in the terrifying darkness. Three of his fingers closed on hers in a gentle squeeze. Suze closed her eyes feeling Claire press tightly against her back as the heat was followed by noise. Wind howled around the legionaries' shields, fragments of pumice knocked against the thin wood and metal bosses. And dust swirled everywhere. It was the end of the world.

*

Birdsong.

Messalina opened her eyes slowly, almost unwilling to believe what she could hear. The sky was blue, she could feel stunted, sun scorched grass under her hands. She closed her eyes again as a car horn ripped the tranquillity of the morning and jarred her aching head.

Slowly she sat up. She felt bruised all over, her head pounded and she had only vague memories of the past few days. A group of teenagers, mostly girls, stood a little way to her right. Their words made little sense to her, English perhaps, although they seemed familiar somehow. She moistened her lips thinking to call out to them and see if they knew what had happened or why she was there. But before Messalina could say a word, a blonde girl in a white flowing dress let out a scream that pierced her brain. In the middle of the group she could see a boy, a young man covered in blood, lying on the ground.

Closing her eyes again she tried desperately to recall how she was outside, and what had happened. The last thing she remembered clearly was reading bird entrails in her secret basement. She shuddered at the memory and opened her eyes as a shadow fell over her. The short brunette stood there, looking down at her and Messalina had a flash of recollection. This was the girl with the sword, she was sure of it. 'No sword this time?' she asked in her heavily accented English.

The girl gave a nervous smile. 'Do I need it?'

Messalina shook her head, she didn't think so. Her head felt clear for the first time in almost forever. 'You saved me from him,' she said, looking towards the blood-soaked Spaniard still unconscious on the floor and feeling a pang of guilt, it was her fault that he was injured. 'Will he survive? It was never my wish to kill anyone.'

Suze shook her head. 'I was saving him from himself,' she sighed, watching Lisa fuss around her unconscious boyfriend. 'He'll be fine,' she said forcefully, 'he has to be.'

Recognising the emotion in the girl's voice Messalina smiled and looked down. She'd been a love-struck teenager once too. She hoped that her actions hadn't damaged any of their young lives too much, but she was also amazed that a small group of teenagers, with so much of life's learning still ahead of them, had managed to defeat the priestess. She watched almost absently as a tall boy and another girl appeared and began walking across the circus to join the group, catching the excited attention of the green-haired girl with her arm in a sling. Still kneeling on the floor, the blonde girl in white responded to something that the boy on the floor had mumbled. His left hand moved slowly and touched her face and the girl leaned down planting a soft kiss on his lips. The sight made Messalina smile. They would be all right.

The small brunette by her side looked away, pretending to make a detailed study of the grass in the Circus. Messalina turned her gaze away from the teens too. She understood the younger girl's feelings, the Spaniard was handsome. But she had her own reasons to be looking inward. The priestess was gone, her brain was empty at last, save for a splitting headache. She smiled slowly to herself in disbelief at the facts as she could recall them, she'd been saved by teenagers. The priestess, that age old power that had manipulated Rome for centuries had been thwarted by teenagers. It was impossible to believe, but it was true. She knew that she would have to face the consequences of her actions, the problem was that she could barely recall what she had done, just a relief that she didn't seem to have hurt anyone too badly. The blonde girl appeared cured and her dashing hero looked like he would survive once patched up. Messalina's eyes flickered and she sank softly back into the grass of the Circus as the flashing beacon of an ambulance arrived on the scene.

Epilogue

It was the thirty-first of October, two days since the Circus, three since Simon's eighteenth birthday. Still aching from the events, he was sat in the sun with his friends at a café outside the Pantheon, enjoying the buzz of people in the square.

'Wait, I got a good one this time,' said Jerry with a delighted grin on his face. Since they'd returned the silver wren safely to the museum that morning, he'd been making up Roman limericks, and was driving the others crazy. 'I promise this one's good,' he insisted. Ignoring Mell's eye roll and the knowing look that Suze and Sarah shared, he cleared his throat and continued. 'There once was a soldier called Vericus, who could not sleep in his bedicus, he rose late, due to something he ate, they say it was garlicus breadicus,' Jerry gave a triumphant bow as Suze swatted at his head.

'You're an idiot, adding icus to it doesn't make it Latin,' Suze said, shaking her head.

Jerry shook his head and laughed. 'Thaticus isicus whaticus youicus sayicus,' he grinned, finally taking a seat.

'Nah, Suze is right. You are an idiot,' agreed Simon.

'Did you seriously just say "nah", instead of no?' said Mell, shooting Simon a curious look. 'Did we finally break you out of your posh shell this time?'

Simon laughed. 'Oh no, there is no breaking out of the posh prison, although,' he glanced down at his broken fingers, 'you may have dented it a bit.'

'Aww we dented him. He's damaged goods,' Jerry laughed, draping an arm around his friend's shoulder, as Lisa and Claire arrived, laden down with shopping bags. Claire had finally managed to get rid of the green dye in her hair, and was now a brunette, the colour suiting her cropped 1920s bobbed style well. Lisa simply looked radiant.

'Simon!' Lisa threw her arms around him, planting a kiss on his cheek, leaving a smudge of peach lipstick. She was much more forward now, threading her arm through his, challenging the other girls with her eyes, as if daring them to even try laying a finger on her man. 'Listen I need to show you what I bought, Claire was helping me, but neither of us have been hiking and we weren't sure what I needed. I have boots, poles, the cutest little hat, a new backpack ...'

'Slow down,' Simon interrupted. 'You. Lisa, you bought hiking gear?' he looked confused. She had never wanted to do anything like hike before.

'Mmmhmm,' she nodded. 'You have always wanted to take me walking in Valencia, to show off your home,' she registered the surprise on his face. 'I know, I was never interested before, but I sort of enjoyed scrambling around the Colosseum, and being free of my father telling me what to do. Think of how many more adventures we can have now,' she glanced over at the counter of the cafe. 'Ohmigod, Claire!' she screeched, enveloping Claire in a huge hug as if they were new best friends. 'Look they serve pink cocktails here! We have to get some, come on!' Dragging Claire behind her she made straight for the café counter.

'What just happened?' said Mell, feeling as though a whirlwind had just landed at the table.

'I have no idea,' Sarah replied. 'Sounds like Claire didn't enjoy herself as much as she thought she would though. She said she'd been wishing for a shop mannequin to come to life, or a spiked ceiling to descend.' The rest of the group laughed as Sarah tactfully changed the subject. 'I'll get us some ice cream,' she offered, taking Mell with her to the *gelateria*.

The peace of the *piazza* was suddenly shattered by music booming from a stereo and a group of British girls, on what looked like a hen party, began collectively murdering an old Kylie Minogue song on the karaoke.

'Ooh,' Jerry cracked his knuckles, staring over at the karaoke machine. 'Jerry likes karaoke,' he said with a grin. 'Hey Si, you and Suze should do a duet, you know she has a monster crush on you right?' he winked at them both, before bounding over to the machine to find a song book.

Suze flushed a mortified red and stared at the table. 'I will murder him,' she hissed through gritted teeth. Jerry had always teased her about Simon, although never when Simon was around, and with her thoughts as churned up as they were, she wished the ground would swallow her.

'What for?' Simon asked, glancing over at her. 'So, Jerry embarrassed you, we both know he was joking. Of all the women in my life, I know I can count on you not to think of me like that. You have seen me fail, several times, you know my ...' he broke off and flexed his broken left hand, 'imperfections.'

'That's not an imperfection, that's the real you,' Suze replied, wounded by his words, but trying not to let it show, as Mell and Sarah re-joined them.

'Oh hell, Jerry's not going to sing, is he?' said Mell, placing a tray of various *gelatos* on the table and spotting Jerry down by the stage. 'He's insufferable enough when he's not the centre of attention. Simon, do you know what happened to Messalina this morning?'

'She handed herself in to the police,' he replied, casting an eye over the various flavours before him. 'But her fingerprints do not match either of those found on the remains of the silver eagle, or in the curator's office, and Remus's body has not been found, so ...' he spread his hands.

'They're letting her go?' Sarah said, taking a little tub of ice cream and almost spilling the cold dessert as Jerry returned and nudged her in the back with the karaoke book. He stared up at the sky, hands behind his back, as she looked around, feigning his innocence and then nudging her in the back again as she turned away to hear Simon's response.

'A little difficult to convict her when there is no evidence. Although I suspect that she may have connections in the right places,' Simon reached for an ice cream, then paused. 'Is this chocolate or coffee?' Mell just shrugged, and he decided to gamble and take it anyway, before answering her original question. 'Messalina was with some workmen when I left the hotel, she is turning the basement into a wine cellar and looking at further restoration of the building's façade, along with refitting the second-floor corridor.'

'Do you mean ...' whatever Sarah had been about to say was lost in an exasperated sigh, as Jerry's latest nudge succeeded in pushing her nose into her ice cream. She put the little tub down and turned to face him. 'I really want to be annoyed with you ... but, I've kind of missed you irritating me.' Jerry's face cracked a broad grin. He'd missed their easy relationship too.

'Yeah me too! We should totally go out sometime!' Jerry pronounced, a little too loudly, drawing looks from Mell and Suze. Sarah flushed red and stared at the table wondering whether to be angry or flattered, and wishing furiously that the others were not around to see. Jerry noticed the stares and faltered, suddenly shy. 'Well ... if, if you wanted to. Umm, you know, I thought you might like to ... sometime er... shit,' he turned away, scuffing the toe of his trainer on the floor.

'Tell you what,' said Sarah, a smile creeping over her face, as she realised he wasn't just joking around. 'This may be the ice cream talking but, you get this entire *piazza* dancing and I will allow you to take me out for one date,' she held a single finger up to emphasise the point.

'Challenge accepted!' Jerry replied, offering his hand to seal the deal, and dropping the song book on the table in front of Suze and Mell. 'Ladies choice.'

'This one,' Mell said, jabbing her finger at a random spot on the page, as Claire and Lisa returned, a waiter carrying a tray of hot-pink cocktails following behind them.

Jerry squinted over her shoulder at it. 'Well I don't have the shoes or the wig, but I'll give it a go!' He snapped his fingers in a pistol shape at Sarah and began singing under his breath, 'Jerry's gettin a da-ate.'

Ignoring him, Lisa reached for one of the lurid pink cocktails. 'Simon, we totally missed your birthday,' she said, handing her boyfriend a glass and taking another for herself, gesturing at the others to help themselves as she clinked her glass against his. 'Happy Birthday *mi amor*,' she raised her glass towards the rest of the group. 'So, where is our next adventure going to be?'

The girls glanced nervously at one another but were saved from having to answer, as Jerry chose that moment to hop up onto the stage and commandeered the attention of everyone in the area.

'Buennas evening!' he yelled, and launched into his song. 'Woooohoa oh oh ohohoh ...'

'I so just lost this bet,' said Sarah, recognising Lady Gaga's '*Bad Romance*' and reaching for a cocktail. 'Oh well,' she raised her glass with a smile, 'here's to terrible choices. Come on, let's go dance.'

As the girls threw themselves into dancing to Jerry's wild performance, Simon took the opportunity to visit the Pantheon, his mind was confused and he wanted to be alone. He timed it just right and slipped into the ancient church as a huge crowd of tourists left to watch the spectacle in the square. The early evening sun fell in a column of golden light through the oculus in the domed roof. Simon let out a heavy sigh and stretched, wincing at the stabbing pain in his side. The wound would heal, but he wasn't certain his relationship would.

Lisa remained blissfully unaware that she was the cause of the four-inch gash in her boyfriend's side. She'd nearly killed him. And sure, Simon understood that she'd not been herself, that it had not really been her. But the experience had changed her. It had changed him too and right now he felt adrift, less certain of himself. Not enough to return the sapphire engagement ring to the shop, but certainly enough to wish he'd waited on the long shipping period, rather than flying to Italy to collect it.

He massaged his forehead. He still loved her, it was just that events had confused things. Everything would be fine. Lisa discovering that she was stronger than she thought, could only be a good thing. She had surprised everyone by refusing the summons home from her father in order to remain with Simon in Rome. It was something that she would never have considered before. And it had been fantastic, two whole days together with no one watching. For the first time in their entire relationship they were not having to snatch quiet moments. So why the feeling of disquiet?

A low cough caught his attention, although, when he looked up the round church was still empty. A smile graced his face as he realised that he'd been watched for the last few minutes. 'Tiberius?' he asked the empty space.

'*Dominus*.' The little ghost shimmered into view as he spoke.

'Tiberius what are you doing here? You returned the golden eagle to the tomb of Romulus as I asked?' The ghost nodded and Simon glanced at the door. Jerry was still singing; his absence would not have been noticed yet. 'Then you have served the family of Caesar well, my friend.'

The little ghost flushed pink. '*Dominus* calls Tiberius his friend? Not even the divine Romulus offered such words.'

Simon shook his head. 'I am not Romulus, although, events suggest that I may have a link to Caesar,' he sighed and shook his head. 'But how can it be possible, Caesar had no living heirs?'

'Not all history is written down *Dominus*,' Tiberius replied.

Simon laughed, and raked a bandaged hand through his hair. 'Master no more, be free Tiberius. Stop loitering in the Colosseum. Be at peace.'

Tiberius's mouth hung open. 'You have true greatness *Caesare*. I may be free of my earthly chains, but forever in your debt.' The ghost hung suspended in the sunlight below the oculus a moment longer, then faded slowly into the dancing dust motes leaving Simon alone.

With a smile, the Spaniard turned to leave the church. He'd lost the chance to obtain answers by letting Tiberius go, but he rather liked the shadow shrouded mystery of the ring's past. The future however, was a different matter. Where the dratted thing's prestige had saved him and Suze from the wrath of the legion, its future promised something more akin to a prison. Mell had been right, at some point Simon would have to figure out who he really wanted to be. He twisted the ring around his finger, Rome wasn't built in a day, the decision could wait.

Author's Notes

There is a huge amount of history to ancient Rome and I have no intention of explaining all of it here. What I want to do is to clarify where I used reality and what was myth, and explain some of the reasons behind events in the book.

The Founding of Rome and the Eagles

The legend of the founding of Rome by the twins Romulus and Remus is most likely just that, a legend. The name Romulus literally translates as 'little boy from Rome'. Rome probably developed the same way most other places did, from small tribal settlements into one unified centre. Besides the legend of the twins themselves, my novel focusses on one of the most famous aspects of the Roman Empire and the Roman military; the eagle standard. The gold and silver eagles belonging to the twins Romulus and Remus are entirely a work of my imagination based on the military standards that the Romans carried into battle. The real eagle standards were introduced to the army during the period of Roman Republic by a Consul, Marius, during a reformation of the army in 107/106 BC.

There are several references to Messalina being in thrall to, or possessed by, an Etruscan priestess in the novel. The Etruscans were a people who pre-dated the founding of Rome but lived in the area of the seven hills. They were known to practice Haruspicy, which we find Messalina doing in Chapter Five. This is the study of animal entrails to foretell the future. A kind of gruesome horoscope.

Characters

Messalina was based on a famous Roman woman of the same name. She was the third wife of the Emperor Claudius, a second cousin to Emperor Caligula, paternal cousin to Emperor Nero and grand-niece of the first Emperor Augustus. Messalina was therefore a powerful woman with a particular reputation for being ruthless, predatory and sexually insatiable. There is a famous story that she challenged a local whore to see who could undertake the most "business" in one night... and won. It is said that she was a schemer who arranged the downfall and murder of some of Rome's more powerful senators and a number of her rivals. She was eventually accused of plotting to murder

death he simply asked for another cup of wine. The Roman senate ordered a
Damnatio Memoriae and had her name scrubbed from all monuments and public
places. Unlike her namesake, the Messalina of my story survives her wrongdoings
and may have the chance to reform.

Simon's lineage to Julius Caesar is a work of fiction. As Simon points out in
the book, Julius Caesar had no living heirs. His sole legitimate child was a
daughter named Julia, married to Caesar's old friend, later enemy, Pompey. Julia
died in childbirth whilst Caesar was campaigning in Gaul and her child did not
survive. A second child, Caesarion, was the illegitimate child of Caesar and
Cleopatra. He is considered to have been executed by Octavian in Alexandria
shortly after the deaths of Antony and Cleopatra, although exact circumstances
of his death are not known.

The Tenth Legion

Famous for being Caesar's legion, the tenth was recruited in Hispania (Spain)
by Caesar himself in 61BC. Early in its history it was known as the Legio X
Equestris (mounted). The legion fought for Caesar in his campaigns in Gaul,
took part in his crossing to Britain in 54BC and remained by his side throughout
the civil war with Pompey. The legion was disbanded in 45BC and given lands
in Gaul and Hispana.

In 42BC the legion was reconstituted to fight for Augustus, Marc Antony and
Lepidus in a campaign against the murderers of Julius Caesar. After this they
went with Marc Antony to Parthia (Iran) and subsequently were with Antony
and Cleopatra at the battle of Actium where they suffered defeat.

When the legion rebelled under Augustus, it suffered decimation – the
execution of every tenth man in the legion. Replacements were added from other
legions and the legion was renamed Gemina (Gemini) and was sent to Hispana
for a number of years. From there the legion survived, moved about the empire
by various emperors until the fourth century AD when we find no further
references to it. The tenth legion's symbol was actually a bull, but the
constellation of Gemini fitted my story better so I changed it.

Within the text I have greatly simplified the Legion giving only the ten
cohorts and suggesting only a single standard and standard bearer. In reality, the
legion would have had several standards each bearing a different image, the eagle,
the emperor, and a symbol unique to that legion. There would also be an attached

baggage train. The command structure begins with the General in command of the province who may have several legions under him, the Legate had charge of a legion, below him was the Camp Prefect, then the First Spear Centurion, commanding cohort one, then nine other Senior Centurions commanding a cohort each. Below the Senior Centurions are the Junior Centurions, each in command of a century, each of which includes Optios, Standard Bearers, Decurions and the soldiers themselves. All this before considering mounted contingents and administration officials.

I simplified things with Simon assuming the role of Commander (in place of Legate) and Mell being referred to once as Prefect with the Centurions below her.

To learn more about the Roman Army I highly recommend the books of Adrian Goldsworthy – "The complete Roman Army" being a very good starting point. However, "The Complete Roman Legions" by Nigel Pollard and Joanne Berry is also very useful for those wishing to know more about specific legions.

Mote-Cavo and the Alban Mountains

My description of the eruption is based on the text of Pliny the Younger (Letters LXV and LXVI) who described the Eruption of Vesuvius and its destruction of the towns of Pompeii and Herculaneum. Pliny is coming under fire these days for recording the date of the eruption as August, when some archaeological evidence appears to indicate an October date, but irrespective of time of year his description is a good one and I have borrowed odd lines to lend weight to the eruption here.

The Colosseum

Built by Vespasian (who had previously commanded the second legion in the invasion of Britain) and dedicated by his son Titus, the Colosseum was known as the Flavian Arena, obtaining the name Colosseum apparently from a colossal statue of Nero that stood nearby. There are at least two levels to the Colosseum and the 'lift shafts' do exist. There were roughly forty holes in the arena floor through which gladiators and wild beasts could be brought into the arena. The central lifts had capstans big enough to lift a lion. The entire building is a marvel of engineering.

There is only one definitely recorded instance of naval battles within the Colosseum which is during the opening games.

The Ludus does still exist and can be visited, although the passage through to the Colosseum is not visible, and is likely lost below the modern roads.

The Gladiators

There are lots of online websites where information on gladiators can be found, so I will not go into much detail here, I will simply explain what I used.

The Retarius (net man), Therax (Thracian) and Sicissor were all real types of gladiator appearing as described in the book, in fact both the Retarius and the Therax have their own Wikipedia pages. Less is known about the Sicissor, which is why I chose it although I added the faceplate, which itself, is loosely based on a Roman cavalry helmet mask (see the Crosby-Garrettt helmet). I also chose to make this gladiator female. Female gladiators were rare, but not unheard of. The term Gladiatrix that I have used to describe her though is a modern concept and not one that the Romans would have known. Their gladiators were simply gladiators irrespective of gender.

The Circus and the Chariots.

I love the Chariots, one of my favourite pieces of cinema is the William Wyler 1959 Ben-Hur chariot race. The Circus of Rome is not so well preserved, but its outline can still be seen as the area is parkland and retains its complete shape. It is a surprisingly narrow structure considering the sporting events held within it, imagine Formula 1 on a 200 yard stretch of duel carriageway with a hairpin turn at each end.

The chariot races were by far the most popular sport in Rome, everyone, even the emperors had their favourite teams, and fan rivalry was similar to football fan rivalry today. It is also a Roman Charioteer who still holds the title of highest paid sportsman in history. Unsurpassed by even today's sporting greats, was a charioteer Gaius Appuleius Diocles. He won 1,462 races out of 4,257 raking in the Roman equivalent of £12 Billion.

Fun points you may have missed during the timeslip and elsewhere (for real history nerds)

The name of the gladiator 'Flamma' on one of the statues in the Colosseum. The statues are a work of my own imagination however, Flamma was a real gladiator and a very successful one at that. He was a Syrian soldier, captured and thrown into the arena as punishment. He survived thirteen years of battles with thirty-four recorded matches of which he won twenty-one. He was awarded the 'rudus' or wooden sword of freedom four times but declined it each time.

The crucified bodies on the Appian Way. Not just the end of the 1960 film starring Kirk Douglas (another favourite of mine), but a grim reality. Having crushed the slave revolt led by Spartacus, the Roman General Crassus did indeed crucify six thousand survivors of the revolt along the Appian Way, from Rome to Capua. Three sources claim that Spartacus himself was killed in the battle, although Appian states that his body was never found.

The body in the road on the Appian Way. I couldn't resist putting this one in, I wonder who spotted it? This is the murdered body of Publius Clodius Pulcher, an ambitious Roman politician, although more famous for his feud with the orator and lawyer Cicero. The trial of his killer 'Milo' became famous as Cicero spoke as his defence, a defence which ultimately failed but secured Cicero's place in history, the text of this defence speech is perhaps his greatest. A very good fictionalised version of this scrap of history is 'A Murder on the Appian Way' by Steven Saylor.

The men covered in blood running through the streets screaming that the tyrant is dead are of course the murderers of Julius Caesar. Some forty senators were involved in some extent in the plot to kill Caesar, although not all were involved in the actual murder. On March 15th 44BC Caesar was stabbed to death in a meeting of the senate. The action was one of the final catalysts that brought about the fall of the republic.

Simon's speech, as Suzi points out, is a heavily edited version of one recorded by Caesar in his Civil War commentaries. Caesar's own account of his battles are somewhat dry, but worth a read.

If you would like to find out more about The Colosseum, the Circus, Gladiators, Chariot races, the founding of Rome and more then please check out my YouTube channel, where I have a series of short HistoryBites videos detailing fun parts of history in 5 minutes or less.

I can also be found on Facebook and Twitter @smporterauthor.

Printed in Poland
by Amazon Fulfillment
Poland Sp. z o.o., Wrocław